# Perfect
# Little Children

## ALSO BY SOPHIE HANNAH

# Perfect Little Children

## Sophie Hannah

HARPER LARGE PRINT

*An Imprint of* HarperCollins*Publishers*

PERFECT LITTLE CHILDREN. Copyright © 2020 by Sophie Hannah. All rights reserved. Printed in the United States of America. No part of this book may be used or reproduced in any manner whatsoever without written permission except in the case of brief quotations embodied in critical articles and reviews. For information, address HarperCollins Publishers, 195 Broadway, New York, NY 10007.

HarperCollins books may be purchased for educational, business, or sales promotional use. For information, please e-mail the Special Markets Department at SPsales@harpercollins.com.

Originally published as *Haven't They Grown* in the United Kingdom in January 2020 by Hodder & Stoughton.

FIRST HARPER LARGE PRINT EDITION

ISBN: 978-0-06-299716-6

Library of Congress Cataloging-in-Publication Data is available upon request.

20 21 22 23 24  LSC  10 9 8 7 6 5 4 3 2 1

For Dan, Phoebse, Guy and Brewstie

# 1

Here we are, in the wrong place: Wyddial Lane. It's a private road, as the sign unsubtly proclaims in letters larger than those spelling out its name, in a village called Hemingford Abbots. I switch off the engine, stretch my back to release the ache from two hours of driving, and wait for Ben to notice that there's no football ground in sight.

He's buried in his phone. I can't help thinking of it like that—as if he's stuck inside the machine in his hand, unable to get out. Quite happy about it, too. Zannah's the same. Most teenagers are, as far as I can tell: they spend all day and half the night in lock-eyed communion with an addictive device. No amount of my children telling me it's "the way life is these days, so stop being so old and just chill" will ever persuade me to think it's okay. It's not. It's frightening and depressing.

Sometimes it's also useful, to a parent who doesn't want to be scrutinized. It's likely to be a while before Ben notices the intense quiet—almost total silence, apart from the occasional bird chirp or gust of wind rustling the branches of the trees that line Wyddial Lane on both sides—and realizes that there are no teenage boys in football shirts traipsing past our car or anywhere nearby. He's completely immersed: head down, lips moving as he types with his thumbs. I've probably got two minutes at least.

Plenty of time. You can take in a lot in a hundred and twenty seconds, and that's all I came here to do: have a good look. Many times over the past twelve years, I've wondered about Flora's new house. Technically it ceased to be "new" at least a decade ago, though that's still how I think of it. I checked last year to see if the "Street View not available in this location" message still came up, and it did. Maybe that's got something to do with it being a private road. I can't think what else it would be. Until today, I assumed that Wyddial Lane was very remote, but it isn't. Despite the peaceful rural vibe, it's only two minutes from a main road.

I've no idea what kind of house I'd buy if, suddenly, money were no object, and I've always been curious to see what Flora and Lewis chose—certainly not curious enough to devote half a day to the four-hour round trip, especially when I might be spotted on my spying mission and I'd have no way to explain my presence, but interested enough to recognize a perfect opportunity when one presented itself. As soon as the list of impending football fixtures arrived and I saw "St. Ives, Cambridgeshire," I knew what I was going to do. It felt like a reward for all those Saturdays spent driving Ben around, all the hours I've stood shivering by the sides of muddy fields far from home while he played. Finally a perk had been handed to me and I resolved on the spot to take full advantage of it.

Today, if by any chance Flora or Lewis catches sight of me here, my excuse will be so close to the truth that it might as well be the truth: I'm driving my son to his Regional League match nearby and I took a wrong turn. Ben, sitting beside me in his red and white football gear, would be all the proof I'd need. Only the "wrong turn" part of the story would be false.

For a better view, I've parked across the road from

number 16, not directly outside it. To the left of the thick wooden gates, there's a square sign, gray stone, attached to the high brick wall that protects all but the very top of the house from prying eyes like mine. The sign says, "Newnham House."

I shake my head. Unbelievable, that they chose to call it that. And those gates, a foot higher at their uppermost point than the top of the wall . . . Most of the houses here have high walls surrounding them. Being on a private road doesn't offer these people enough privacy, apparently.

Of course the home of The New Flora and Lewis Braid looks like this. I should have been able to predict it all: the ugly, sprawling modern mansion, the private road, the gates kidding themselves that they don't appear superior and unfriendly because they've got curly flourishes at the top that look marginally more welcoming than the seven feet of dense wood immediately beneath them.

There's a silver box with buttons below the "Newnham House" sign—an intercom. I'd need to press those buttons if I wanted to gain access, which I definitely don't.

Is this what too much money does to people? Or is it only what too much money does to Lewis Braid? There's no way this house is Flora's choice—not the

Flora I knew. And Lewis had a knack for getting his way whenever they disagreed.

"Where are we? This isn't the ground." My son has finally noticed his surroundings.

"I know."

"Then why've we stopped? I thought you knew where we're going?"

"I do."

"The warm-up starts in, like, fifteen minutes."

"And it'll only take us ten to drive there. Lucky, eh?" I smile brightly, switching on the engine.

Ben turns back to his phone with a sigh. He is considerate enough not to say, "I wish Dad was driving me." According to our family folklore, Dominic is a good driver who plans well and allows enough time, and I am the opposite. This week was Dom's turn to do football duty. He couldn't believe his luck when I said I fancied an outing and offered to go instead. I doubt he remembers that Flora and Lewis moved to very near St. Ives soon after we last saw them. Even if he does, he wouldn't suspect I had a secret agenda. Dominic would never take a ten-minute detour in order to see the current home of someone he hadn't seen for twelve years—therefore, in his mind, neither would I.

"Fuck off!" Ben says to his phone.

"Ben. What have we—"

"Sorry." He makes that sound like a swear word too. "Do you have a list of everything Dad's ever done wrong?"

"What? No, of course not."

"So it's not normal, then? Most people in relationships don't do it?"

"A written list? Definitely not."

"Lauren's got a list on her phone of everything I've done wrong since we've been a thing."

Lauren, a model-level-beautiful girl who is excessively polite to me and eats nothing apart from noodles according to both my children, describes herself as Ben's girlfriend. He objects to this terminology and insists that they are merely "a thing."

"But you've never done anything wrong to Lauren, have you? Or have you?" They've only been together—if that's the right way to put it—for three weeks.

"I put two 'x's in my last message instead of three. That's the latest thing."

"Did you do it deliberately?"

"No. I didn't even know I'd done it. Didn't think about it."

I indicate to turn onto the main road, wishing I had a choice and could stay a bit longer on Wyddial Lane.

Why? I did what I wanted to do, saw what there was to see from the outside. That ought to feel like enough.

"Who the fu— Who *counts kisses* in a message?" Ben says.

"Girls do. Some girls, anyway. Lauren's obviously one of them."

"First the problem was me not doing it—she'd always put a line of 'x's at the bottom of her messages and I never would, and she thought that meant I don't care about her—so I started putting them in, and now she's counting how many, and thinking it *means* something if I do one less than in the last message. That's crazy, right?"

"Ask Zannah if she counts how many kisses Murad puts in each message." Murad, to my knowledge, has only once done something wrong in the year and a half that he and Zannah have been whatever-they-call-it, and he turned up looking tearful the following morning, clutching a dozen red roses. Zannah was delighted, both by the roses and by the news of the sleepless night he'd suffered after "criticizing me when I'd done fuck all wrong. Mum, I literally don't care what you think about me swearing right now. Sometimes I *need* to swear, or I'd throw myself off a bridge."

I would be very surprised if my daughter did not keep on top of the kisses-per-message statistics.

Ben groans. "And now, because I didn't instantly reply and say 'Oh, sorry, sorry,' and send a long line of 'x's, she's going to accuse me of blanking her."

"So why not reply and send more kisses?"

"No! Why should I?"

"You're right. You shouldn't." Poor boy. He's fourteen, for God's sake—too young to be engaged in fraught relationship negotiations.

"I've done nothing wrong. Ask Zannah, Mum. Lauren's a high-maintenance, needy—"

"Ben!"

"*Person.* I was going to say 'person.'"

"Yeah. Course you were." I'm glad his instinct is to stand up for himself, and that he's not planning to cry all night and take roses around to Lauren's house tomorrow morning.

Ten minutes later we're parked in the right place. Ben climbs out of the car. "You coming to watch?" he asks, tossing his phone onto the passenger seat. I usually do. I'm not remotely interested in football, but I love to see Ben doing something healthy and worthwhile, something other than being the slave of an electronic device.

"In a bit," I say. "First I want to find a supermarket and get something for dinner tonight."

I watch him run off. Soon he and other red-

and-white-clad boys are pushing each other around happily—trying to trip each other up, grabbing each other's backpacks.

On the passenger seat, Ben's phone starts to ring. "Zannah" flashes up on the screen. I pick it up. "Hi, darling. Everything okay?" Zannah isn't normally awake before noon on a Saturday.

"Where's Ben?" The clipped precision of her words doesn't bode well.

"Football."

"Really? According to Snap Maps, he was on a street called Widdle Lane or something ten minutes ago. What the hell was he doing there?"

"Wyddial Lane. Yeah, that's nearby. Now we're at football."

"Right. When you next see him, can you please ask him to deal with his high-maintenance nightmare of a girlfriend? Thanks. She's just called me and *woken me up* to tell me that Ben blanked her in the middle of an important conversation, and can I ask him to message her? Their pathetic relationship is not my problem, Mum, and I'm not getting dragged into it."

"I—"

"Thanks, Mum. See you later. I'm going back to sleep. Ugh, it's *nine thirty*—grim."

She's gone. "Girlfriend," she said. So using that word

in a teenage context is not entirely disallowed. I add this important clue to my ongoing study of teenage behavior, glad that my investigative interest in every aspect of my children's lives is not reciprocated. Zannah and Ben aren't remotely concerned about the details of my day-to-day life. Neither of them asked me why I drove to Wyddial Lane before going to the St. Ives football ground; neither of them ever will.

There's something comforting about living with two people who never think about or question your behavior. I tried to explain this to Dominic once, when he complained that the kids never ask how our days have been. "They're teenagers," I said. "Anything happening outside of the teenage arena, they couldn't care less. Be thankful—remember the time Ben found cigarettes and a lighter in your jacket pocket, and you told him you gave up ages ago, and they must have been there for at least ten years? You didn't mind then that he didn't pounce on that and say, 'But wait, you only bought that jacket last month.'"

I don't have any bad habits that I'm concealing from the children. I've only ever had one near miss on a par with Dominic's cigarettes-and-lighter scare, and that was when Zannah was four and still interested enough in people outside her immediate peer group to notice strange things her mother did. She walked into the kitchen and found me with a pair of scissors in one hand and a photograph in the other. I must have looked upset and guilty, because she asked me if I was okay. "Of course, darling," I said in a bright voice.

How could I have explained to a four-year-old what I was doing—or to anyone? Dominic was working in the living room, which was next to the kitchen in our old house. He'd have been horrified. I remember holding my breath, praying that my unnaturally high-pitched "Of course" hadn't aroused his suspicions. Four-year-old Zannah looked doubtful, but she didn't ask any more questions.

The photograph she'd caught me holding was of the Braid family: Lewis and Flora and their three children—Thomas, Emily and Georgina. A happy family portrait, taken in the back garden. Flora had included it with their Christmas card. She always sent a photo, just as she always signed the card "Lewis, Flora . . ." His name had to come first because it was traditional, and the Braids cared about things like that. Dominic and I discussed it once. He said, "There's no way Lewis has ever said to Flora, 'Make sure to put my name first.' He'd totally leave the Christmas card sending to her, wouldn't he? I can't see him giving it a single second's thought."

"True," I said. "But he also would never have ended

up married to the kind of woman who wouldn't automatically put his name first on all correspondence."

So often over the past twelve years, I've wanted to tell Dominic what I did to that photograph and ask him which he thinks is worse: that, or what Flora did to me.

If I did, he'd probably laugh and say, "You're mad, Beth," in an affectionate way. He'd say the same—that I must be insane—about what I'm going to do next, which isn't what I've just told Ben.

I'm not going to the supermarket to buy tonight's dinner.

I'm going back to Wyddial Lane.

**I'm amazed** by how much more I notice now that I'm alone and there's no pressure from an imminent football match to distract me: the black metal mailbox attached to a gatepost, with "16" on it in white, the burglar alarm, the row of what might be tiny security cameras or some kind of motion sensors lining the top of the house just under the gutters, like a string of paranoid fairy lights.

As I drove back here, the gray sky gave way to a hazy blue and the sun appeared. Now it's properly warm for the first time this year. Even with the window down, it's already too hot in the car. I don't want to put on the air conditioning—that would involve starting up the engine, and the last thing I need is for Flora to look out and wonder about the stationary car with its engine running.

That's funny: I'm assuming that, if anyone's home, it's going to be Flora. Twelve years ago, when I still knew the Braids, Lewis's job on Saturdays was to ferry Thomas and Emily around by car to their various hobby duties: swimming lessons, drama club, tennis coaching. Five-year-old Thomas and three-year-old Emily had an absurd number of unmissable appointments. Lewis drove them to and fro while Flora caught up on the housework. He often used to say, "When I sell my company for a trillion dollars, we'll have a fleet of chauffeurs and I'll be able to spend weekends watching telly with my feet up." In those days, he was always making jokes about how he would one day be rich. If we went to a crowded bar or café where we had to raise our voices to be heard, Lewis would announce, "When I'm rich I'll have four chefs living in the annex of my mansion—Indian, Italian, French and English—so that I don't have to put up with other people's noise in order to get great food." Flora would tut at his imaginary extravagance and say, "Lew-*is*," in the same voice she used to subdue her small children when they were making a spectacle of themselves in public.

As it turned out, Lewis didn't need to worry about

selling his company in order to get rich. His hoarder-miser grandfather died and left him several million pounds that nobody in the Braid family had known the old man had. Lewis and Flora moved from a three-bedroom basement flat to 16 Wyddial Lane, which looks as if it must have at least eight bedrooms, and now perhaps Lewis has all those chefs and chauffeurs he used to joke about acquiring. Maybe he and Flora and their kids are all inside the house now, staring at their iPhones.

What age would Georgina be? Twelve, so not quite a teenager. We didn't let Zannah have a phone until she was thirteen, but her teenager behavior had definitely started by then. She was eleven the first time she raised her eyebrows and asked me why I imagined in my wildest dreams that she might want to go into town with someone wearing a carpet. (I was dressed in a beautiful woolen poncho at the time.)

I feel ashamed when I think about Georgina Braid, so I concentrate on the house instead. I got it wrong before—I glanced at it and decided it was modern, but, on closer inspection, it looks as if only the sides of it are newly built. The middle third of the building sticks out in front of the grand wings to the left and right, which are flat-fronted and have been added much more recently in what Zannah would call a "glow-up." The dark-red pantiled roof of the newest sections starts higher up than the roof of the middle part, which has two dormer windows set into it. Presumably this was once an average-sized cottage. Only just visible above the closed wooden gates is a lychgate-style roofed porch, with the same red tiles. Apart from the two roofs—house and porch—the entire frontage is gleaming white. It looks as if it might have been painted yesterday. The overall effect is of a sleek, contemporary white-cube-style house that has swallowed a lumpy old cottage and been unable to digest it.

There's a second building, long and low, standing between the house and the high wall, separating the two. Most likely it's a double or triple garage. If there's this much space at the front, there must be three times as much at the back, at least. I picture a long, striped lawn, alternating shades of lush green, and a smooth stone patio area, complete with top-of-the-range outdoor chairs and sofas: dark brown with plump cream cushions.

I wipe beads of sweat from my forehead. One open window isn't enough. How has it become so hot, suddenly? I open my door slightly, to let more air in.

Could I . . .

No. Absolutely not. I can't ring the bell and smile and say, "Hi, Flora. I was passing, and I thought I'd pop around on the off chance." Not after twelve years.

Is that why I came here, really? Not only to see the house but because I'm secretly hoping to rewrite the story?

*The Braids and the Leesons were best friends. Twelve years ago, they did not have any sort of argument, nor did they exchange harsh words. The last time they saw each other, everybody smiled and laughed and kissed and hugged good-bye. They talked about getting together again very soon—maybe next week, maybe taking the kids to the summer fair on Parker's Piece. As they enthusiastically agreed to ring each other to arrange this outing, Flora Braid and Beth Leeson both knew that there would be no phone call in either direction, and no trip to the fair. Dominic Leeson and Lewis Braid did not know this, because no one had told them that the two families would never meet or speak again.*

On the face of it, it makes no sense. Only Flora and I understand what happened—and I'll never know whether our understandings of it are the same. I've tried to explain to Dominic what happened from my point of view, and I suppose Flora must have told Lewis something, though perhaps not the truth . . .

This is ridiculous. I should be watching Ben play football, or finding a supermarket. I really do need to get something for dinner. Who cares where the Braids live now? I've seen everything there is to see—cream curtains at the upstairs windows, fat, square redbrick gateposts topped with large balls of gray stone, perfectly smooth and round, clashing horribly with the red brick.

I should go.

I'm about to start the car when I notice one coming up behind me: a Range Rover driving extra slowly. Wyddial Lane is a twenty-mile-an-hour zone, and this car's going at no more than ten. I'm watching it, willing it to speed up, when I notice a movement from another direction.

It's Flora's gates—they're opening.

The silver-gray Range Rover slows still further as it approaches the Braids' house. It inches forward, now almost level with my car. That's where it's heading: through the wooden gates, into the grounds of number 16. Of course: there's no way Lewis and Flora would have gates that you have to get out and open; they'd have some kind of remote-control setup.

I see glossy dark brown hair through the Range Rover's half-open window. It could well be Flora. It's bound to be.

*Shit.* Why did I think I could get away with this? She's going to see me.

*No, she won't. No one looks at a random parked car. She'll drive in through the gates and then they'll close again, and she won't think about what's beyond her property.*

I turn my face away, making sure to lean close to my open window in case there's anything to hear.

There's nothing for a few seconds. Then a crunch of tires on gravel, and the sound of the Range Rover's engine cutting out. A car door opens. Feet land on gravel and a woman's voice, halfway through a sentence as it emerges into the open air, drifts across to me: ". . . said I'm ready now. You can start. Yes. Start."

It's Flora. Unmistakably. She doesn't sound happy. She sounds . . . I don't know how to describe it. Afraid, resentful, prepared for the worst. Is something horrible about to happen?

*Don't be ridiculous. You heard, what, six words?*

I listen for a response but I hear nothing. Flora's probably on the phone.

*I've never heard her sound like that before.*

I can't not look. I have to risk it. If the worst happens and she spots me and I decide I can't face talking to her, I can just drive away, fast. That'd give her twenty-mile-an-hour-zone neighbors something to talk about. They could lobby to have Wyddial Lane sealed at both ends so that no one who doesn't live here can enter in future.

The gates of Newnham House are still wide open. And there's Flora: twelve years older, but it's definitely her. Her hair hasn't changed a bit: same dark brown with no hint of gray, same style. She's wearing white lace-up pumps, a pale gray hoodie and jeans.

"Home," she says, holding her phone half an inch away from her ear. "I'm at home."

I tried to push it away but it's back again: the strong sense that what I'm seeing isn't an ordinary conversation. There's something wrong.

A short silence follows. Then she says, "Hey, Chimp." She stops, raises her voice slightly and says, "Hey, Chimpyyy!"

Strange. The words don't match the expression on her face at all. She looks upset and worried, not in relaxed-greeting mode.

Is she talking to a new person now? Did the person she told she was ready put a child on the phone? It must be a child, surely. Who else would allow themselves to be called Chimpy? Her change of tone, too, from normal to deliberate, slower, louder . . .

Suddenly, she turns away and stretches out her arm, holding her phone as far away from herself as possible.

Then, a few seconds later, she brings it back to her ear and wipes her eyes with her other hand.

*She started to cry and didn't want Chimpy to hear.*

"Peterborough," she says in a more normal tone of voice. "Lucky. I'm very lucky."

Tears have filled my eyes. I can't blink. They'd spill over and then I'd be officially crying, which would be insane. This woman has been no part of my life for twelve years. Why should I care that something about this phone conversation has upset her?

"Yes. Tomorrow," she says. "I'll speak to you tomorrow." I watch as she puts her phone back in her bag. For a few seconds she stands still, looking tired and defeated, relieved that the conversation is over.

She opens the back door of the Range Rover, sticks her head in and says, "We're he-ere!" The deliberate jolly tone is unconvincing. Then she stands back. Nothing happens.

No surprises there. When the destination they've arrived at is their own home, teenagers don't get out of the car unless nagged extensively. If you're dropping them at a friend's house, it's a different story.

I hear Flora sigh. "Thomas! Emily!" she says in a singsong voice. "Come on, out you get!"

"Why are you speaking to them like they're still toddlers?" I mutter. "No wonder they're ignoring you."

Even when her kids were little, Flora's speaking-to-babies-and-children tone annoyed me. Thanks to her, I made sure I always addressed Zannah and Ben as if they were proper people.

Flora stands back as if someone's about to get out of the car. "That's it!" she says encouragingly.

*Quit it, woman, unless you want them to run off and join a cult. They ought to be able to get out of a car without a pep talk from their mother.*

A small, bright blue backpack tumbles from the car to the ground. I see a leg emerge, then a boy.

A very young boy.

What the hell?

"Come on, Emily," says Flora. "Thomas, pick up your bag."

A little girl rolls out of the car. She picks up the blue bag and hands it to the boy.

"Oh, well done, Emily," says Flora. "That's kind. Say thank you, Thomas."

This cannot be happening.

I touch the skin of my face with my right hand. Both feel equally cold. All of me feels frozen apart from my heart, which beats in my ears like something trapped in a tunnel.

I lean back in my seat, close my eyes for a few seconds, then open them and look again.

Nothing has changed. The little girl turns and, for a second, looks straight at me.

It's her. That T-shirt with the fluffy sheep on it . . . *Le petit mouton.*

The girl I'm looking at is Emily Braid, except she's not fifteen, as she should be—as she *must* be and is, unless the world has stopped making sense altogether.

This is the Emily Braid I knew twelve years ago, when she was three years old. And Thomas . . . I can't see all of his face, but I can see enough to know that he's still five years old, as he was when I last saw him in 2007.

I have to get out of here. I can't look anymore. Everything is wrong.

My fingers fumble for the car keys. I press them hard, then realize I'm pressing the wrong thing. It's the button on the dashboard, not the keys. I'm waiting for the engine to start and it won't because I'm not doing it right, because all I can think about is Thomas and Emily Braid.

Why are they—how *can* they be—still three and five? Why are they no older than they were twelve years ago?

Why haven't they grown?

# 2

Several hours later, walking back through my front door and closing it against the world feels like an achievement.

*I made it. Me and Ben, safely home.* How I was able to concentrate on driving properly, I've no idea. I probably shouldn't have risked it.

I lean against the wall in the hall, shut my eyes and let the sound of Ben telling Dominic about the match wash over me. His voice broke a few months ago, and we're still getting used to this new deeper one. His music teacher described him as a "bass" the other day, and it gave me a strange, dislocated feeling. My sweet little boy, a bass—the lowest and most booming kind of male voice there is. How did that happen?

How do I tell Dominic, or anyone, what I saw on Wyddial Lane?

I want to be in the living room, in a comfortable chair with my feet up, so that I can think about what to do. This seems an impossible goal. I can't imagine getting to that chair, even though the living room is only a few feet away. Nothing makes sense anymore, so I might as well stay here in the hall, looking at the clumps of mud from Ben's football boots that I'm going to need to pick up at some point.

Where was Georgina Braid? Why wasn't she in the car with her brother and sister? The last thing I saw before I drove away was Flora aiming her remote-control fob at the car to lock it, and then at the gates of her property, which started to glide shut. Maybe Georgina was inside the car and hadn't climbed out yet.

*She wouldn't have been able to climb. She's only a few months old. Flora would have lifted her out in her car seat and . . .*

I push the thought away, appalled by it. How can I, an intelligent adult woman, be thinking this? Georgina Braid was a few months old *twelve years ago*. She's twelve now. Thomas is seventeen and Emily fifteen. These are facts, not something to speculate about. There is no other possible outcome, for someone who was five in 2007, apart from to be seventeen now, in 2019.

*Unless they're dead.*

That's not a thought I want in my head either. Thomas, Emily and Georgina Braid are not dead. Why would they be? Two of them can't be, because . . .

*Because you've just seen them? Aged five and three, which we've established is impossible?* I didn't imagine what I saw. That's impossible too.

Ignoring the mud and the discarded football boots, I walk into the living room and sit down, like someone waiting for something momentous to happen.

There's a clattering of footsteps on the stairs, followed by Zan's voice: "You need to stop blanking Lauren, like, *right now*."

"Blanking? What does that mean?"

"You'll never understand, Dad, so don't make me explain."

"I'm not blanking her," Ben says. "I'm just not replying to her."

"Yeah, and she's been spamming me all morning about it—so please deal with her, so I don't have to."

The living room door bangs open, hitting the wall. Zannah walks in wearing a black sleeveless top and turquoise pajama bottoms with white spots. There's a lilac-colored towel wrapped around her head and a grainy-textured green substance all over her face. "Mum, can you make him sort Lauren out?" She squints at me. "What's up with you? You look weird."

Great: she's picked today to notice that I'm someone whose behavior might mean something. She stares at me, waiting for a response. In the hall, Dominic is saying that Gary, Ben's football coach, must regret taking Ben off at halftime, because the other team scored their two goals within seconds of Ben being replaced by an inferior defender. This irritates me in a way it wouldn't normally. Dom wasn't there. How does he know? From my brief exchange with Gary at the end of the game, he didn't strike me as a man racked with regret.

"Dad!" Zannah yells. "Come and look at Mum. There's something wrong with her."

The easiest thing would be to say I feel ill. No one would question it. It's hot. I'm not good with heat. It's a joke in our house. Ben and I have pale, Celtic complexions, and constitutions that function better in cooler weather. Dom and Zannah are dark, with olive skin, and love stretching out in the sun for hours at a time.

"Dad, get in here, seriously."

By the time Dom arrives, I've convinced myself that the most sensible thing is to pretend to be fine in the hope that I soon will be. Maybe by dinner time I'll have convinced myself that I didn't see five-year-old Thomas and three-year-old Emily, that the heat made me hallucinate.

"You okay?" Dominic asks me.

"She's *obviously* not okay."

"Zan, can you give me and Dad a minute?"

"What? Why? You're not getting divorced, are you? If you are, can I hit all the people I've been not hitting till now? Callie's parents are splitting up, and she's started punching and pushing me—in a jokey way, but, I mean . . . I have bruises! Actually, I'm so done with that girl."

"We're not splitting up," I tell her.

"Beth, what's wrong?" Dom asks. "Should I be worried?"

From the hall, Ben calls out, "Can you all stop causing drama?"

"Yeah, when we're *dead*," says Zan. "Life *is* drama, little bruth."

"Zannah, please," says Dom. "Upstairs."

"Mum, why can't I stay?"

"Suzannah. We very rarely ask you to—"

"Uh-oh. Dad's full-naming me. It must be serious. All right, I'm going." Zan flounces out of the room, slamming the door behind her.

I still approve of my advice to myself to say nothing

and try to pretend it didn't happen, but I know I can't follow it. The words are swelling inside me, preparing to burst out.

"I went to Hemingford Abbots while Ben was playing football."

Dom frowns. "Where's that?"

"Near St. Ives, where football was." I take a deep breath. This isn't the difficult part of the conversation. This bit should be easy. "It's where the Braids moved when they left Cambridge."

"Oh, right. Yeah, I remember—before they moved to Florida."

"What? Who moved to Florida?"

"The Braids did."

The door opens and Zannah reappears. "You're never going to get anywhere at this rate. You need me to interpret." She performs some invented-on-the-spot sign language.

"Were you listening outside the door?" asks Dom.

"Course I was." She rolls her eyes. "Who wouldn't?"

"The Braids didn't move to Florida," I say.

"They did. Something Beach."

"What makes you think that?"

He looks puzzled. "I don't know. I just . . . oh, I know. It might have been LinkedIn. I'm barely on it, but I think I got a message inviting me to follow

Lewis, or befriend him, or whatever it is people do on LinkedIn. I had a look at his profile and he was CEO of some company in Florida."

"They might have been in Florida at some point but they aren't anymore," I tell him. "While I was parked outside their house in Hemingford Abbots, a car drove through in the gates. Flora got out."

"I don't know who these people are, but maybe they've split up," says Zannah. "He's in Florida, she's here."

"Zan, please, can you let me talk to Dad alone?" If she hears what happened, she'll either be worried about me or scathingly sarcastic; I want to avoid both.

She looks disappointed, but, for once, doesn't argue. We listen as she stomps back up the two flights of stairs to her bedroom.

"I suppose they might have moved back," says Dominic.

"To the same house? It's the same address they gave us when they left Cambridge twelve years ago: 16 Wyddial Lane."

"They could have rented it out while they went to Florida temporarily. Either way, I'm not sure why it matters. To us, I mean."

"The children haven't aged," I blurt out, aware of how ridiculous it sounds.

"*What?*"

"Thomas and Emily. They should be seventeen and fifteen. Right?"

"Sounds about right, yeah."

"I saw them, Dom. Flora opened the back door of the car and said, 'Thomas! Emily! Out you get!' in a stupid singsong baby voice, and I thought 'Who talks to teenagers like that?' and then the children got out of the car and they weren't teenagers. They were little children."

Dom looks confused. Then he laughs, but tentatively—as if someone might stop him at any moment.

"Beth, that's impossible."

"Yeah. It is, isn't it? I didn't see Georgina . . ."

"Who?"

"Their youngest."

His eyes widen. "Shit—you know, I'd totally forgotten they had a third."

This doesn't surprise me. Lewis and Dom were never as close as Flora and I were. Dom probably hasn't thought about the Braids much since we last saw them.

He smiles. "Remember the two-thousand-pound changing room, in Corfu? That's something I'll never forget."

"I can't believe you didn't tell me they'd moved to Florida."

"Why would I? I deleted the message and forgot about it. We hadn't seen them for years."

"Since Thomas was five and Emily was three." I can't help shivering as I say it, despite the heat. "Which they can't still be."

"No, they can't."

"But, Dom, they *are*. I saw them. I heard Flora call them by their names, I saw their faces. Emily was wearing her 'Petit Mouton' T-shirt. You won't remember it, but . . . Thomas's clothes were the same too. It was them—today, but exactly as they were twelve years ago. And other things were wrong, too."

"Like what?"

I'm grateful that he hasn't laughed in my face, and even more grateful when he sits down next to me and says, "Tell me from the beginning, the whole story."

**It's several** hours later, and I haven't woken up yet, so I guess it wasn't a dream.

Dom, Zannah and I are sitting at our kitchen table. They're eating Italian food from our favorite local restaurant, Pirelli's. I'm trying to persuade myself to take a mouthful of the spinach and ricotta cannelloni Dom bought for me. I haven't felt hungry since this morning. Ben is staying overnight at his friend Aaron's house, and is the only member of the family who doesn't yet know what I saw, or what I cannot have seen, depending on your point of view. Zannah knows nearly everything, mainly from sneaking silently downstairs and listening at the living room door.

After wolfing down a shrimp and red pepper pizza, she pushes her plate aside, reaches for her notebook and pen and pulls them toward her. "Okay," she says. "Let's list all the possibilities."

"I had a funny turn because it was hot, and I didn't see what I think I saw."

"When Dad suggested that before, you said, 'I know what I saw.'"

"That's true."

"Mum, you're not making sense."

"If we're listing all the possibilities, we have to include me being . . . wrong. Deluded. However sure I am that I'm not."

"All right." Zannah makes a note. "That's possibility one."

Shouldn't we break it down a little further? A) There was no one there, and I hallucinated three people. B) I saw three people get out of a Range Rover, but they weren't Flora, Thomas and Emily Braid. There's probably a C) and a D) but I can't think what they might be.

"What are the other possibilities?" Zannah looks around the table, like a manager in a meeting waiting for her team to make helpful suggestions. "I can think of one."

"Go on," says Dom. I find it hard to believe we're having this conversation.

"Thomas and Emily, the ones you knew, died. Lewis and Flora then had two more kids, a boy and a girl, and gave them the same names, as a way of honoring the memories of Dead Thomas and Emily."

"Very, very unlikely," says Dom. "Though not impossible, I suppose. It'd explain a lot—the clothes, for example. Lots of families keep clothes their oldest kids have outgrown, and then, if you have more kids . . ." He turns to me. "If the two children you saw today were also Lewis and Flora's, there could well be a strong facial resemblance to Older Thomas and Emily."

"If Thomas and Emily Number 1 are dead, whatever killed them might have killed Georgina as well," Zannah points out.

"There should be an easily found record of it online if they're dead," says Dom.

"No, you're wrong," I say, realizing with a small jolt

of shock that I'm supposed to be part of the conversation. This isn't some kind of weird play and I'm not the audience. Dom and Zan are jumping from one thing to another too fast. "*If* Thomas and Emily had died, then yes, Flora might have wanted to have more children, but there's no way she'd give them the same names. No one would."

Dom shakes his head. "There's always somebody who'd do the bizarre thing you think no one would do."

"Not Flora. And . . . I'm not sure anyone would do it. Wouldn't you feel like you were trying to replicate your dead children in a sick way?"

"*I* would, yeah," says Dom. "But I'm not them. Lewis Braid's a weirdo. Always was. Flora wasn't, but . . . if she really did lose her children in some terrible accident, and she's traumatized, who knows what she might do?"

Zannah taps her pad with the pen. "All right, so, option one: Mum had a funny turn and didn't see or hear what she thinks she did. Option two: Mum saw a new, different Thomas and Emily who were named after their dead older siblings. What else?"

I don't feel that option two is in any way a possibility, but I don't have the energy to protest. *Flora wouldn't do that. No version of her, past, present, future, however freaked out, would do it.*

"Do we want to include a supernatural possibility?" asks Zannah.

"No," Dom and I say together.

"How about: Mum *did* see Thomas and Emily Braid, the same Thomas and Emily Braid she knew twelve years ago, and they're now teenagers, but they look like little kids because they've got some messed-up genetic disease?"

"That's ridiculous," I say.

"There are definitely some conditions that make you age faster, or slower," Zan insists. "If Lewis and Flora both had some kind of recessive gene that was a really bad fit with the other one's recessive gene . . . or something like that. See, Mum? A teacher at school actually taught me something—recessive genes. It might explain who Chimpy is, too."

"How?" asks Dom.

"If Thomas and Emily have both got this genetic thing, chances are Georgina has too. Chimpy might be her nickname. Maybe she needs to live in a home, which would obviously upset Flora, which explains why Mum said she looked and sounded so upset."

"No. This is stupid." Zannah looks hurt, and I feel guilty for cutting her off. I can't stand to think about Flora's children dying or having genetic diseases. I don't want to imagine every possible grotesque scenario.

"The two children I saw looked perfectly healthy and normal. There's no—" I break off and start again, trying to sound less dogmatic. "I don't believe there's any medical condition that could make two teenagers look like healthy, normal, much younger versions of themselves."

"Agreed. Overwhelmingly unlikely, verging on impossible," says Dom. "Still, it would explain why they suddenly dumped us as friends. Lewis was obsessed with perfection. He wouldn't have wanted us around to witness the non-growing phase of his children's lives."

"I'm still putting it on the list as option three," says Zannah. "Same Thomas and Emily, genetic condition that makes them look younger. What do Lewis and Flora do? What are their jobs?"

"They're both scientists by training," Dom tells her. "He's been working in IT for years, inventing systems that do all kinds of fancy things. She did the same kind of stuff. They worked together for years, until they had kids, and then Flora gave up her job and became a full-time mum."

"Scientists?" Zannah chews the lid of her pen thoughtfully. "No. Even if a science genius invented a drug that stopped people aging, they wouldn't freeze their kids in time at three and five. Those are pain-in-the-arse ages. You might freeze your kids at, like, nine and eleven."

"Trust me, if Lewis Braid had invented a way to halt the aging process, he'd have patented it, publicized it widely and made millions from it," says Dom. "He wouldn't keep quiet about it."

It ought to be possible for me to listen to this jokey back-and-forth and feel comforted. Instead, it's making me feel lonely. *No one but me saw what I saw.* No one saw how wrong it was. Flora wasn't okay—she didn't look it and she didn't sound it. Nothing about it was right.

"Mum, you've not eaten anything," says Zannah.

"I'm not hungry. You can have it if you want."

"Flora'd be what age now?" Dom asks. "Forty-three, like us?"

"Forty-two," I say. "She could easily have had two more children."

Zannah says, "What about this possibility: Flora *did* have two more kids after her first three. The youngest two look very similar to young Thomas and Emily, because they're siblings, and you saw them and freaked out, Mum. That's why you thought you heard Flora call them Thomas and Emily, but actually she called them by their real names, whatever those are—Hayden, Truelove, whatever."

"No. I heard her say, 'Thomas, Emily, out you get' before I saw their faces."

"Truelove?" Dom raises his eyebrows.

"That's what me and Murad want to call our first baby. Boy or girl."

"Truelove Rasheed?"

"Rasheed-Leeson—I don't know why you'd think I'm ditching my surname, Dad. Think again."

"Truelove? Really?"

"*Did* the Braids dump you as friends?" Zannah asks me. "Why?"

I look at Dom.

"What?" he says.

"I'm waiting to hear your answer."

"I've no idea what happened. All I know is, one minute they were our friends and then we never saw them again."

"Wait, what?" says Zan. "Dad, a minute ago you said they dumped you."

"Well, I assumed . . . Was it us who dumped them?" he asks me.

"By 'us,' do you mean me? You'd remember if you'd been responsible for ending the friendship, presumably." Why am I pushing this? It's the last thing I want to think or talk about.

I need to get away from this for a while.

"Have I done or said something wrong?" Dominic looks at Zannah, then at me. In a different frame of mind, I would find this endearing. Of the four of us, he's always the most willing to accept that something might be his fault.

"Dad has no idea why our friendship with the Braids ended," I tell Zannah, on my way out of the room.

# 3

I wake up. The curtains in our bedroom are open. It's dark outside, in that thorough way that looks like the night trying to tell you it hasn't finished.

I reach out and pat the top of my bedside cabinet but my phone's not in the place it always spends the night, plugged into the charger. And I'm still in my clothes, lying on the bed, not in it. That's right: I left Dom and Zannah in the kitchen and came in here, when I couldn't stand to hear any more stupid, outlandish theories. I must have closed my eyes . . .

I hardly ever remember my dreams but this time I've dragged a vivid one out of sleep with me: Dominic and I found three new rooms in our house that we'd never noticed before, and were really excited about having more space.

Maybe it was real. Maybe if I looked now, I'd find those three extra rooms. It's no more implausible than what happened in Hemingford Abbots.

Now that I'm less tired, my certainty has returned: I saw them. I saw five-year-old Thomas and three-year-old Emily. Not different children with the same names. I saw the same Thomas and Emily Braid, the ones I knew twelve years ago.

*Except that's impossible.*

"Dominic?" I call out.

The house responds with silence. I get up, take a sip of stale water from the glass by my bedside that's still half full from God knows when, and go upstairs to where Zannah and Ben's rooms are, and Dom's office. Our bedroom is on the ground floor, with what the estate agent called a "dressing room" attached to it. It's a large, modern room that the previous owners added on. I knew as soon as I saw it that I could add an extra door to make it directly accessible from the hall and it would be the perfect treatment room. Who would want to waste a brilliant space like that on getting dressed?

I told the agent how I planned to use the room. He blinked at me, and continued to refer to it as the dressing room for the rest of the viewing. His final words of wisdom before we left were: "People worry about curb appeal, but bear in mind, the inside of the house is the bit you're going to be seeing day in, day out."

"What a dick." Dom laughed as we drove away. "Does he think we're going to blindfold ourselves every time we get out of the car and walk to the front door? He basically told us he thinks the house is hideous."

I can't understand how anyone could think Crossways Cottage looks anything but beautiful from the outside. Unusual, yes, but lovely. As soon as I saw it, I adored the strange, two-buildings-stuck-together effect. It seemed so perfect for a house on a village green. Half of it's a white-fronted traditional cottage with a thatched roof and the other half is a joined-on barn conversion: black-painted wood. The two completely different roofs meet in the middle, and are different heights—one around a foot lower than the other. The overall effect is charming, not ugly. Unlike all the houses around it, which face the green head-on, ours stands at an angle, hence its name. If we ever have to move, I'll show people around myself instead of leaving it to a useless estate agent. I'll say, "Look how stunning it is—you'll be lucky if I agree to sell you this house at any price."

On the first floor, Zannah and Ben's bedroom doors

are wide open. Both of them close their doors whenever they're in their rooms, to remind intrusive parents to stay out. Dom's office door is closed, with a sliver of light visible underneath it. I can hear his fingers tapping at the keyboard.

I push open the door and find him slumped at his computer. "Sit up straight. Your back," I remind him.

"I wondered why it was aching." He stays in the same position, staring at the screen, which is full of different versions of the same logo: three letters twisted artfully around one another, a well-known local company's initials. "Which do you think's the strongest?" Dom asks. "I mean, obviously no one apart from the woman who commissioned them will notice the difference or care, but I have to pretend to have a strong opinion by next week."

"What time is it?"

"Five to . . . uh . . . twelve. Shit. It's nearly midnight."

For the first time since seeing what I saw in Hemingford Abbots, I wonder: could something be wrong with me? I've slept through the whole evening.

No. I'm fine. I needed to recharge, that's all.

*Is it? What about seeing the impossible?*

"Where's Zan?" I ask.

"She went to Victoria's."

"Is she staying overnight?" It's not unheard of for lifts home to be requested as late as 2 a.m.

"Yup. We can go to bed with no fear of chauffeur duties."

"I've just been asleep for three hours. I'm not tired."

"Well . . ."

"What?"

"I think you're more exhausted than you realize, Beth."

"Dom, I'm wide awake. I've just—"

"I'm not saying come to bed now if you don't want to, but . . . what happened to you today, and then sleeping all evening . . ."

"For God's sake, Dom. You have naps all the time." I'm unreasonably annoyed with him for having the same worry I just had; it makes it harder to dismiss.

"I think you've been stressing out and pushing yourself too hard for too long. You have clients from 8 a.m. till 6 p.m. five days a week. You never take a proper lunch hour—"

"That's a normal working week. We have a huge mortgage to pay off, university costs coming up in a few years . . ."

"I know. I just . . . it's evenings too. You're doing chores and admin till midnight, sometimes."

I wish I could deny it, but I can't. And there's no point saying that he's the one who's working late tonight; we both know that if I hadn't fallen asleep, we'd have spent the evening talking and Dom wouldn't have considered coming up here to work on logos. He'd have gone to bed at half past ten or eleven and . . . yes, I'd then have done a couple of hours of admin. Is there any woman with a full-time job and a family who doesn't need those hours between 11 p.m. and 1 a.m. to catch up and stay afloat? Probably. I don't know any.

Dom has a great talent that I lack: the ability not to give a toss about most things. He regularly announces that some project or other has been delayed, and seems amused by his colleagues' panic over missed deadlines. We've had the conversation dozens of times: me saying that if his work bores him, he should do something else, him telling me I don't understand, and that not caring about his career is his favorite hobby.

He reaches for my hand, squeezes it and says, "I also think you're stressing out about Zannah and Ben more than you realize."

"Zan and Ben are fine."

"I agree. But they're teenagers, and more demanding than they used to be, and you let it get to you in a way that I don't. Is their school good enough, is Zannah too cheeky and rebellious, is it our fault?"

"No, yes and yes, in that order." I sigh.

"Beth, everything's fine. You know my life's great guiding motto."

"I don't, actually."

"Let it wash over you."

I smile. "You've never told me that before."

"That's because I just made it up."

"But you're right: that *is* your life's guiding motto."

"I wonder if maybe it's not a coincidence," Dom says.

"What?"

"This idea of Thomas and Emily Braid, who are teenagers the same age as ours, being suddenly little kids again." He looks nervous. As if he knows he's taken it too far.

"Wait, are you saying . . ." I laugh. "You think I have a secret desire for Zannah and Ben to be little again, and it made me hallucinate five-year-old Thomas and three-year-old Emily?"

Dom looks suitably embarrassed. "That's crazy, isn't it?"

"Totally. Whatever I saw, whatever happened, it's not that. I think—" I break off, too proud to say it: *I think I'm handling the challenge of parenting two teenagers really well. My kids like me. I like them. How bad can it be?*

"Was Zan . . . okay?" I ask. "When she left, I mean."

"Fine."

"She wasn't worried by . . . any of it?"

"Not at all. I think she's enjoying the mystery. Which I'm a bit closer to solving." Dom smiles proudly, tapping his computer screen.

"You've searched online?"

"Extensively."

So he hasn't been working all evening.

"The good news is, nobody's dead. They're still in Delray Beach, Florida."

"If you're waiting for me to say I didn't see what I saw . . ."

"All I'm saying is, they live in America."

"That doesn't mean they're there right now, today."

Dom frowns. "True," he concedes.

"Maybe they never sold the Hemingford Abbots house. Rich people don't have to sell a house in order to buy a house. They might divide their time between England and Florida."

"You're right. Although . . ." He breaks off with a yawn.

*Although, even if the Braids still own the Wyddial Lane house, you didn't see what you think you saw— because that's not possible.*

"You should go to bed. Can I . . . ?" I point at his

computer. My laptop's in the car. I can't be bothered to go and get it.

"Sure." He stands up. "Look at the search history and you'll find everything I found. It'll make you feel better."

"Only if realizing that I'm having psychotic delusions is a good thing," I mutter, sliding into his chair.

"Well, no one's dead—that's a good thing. And I wouldn't call it a psychotic delusion. More of a—"

"I saw Flora, Dom. And Thomas and Emily, as they were twelve years ago. I saw and heard it all, everything I described."

He squeezes my shoulder. "I'm exhausted, Beth. We'll talk about it again tomorrow. Okay? Want me to bring you up some reheated cannelloni before I go to sleep?"

"No, thanks. I'll get some later." I still don't feel remotely hungry. "Oh—guess what they've called their house."

"Who?"

"The Braids."

"You mean the people living in the house in Hemingford Abbots that used to be the Braids'," Dom corrects me.

"It was named by them for sure, whether they live there now or not. It's called Newnham House. Typical Lewis. They lived in Newnham in Cambridge, so when they left Cambridge, they called their new house Newnham House, thinking it's a nice way to remember where they used to live."

"And . . . it isn't?"

"No. It's silly. It's clinging to the past in an artificial way—trying to pretend your new place is your old place." When Dom doesn't look convinced, I say, "We also moved out of Newnham. If I'd suggested calling this house Newnham House, would you have agreed?"

I never told Dominic why I wanted to leave Cambridge. Or, rather, I told him, but my explanation was a lie. It had nothing to do with wanting to live closer to my mum, though that's where we've ended up—in Little Holling in the Culver Valley. Mum's about fifteen minutes away by car, in Great Holling. Every time one of her friends pops in while I'm there, she says—and her wording of the line never varies—"What with me living in Great Holling and Beth living in Little Holling, it's like Goldilocks and the three bears!"

I've tried to tell her that it's nothing like that, and that nobody knows what she means. "Of course they do!" Mum insists. Once, Zannah heard this exchange and said to me later, "You're ruder to Gran than I am to you," which made me feel awful.

Mum also doesn't know why I was determined to

leave Newnham, having once thought I'd live there all my life. It was because of the Braids. Once they'd left, I couldn't bear the thought of staying there like something they'd discarded, of being the left-behind friends while they moved on to something bigger and better. If they were going to have a new start, then so were we.

"I'd happily swap the name Crossways Cottage for Newnham House," says Dom. "Or for anything less twee. Remember, I suggested getting rid of the name and making do with 10, The Green, but you—"

"Forget it." I wave his words away.

"Beth, I don't see anything wrong about the house name. Sorry. Can I go to bed now?"

He doesn't wait for an answer.

"Night," I call after him.

Once he's gone, I look at his computer's search history: LinkedIn, Instagram, Twitter. He's been busy. No Facebook, though. Why didn't he check to see if the Braids were on Facebook? I haven't either, not once in twelve years. I assumed I knew everything I needed to know about Flora and her family. I knew they'd moved to Wyddial Lane because they sent us a "new address" postcard—nothing personal written on it, just the address, minus the house's name. They must have added that later.

I remember thinking it odd that we'd be on their list;

Flora must have known, just as I did, that our friendship was over. Why would she want me to know where she was moving to? Perhaps she thought a complete cutoff would be too stark and obvious; easier to shift to a Christmas-cards-only friendship, allowing us both to pretend nothing was wrong, that we were simply too busy ever to meet.

I go to the bottom of the list of Dom's search results and click on the one he went to first. Might as well follow the same chronological order. I feel more alert than I have for a long time.

It's time to find the Braids.

**Lewis is** on LinkedIn, though there's no photograph of him, only a gray-man silhouette. So he couldn't be bothered to upload a picture. I skim over the list of his former jobs, several of which he had while I knew him. His current position, "2015 to present," is "CEO of VersaNova Technologies, an application software company based in Delray Beach, Florida."

Dominic was right. How absurd that I needed to see it with my own eyes to believe it, given that my eyes have been seeing the impossible lately, in broad daylight.

Still. Lewis working for a company in America doesn't mean Flora couldn't have been in Hemingford

Abbots this morning. *Yesterday morning*, I correct myself. It's after midnight; tomorrow is now technically today.

In Lewis's "Contact Information" there's a Versa Nova email address for him, and a link to a Twitter account. Clicking on the link, I find myself staring at his smiling face. The photo that he's chosen to represent him on his Twitter page, the one that appears in a little circle next to each of the short messages he's posted, is of him suntanned and grinning, wearing a black and gray baseball cap.

Like most people, after a gap of more than a decade, he looks older than when I last saw him.

*Like everyone except his children, Thomas and Emily, who look exactly the same as they did twelve years ago.*

His official name on Twitter is @VersaNovaLewB. I remember Ben joining Twitter and having to choose a name like that. He called himself @boycalledBen, which prompted Zannah to say that she was embarrassed to be related to him.

Lewis's smile is exactly the same: wide and full enough to dimple his cheeks and narrow his eyes, and alarming in its intensity, as if he might be about to start teasing you in a way you're not going to like very much. He used to do that a lot. There was no point in asking him to stop—he'd only do it more. For nearly a year he called Dominic "Rom-com Dom" after we all went to see a movie, *About a Boy*, that Dom liked as much as Flora and I did, despite being a man. Eventually Lewis professed to find this hilarious, though at first he found it implausible. On the way home from the cinema, he hounded Dom relentlessly: "Really? You liked it? I mean, *liked* liked? You actually thought it was good?"

There's a larger photograph, a kind of personalized banner at the top of his page. This one's a picture of Lewis and two other men in suits and ties, all grinning as if in competition to look the most triumphant. Lewis is in the middle and holding a knife, about to cut into a large, square cake covered in white icing and decorated with blue piped writing. The cake has four candles. Farther down Lewis's Twitter page, I find this same picture again, underneath the words "Happy 4th Birthday, VersaNova Technologies!"

That was posted on January 28 of this year. So Lewis's company is four years old.

"If it looks like it's four, it's probably sixteen," I mutter, then laugh. "Like Thomas and Emily." *Sorry, Lewis. You always hated my sense of humor.*

I'm exaggerating. He didn't hate it, but he didn't understand it either. Any joke that was eccentric or surreal, he used to object to. "But why's that funny?"

he would demand. "Tell me. I don't get it." His idea of funny was saying something and then contradicting it a few seconds later, especially if he knew it would disappoint you. The more crushed you looked, the funnier he found it. Like the time the four of us went on holiday together to Mexico. At Heathrow Airport, Lewis grabbed me by the arm and whispered in my ear, "Hey, see that lady over there? She said they were going to upgrade us to first class. Not just business class. *First.*"

"That's amazing," I said. "Do Dom and Flora know?" I couldn't understand why he was telling me alone, when the other two were standing only a short distance away.

"Actually, she didn't say that at all," said Lewis casually. "I made it up." Then he spent the next hour laughing at my gullibility.

*Imagine if he knew that you're gullible enough to believe Thomas and Emily haven't aged in the last twelve years . . .*

Dom's words from earlier replay in my mind: "Lewis Braid's a weirdo. Always was."

We liked him, though. Didn't we? We must have. We went on holiday with him more than once. He was one of our best friends.

All the same . . . Now that I come to think of it, I'm not sure I ever wholeheartedly liked him. I was always wary of what he might do or say. I found his confidence impressive, and he had a great line in entertaining rants, but I also felt unsettled by him. He suggested more activities that I felt a strong and defensive need to resist than most people I knew: marathon boozing sessions, terrifying-sounding hikes up the sides of remote mountains, unpleasant prank campaigns against anyone that any of us disliked.

He was interesting and unpredictable, and could liven up a room purely by walking into it.

He had a strange habit of bursting in, like a cowboy crashing into a barroom, about to pull a gun. Instead of a gun, Lewis would typically produce an unexpected declaration of some kind, something that made everyone look up and take notice. It could be anything from "Your lord and king is here, motherfuckers!" to "Hey, Dom, Beth—your next-door neighbor's wanking over his computer. I've identified the optimal vantage point, if you want to catch some of the action."

He was horrified when we all said we had no desire to watch. "What is wrong with you freaks?" he yelled, actually upset that we were missing out. "It's the most grotesque and embarrassing thing you're likely to see all year! You're a bunch of fucking *philistines.*"

Dom was right: Lewis Braid was weird, and he could be a giant pain in the arse, but we'd have had less fun without him around, no doubt about it. Life would have been much less colorful.

I read a few of the posts he's put on his Twitter page. There's no hint of his more outrageous side here. It's all bland and professional: "Small can be beautiful at VersaNova—great team, fantastic colleagues and a mission worth working for!" "It's a beautiful day for the opening of the ATARM conference here in Tampa, Florida. Proud to be one of the sponsors of this fantastic event, April 18–20!" "VersaNova named in @technovators Top 10 Tech Companies to Watch in 2019" "Great to see our technology director Sheryl Sotork featured in *CapInvest* Magazine" "'Patient Capital Delivers Results'—thrilled to be one of the software companies featured in this article."

I don't know what I was hoping for. *"Hey, guys, it's a bit strange but my oldest two children seem to have stopped growing . . ."*

I keep scrolling farther down, reading tweets from last week, last month, the end of last year. Lewis doesn't post on here very often—only once or twice a month. There's nothing interesting in December last year, or November.

*Wait. What's this?*

In October, he posted a link to what looks like an Instagram account in his name. I click to open it. I have no idea what a grown man's account might look like. I'm more familiar with Instagram than with Twitter or LinkedIn. Zannah sometimes shows me selfies posted there by girls at her school and asks me if I think they're flames, mingers or donkeys, which apparently, as everyone who is not "so lame" knows, are the only three categories.

Soon I'm staring at a photograph of Lewis on the deck of a boat, with a beautiful sunset behind him. He's been much more active on Instagram than he has on Twitter. There are a lot of photos on his page. I work through them methodically, opening them one by one: Lewis bare-chested in denim shorts, holding up a fish, Lewis with two other people, walking along a . . .

*Two other people.*

Are they . . . ?

I try to tell myself that I can't possibly know for certain, but I do. It's them. It's Thomas and Emily. Teenagers. As they should be. This is how the children I knew twelve years ago would look now. When I look at their faces, I have the same feeling I had when I first saw Lewis's photograph on Twitter: absolute recognition.

*If this is them, then who were the Thomas and Emily you saw in Hemingford Abbots?*

Suddenly I feel dizzy, as if I'm tumbling forward

without anything to stop me from falling. I hold on to the sides of Dom's desk with both hands and breathe deliberately until the fuzzy dots in my head start to clear.

*Come on, Beth, get a grip.* Nothing has changed, except in a good way. If these two golden, perfect, healthy-looking teenagers are Thomas and Emily Braid—and they are, I know they are—then they didn't die and get replaced by a new Thomas and Emily. And, all right, I still don't know who the two children were that I saw at 16 Wyddial Lane, but I never knew that, and so nothing has changed, nothing is any more frightening now than it was before. The Hemingford Abbots children could never have been Thomas and Emily Braid; they were too young. I should have known that from the start. I *did* know it, but I didn't fully believe it—not until I saw these photographs.

Do all Florida teenagers look radiant, sun-kissed and wholesome or is it just Lewis Braid's children? They certainly all seem to have a great life in America. Lewis's Instagram is an apparently endless pictorial log of every pleasure available to humankind: glasses of champagne, cheese-and-salsa-drizzled nachos, sunsets, beaches, swimming pools, balcony terraces in fancy-looking restaurants . . .

I take in all these things at a glance, but I don't care

enough about the details to look at them properly. The Braids are lucky and rich; I knew that already. Now, in Florida, they're luckier and richer. Of course they are.

Thomas and Emily are all I'm interested in. I scroll down, hoping for more photos of them.

Here's Emily in very short black shorts, a long, floaty white blouse and a red-and-navy-blue-bead ankle bracelet. Thomas, in the most recent pictures, has a surfboard under his arm and sun-bleached hair almost down to his shoulders. Unlike his sister, he seems to favor longer shorts, right down to his knees.

*His sister . . .*

My breath catches in my throat.

*Georgina.* Where is she?

I search two, three times to make sure. She isn't here. There are no children in these pictures apart from Thomas and Emily. And no Flora either.

Why would Lewis fill his Instagram with many pictures of two of his children, but none of the third? And none of his wife?

A memory surfaces suddenly, from the last time we were all together. Lewis said that if he were Thomas or Emily, he would hate Georgina, because now their parents' sizable estate would have to be divided between three people instead of two. Instantly, Flora looked unhappy. She often used to roll her eyes at him affectionately, as if he were a lovable but disobedient puppy, but this time she looked seriously uncomfortable. He put his arm around her and said, "I'm joking. Relax. There's plenty for everyone."

I only saw Georgina once, but she was a beautiful baby. And Lewis loves to show off all the wonderful things in his life—this Instagram account is proof of that—so why not Georgina? Why not Flora?

Other questions crowd my mind: *Why wasn't Georgina in the car yesterday? Why did Flora start crying when she spoke to Chimpy on the phone? Is there some kind of pattern here that I'm missing?*

Has something happened to Georgina Braid? No, there's no reason to think that. Flora's not in these pictures either, and I know nothing's happened to her. I saw her yesterday.

*I did. I saw her.* The rest of what I saw makes no sense, granted—but nothing is going to persuade me that I didn't see Flora.

I think back to the conversation at the kitchen table. When I told Zannah that the Braids had a third child in addition to the two I was sure I'd seen that day, Dom said, "Did they?" He didn't seem to know. If I hadn't told him, would he have remembered? *Did* he remember, genuinely, or did he simply take my word for it, assuming that I was bound to know better than him?

*No. It's not possible that I imagined the existence of Georgina Braid.* I can prove I didn't. It's the easiest thing in the world: all I'd need to do is dig out the pieces of a photograph I cut up many years ago and then kept, in its vandalized form, because it felt like the only way I could make amends for that small act of violence.

I stay where I am.

Of course Georgina Braid was real. I don't need to prove anything to anyone. I'm not crazy.

# 4

"It's seven in the morning, Beth." Dom blinks as I pull open the bedroom curtains. "I've been awake less than five minutes."

"I'm not asking you to do it now."

"I need coffee before I do anything."

"In the kitchen, all ready. Proper tar sludge." My name for Dom's preferred style of coffee is a running joke, as is his for mine: beige water.

"Thanks, but . . . Beth, I'm not bothering Lewis Braid. If you want to, fine, but I don't."

"I'm not on Twitter, LinkedIn or Instagram, and he's not on Facebook—or at least, I didn't find him there if he is. I'm asking you to send him *one* little message, that's all."

"Saying what? How are you after all these years,

and are your children by any chance five and three in Hemingford Abbots as well as being seventeen and fifteen in Florida?"

"Obviously not that."

"Then what?"

"Just 'How are you?' would be a start."

Dom laughs. "I see. So this one message, the only one I needed to send a minute ago, is now 'a start.' Start of what? A long back-and-forth?"

"Hopefully, yes. A chat. At some point you could say 'Beth said she was in Hemingford Abbots the other day and saw a woman who looked exactly like Flora,' or something. You could ask after Georgina, say, 'Hey, I was looking at your Instagram photos and there are loads of Thomas and Emily but none of Georgina—'"

"Whoa, hold on . . . I'm not going to message a guy I haven't seen for twelve years, and accuse him of discriminatory parenting. Look . . ." Dom hauls himself into an upright position. "You want a definitive answer, I get that. But you're never going to get one. There are loads of reasons—nonsinister ones—why Lewis might not put pictures of Flora and Georgina on Instagram."

"Such as?"

"Maybe Georgina's shy and doesn't like having her photo taken, or doesn't like the idea of pictures of her being online. Maybe Flora's . . . I don't know, a school-teacher, and doesn't want pictures of her private life online for her pupils to see. Or it's a coincidence that means nothing: Flora and Georgina happened to be somewhere else on the days Lewis took those photos."

"Flora, a schoolteacher?"

"It's possible, Beth. We haven't seen them for twelve years."

"I saw Flora yesterday," I say quietly.

Dom looks at me hard. "I need coffee," he says.

Five minutes later we're in the kitchen: Dom leaning against the counter, me sitting at the table waiting for whatever speech he's about to deliver. I know him so well, and can feel him preparing to say something labeled in his mind as "difficult but necessary."

Finally, he says, "You want me to contact Lewis in the hope that it'll help to make sense of what you saw yesterday. I understand that, but . . . it won't work, because there's no sense to be made of it. Think about it. We've seen Thomas and Emily on Lewis's Instagram, we know they're teenagers, we know they're in Delray Beach, Florida. Yes, they might divide their time between America and the UK, they might still own that house . . . but they can't still be five and three, can they?"

"No."

Dom looks relieved. "Right—and that means you

can't have seen what you thought you saw. You might have seen another woman with two different children, but you didn't see Flora Braid with Thomas and Emily twelve years younger than we know they are."

"So we're going with the 'I had a funny turn' theory?"

"I mean . . . unless Flora and Lewis have had two more kids and were crazy enough to name them after their two oldest kids. Does that seem likely to you? It'd explain the strong resemblance, but . . . no."

Five children: Thomas, Emily, Georgina, Thomas and Emily. No. That's not the explanation. Lewis might be weird, but he's not that weird.

"Beth, there's no point in contacting Lewis Braid. Seriously. The only way he could give you the closure you want is if he says, 'Oh, yeah, my kids exist in two different time streams. They're simultaneously teenagers and toddlers.' Since we know he's not going to say that, because it's factually and scientifically impossible . . ." Dom shrugs and takes a sip of his coffee. "I've got a better idea. We can sort this out without any help from Loony Lewis."

"How?"

"By going back to Hemingford Abbots."

"What? Really?" My mood lifts a little. The only thing I can't face is the prospect of doing nothing at all, which was what I expected Dom to suggest: do nothing, forget about it, assume I imagined the whole thing.

"Really," he says. "It's Sunday, neither of us is working. Let's do it, and draw a line under this today. My guess is, there's a brunette woman who looks superficially like Flora living in that house, and she's got two small kids. If you see them again, you'll realize . . . what must have happened."

"I'm up for it if you are." Is it possible that, a few hours from now, I'll be saying, "I can't believe I was so certain that three complete strangers were Flora, Thomas and Emily"? If that happens, what should I do? Go to the doctor and get my brain tested? I'm not sure which is worse: seeing the impossible and being the only person who knows it's real, or not being able to trust my own senses.

"What about the kids? Our kids," I clarify.

Dom pulls his phone out of his bathrobe pocket and starts tapping out a message. "Zan's got her key. I'll tell Ben to make sure she's home before he comes back."

While Dom has a shower, I go back to his computer, back to Facebook. Is it possible that the Braids aren't on here at all, any of them? It seems they're really not. Maybe they were until recently. I heard something on the radio a few weeks ago about people deleting their

Facebook accounts because they objected to something or other that the company had done.

I go from Facebook back to Lewis's Instagram to check that he hasn't posted anything new in the past few hours. He hasn't. I go to his Twitter page: no new posts there either.

I notice something that I didn't spot last night: a row of numbers underneath the company-birthday-celebration banner-photo. Lewis's "Following" number is 432. I click on it, not thinking it will work the way I want it to. Surely I won't be allowed to see who Lewis is following if I'm not one of his Twitter friends or whatever it's called.

Unbelievably, there seems to be no such restriction. The screen fills with names, and small pictures of smiling faces. My heart starts to pound. If any other Braid family members have Twitter accounts . . .

I scroll through as fast as I can. Grinning man, grinning man, cartoon character, business logo, business logo, woman in sunglasses, baseball team . . .

I force myself to slow down. I can't afford to miss any account that might be Flora or one of the children.

After a minute or so of doing this, my right hand starts to ache. I take a break to release a couple of trigger points with my left—one of the useful things about being a massage therapist is knowing exactly where to press, on the parts of my body that I can reach.

Once I've smoothed the ache away, I scroll down again and almost immediately find what I'm looking for. Thomas Braid is on Twitter. He's @tomtbraid2002. The "t," I remember suddenly, is for Tillotson—his middle name and Flora's surname before she married Lewis.

*2002. Thomas's birth year. Making him seventeen now.*

He has fewer followers than his father—only twenty-seven. He also hasn't put anything up on his page since June last year, when he reposted something from someone called "Bav" saying, "If you hear them chat shit about me, remember there will have been a time I was good to those goons."

A lot of Thomas's followers look similar to him: long-haired surfer types. Oh—and here's Emily Braid, who of course follows her brother. I click on the little picture of her and her page appears. I read her biographical blurb, and . . . wait. Does this mean . . .

My heart staggers an irregular beat, like a dancer out of time with the music.

"Soulmate of @ScobyJoe, sister of @tomtbraid 2002, daughter of @VersaNovaLewB #LoveFlorida

#sunshine #goodvibetribe." Followed by three small red hearts.

No mention of Georgina or Flora.

All right, so they're not Twitter users. That's the obvious answer. She's only included the important people in her life who have "@" names on this site. That makes sense.

But Flora and Georgina are also the only two family members missing from Lewis's Instagram. So . . . they don't do Twitter, and they don't like having their photographs taken?

I read through Emily Braid's Twitter posts. She's done many more than Thomas. They're generally dull: "Can't wait for Friday!" and "Need to have my lashes done again!" above a photograph of the top half of her face that is presumably meant to reveal the woeful state of her eyelashes. They look fine to me.

Dom appears behind me, showered and dressed. "All sorted on the Ben and Zan front. Shall we go?" He squints at the screen. "What are you doing? Is that Emily Braid's timeline?"

"It's her Twitter."

"Same thing."

There's no point drawing his attention to the missing mother and sister in her blurb about herself. I know what he'd say; I've just said it to myself.

And I'm not convinced. Irrational though it may be, I'm increasingly certain that something must be wrong in the Braid family.

I turn to face Dominic. "Please answer the question I'm about to ask you honestly, without trying to please me."

"Okay."

"Do you remember Georgina Braid? When I mentioned her yesterday, you'd forgotten all about her."

"There's not much to remember. She was a tiny sprog the only time I met her."

"But you remember her? You remember them all coming around, and Georgina being there—a baby? Flora carried her in and rocked her in her car seat, in our living room."

"I don't remember the car seat or the rocking, but, yeah, I remember the baby."

Good. That means I didn't imagine Georgina Braid and I don't need to go and look at the photograph I cut up all those years ago. The thought of holding the pieces in my hands makes me feel slightly nauseous.

"Ready?" Dom says, his voice full of confidence. He's eager to get going, sure we'll be back from Hemingford Abbots before lunchtime, having sorted out this mess once and for all.

I don't see how he can be right, but I hope he is.

**Wyddial Lane** hasn't changed. But then, why would it?

We're in Dom's car, not mine, parked across the road from Newnham House. Yesterday's heat has disappeared and it's cool and damp, the sky as gray as wet slate.

"Right." Dom claps his hands together. "Are we doing this, or what?"

There's something I've been trying not to say for a while now. I decided I wasn't going to ask him. I still think I shouldn't, but I know I'll blurt it out eventually, so I might as well get it over with. "Do you really not remember why it ended?"

"Why what ended?"

"Our friendship with the Braids."

"Did Lewis decide we weren't bling enough, once he'd inherited all that money?"

"Why would you think that?"

"Beth, I've no idea. I *don't* think that. You're right, I don't know why we stopped seeing them. I might have known once, but I've forgotten." He says all this in a God-help-us tone, as if it's petty to care why a long friendship suddenly ended.

"Money had nothing to do with it," I tell him. "It was because of Georgina."

*Chimpy.* It's the kind of nickname you might give

your youngest child . . . but then why did talking to Georgina, if it was her, make Flora cry? Is the answer to that question something to do with Georgina being nowhere in evidence on Lewis's Instagram? Is she, for some reason, a source of misery to both her parents?

"Who's Georgina?" Dom chuckles. "Just kidding."

"For God's sake, Dom."

"Beth, lighten up. And also . . . focus. We're here to investigate number 16, not to analyze the breakdown of our friendship with the Braids or discuss the miscarriage."

"The miscarriage?" Not a word I was expecting to hear today. "You mean *my* miscarriage?"

"Yeah. Should I not have mentioned it? You said the friendship ended because of Georgina. I thought you were implying that Flora having a third child just after you lost a baby . . . I guess I was wrong."

"I was nine weeks pregnant. I didn't think of it as losing a baby. Do you really think I'd allow my closest friendship to end for such a stupid reason—my jealousy because Flora had successfully had a third child when I'd failed? Am I that pathetic?"

"No, I . . . I'm sorry, I didn't mean—"

"I wasn't jealous. Not at all."

"I believe you. But then what did you mean—" He

PERFECT LITTLE CHILDREN · 73

breaks off. "Look, shall we do what we came here to do? When Captain Cook arrived at Botany Bay after sailing all the way from England, did he disembark and explore the terrain or did he sit in his boat, chatting about his friends' babies?"

I couldn't know less about Captain Cook if I tried, but I play along. "The first, I'm guessing. Who's going to do the talking, assuming someone's home?"

Will he ask me later, or forget about it, content never to know in what way Georgina Braid caused the end of my friendship with Flora?

"What if the door opens and Lewis is standing there?" I ask.

"That won't happen, because Lewis lives in Delray Beach, Florida, but if it does—if he still owns this house too, and he happens to be in it today—I'll say, 'Hi, Lewis. Long time no see. Would you mind showing me your secret stash of tiny cloned children?'"

Soon Dom and I are both laughing uncontrollably. It's probably nerves. We're about to do something a lot of people would never dream of doing.

Once we've pulled ourselves together, we get out of the car and walk briskly across Wyddial Lane toward the large wooden gates of number 16. Dom presses one of the illuminated buttons on the intercom. We stand and wait.

Nothing.

"Fuck," I say. "They're out."

"Then we wait," says Dom.

"How long?" *Please say, "All day."*

"Half an hour?"

It's not long enough. I want to wait until these gates open, however long it takes.

"Maybe an hour," Dom concedes. "Not longer, surely? They might have set off on a family holiday last night and not be due back for a week. Why don't we go for a walk and come back in a bit? It's better than just standing here."

"No. If we go anywhere, we might miss them. What about the neighbors? We could try them. The people at numbers 14 and 18 will know the name of the family at number 16. I bet everyone knows everyone on this street. It's a private road, so the council don't deal with it—and yet look how well maintained it is."

"Tarmac smoother than a baby's ass," Dom agrees.

"That means the neighbors will have regular meetings, and a residents' committee, coffee mornings . . . It's that kind of street."

"I know some of our neighbors' names, but I wouldn't give them out to a pair of strangers who turned up unannounced and said, 'Please tell me who lives next door.' I'd say something bland like, 'I'm afraid I couldn't possibly divulge . . .' or words to that effect. Which is what numbers 14 and 18 will say if we ask them."

"It's worth a try. We've come all this way. I'm not going home with nothing."

"Beth, we might have to."

I shake my head.

"All right, if you want to do it, let's do it," Dom says wearily. "I suppose the worst they can say is no. Or they might not be home."

I don't care. I'm waiting here on Wyddial Lane until I find someone who can answer my questions. I don't care if I'm being obsessive. Something inexplicable has happened, and I want to know why. Dom would be exactly the same if it had happened to him, if he knew he'd seen something he couldn't possibly have seen.

"I'm going to tell the truth," I say.

"To?"

"Any neighbors I talk to. Everyone. Until we got here, I was thinking I'd invent some story, but it's better to be upfront. Don't say anything, okay? Let me do the talking."

I head for number 14 and press the buzzer on the

intercom next to the wrought-iron gates. Immediately, there's movement.

"Dom, look."

"At what?"

I point through the gates' metal bars. "The front door's opening."

## 5

"No, it isn't," says Dom.

"It is. Just very slowly. Wait. Now it's stopped. It opened a tiny bit. Look, now it's moving again."

The door edges farther open but I can't see anybody, and no one comes out of the house.

Number 14 is a completely different kind of house from number 16: mock-Tudor, black and white lines all over it in a diamonds-within-squares pattern that would make my eyes ache if I looked at it for too long. There's a round pond in the middle of a turning circle in front of the house, with a squat little water fountain at the center of it.

"The door looks closed to me," Dom says.

"It's opening. I think someone's spying on us from inside."

As I say this, the front door of 14 Wyddial Lane closes with a click.

"Did you hear that?" I say. "Whoever's in there decided they didn't want to talk to us."

Dom nods. "You were right. Come on, let's try number 18."

"Wait. Look." Number 14's door is opening again. Slowly, it moves until it's all the way open. A woman emerges from the house: midsixties, short gray hair, large pearl earrings, beige trousers with sharp creases ironed into them. A white blouse with a fussy, flouncy bit at the top that looks like an attached scarf. Pinned to this is a coral-pink and white cameo brooch.

She approaches slowly, as if hoping to work out who Dominic and I are before she reaches us. Eventually she arrives at the gate, which she doesn't open.

"Is everything all right?" she asks me sharply.

This throws me. "Yes, thanks."

"I heard an argument. Raised voices."

It was hardly an argument, but I'm not going to quibble. "Yes, that was us, but we're fine, thank you. I wanted to—"

"If this gentleman's bothering you, I can summon help." Keeping her eyes on me, she nods at Dominic.

"Everything's fine, honestly. He's my husband."

"That, I'm afraid, is no guarantee of anything," the woman says sternly.

I'm not sure how to reply. "There's no problem, really."

"What can I do for you, then, if you don't need help?"

"My name's Beth Leeson," I tell her. "This is going to sound a bit weird. I was here yesterday, and—"

"I know you were."

"You do?"

"Yes. You parked your car over there, as you have today, except it was a different car. You had a boy with you. Then you drove away, and returned a short while later without the boy."

I smile at her. "You're very observant."

"One needs to be."

"That was my son, Ben. I dropped him off at his football match and then I came back."

"What business do you have on Wyddial Lane?"

"None, probably. That's what I'm hoping you can help me with. I had some friends who lived next door, at number 16, a few years ago. Lewis and Flora Braid."

"Before my time. When did they leave? I've only been here three years."

"I'm not exactly sure. But . . . I'm assuming

you know the names of the people who live in the house now?"

Her eyes narrow. "I do, yes."

"Are their names Lewis and Flora Braid?"

"No. Didn't you just tell me that your friends have moved away?"

"Yes. I was pretty sure they had, but I wanted to check."

"Well, now you've checked. A different family lives in the house now. No one by the name of Braid."

"Thank you," says Dom. "That's incredibly helpful to know."

She gives him a curt nod.

"Come on, Beth."

"Hold on. Would you mind telling me the name of the family that lives at number 16 now?" I ask the woman.

"I think I would, yes. I wouldn't appreciate it if they gave my name to complete strangers. Why do you care what they're called? I thought it was your friends the Braids you were interested in."

"It is," says Dom. "Thank you. Sorry for bothering you."

"Wait a second," I say. "Maybe if I tell you—"

"Beth," says Dom forcefully. He puts his hand on my arm and tries to steer me away.

"I'm not ready to leave yet," I snap at him. Great. Now the woman behind the gate will be confirmed in her suspicion that he's a tyrannical wife beater.

"They're called Cater," she says unexpectedly. "Kevin and Jeanette Cater."

"Thank you so much. Do they have young children? Is one of them known as Chimp, or Chimpy?"

The woman looks affronted. She takes a step back.

"Why on earth would you ask me that?"

"Does either of them drive a silver Range Rover?"

"May I ask what is going on here?" She stares at me with undisguised suspicion. "This is starting to feel more than a little irregular. A great deal more is involved, I suspect, than a desire to know if an old friend is still in the same house."

"Yes. You're right." If I want more information from her, I'm going to have to tell her. "My friends—the Braids—are supposed to have moved away. To America. But when I was here yesterday morning, I saw a silver Range Rover drive up and go in through the gates. A woman and two kids got out, and . . . they were my friend and her two oldest children. They were the Braids. I . . . I recognized them."

The woman shakes her head. "I'm afraid your story doesn't add up, Mrs. . . ."

"Beth Leeson. You can call me Beth."

"*My* name is Marilyn Oxley." She says this as if she thinks it should make a difference to what happens next. "If you knew your friends had moved away, why on earth would you come and park outside their former home? Hmm?"

"I didn't know at that point."

"The silver Range Rover you saw is Jeanette Cater's car."

I swallow hard.

"What's more, I heard a voice that I recognized as the voice of Mrs. Cater. As you can imagine, I know her voice rather well, from living next door to her. Now, if you're telling me that your friend Mrs. Braid got out of the car with her two children, why on earth didn't you rush over and say hello? You didn't do that, did you? You waited and you watched, while Mrs. Cater got out of her car and spoke to somebody on the telephone. I saw you, from my bedroom window."

"You were watching me?"

"I was. It's not common for cars to appear on our street and for nobody to get out of them. We residents of Wyddial Lane take our home security seriously. I decided your behavior was suspicious, so, yes, I watched you until you left."

"It's not at all suspicious once you know why," I tell her. "If I could maybe . . ." *Stop it. You can't invite yourself into her house.* "If we can talk properly, I'll tell you the whole story. Flora Braid and I were once best friends, but we're not anymore."

"I think I've heard enough," says Marilyn Oxley. "You'd better be on your way. I've told you who lives next door, against my better judgment. Let's leave it at that, shall we?"

"Please, just one more thing. You've been so helpful. If you could tell me . . . is Jeanette Cater around five foot six, with wavy, dark brown, shoulder-length hair?"

A long, tense pause follows. Then, "Yes, that is an accurate description of Mrs. Cater. Good-bye, Mrs. Leeson."

"Does she have two children, about five and three?"

She must have heard me, but she keeps walking in the opposite direction.

"Thomas and Emily?" I call after her.

She stops. Turns to face me. Her expression makes me gasp. She didn't look this angry or disgusted a moment ago.

"Never come back to Wyddial Lane again," she says. "If I see you here, I shall call the police."

She walks briskly back to her house.

"Wait . . ." I whisper.

The front door of number 14 slams shut.

---

**"I'll be** the judge of this." Zannah flops down on the sofa next to me. She's wearing pajamas again—different ones: white, dotted with pink and green watermelons. Her hair is wet, her face pink and glowing. She smells as if she's spent the last few hours marinating herself in some sort of rose and lemon mixture.

"The judge of what?" says Dom.

"Your and Mum's stupid argument."

"Not an argument," I say. "A discussion."

It's one that's been in progress ever since I typed the names Kevin and Jeanette Cater into Google's search box several hours ago. LinkedIn soon offered me a Kevin Cater who worked for a company called CEMA Technologies in Cambridge between 1997 and 2008. In 2008, Kevin left CEMA and went to work for a different company, also in Cambridge, that went bankrupt two years later. We could find nothing online about what he did after that.

Both Lewis and Flora Braid used to work for CEMA Technologies. Dom has been trying to persuade me that this is pure coincidence.

There were a few Jeanette Caters in our search results, but none who could conceivably be the woman living at Newnham House. A search for the name

"Cater" along with the Wyddial Lane address yielded nothing.

"I agree with Mum," Zannah says. If she's able to take a side, she must have been eavesdropping. Again. "It's too big a coincidence. It's another link between the new owners of the house and the old: first Mum sees the Braids outside the Caters' house when they're supposed to have moved to Florida, then it turns out Lewis and Flora and this Kevin guy all worked together. That's weird. Like, significant weird."

"They didn't necessarily work together," says Dom. "They worked for the same company."

"At the same time," I mutter.

"All three of them were Cambridge-based science-and-tech types—in 1997 there weren't as many of those kinds of companies in Cambridge as there are now."

"Dad, how often have you bought a house from someone you used to work with? Never, right?"

"Zannah, mock all you like, but in real life there are plenty of coincidences. Did Mum tell you what happened when we went to Hemingford Abbots this morning?"

"Yup. And the Twitter and Instagram stuff from last night—which is also just too messed up. If I ever have three kids, there's no way I'll put photos of only two of them on my Instagram. I think something freaky's going on."

"So do I. I'm sure of it." I have the confidence to say this out loud, now that my brave daughter has said it first.

"I've no idea what, though. I can tell you what Murad and Ben think, if you like?"

"You've told them? Zan!"

"Was I not supposed to? You didn't say it was a secret. Why shouldn't they know? Ben's your son and Murad's your future son-in-law." As an afterthought, she mutters, "Unless he bails on me, which he'd better not."

It seems my daughter is unofficially engaged. I wonder if she's ever going to tell us more formally.

"When did you tell him? You haven't seen him since I told you."

Zan rolls her eyes. "I communicated with him using my electronic device, Mother. Relax. He's not going to tell anyone."

Dom says, "Shouldn't you be revising? Your GCSEs start in a month."

I wait for Zannah to blow up, but instead she says with a knowing weariness, "Ugh, Dad. Yeah, I should be doing a lot of things," as if he couldn't possibly imagine the full horror of everything in her life that's getting neglected at the moment.

She's right—he can't. I can, though. I never see her do any homework. Whenever I walk into her bedroom, I find it full of old plastic water and Diet Coke bottles, bowls of congealing cereal, used makeup pads covered in patches of beige foundation, false painted nails, torn pairs of tights. It takes me at least an hour to sort out the mess each time and make the room look nice again.

When I was a child, I didn't need to tidy my room. Not once. It never got messy. Tidiness was a house rule, one of the most important to my retired navy officer father. I would never have dreamed of leaving a discarded pair of tights on the floor overnight; I'd been trained to believe it wasn't a possibility.

Dom and I have left it too late to introduce a strict tidiness policy with Zannah and Ben, and I'm not sure I'd want to. I look at their lives and feel instinctively that they're much harder than mine was at their age. They both complain about stress in a way that I never did. Their friends are more troubled and difficult; their school is full of self-harmers, drug takers and kids with a whole range of conditions I hadn't heard of until I was at least thirty. I'm pretty sure Zan and Ben aren't being taught properly, even in the lessons that aren't sabotaged by out-of-control behavior from the most chaotic students.

I didn't love school as a teenager, but I didn't hate it either—not the way Zannah and Ben hate Bankside Park. And I don't remember resenting my teachers anywhere near as much as I resent theirs for the way they gleefully dish out detentions to anyone who doesn't hand in their homework on time, while at the same time marking and returning only a tiny fraction of the work their pupils submit. Neither Zannah nor Ben has ever had a piece of English homework returned with a mark or a comment from a teacher on it—not once since they started secondary school. I've talked to the head about it several times. He makes soothing noises, but nothing ever changes.

"What do Murad and Ben think?" I ask Zan.

"About the Caters and the Braids?"

This throws me a little. *The Caters and the Braids. As if they're a kind of foursome.*

"About what I saw. Or what I think I saw."

"They both think Jeanette Cater *is* Flora Braid—same person, new name."

"Why would she change her name?" Dom asks.

"Dad, I'm not psychic. But it'd explain Mum being sure she saw Flora, and the old woman saying she heard the voice of Jeanette."

"Hold on. No." Dom paces up and down the room. "That particular neighbor hasn't lived on Wyddial Lane for very long, but others must have been there longer. They'd have noticed if Flora Braid suddenly changed her name to Jeanette Cater."

"Maybe they did notice," I say. "We don't know that they didn't."

"Murad thinks it's too much of a coincidence for both the Caters and the Braids to have kids called Thomas and Emily." Zannah picks up the remote control, turns on the TV and immediately mutes it. She and Ben always do this; I've no idea why.

"Right," says Dom. "So, he thinks they're the same two kids, then? Do they belong to the Caters or the Braids? If the latter, how does he explain their failure to get taller or older, despite the passing of twelve years? And the fact that they're also teenagers living in Florida?"

"He can't explain any of that, and neither can you," Zannah fires back triumphantly.

"I think I might be able to. We know a lot more than we did yesterday. Jeanette Cater is the same physical type as Flora Braid, with the same hair color and style." Dom looks at me. "The car you saw her get out of is Jeanette Cater's car, according to her neighbor. And you saw her outside a house that you believed, at the time, belonged to Flora. So . . . here's my best guess: the Caters have two young children. They might be called Thomas and Emily—"

"No," Zan talks over him. "Another huge coincidence? No way."

"I agree, it's unlikely. So maybe one of them's called Thomas and the other's called something else." He's making it up as he goes along. "Superficially, they look like Thomas and Emily Braid did when they were little . . ."

"So did I imagine hearing Flora's voice, then?" I ask him. "Did I imagine recognizing her face, and hearing her, clearly, call them Thomas and Emily? You saw and heard what happened when I asked Marilyn Oxley about the Caters' children. How do you explain that?"

"What happened?" Zannah asks.

"Her whole demeanor changed. She went from restrained and suspicious to . . . full-on contempt, threatening me with the police."

"She probably thought you were a pair of pedos," says Zannah. "Lurking outside the house, asking weird questions about little kids."

"Why would she think that? The natural thing for her to think at that point is that I'm having trouble accepting that I got it so wrong. I've already asked her if Jeanette has dark wavy hair and a silver Range Rover—

two of the things I saw, two identifying details. The logical next thing for me to ask about is the only other thing I saw: the two children."

"But you said she also assumed, based on nothing, that Dad was a wife beater. So she's not logical. 'Yes, great point, Zannah,' said nobody."

I stand up and walk over to the window. Our house's location is about as un-private as you can get: the village green—no walls or gates to protect us from prying eyes. There are always people out there walking dogs, parents pushing kids on the swings, people strolling past on their way to the village's only pub, The Olde Jug.

"Beth, Zan's right. There's no reason to think Marilyn Oxley's capable of rational behavior and there's some evidence that she isn't. All that faffing around with her front door, as if she wasn't sure whether to open it or not. And why the hell is she staring out of the window every second of every day? If she's normal, I'm King Harold of Wessex."

"It wasn't me asking about Jeanette Cater's children that made her turn like that."

Dom and Zannah exchange a look.

"Mum, you just said it was."

"Not at first. When I first asked her if Jeanette had kids of around five and three, she was already heading back toward her house, having decided the conversation was over. She heard my question and kept walking. It was when I said their names that she got angry and turned on me. I shouted after her, 'Thomas and Emily.' It was hearing those two names that made her flip out."

"So what do you think that means?" says Dom.

"Wait. Does it mean . . ." Zannah narrows her eyes. "This is insane, obviously, but . . . might it mean that the two little Cater kids *are* called Thomas and Emily?"

Thank goodness someone understands the way my mind works. I'm grateful for any scrap of evidence that proves I'm not losing the plot.

"You're going to have to fill me in," says Dom. "Why, *how*, could it mean that?"

"Think about it," I say. "Marilyn Oxley moved to Wyddial Lane after the Braids left, so there's no reason to think she knows any of their names. Let's assume the Cater children *are* called Thomas and Emily—the two names I heard the dark-haired woman say. When I ask if those are their names, what's Marilyn Oxley likely to think?"

"You mean . . . she'd think you've just presented yourself as someone who knows nothing about the Caters, you don't even know their last name, yet you seem to know the names of their children?"

"Precisely. When she heard me say those names, she must have thought everything I'd told her was a lie. If I've been lying, and I'm suddenly revealing an interest in Thomas and Emily Cater that I've kept hidden until so late in the conversation . . . That's the only way I can make sense of her police threat."

"But that only works if the Cater kids are called Thomas and Emily, which we agreed would be too much of a crazy coincidence." Zannah groans. "Mum, this is doing my head in. I need answers. Can't you go back there and—"

"Get arrested? No." Dom is keen to rule this out as an option.

I'd willingly spend a night in a cell if it would get me the answers I want.

"How about contacting the Braids in Florida?" Zannah suggests. "If they used to work with Kevin Cater, and he bought their house, there's a chance they've kept in touch with him. If he's got kids with the same names as their oldest two, they might know."

"That's not a bad idea," I say. The Caters might be on Flora's Christmas card list—the same one we were removed from after the photograph incident. "But . . . I'd have to explain how I came to know about the Caters in the first place."

"The Caters *cannot* have kids with the same names

as the Braids *and* live in the same house, *and* look the same," Zannah says. "That just can't happen. It's like something out of a horror film. I mean . . . one name the same, maybe, but two?"

"Zannah's right, Dom. We need to make contact with Lewis in Florida."

"I wouldn't say we need to, but—"

"Dad!"

One of my husband's best qualities is that he knows when he's lost an argument.

"All right. If I have a spare minute tomorrow, I'll—"

"I'll do it," I say. "And not tomorrow. Now. Right now."

# 6

An hour later, thanks to my son, I have an Instagram account. He's put it on my phone, too—a little pink and orange camera icon—so that I can correspond with Lewis Braid more easily.

*If he replies.*

I'd have preferred to contact Flora directly, but I've searched the whole house and can't find the old address book where I wrote down her number. I probably threw it away years ago.

So far I've sent Lewis one message: "Hi Lewis, Beth Leeson here! Could you send me a phone number where I can contact you? It's fairly urgent."

Zannah was watching over my shoulder as I typed. "Is that . . . Oh, my God! Ben! She's using punctuation."

"Lewis Braid uses punctuation on Instagram too," I said as both my children laughed at me.

Then I pressed send. Ever since, I've been picking up my phone approximately every ten seconds, and using the other nine of each cycle to prepare dinner.

"Beth," says Dominic from the kitchen table.

"Mm?"

"You know it might be hours before—"

"I know."

"Then stop looking."

"I can't."

"Can you come and sit down for a minute? I want to talk to you, while the kids aren't around."

"I can talk while I chop peppers."

"I know, but I'd like to . . ."

I listen to the silence as he reworks his plan and decides it doesn't matter if I sit down or not. It's lucky we're not both equally stubborn; we'd have had to get divorced long ago.

"All right. I get why you want to try and understand what you saw yesterday. Anyone would want to. But . . . have you considered the possibility that you'll never know for sure?"

"Of course I have."

"And you're okay with that?"

"No. Which is why I'm trying to find out."

"And hopefully Lewis'll get back to you. But what do you think he's going to say?"

"If I knew that, I wouldn't need him to phone me."

"Here's what I think he's going to say." I hear Dom pouring himself another glass of wine from the bottle on the table. "'Hey, Beth, great to hear from you! What? No, Flora wasn't in Hemingford Abbots yesterday—she's here in Florida with me. What, the children? Yeah, they're all here too. Sorry? Kevin Cater? Yeah, we knew him vaguely. Couldn't believe it when he and his wife turned up to view our house—and then they bought it! No, sorry, I've no idea if they've got kids or what they're called.'"

"He might say all that," I agree. "We don't know that he will."

"What if he does? Will you accept that you've found out all you can, and leave it alone?"

I laugh. "Why would I do that?"

"What else could you do, at that point?"

"If Kevin and Jeanette Cater have two young kids, I can find out their names. I can talk to other neighbors on Wyddial Lane, find out if any of them knew Flora *and* Jeanette Cater. Or if any of them say, 'She's the same person, and we have no idea why she suddenly changed her name.'"

Behind me, I hear Dom's long, slow sigh. Clearly my answer wasn't the one he was hoping for.

"Put that knife down, and the peppers, and come and sit here," he says. He sounds so reasonable and hopeful, it's hard to resist. From his tone, I can almost believe that something brilliant will happen as soon as I sit down at the table, something that'll solve every problem.

I compromise by bringing the chopping board and knife with me, so that I can sit and chop at the same time. Dom thinks if we're face-to-face, he'll be able to persuade me. Looking straight at him isn't going to change what's in my head.

"Yes, you could find out the names of the Caters' kids if you tried, but what good would it do? If they're called Thomas and Emily, then yes, it's a massive coincidence and bloody strange, I agree—but so what? And if they're not called Thomas and Emily, then . . . well, you probably didn't hear anyone call them Thomas and Emily. People can get things wrong, Beth. Even you."

*Don't get defensive. Answer as calmly as possible.*

"That's true. But why would that happen to me, when it never has before? It was hot yesterday, but not that hot. And . . . everything else I've seen before and since is real. The bottle, our wineglasses, these chopped red peppers . . . you can see them too, right?"

"Beth . . ."

"I'm not being facetious. I'm serious. I've had no other delusions or hallucinations. This isn't part of a pattern. That makes me a reliable witness. I *trust* myself. I know who I saw yesterday. I saw Flora Braid. I heard her speak. She was my best friend for more than a decade. I'm not wrong about this."

"All right, let's say you did. You saw Flora. And with her were two small children—who we *know* can't be Thomas and Emily because they're not little kids anymore. So, fine. You saw Flora with two kids. She called them Thomas and Emily. Maybe she's calling herself Jeanette Cater these days. Who cares? None of these people are anything to do with us. We can forget about them and get on with our lives. Or at least I hope we can. So far, Zan and Ben don't seem too freaked out by all this, which is great, but if it carries on . . ."

"They're fine, Dom. Zannah's loving it."

"Too much, yes. She's got her GCSEs coming up. It's hard enough convincing her they matter as it is. Having her mother fall apart at the exact time that—"

"Wait. Who said anything about falling apart?" I take the chopping board back over to the counter and

start to chop an onion. "Wanting to find an explanation for something isn't the same as having a nervous
breakdown, Dom. Look, here I am, cooking dinner.
I'm not crying, screaming, disintegrating."

"No, but you are obsessing. We've talked about
nothing else since yesterday morning—which is fine,
because it's recent and it's peculiar, I'm not denying
that, but . . . you know."

"You want me to just forget all about it?"

Will he have the guts to say it?

"Not immediately—speak to Lewis if you can—but
at a certain point, yes. We're going to need to forget
this and move on. Accept that we'll never know the
answer."

"That's not fair," I say quietly.

"What isn't?"

"Pushing something you know you'll be able to do
and I won't."

"Beth, it makes no sense to pursue this beyond a
certain point if no answer presents itself soon. Let's not
allow it to take over our lives."

Dom's right: it's not ideal for my thoughts to be
full of an unsolvable mystery when Zannah's GCSEs
are coming up. Could it be some kind of stress-escape
fantasy? Would that be enough to make me imagine
I saw . . .

*No. No way.*

I might never know what it means, but I'll always know what I saw.

I check my phone. There's a new notification, from Instagram. *Lewis.* "He's replied. 'Call me!' with an exclamation mark. He's sent a number."

"Good. Then let's call him," says Dom.

**The Olde** Jug, our local village pub, has been around since the seventeenth century, but has only been called The Olde Jug since the new owners took over last March, added on a conservatory at the back, and hung hundreds of pottery jugs from the dining-room ceiling. These changes caused a rift in the village that's still noticeable more than a year later.

The discouraging estate agent warned Dom and me about village life. "Personally, give me the city any day," he said. "I live two minutes' walk from Rawndesley station, shops all around me. Don't need to get into my car to go anywhere, apart from for work. Villages are all well and good if you like that sort of thing, but they're not right for everyone—your neighbors popping in all the time, wanting to know your business."

This was the one consideration that made me anxious about moving to Little Holling. Dom reassured me. "Think of it this way: how much fun would it be to live in a village if you couldn't give less of a shit what the other villagers think of you?"

So we decided to eschew the film club, the book group and all other such delights, and hope for the best. Dominic often boasts that he's avoided our neighbors so successfully that he has no idea what any of them think of him. The only exception to this is The Olde Jug's new owners. When they first arrived and changed the pub, the opposition to their proposed new-conservatory shake-up was so loud and hysterical that it reached even Dom's ears. At first it seemed as if the entire village might boycott the pub, so Dom decided we had to go there as often as we could. For a while, we ate there four times a week, even though it was a stretch, financially. "I'm not letting a perfectly nice pub go out of business because some idiots can't cope with change," Dom insisted.

He also went around knocking on doors one day, trying to persuade people to see sense. Many of them did—chiefly, those who had most missed their evening pint or four while the whole-village boycott was in progress—and that was how Little Holling divided into two factions, the one led by my husband and the one led by the deeply obnoxious Val and Geoff Monk, who, now, turn and walk the other way if they see any member of my family heading in their direction.

Robin and Ruth, The Olde Jug's new owners, have become our close friends, even though we no longer bankrupt ourselves eating their Sunday roasts and Friday fish-and-chip suppers every week. I've told Dom I know they'll understand, and they will.

"Well, I don't," he says. "Why not ring Lewis from the car, if you don't want to do it in our house?" he asks as we walk across the green to the pub. It's an odd-looking building: tall and narrow, with a white-painted brick frontage and red-painted stonework above and below the windows. It doesn't look like a typical village-green pub.

"With people strolling past, nosy villagers knocking on the window, dogs barking on the green?" I say. "No thanks. I want to be in a quiet room, alone, where I know Zan and Ben aren't going to stick their heads around the door and yell, 'Can we go into town and get a Nando's?'"

"You're building this up too much, Beth. Going to a special place to make the call . . ."

"Dom, I'm nipping across the green, that's all. I mean, here we are."

"You're hoping and secretly believing that Lewis

Braid is going to tell you something mind-blowing that solves everything, and you're going to be disappointed."

"I want to be able to focus, that's all."

I've never said so to Dom in case it would sound disloyal, but I can't concentrate at home—not on anything important that requires focus, not while Zannah and Ben are in the house and awake. That's why I do my work admin late at night. Teenagers are even worse than nosy villagers when it comes to smashing through your carefully constructed boundaries.

The Olde Jug is quiet and smells temptingly of roast beef. Soon it will start to fill up with all those who have booked for dinner. There are no tables in the bar area, and the restaurant part of the pub is relatively small—only one room, now with a conservatory extension which has enabled a few more tables to be added—and needs to be booked several weeks in advance. Little Holling folk complain furiously if they've found themselves eating near people who look as if they're from Somewhere Else, even though there's no rule stating that priority should be given to those who live closest.

Robin and Ruth live in a two-bedroom flat above the pub. They're happy for me to use it to make my call, as

I knew they would be. "Don't even ask," Dominic says over his shoulder to Robin as we head upstairs.

"He didn't ask," I mutter.

"Living room or kitchen?" Dom asks.

"Kitchen."

"Shall we make a cup of tea?"

"No. I'm ringing him now." I want to get it over with, whatever it turns out to be.

A few seconds later, I hear a voice I haven't heard for twelve years. "Beth Leeson!"

"How did you know it was me?"

"International call. Actually, you're right—as a hot-shot CEO, I get loads of international calls." Lewis has always done this: mocking his own boastfulness at the same time as indulging it to the full. "But I've been waiting for you to call since I sent you my number. How are things? How's Dom and the kids?"

"Fine. We're all fine. How . . . how are things with you?" There's a lag after each of us speaks.

"Amazing, thanks. The kids are so American now, you'd barely recognize them."

I close my eyes. When I open them, Dominic is gesturing for me to put my phone on speaker so that he can hear Lewis's side of the conversation. I shake my head. The look I get in response tells me I'm being silly, but I don't care. I'm not risking pressing a button that might cut Lewis off.

"Flora's doing great. Loves the climate here. Keeps saying she can't believe she put up with the gray, gloomy English weather for so long. When are you guys gonna get your lazy asses out here to visit us?"

Another classic Lewis Braid move: making you feel guilty for not accepting an invitation you never received.

"Do you ever come back to the UK?"

"Yeah, when we can. We were back for Christmas, stayed with Flora's parents. They're still in their little place in Wokingham. Bit of a squeeze with seven of us!"

*Seven.* Lewis, Flora, Thomas, Emily, Flora's parents . . . and Georgina. She has to be the seventh person. Still, no harm in checking . . .

"How old is Georgina now?"

"She's twelve. Terrifying how quick time passes, isn't it? Did you and Dominic ever have any more?"

"More time?" I'm confused.

"No, more children. Though, come to think of it . . ." Lewis laughs. "God, what I wouldn't give for more time. Bet you're the same. Remember before we had kids, how we used to spend whole days lying around by the river, or watching movies?"

"Yes."

"Anyway, enough about the past! As my favorite life coach always says: memories of the past are not the past. They're thoughts you have in the *present, about* the past."

I shiver. Dominic mouths "What?" I turn away from him so that I'm not distracted. Lewis talking about the present and the past makes me feel . . .

*What? That he's more likely to have frozen his children in time to prevent them from aging? Ridiculous.*

"Your favorite life coach?" I say, forcing out a laugh. "How many do you have?"

"I don't *see* them, I just listen to their podcasts. But enough about my perfect life in sunny Florida—tell me what you've been up to. Are you working again, or still a slacker?"

I'd forgotten this: that Lewis described it as "slacking" when Flora and I gave up our jobs to look after our babies. He loved that joke; it became one of his regulars. I never minded it. It was like his boasting: so outrageous, we all assumed he didn't mean it.

*Except Flora.*

I didn't think of it at the time, but now I wonder: was that why she always looked worried and said, "Lew-*is*," while Dom and I were busy saying, "It's fine—we don't take him seriously"? Was Flora scared he was revealing too much of his true character?

"No, I'm working," I say.

"Aha! Hunting heads again!"

"I'm not in recruitment anymore. I retrained as a massage therapist."

Lewis laughs loudly. "A masseur! You mean a hooker, right? Is that what this call's about? Are you a hooker hoping for a handout from an old friend? Or, should I say, a hand *job*? No, wait—that's the wrong way around. If you're a hooker, you'd be offering *me* a hand job. I'm mixing up my hooker metaphors."

I do some fake laughing and try to move the conversation on, but Lewis insists on knowing what I actually do, if not hookering. I explain to him about trigger-point massage, what led me to it, the principles involved. "Hmm," he says when I've finished. "Reckon you could sort out my tennis arm?"

"Definitely," I say. "What about Flora? Is she working now, or—"

"Hardly. She's committed to slacking for life."

"You know, I . . . I drove past your old house."

"The Newnham flat? How's it looking these days?"

"No, the house you moved to afterward. In Hemingford Abbots."

"Wyddial Lane?"

"Yeah."

"What the hell were you doing there?"

My heart thuds. Is he suspicious? *No. He's just being Lewis.*

"Ben's football team was playing nearby, in St. Ives, and I took a wrong turn on the way. I recognized the street name from the change-of-address card you sent when you moved." *Shit.* That sounded so obviously like a lie. I hold my breath, waiting for Lewis to question it.

Instead, he says cheerfully, "So, you really think you could un-fuck my arm? I've tried sports massage. Didn't work."

"Because the trigger points in your shoulder and neck need releasing, probably. Your arm is where the effects are manifesting, but not where the problem's located." It's hugely frustrating that so many people charging for massages all over the world don't know this basic fact.

"What the fuck?" Dominic murmurs behind me. I wave my arm frantically: sign language for "Be quiet or leave."

"Inneresting. Hey, Flora!" Lewis yells. "Guess who's on the phone? Beth Leeson! She reckons she can sort out my tennis arm!"

"Can I speak to Flora too?" I ask, my throat suddenly dry.

"You trying to get rid of me, Beth?"

"Haha. No, not at all. I mean after."

"She's in the bath. Hang on, she's getting out. Seriously, though, you should all come over and stay with us. We've got a three-bedroom guesthouse in our garden, a swimming pool, a tennis court. You'd have fun! Oh, wait, here's Flora."

I hear a woman's voice in the background. I can't hear what exactly she's saying—something about being lucky, I think—but . . . it sounds like Flora.

How can it be her?

"What, hon?" Lewis calls out. "Can't you do that later? Oh, okay. Beth, she'll ring you back in five, ten minutes. Is that okay?"

"Sure," I say.

*Lucky. Where have I heard that word recently?*

"Sit tight. And get your diary ready. Let's schedule a visit for y'all to the good old US of A!" The line goes dead.

I put my phone down on Ruth and Robin's kitchen table.

"That's it?" says Dom.

"No. Flora's ringing me back."

"When? Can we go home, and you talk to her there?"

"No, she's ringing in five minutes, Lewis said. Dom,

I heard her. In the background. Well, I heard a woman. It sounded like Flora."

"You didn't ask him why there's no Flora or Georgina on his Instagram, or who Chimpy is."

"I haven't spoken to him for twelve years. I didn't want to sound like I was interrogating him."

"So how long are we going to sit here? I mean—"

Dom doesn't get a chance to tell me what he means because my phone starts to ring.

"Hello?"

"Beth! I can't believe this! Is it really you, after all these years?"

*Is it really you, Flora?*

I don't need to ask. I know it's her, without a doubt. I'd know that voice anywhere. It's the same one I heard yesterday morning, on Wyddial Lane. I can't pretend anymore, not now that I've heard her speak. "Flora—sorry to just go straight in with this, but . . . can I tell you about something really strange that happened to me yesterday?"

Dom covers his face with his hands.

"Of course," says Flora.

I tell her the same lie I told Lewis—that I ended up on Wyddial Lane by accident. Then I tell her what I saw, and what happened when Dom and I went back there this morning. When I get to the end of the story, she says, "Beth, that's . . . the strangest thing I've ever heard. I can promise you, Thomas and Emily are no longer five and three." She laughs.

"Obviously," I say. "I know it sounds like I've gone mad, but I haven't. I don't think so, anyway."

"Is this why you contacted Lewis?"

"Yeah. Dom told me you'd all moved to Florida— I didn't know that, but as soon as I heard it, I realized I could . . . well, I could find out if you were there or here."

"I'm here." Flora laughs. "Which, for you, means I'm there, and you can't have seen me on a street in England where I used to live. Beth, I'm really sorry, but I'm going to have to call you back later. Someone's at the door. Lovely to talk to you—we've left it far too long! Bye."

"Wait," I say.

Too late. She's gone.

She lied. No one was at her door. She could have ignored it, or let Lewis answer it. She hasn't spoken to me for twelve years, I tell her the most bizarre story she's ever heard and she chooses to end the call because "someone's at the door"?

I know where I heard the word lucky. Flora said it, standing outside Newnham House yesterday, talking on the phone. As well as saying she was home, talking about Peterborough and saying hello to someone called Chimpy, she said, at the very end of the phone call, "Lucky. I'm very lucky."

I pick up my phone again.

"What happened?" says Dom. "Where did she go? Who are you ringing now?"

"No one. Look. Look what it says for the last call." I pass him the phone.

"No caller ID." He says it as if it's an answer that raises no questions, and hands the phone back to me.

"What does that mean?" I try Lewis's number again and get a busy signal.

I can't call Flora back, or see where she called me from. If she's in Hemingford Abbots and not Delray Beach, for instance. Which would explain why there had to be a separate call—why Lewis couldn't pass his phone to her so that she could speak to me.

Then who was the woman I just heard saying "lucky"?

"It could mean many things," says Dom.

"No." It could, but it doesn't. "It means one thing. It means that Flora deliberately withheld her number."

# 7

The nearest school to Wyddial Lane is in a village called Wyton. Houghton Primary has a large, square courtyard playground bordered by an L-shaped beige-brick building and another L made from green prefabricated units. There's a tree in one corner, tall and thick with pink flowers, pushing up the concrete on either side of it. I think it might be a cherry tree. Dom and I have often agreed that trees are like fish—we ought to know more than we do about the differences between the various types, but we've reached our forties and can still only identify weeping willows and salmon with any certainty.

The tree, together with a fence painted the same green as the prefabs, allows Houghton Primary School to make a welcoming first impression. It's eight forty-five. The bell signaling the start of morning school rang a few seconds ago, and the children are shrieking with delight and running circles around one another. I can't imagine what it must feel like to have so much energy. I got up and left the house at five this morning, having had only about two and a half hours' sleep. I wanted to make sure to get here before the pre-school breakfast club part of the day, so that I wouldn't miss any parents who dropped their children off early.

*Flora Braid—that's who you didn't want to miss. Dropping off Thomas.*

I'm no longer correcting every thought that passes through my mind. I know why I'm here and I'm not going to argue with myself about it: I'm waiting for Flora to bring her son, five-year-old Thomas, to school. Emily, at only three, is still too young for school. Maybe she'll be getting dropped off at nursery school on the way.

So far, it's not looking promising. I've seen two black Range Rovers, but no sign of the silver one I saw outside Newnham House. When the children start to form a line to enter the building, I know it's not going to happen. They're not coming. Flora wouldn't allow Thomas to be late for school. Lewis always used to tease her for wanting to get to the airport two and a half hours before even a domestic flight. When we went to

Corfu, he grumbled all the way to Gatwick about how early she'd insisted on leaving. "When I've got my own private jet, I'll get picked up from my house," he said matter-of-factly, as if this was something inevitable that would one day happen.

"No messing about, no lining up for hours with half of London."

*Damn.* How could I have been so stupid? Houghton Primary is a state school. Anyone who lives locally can send their five-year-old here for free. If I wasn't so tired, I would have realized this much sooner. There's no way on earth that Lewis Braid, with the money he must have now, would send his kids to a state school. Thomas—both Thomases, the seventeen-year-old one in Florida and the five-year-old one in Hemingford Abbots—will be receiving an expensive private education.

That's how I'm thinking about this until I've gathered enough information to make sense of all the contradictory evidence: there are two Thomases. I've *seen* two Thomases—one in real life, the one I can't possibly have seen, and one in photographs online, the one that other people believe in too.

My phone starts to ring on the seat next to me. It's Dom. He was still asleep when I left the house, and has no idea where I am. I'll text him, but not now. If I take the call, we'll only end up having the same conversation we had last night; he'll tell me I need to stop wanting the answers I'm always going to want until I get them.

Flora never called me back, though she promised she would. Lewis didn't answer his phone again, though I tried calling it many more times.

"When are you going to accept that there's nothing more you can reasonably do?" Dom asked me.

I didn't reply, apart from in my head: *When are you going to realize how fucking bizarre and creepy it is that a woman in the same room as Lewis Braid in Florida said the same words I heard Flora say outside Newnham House yesterday? "Lucky. I'm very lucky."*

Once Dom's name has disappeared from the screen, I pick up my phone and put the words "Private primary schools near Hemingford Abbots, Cambs" into the search box.

Various results come up, enough to convince me that there isn't one obvious next port of call. I try to look at the first few search results, but it's no good. My screen is too small, and cracked from when I dropped it on the tiles at St. Pancras station last year. I'm not ready to go home. Where can I go that might have Internet access and computers?

Half an hour later I'm at Huntingdon Library, staring at a screen large enough to contain all the information I need at a glance. There's no obvious answer to the question of which school five-year-old Thomas is likely to attend. There are plenty of private prep schools in Cambridge but, having lived there for many years, I know how impossible it can be to get in on the A14 in the morning. From Hemingford Abbots, in rush-hour traffic, it could easily take an hour or more. Still, as a proud University of Cambridge graduate, Lewis would certainly believe that Cambridge was where the best education was to be had. No doubt about that.

*He also believed in ease and convenience, and not waiting in lines, whether at airports or on busy commuter roads . . .*

Would Flora be willing to expose her children to exhaust fumes for an hour twice a day? I wouldn't. What would I do, if I lived in Hemingford Abbots and wanted my children to attend a straw-boater-and-striped-blazer sort of private school, but didn't want to see, or inhale, too much of the A14?

I start to look through the other options and find one that looks promising: Kimbolton Prep School. Not too long a drive from Wyddial Lane, and possible to reach without getting snarled up in the Cambridge traffic.

A woman's voice behind me says breathlessly, "You'll never guess who's upstairs!"

I turn, but she's not talking to me. The white-haired

man at the computer next to me, without turning his head, says, "Who?" as if bracing himself for bad news.

"John Major—well, a statue of him, anyway. Bronze or copper or something like that. What a funny thing to have in a library. John Major," she says again wistfully. "I never thought I'd miss him, but I do. Should have appreciated him when he was prime minister. He'd never have landed us in this mess."

The white-haired man harrumphs in response.

I pick up my bag and make my way outside. Kimbolton Prep School. That has to be what Zan and Ben would call "a good shout." There's nowhere else nearby that looks like the sort of place Lewis Braid would choose for his child. And he always made all the important decisions.

Did Flora want to ring me yesterday or did he force her to, and then tell her when to end the call and that she mustn't ring me back? Did he make her withhold her number so that I couldn't phone her back later?

Dom didn't originally want me to contact Lewis, but he couldn't stop me, just like I couldn't stop him from spending too much money on pub meals all those years ago, to support The Olde Jug's new owners before they were our friends. That's because neither one of us controls the other; we're both free agents. Flora and Lewis, on the other hand . . .

What if he's always manipulated her, and I just didn't realize? So often she would say, "Lew-*is*," as if she wished he would stop whatever he was doing. I interpreted it as her trying and failing to control him, but what if it was the other way around: him controlling her, keeping her alert and in check by demonstrating how far he was willing to go? *Like the two-grand changing room* . . .

When you're young, you don't seriously wonder whether your friends might be terrible people. You're naive and optimistic; you assume anyone occupying the structural position of best friend must be a good person deep down.

What if Lewis isn't? What if, as well as being an entertaining, outrageous and occasionally offensive weirdo, he's also something much worse?

Or I might be getting stupidly carried away. There's no way of knowing, not without an answer to the more immediate question: what are he and Flora so determined to hide, and how does it relate to all the bizarre things I've seen and heard? That's the mystery—the one Dom can forget all about, apparently, and I can't. At least we agree on one thing: the Braids are hiding something.

In my hurry to get to the library, I forgot to notice where I left my car, and I have to walk up and down the car park for a few minutes before I spot it. I'm reaching into my bag for my phone when I feel someone's eyes on me.

I look up, and my phone slips from between my fingers. She's standing directly in front of me, about ten feet ahead.

It's Flora.

**She must** have been coming this way, then seen me and come to a standstill. Her eyes are wide with shock, and she's lowering her arm, as if she's been pointing at me, or pointing me out to somebody . . . but there's no one with her. She's alone.

She stares at me as if she's never seen anything more terrifying. Feeling as if the ground I'm standing on is falling through space beneath my feet, I take a step toward her, opening my mouth to speak, but she's already turning away, walking fast in the opposite direction. Running.

"Flora! Wait!"

I think about chasing her, but there's too much distance between us already and something's nagging at the back of my mind, telling me I mustn't go anywhere, not without . . .

My phone.

I dropped it. It made a crunching noise. The screen

was already cracked; now it's probably damaged beyond repair. In normal circumstances, I'd be feeling sick about the cost of a new phone.

Amazingly, it still works, though it looks like something anyone sensible would throw in the trash. Dom has tried to call me four times. I send him a quick message saying, "Out for the day. Don't worry, all fine!" and end up with a small piece of glass in my forefinger. Parts of the screen are missing around the button at the bottom. I can see silver-gray innards. And more silver in front of me, now that I've turned around: Flora's Range Rover, standing out glossily in a row of smaller, less shiny cars. I must have walked straight past it and not noticed—because I wasn't looking for it, not here.

To be strictly accurate, I suppose I should say, "A silver Range Rover." I didn't notice the license plate on Saturday, so there's no way of knowing if this one is Flora's.

*It is. It's her car. She was on her way back to it, walking across the car park, when she saw you and turned and ran.*

A text arrives from Dom. "No clients today? Out where?"

"I rearranged two appointments," I text back.

"Why? What are you doing?" is his response. Then, "When back?"

If I set off now, I could be back by noon. I send a reply saying, "Not sure when back yet, will keep you posted!," put my smashed phone back in my bag and walk over to the silver Range Rover. The windows are tinted, making it hard to see what's inside, though I can see the outlines of car seats.

I don't know what makes me try the door. It opens with a soft and fluid thunking sound. I close it, then open it again. *Thunk-thunk.* My car doors make a much harsher noise. No one would leave a car like this unlocked. It must be worth at least fifty grand.

The answer comes to me right away: she didn't. Flora didn't leave the car unlocked while she went and did whatever she had to do in Huntingdon. She unlocked it just now, thinking she was about to drive home, and then, in her shock at seeing me, she forgot to lock it again before running away.

I walk around to the other side of the car, open the door, get in and sit in the driver's seat. If Flora wants to come back and ask me to get out, let her do that. I've got plenty to ask her; she can give me some answers and maybe then I'll agree to move.

I open the glove compartment and find nothing useful, only the Range Rover's official manual. I get out again, open the boot and see a black backpack with green straps and zips, a pink and white duvet with white press-studs along one edge, a creased sheet of paper with some writing on it in large handwriting. This turns out to be a spelling test. There's no name at the top, only the numbers one to five in the margin and the answers written in a child's hand: "friend, school, house, father, shugar." All have red ticks beside them apart from "shugar." Next to it, the correct spelling of the word is written in smaller, adult handwriting.

Is this a test that Thomas Braid, or Thomas Cater, was given at school? My eyes linger on the words "house" and "father." There's nothing here to identify who the Range Rover belongs to—no "Braid" or "Cater" written on anything. Also no mud, dirt, no crumbs, no wrappers. The boot looks as if it has been recently vacuumed, which is what I'd expect from a car belonging to the Braids. They used to hire carpet cleaners every two months when we all lived in rented flats in Newnham. Dominic used to rib Lewis about it. "You're paying, out of your own pocket, to have a carpet professionally cleaned that's still clean from the last time?" he would say, and Lewis would shake his head and say, "You live in filth if you want to, mate. Some of us have higher standards."

On the backseat, there's a bunched-up navy-blue raincoat that would fit a woman of Flora's size, and two child car seats. They're not baby seats. They're the kind that a five-year-old and a three-year-old would need.

*Two car seats. Not three.*

I'm not crazy. I didn't imagine anything. This is all real.

This is where two small children were sitting on Saturday morning, in these car seats, when Flora opened the door and said, "Thomas! Emily! Out you get!" And that's what she said. I didn't mishear or misremember. She called them Thomas and Emily, and they were wearing Thomas and Emily Braid's old clothes.

I open the driver's door again, get in and close my eyes. Next thing I know, I'm waking up with a sharp pain down one side of my neck. How long was I asleep for? *Shit.* I guess that's what happens when you get up at five a.m. after sleeping for less than three hours. What if Flora had come back and caught me in her car? She's going to have to come and get it at some point.

I pull my phone out of my bag. I've only missed twenty minutes. Not too long, but still, what if . . .

It occurs to me for the first time since this started that I might be in danger. I force myself to laugh out loud. *Don't be ridiculous, Beth. Danger? Seriously?*

I try to feel lighthearted and brazen about it, and fail. People who are hiding something will sometimes go to extremes in order to protect their secrets. Indulging my curiosity is one thing, but Zannah and Ben need a mother who hasn't been strangled in a car by an assassin sent from Florida. Or maybe there are more affordable hit men for hire in Huntingdon, who knows?

The trouble is, it's not only curiosity. On Saturday morning, when I saw Flora, I thought that something was badly wrong. Now, two days later, I know something must be. Because of everything that's happened, because she ran away from me. And there are children involved . . .

Before I can think it through any further, there's a sharp knock on the window next to my head. It's a woman I've never seen before.

I open the car door, my heart hammering, and get out. She's a few inches taller than me—with thin, straight dark hair, chin length, cut in an angular style. "Would you care to explain yourself?" she says in an accent I can't place. Italian, maybe.

"Pardon?" I stammer.

"What are you doing sitting in my car? How did you get in?"

"It was unlocked. It's . . . it's not your car."

"Not mine?" She produces a set of keys from her

pocket and dangles them in front of me. She slams the driver's door, locks the car, then unlocks it again. "This is not my car, you think?"

"This is Flora Braid's car."

"Who?"

"Flora Braid," I say with more confidence than I feel.

There's nothing this woman can do to me. This is a busy car park. There are people all around us. She wouldn't risk it.

"Are you all right?" she asks me.

"Who are you? Where do you live?"

"Where do I live?" she laughs. "Who are *you*, and why were you in my car?" She shakes her head, waving one hand dismissively. "I don't even care. Just go away from me. Get some help."

"Do you live on Wyddial Lane? At number 16?"

She looks surprised. "How do you know this? Have you . . . are you following me?"

"Is your name Jeanette Cater?"

"You have no right to ask me one single thing. You get into my car without permission, and then you think you can bombard me with question after question? What is this about? What do you want?"

"Answer me and I'll tell you. Is your name Jeanette Cater?"

"Yes. Yes, it is. Are you satisfied now?"

I'm not. But I'm not scared anymore. "Why did you say 'Who?' when I mentioned Flora Braid?" I ask her.

"Because I do not know who you mean! And if I don't get an explanation—"

"Surely you remember Flora Braid. She's the woman who sold you your house. Lewis and Flora Braid."

Jeanette Cater nods. "So, this is true," she says after a few moments. "I had forgotten the name."

I don't believe her.

"Flora was in this car park less than an hour ago," I tell her. "She was on her way back to her car, *this* car, the one you're saying is yours, when she saw me and ran away. What did she do: send you to collect it for her because she's too scared to face me? She also lied to me on the phone last night—pretended she was in Florida when in fact she was in her house on Wyddial Lane, probably."

"Please." Jeanette Cater puts out a hand to stop me. "This is insanity, what is happening here. This is my car. I am the only person who drives it apart from my husband. Flora Braid has never driven it. I can promise you this."

"That's a lie. I saw her drive it through the gates of 16 Wyddial Lane on Saturday morning. I *saw* her."

"I'm sorry for you, but you are seeing things that do

not happen, in that case. Good-bye." She nods formally, evidently hoping this dismissal will cause me to walk away. That's when I notice it, when she stops talking and stands completely still: the green jacket with large lapels, and two-line checks designed to have a sort of double-vision effect. Black trousers, black boots with square heels . . .

This woman I've never seen before is wearing the exact same outfit that Flora Braid was wearing when I saw her less than an hour ago.

# 8

Things can change a lot in hardly any time at all.

My third visit to Wyddial Lane, the day after my encounters in a Huntingdon car park with Flora and the woman calling herself Jeanette Cater, is not furtive and illicit like the first two. It has been prearranged by my husband—the same Dominic Leeson who recently told me I mustn't ever come back here in case Marilyn Oxley from number 14 calls the police.

I remind him of this as we drive in through the open gates of Newnham House. He says in a resigned tone, "Forgetting about the Braids and the Caters is still my top option. But you won't or can't do that, so I thought I might as well try and sort it out."

*Wouldn't that be nice.* Dom thinks that sorting out is what's about to happen because he's spoken to Kevin

Cater, and they've made an agreement. Kevin Cater is listed in the phone directory, and therefore must be helpful and trustworthy. He sounded like a reasonable bloke, Dom said, and no part of their phone conversation failed to make sense. He's expecting progress to be made today.

I'm not sure what to expect, or that I want to know what we're going to find inside this house.

"This is what normal, sane people do," says Dom. "If there's a problem then they arrange to meet, they talk, they sort things out. They do not get into strangers' unlocked cars without permission and fall asleep in them."

I sigh. "You keep going on about that as if it's some terrible transgression."

"It is! It's crossing a line. You can't do things like that, Beth. It's not good. If you carry on in that vein, anything could happen to you. I don't want to worry every time you leave the house that —"

"Dom. I sat. In. A car. You're overreacting. Let's not have the same argument we had last night. You win, okay? I'm not going to be making a habit of it. What if I say 'I promise never again to enter a stranger's car or touch their property without permission'?"

"Then I'll be very happy." He exhales slowly. "Right. Good."

I haven't actually said it. I only asked "What if?"

We get out of the car. It's strange to think I'm standing in the exact spot where the three of them stood on Saturday morning: Flora, Thomas and Emily.

Dom presses the doorbell. A few seconds later it opens and a man appears. He's wearing a blue-and-gray-checked shirt tucked into jeans, and white socks, no shoes. He looks at Dominic and me as if we're a delivery that someone has left on his doorstep, which he now has to decide what to do with. He has a square face and mid-brown hair in a short, serious-businessman style.

"Dominic and Beth Leeson?" he says, unsmiling.

"Yes. Thanks so much for agreeing to see us at such short notice," says Dom.

"I agreed for Jeanette's sake. She was disturbed by what happened in the car park yesterday." He looks pointedly at me. "So . . . I'm hoping we can resolve the matter swiftly and avoid any further . . . incidents."

"That's exactly what we want too," Dom assures him. "The last thing Beth wants to do is upset your wife, Mr. Cater. If we can—"

"I think you'd better call me Kevin. And let's not have this conversation on the doorstep."

"Of course not."

"What time is it?" Cater consults a watch that looks

expensive. "Yes, it's noon. All right, follow me. Close the door after you."

He takes us through a spotlit lobby that's too sleek and professional-looking to be called an entrance hall. There's nothing homely about it. It's entirely white—like a nonslippery ice rink—and dotted with square pillars. We pass the entrance to an enormous kitchen with a concertina-style door that's standing open. It's made of padded white felt, with rows of silver studs marking out the lines along which it folds. I think it's supposed to look stylish.

There's a hefty white rectangle of kitchen island with a ring of silver pans hanging from the ceiling above it, three beige sofas at the far end of the room, and a wooden table with at least twelve chairs around it, though it's hard to be precise after a quick glance while walking past.

Dom looks back, glares at me and beckons me to hurry up. He thinks I'm snooping and he doesn't want our host to catch me in the act. I wonder if he's noticed: every single thing I've seen so far inside this house could have been chosen by Lewis Braid. Or by the kind of interior designer he'd hire.

Kevin Cater shows us in to a large, rectangular sitting room with unusually high caramel-colored skirting boards, ornate bronze radiators, a herringbone-

patterned dark-wood floor, gold floor-length curtains and striped wallpaper: mustard alternating with
fawn. Around the room, in a strictly rectangular ar-
rangement, are sofas and chairs, all white, cream or
gold, with wooden occasional tables dotted between
them here and there.

When I see the framed photographs on the walls, my
breath catches in my throat. There are eight in total, and
every single one is of a murmuration of many hundreds
of birds against a sky. Sunset, broad daylight . . . the
skies are all different, as is the shape made by the birds
in each picture, but the theme is very much the same.

When I knew him, Lewis Braid used to go wild
with glee if he saw a murmuration. I didn't know it
was called that until he told me. He would stare and
stare, and sometimes chase the birds, and swear loudly,
more often than not, when they finally flew out of
sight. "Isn't that the most incredible thing you've ever
seen?" he'd demand. Once he snapped at Flora for
not bringing a camera to a picnic, as if she could have
known that there would be a murmuration of starlings
above our heads that day. Another time he leaped up
and started flapping his arms like an idiot, yelling,
"Why can't I be a bird, flying in a beautiful, perfect
flock in the moonlight?"

Lewis Braid arranged for these photographs to be

framed and hung on the walls of this room. How could it have been anyone else? Does anybody care as much as Lewis does about birds flying in large groups? I've never met anyone else who's even mentioned a murmuration, let alone made a fuss about one.

"Did you do up this room?" I ask Kevin Cater. It comes out harsher than I intended it to.

"Beth . . ." Dom warns.

"It's all right," says Cater. "Actually, we didn't. We inherited it from the previous owners. Everything had been done so beautifully, with no expense spared. Jeanette and I hardly changed anything."

*No. Lewis wouldn't leave his murmuration pictures here for another family. He'd take them to Florida. He'd take them with him wherever he went.*

Kevin Cater's eyes rest on me a little too long. A smile plays around his lips. It's not a friendly one.

"Take a seat," he says. "I'll go and track down Jeanette. In a house this size, it's easier said than done."

Once he's gone, I walk over to the door and close it.

"Did you see the look he gave me before he left the room?" I ask Dom. "He was taunting me."

"What?"

"He wanted me to get the message: 'If I tell you I haven't changed anything about this house, then you won't be able to prove that the reason it still looks like

Lewis Braid's house is because it still *is* Lewis Braid's house.' He's not a good guy, Dom. I don't trust him."

"For Christ's sake, Beth."

"And I don't like him. Did you hear how he said, 'Let's not discuss this on the doorstep,' when *he* was the one who started doing that, not us? And what about 'What time is it? Ah, yes, it's noon, so you can come in'—he virtually accused us of arriving rudely early, when it was easily five past twelve by the time we rang the bell. And he must have known that. If we'd been two minutes early, would he have made us wait outside? That was how it sounded."

"Beth, shut up. I mean it. He's going to walk back in any second now."

"So? I'm not scared of him. Or fooled by him. Everything he's said and done so far is an attempt to manipulate us and make us feel small."

"Shh. Keep your voice down."

"Why? Remember how huge his house is, like he just told us? He's probably in another wing, miles away, and wouldn't hear me if I screamed the place down."

Dom's face is flushed. "I can't be bothered to think of a way to put this tactfully, so I'm just going to say it. You're sounding crazier by the minute. Manipulate us? Come on! The guy's understandably pissed off because he's having to waste his day proving to you that his wife is in fact his wife and not a woman who used to live here and who's currently in Florida. If he's falling a bit short of warm and friendly, that's why."

"Really? If you think that, then you can't possibly understand . . ."

"What?" Dom asks in a whisper. "What don't I understand?"

"You keep saying you agree that everything that's happened is bizarre, but if you really thought that, you'd know that Kevin and Jeanette Cater have to be involved in it, whatever it is. She was wearing the *same clothes.*"

The door opens. Kevin Cater walks in, followed by the woman I first met yesterday in the car park in Huntingdon. She's wearing a knee-length black pleated skirt with a red and black leopard-print top and black slip-on pumps.

She's taller than Flora, who's the same height as me. The black trousers she had on yesterday were probably much too short for her legs, but the black boots hid the problem. Convenient for her.

Pleasantries are exchanged by everyone apart from me. The woman offers us drinks; Dom and I both say no. He adds a "Thank you." As I listen to the small talk they're all using to ward off the moment when things might turn awkward, I wonder if Dom has noticed that the Kevin who has returned to the room is considerably friendlier than the one who left it a few minutes ago.

*It's all a show.*

"So, Beth," says the woman eventually. Is she Jeanette? Didn't Marilyn Oxley tell me that Jeanette Cater had wavy hair, like Flora? This woman's hair is ruler-straight. I wish I could remember exactly what Marilyn said. Not that it matters. Hair can be artificially straightened. "We should talk about what happened yesterday. I . . . perhaps I did not react to you in the best way. I am afraid I was very shocked to find you in my car."

I swallow the urge to tell her it's not her car, it's Flora's. Instead, I say, "I understand. May I ask you a question?"

"Of course."

"Where were you on Saturday morning, and where was your car?"

"I went out, with the children, early, to do some shopping. We arrived back at about nine thirty, I think, or just after."

Her getting the time right means nothing. Marilyn Oxley could have told her what time I returned to Wyddial Lane, or Flora, if she saw me there. I don't think she did, but I can't absolutely rule it out.

"In the silver Range Rover?" I ask.

"Yes."

"Where's your accent from?"

"Beth!" Dom barks at me.

"It's okay," Jeanette says. "The Ukraine. I was born there and grew up there."

"With a name like Jeanette?"

"Actually, that is what I named myself when I moved to England." She smiles at Dominic. "My real name is a full-of-mouth for an English person to say, so . . ." She shrugs.

"I'm so sorry about the interrogation," Dom gushes, determined to ingratiate himself. "I'm assuming you know the, er, situation?"

"Kevin told me what happened, yes." To me, she says, "You were here on Saturday and you saw me with my children. You mistook me for your friend."

"That's right," says Dom. Kevin Cater nods.

I say nothing, determined not to agree with her version of what happened.

"How old are your children?" I ask.

"Five and three years old."

"What are their names?"

"Toby and Emma."

I have the same feeling I had in the car park in

Huntingdon: the ground falling away beneath me. Those weren't the names I heard. They weren't the names she called out and it wasn't her who did the calling. Toby and Emma, Thomas and Emily—just similar enough to make me think I could have misheard.

*Right, Kevin?*

I'll never think that. I don't trust these people. I trust myself: what I saw and heard.

"Which is the older one?" I ask.

"Toby. He is five. Would you like to see a photograph of them?"

"Is that necessary?" Kevin Cater asks.

"No," says Dom, at the same time as I say, "Yes, please."

"It's all right, Kevin." His wife lays a hand on his shoulder as she leaves the room. Kevin takes the opportunity to tell us again how big the house is, which leads to a discussion—one in which I play no part—about whether having too much space can actually be as inconvenient as having too little, if not more so.

Jeanette returns with a photograph in a frame and brings it over to me. I want to scream.

"Well?" says Dom impatiently. "Beth?"

I pass the photograph to him. He holds it close to his face, then at a distance.

"Right, well!" He laughs. He sounds relieved. "These children are *not* Thomas and Emily Braid, I think we can safely say. Not as they are now and not as they were at three and five."

"No, they're not," says Kevin Cater, looking at me. "They're Toby and Emma Cater. *My* children."

Dominic turns to me and says, "I remember quite clearly what the Braid children looked like when I knew them, and these are not their faces."

"I agree," I say. "They're not Thomas and Emily."

"I suppose from a distance, if you were in a car on the other side of the road . . ." Now that he believes I've conceded, Kevin is ready to be generous. "An easy mistake to make, maybe."

"Those aren't the two children I saw. Whoever they are, I've never seen their faces before. Dom, did you notice anything else about that photo—anything interesting?"

"What do you mean?" Dom's face reddens. "Beth, come on."

"What? You think I'm being rude? I asked a simple question: do you notice anything else about the photo?"

"No."

"Like what, exactly?" Kevin Cater snaps.

I stare at him.

"There's nothing to notice, Beth," says Dom. "It's a photo of two children. Come on. I think we've taken up enough of these people's time." He stands up.

Cater follows his lead. Jeanette too. I'm the only one still seated. All three of them are thinking that this will soon be over.

"Who's Chimpy?" I ask Kevin Cater.

"I've no idea," he says. "I don't know what you're talking about." He looks at Jeanette, who shakes her head.

"Means nothing to us," says Kevin. "Sorry."

My sense is that they're telling the truth—but only about not knowing who Chimpy is. About everything else, they're lying. Watching them now, the way they're rearranging themselves, getting into position for the next rehearsed lie, I feel as if we're back in the charade after a small interlude of honesty.

"I hope we were able to help?" says Jeanette.

"Hugely," says Dom.

"I'm not sure your wife agrees." Kevin stares at me.

"Oh, I do," I say, adjusting my tone carefully. "I'm very glad we came. It's been extremely useful."

"I don't want to find you outside my house or in my wife's car again, Mrs. Leeson."

"I know you don't, Kevin. I wouldn't want that either, if I were you."

---

**I'm sitting** in my room in the dark when Zannah comes in and switches on the light. "Are you hiding?" she says. "Dad said he couldn't find you."

"He didn't look very hard, then. What time is it?"

"Twenty past ten."

I'm about to say "at night?" but stop myself in time. The curtains are open and it's dark outside. "Ben's not still playing Fortnite, is he?" I ask.

"No, he's in bed—teeth brushed, clean pajamas, room tidied." She smiles proudly. "I am going to make *such* a great parent one day."

"Dad should have sorted Ben out," I say, and it feels like a monumental effort to push out each word.

"Yeah, or you should, as you're his mother," Zannah quips. "Dad's snoring in front of the world's most boring documentary. Mum, what's going on? Dad said you've barely said a word since you left the Caters' house. Are you pissed at him? Was he, like, really annoying?"

I smile. "Not really. He did and said what almost anyone in his situation would do and say."

"So you're all good, you and him?"

"I'm not annoyed with him, if that's what you mean."

"He also said you threatened Kevin Cater."

"Not in so many words."

"But you kind of threatened him."

"Kind of. Nonspecifically. I just let him know that I think he and his wife are creepy liars."

"Mum, you should be careful. At this rate Ben's going to have to get some of his baddest roadman mates to back you on ends."

"Back me on what?"

"Ugh, you're so old. Never mind. But that's why you shouldn't go around starting trouble."

"Because I'm too old? I'm really not that old, Zannah."

She flops down on the bed next to where I'm sitting. "So what happened then?"

"Didn't Dad tell you?"

"He said the kids living in that house aren't Thomas and Emily Braid, and don't look anything like how Thomas and Emily used to look when they were little."

"We were shown a photo of two young children who looked nothing like Thomas and Emily Braid. That's true."

"So . . . how come you're not saying, 'I made a mistake, it's all over'?"

"Because the more I'm told and the more I see, the more certain I am that I *didn't* make a mistake."

"Fair enough," she says easily.

"Have you been revising?"

She snorts. "No."

"Zan—"

"Tell me about the Greek changing room."

"What?"

"Your Lewis Braid story about the two-thousand-pound changing room in Corfu."

"If I tell you, will you start revising?"

"Definitely. Immediately afterward. All night long." She grins. "Please?"

"It's nothing important or particularly interesting. Just something funny that happened when Dad and I went on holiday with Lewis and Flora to Corfu before you were born. We'd booked an apartment on a beach—literally on the sand, a few meters from the sea, beautiful sandy beach . . . Anyway, one day we went off in search of a restaurant serving better food than what was available nearby. Flora and Dad and I were all fine with the usual tzatziki and olives and stuff, but Lewis was appalled, pretty much from day one, by the quality of the meat at the two tavernas on the beach. He called it 'gray flesh cubes on sticks.' "

"Sticks?"

"Kebab sticks. Anyway, he made a fuss—and when Lewis kicked off, it was impossible to ignore—so we went off looking for somewhere better and we found this hotel. It wasn't exactly posh—really good hotels are in short supply on Greek islands—but it was certainly a step up from where we were staying, and the closest to posh that we were likely to find, and we had a lovely lunch there with meat that Lewis thought was good, but he still wasn't happy. He was always such a perfectionist. Like, *nothing* could be wrong. Nothing unsatisfactory could be allowed to stand."

"He sounds like a twat." Zannah yawns.

"You know what? I think he is, and was, but I somehow didn't fully realize it. I was young and easily impressed and he was so entertaining, and confident. We all just kind of assumed he was brilliant because he acted as if that was beyond doubt. Anyway . . . the hotel's restaurant opened out onto a swimming-pool terrace. Stunning pool: huge, with absolutely no one in it or sitting around it. Apart from us, there were only two other people eating in the restaurant. We got the impression that the hotel was pretty much empty, and by the time we were ready to pay the bill and leave, Lewis was obsessed—completely obsessed, as much as he had been before about finding decent meat—with that swimming pool."

"Why? Shit!" Zannah presses all of her fingers against her forehead, then spreads them out. "I'm trying not to frown, so that I don't get too wrinkly when

I'm older. Antiaging moisturizer can only do so much. I've got to train myself to be surprised without scrunching up my face. Why did Lewis suddenly get obsessed with a swimming pool?"

"He said that no holiday was worth going on unless it had a great swimming pool as well as a great beach. He said it as if it was something he'd always thought and passionately advocated, though he'd never mentioned it before. It was so weird. He was the one who'd booked our holiday, chosen the place, everything. He'd happily booked an apartment on a gorgeous beach, with no swimming pool—but only about thirty footsteps from the most stunning, clear blue sea!—and then suddenly he was in the most horrendous mood because going to the hotel had ruined everything for him. Seeing that pool had made him think that his holiday was beyond flawed."

"Mum, he sounds like the biggest arse that ever lived."

"He certainly acted like one that day. He looked as if he might explode with murderous rage at any moment. Dad was taking the piss out of him, Flora was warning him to stop, and I couldn't stop laughing. Then, suddenly, he leaps up from the table and storms over to reception. No one knows what he's planning to do or say. Obviously we follow him, and find him negotiating with the receptionist: why can't we come and swim in their pool every day if we want to, if we eat at the restaurant? No one else is using the pool. The receptionist explained that the pool is for hotel guests only. An argument started, lasting twenty minutes at least, with Lewis insisting that anyone who eats in the restaurant surely qualifies as a temporary hotel guest, and the receptionist saying, no, it doesn't work like that, a guest is someone actually staying in the hotel."

"Ugh. Weren't you horribly embarrassed?" Zan asks.

"Weirdly, no. Anyone watching would have noticed no one but Lewis, so the embarrassment, I figured, was all his. Not that he felt it for a second. Once he saw that his valid guest argument wasn't going to work, he tried another tactic. He asked if we could pay a small fee to come and swim at the hotel, as day guests. The receptionist was nearly in tears by this point."

"I'm not surprised. I'd have said, 'You like our pool so much? I'll be happy to drown you in it, you fucker.'"

"Zan, don't swear."

"Ugh, Mum, relax. What happened next?"

"The receptionist said no to Lewis's day-membership scheme, even after he told her in great detail about various hotels in the UK that allow people to do precisely what he was proposing." I laugh at the memory. "What does a Corfu hotel receptionist care if the Quy Mill Hotel in Stow-cum-Quy, Cambridgeshire, lets anyone buy a day membership for a tenner? She just kept saying, 'My boss not allow, my boss not allow.' It looked as if Lewis was defeated for once—Dad was helpfully pointing that out, saying, 'Come on, Lewis, you've tried your best. Isn't it time to give up now?'"

"Ha! Dad always thinks it's time to give up. Like, even before you've started trying."

"True. But in this case he was right, or at least we all thought he was. Lewis had other plans, however."

"What did he do?"

"Asked if there were rooms available at the hotel. 'You seem pretty *empty*,' he said, stressing the last word."

"As if the receptionist cares," Zannah mutters scornfully. "It's not her hotel. She's not going to get a share of the profits even if it's full."

"I guess. She looked very confused and said, 'You want to stay here?' Lewis said no, he didn't, he had no intention of staying there, but since the only way he was going to be able to use the pool was to book a room, then that was what he'd have to do—that was what the receptionist was forcing him to do. He tried to book two rooms, there and then: one for him and Flora and one for me and Dad. We said not to book one for us, we were quite happy with the beach, but Lewis wouldn't listen. Trouble was, they didn't have two double or twin rooms in the hotel. They *weren't* empty, whatever Lewis thought, and all they could offer us was some kind of self-catering villa in the grounds that slept six people and was part of the hotel but also self-contained. Thankfully, it counted, for pool-using purposes. Dad and I were begging Lewis to see sense and be happy with the beach, not waste his money, but he was a man on a mission. He booked the villa—'the most expensive changing room I've ever used,' he called it later. Two grand, it cost—in 1997. The craziest thing was, none of us slept a single night there, even though it was much plusher than our beach apartment. Again, Dad and I tried our best to make Lewis see sense—since we'd gotten it now, we might as well use it, we said—but he was adamant. He said, 'I want that receptionist to see that she's made me spend two thousand of my hard-earned pounds on a villa that we're going to use for maximum half an hour a day, and for nothing apart from changing into and out of our swim suits.' "

"Okay, I have a theory and a question." Zannah sits up. "You said before, 'Flora was warning him to stop'—in the hotel restaurant. Warning who? Lewis, to stop making a fuss about the pool, or Dad to stop taking the piss out of Lewis?"

"Dad. Flora has always been a peacemaker. A soother-over of potentially troublesome things."

"That's what I thought you meant. Was she scared Lewis would hit Dad or something, if he didn't stop teasing him?"

"I think she might have been, yes. It's hard to explain when you don't know Lewis, but he could get into these weird states, almost like a maniac, and he'd be so full of passionate determination . . . It didn't happen often, but when it did, he could be scary."

"*Did* he ever hit Dad?"

"No. Of course not."

"Why 'of course'? People hit people all the time. How did you get to be friends with a maniac? Unwise life choice."

"Flora was my best friend at university. She was younger than me, but we met through rowing and clicked right away. Lewis was her boyfriend, and I just accepted him, like she accepted Dad. We became a foursome."

"You rowed?" Zannah looks horrified. "In a boat? On a cold, wet river?"

"Yeah, for my college."

"Oxbridge shit is so weird. I'm not going there."

"What, you mean because you're never going to do any revision?"

"Straight savage there from Mum. Nice one, Mum. You really got the crowd roaring with that one."

"Wanna know something I haven't even told Dad yet?"

"Obviously."

"The photograph Jeanette Cater showed me of her so-called children was a fake. It was a picture of a boy and a girl, around five and three. Kevin Cater probably printed it off the Internet. The picture didn't fit the frame. At all. There were big black margins of backing card at the top and bottom. If you'd seen the Caters' house . . . bland, grand, magazine-photo-ready, if you know what I mean—"

"You mean, not a tip like our house?"

"—but perfect, everything fitting exactly right, no expense spared. I don't believe people who live in a house like that would frame a picture of their two children so . . . badly. Yes, our house isn't the tidiest, but even I wouldn't frame a photo in such a slapdash way. Notice, all the photos of you and Ben all over the house are properly framed."

"Why haven't you said this to Dad?"

"I will. I just . . ." I break off with a sigh. "I think

he'll tell me that I can't possibly know how two strangers would frame a photograph. And he'd be right."

"Okay, here's my theory." Zan tucks her hair behind her ears. "Lewis—the maniac—used to hit Flora, like maniacs do. She eventually left him, and he let her—maybe he was bored with her and fancied getting a new wife—but he had one condition: she mustn't ever tell anyone that he was a violent abuser. She agreed to keep quiet, in exchange for getting to keep the house. She married Kevin Cater—someone she knew from when they worked together. Lewis moved out of the Hemingford Abbots house and Kevin moved in."

"So Flora Braid is now Mrs. Kevin Cater? Then who's the woman I met, who told me and Dad she was Kevin's wife?"

"The woman with a *foreign accent?*" Zan rolls her eyes. "Don't people with huge mansions usually have foreign servants? Like, Polish nannies, Romanian cleaners? Jeanette sounds more like a French name, to be honest."

"It's not her real name. She said—" I stop, gasp and grab Zannah's arm. "Zan. Zan, you're brilliant."

"Why, thank you. What did I do?"

"I can't believe this has only just occurred to me. Oh, my God."

"What?"

"Do you have a different name for French lessons at school? A French name?"

She laughs. "Er . . . no. Mum, no one calls us anything or teaches us anything at Bankside Park. We don't learn shit." Normally this sort of statement would send me into a spiral of panic.

"My French teacher gave us all French names. I was *Élisabeth*. I told Flora that, soon after we met. It came up when we were comparing notes about the schools we'd gone to, and she said, 'We did that too.' I didn't remember until now. Why didn't I think of it as soon as Marilyn Oxley—"

"Mum, slow down. You're making no sense. So what if you and Flora both had . . . Oh." Zan's eyes widen. "You mean . . . ?"

"Yes. Flora's French name at school was Jeanette."

# 9

"Great. We're here," says Zannah, as we pull up on the street outside Kimbolton Prep School. "Now are you going to tell me *why* we're here?"

Three nights—mainly sleepless, for me—have passed since I realized that of course Flora would change her name to Jeanette if she were going to change it at all. I've forced myself to do a full two days of massages, so as not to let clients down, and to prove to myself that I'm still an ordinary person with an ordinary life.

It's ten in the morning. I've timed this trip, unlike my last visit to a school, to ensure that I won't bump into any parents dropping off or picking up their children. I don't want to see Flora, or Kevin Cater—or the woman who called herself Jeanette because, for some reason, I'm not allowed to know that Flora still lives in that house.

Today I'm not here to try and catch a glimpse of any of them; I'm here to find out about the people who live at 16 Wyddial Lane—as much as I can, which will be easier if they're not here. I'm telling myself that if I approach the task ahead with the resolve of Lewis Braid on that day at the Corfu hotel . . .

"You can do it, Beth," I hear Lewis's voice in my mind. He was brilliant at motivating people. Once, when I had a deadline at work that was nearly driving me to a nervous breakdown, he said, "Have you tried telling yourself that it's the best fun ever and you're loving every second of it? You'd be amazed by how much that'll change your attitude *and* the outcome."

"But I'm not loving it," I told him. "I hate it. It's nearly impossible."

"So? Can you do nearly impossible things? Yes, of course you can. You *love* to do nearly impossible things." The following day he turned up at our flat with a sign he'd had made for me, saying, in capitals, "WE CAN DO NEARLY IMPOSSIBLE THINGS." "I'm not leaving till it's up on a wall," he said bossily. Would he be a great boss, or the worst in the world? It's hard to know. Both, probably.

"Er, Mother?"

"Sorry, I was just . . ."

"In a trance. I know. So, why are you so sure the Braid-slash-Cater kids go to this school?"

Excellent question. When I have to explain to Dom later why I let Zannah come with me when I should have made her stay at home and spend her pre-GCSE study leave revising, this is what I'll tell him: she's got a sharp mind and a powerful capacity to get to the heart of a problem. Nothing associated with school ever brings this out in her. Thinking about the Braid-slash-Cater problem does.

"I know what type of school Lewis would pick for his kids," I tell her. "This type—of which this is the closest example to Wyddial Lane."

"But they might not be Lewis's kids."

"I trust what I saw," I repeat my mantra. "I saw Thomas and Emily Braid, aged five and three. Or, at least . . . two children who looked so similar to them that they can only be Lewis and Flora's."

"What school did the other, older Thomas and Emily go to?"

"Thomas had just started at King's College School in Cambridge when we last saw them. Emily was signed up to go there too."

"Mum! Then that's where we should be."

"I thought about it."

"And?"

"Why would Flora have been in Huntingdon doing chores on a school-day morning? She wouldn't. If Thomas—new Thomas—is at King's, she'd drop him off, then do those chores in Cambridge. Bank, post office, nipping to a shop . . . whatever. Why would she drive to Huntingdon?"

"Major logic fail," says Zan. "She could have gone to Huntingdon for a million reasons. Maybe she's got a friend who works there and they were meeting for lunch, or—"

"No. She was coming back to her car in the car park long before lunchtime."

"Coffee, then."

"It's possible, but . . . I don't know. I just figure: someone who's in Huntingdon on a weekday morning is more likely to have a child here, at this school, than at a school in Cambridge. All other things being equal."

"Yeah, but all other things about this situation are so *not* equal, are they? All other things are, like, totally fucked."

"Zannah, stop swearing." I turn to face her. "I mean it. You need to behave properly. Not only to please me and Dad, but because you want to go out into the world as—"

"Mum, stop trying to cram years of proper parenting into one little pep talk. You're not a Mumsnet kind of mum, so don't pretend you are."

I don't know what she means because I've never looked at Mumsnet. Actually, maybe that's what she means.

"Do you want to come in with me?" I nod in the direction of the school.

"Sure—but to do what? No school's going to answer questions about its pupils from someone who just walked in off the street."

"Which is why we can't ask questions. We have to pretend to know already. What's tricky is working out *what* we're going to pretend to know."

"What do you mean?"

"Come on, let's go. I've got an idea. Your job is to stand behind me and smile, looking like the respectable daughter of a respectable mum. And no swearing. First we need to grab something from the boot that might belong to a five-year-old boy." My car's boot operates as a kind of storage cupboard-cum-dustbin. There's plenty in it to choose from.

Five minutes later, armed with a pale blue drawstring sports bag with a pair of socks inside it, Zannah and I are standing at the reception desk of Kimbolton Prep School. I press the buzzer and wait, rehearsing what I'm about to say.

A woman appears. She's young and elegant, with short hair, a long slender neck and lovely earrings: small round pearls that look real, with solid silver flower shapes behind them. She reminds me of a swan, and looks friendly enough. "Can I help you?" she says.

"Yes, I hope so," I say with a smile. "I'm a friend of Jeanette Cater's. She left this in my car boot . . ."— I wave the bag in the air—"and I don't have time to go to her house now and drop it off, so I thought . . . would it be okay to leave it with you?"

"Sure. No problem at all."

I fight the urge to say, "So you know Jeanette Cater, then? Her son is here, at this school?"

The receptionist reaches for a pad and pen that are over on the other side of the desk. "Let me write down your details, just so I can tell Jeanette what happened."

*Shit.*

"Beth Leeson," says Zannah cheerfully, while I'm frantically trying to think of a fake name I can give. *Too late now.* "Oh—sorry, that's my mum. She's Beth Leeson. I'm Zannah."

I try to look unflustered. Zan's probably right: better not to lie. Besides, if the receptionist hands Jeanette Cater a random sports bag later and tells her it was brought in by a person whose name she doesn't recognize and who claims to be her friend, it's going to be pretty obvious who's behind it—especially when Jeanette asks for a physical description of this mysterious woman. My hair is half brown and half blond at the moment; for months I've been too busy with clients and their problems—both physical and emotional—to get it sorted out.

Zan must have worked this out long before I did: I've been lied to, and I'm taking steps to find out why, and what's really going on. I'm not ashamed of any of my actions and, by doing this, I'm letting Jeanette Cater know that I'm not.

It's funny how quickly my thinking patterns have adjusted to all the unknowns. When I think about "Jeanette," there's a shadowy person in my mind who might be either Flora or the woman with the foreign accent. When I think about "Thomas and Emily," sometimes they're the two photogenic teenagers on Lewis's Instagram and other times they're the two small children I saw getting out of the silver Range Rover last Saturday.

The receptionist writes down "Beth Leeson." "Phone number?" she asks me.

"Jeanette has my number."

"Oh—ha, yes. Sorry! I'm so used to taking full details from people. Tell you what, though . . . if you could just let me have your number, just in case?"

Zannah recites our home number, and the receptionist writes it on the pad. When she looks up, I see uncertainty in her eyes. "And you're Jeanette's . . . *friend?*" she says, as if this is an outlandish concept.

"Yes."

Two spots of red have appeared on her otherwise white cheeks. She holds out her hand awkwardly to take the sports bag from me. She's gone from friendly and confident to nervous in the space of seconds. Why?

"What's your name?" I ask her.

"Lou Munday," she says quickly. "Rhymes with the famous song, 'Blue Monday'! Haha. My husband says that's one of the reasons he married me." She's still on edge, but trying to hide it.

I pass her the bag.

We say our good-byes, and Zannah and I are halfway to the door when she calls after us, "Thanks again! I'll give this to Jeanette later when she comes to collect Thomas."

I freeze. Zannah and I exchange a look.

*Thomas. Not Toby.*

Kevin Cater lied. I now have proof, and it came from someone impartial, with no skin in the game. I should make a motivational sign like the one Lewis made for me, with "I trust myself" emblazoned across it, and stick it on the wall in my treatment room. My clients would love it. Lots of them are keen on positive psychology and mindfulness and things like that.

Zan is ahead of me, walking back to reception. "Did you say Toby, Mrs. Munday?" she asks in her fake-sweet voice, the one she only uses on me when she wants me to spend serious money on her. "Jeanette's son isn't called Toby. He's called Thomas."

"I know. I said Thomas." She looks confused.

"And his sister's not called Emma," I say.

"No, she's called Emily. I didn't say anything about an Emma." The red spots on her cheeks are growing.

"I know you didn't. Can I tell you something that's going to sound—"

"Mum," says Zan curtly. She's trying to warn me off.

"No, I'm doing this," I say. "Mrs. Munday—"

"Please, call me Lou."

"I don't know how well you know the Cater family . . . for example, do you know that Thomas and Emily have a younger sister called Georgina? A baby?"

"We don't know that's true," says Zannah.

Lou Munday looks mystified. She says, "The Caters don't have a baby called Georgina, or any baby at all. They just have Thomas and Emily."

"Just to check: we're talking about Kevin and Jeanette Cater, who live at 16 Wyddial Lane, Hemingford Abbots?"

Lou has started to pluck at the skin of her neck with the fingers of her right hand. "I probably shouldn't . . . I mean, I *can't.* I can't tell you where they live."

"I've just told you where they live: 16 Wyddial Lane, Hemingford Abbots. Is that right?"

She starts to mumble about safeguarding issues. It's been a while since she looked me in the eye.

"Does Jeanette Cater have a foreign accent?" Zannah asks her.

"A foreign . . . No, she . . . I'm sorry, but I'm afraid I can't—"

"No? No foreign accent?"

"Zan, wait. Lou, I'm really sorry about this. I don't want to make you feel uncomfortable, and obviously you don't have to tell us anything else. We'll leave in a minute, I promise. Before we go, though, I'd like to tell you something. Tell, not ask."

Am I really going to do this? Is this a strategy, or a burst of recklessness I'll regret?

"I lied to you. I am Beth Leeson—that's true—but the bag I gave you belongs to my son. It's nothing to do with the Caters. I lied because . . . well, it's a long story, but . . . I think there might be something wrong—I mean really, horribly wrong—in the Cater household. It would take too long to tell you every-thing so I'll just say this: three days ago, Jeanette

Cater, or, rather, a woman who introduced herself to me as Jeanette Cater, with a foreign accent, told me that her children were called Toby and Emma. Not Thomas and Emily. And . . . a few days before that, I saw a woman *who is not Jeanette Cater*, because she's my old friend Flora Braid, getting out of a silver Range Rover and . . ." I should probably stop there. The rest would sound too implausible.

Lou shakes her head. "I can't talk to you," she says in a tight voice. "You need to leave."

"You have my phone number. Will you ring me later? I swear to you, whatever you tell me will go no further. No one will ever know you said anything at all."

She shakes her head more vigorously. The pearl flowers on her earlobes jiggle up and down.

"I'm worried about the children. Thomas and Emily. I think you are too."

That one hit home. Her eyes widen. She takes a step back and nearly trips over the sports bag, which she's left on the floor. She picks it up and pushes it across the desk to me. "Please just go," she says.

# 10

The plan was to drive straight home after Kimbolton Prep School; the decision to ignore the plan was unanimous, which is why, for the third time in less than a week, I'm on Wyddial Lane. I turn the corner and pull over as soon as I'm clear, at the top end of the road. Hopefully Marilyn Oxley won't see me, or the Caters.

*Or Flora.*

Zannah says, "If I pass my test when I'm seventeen, will you and Dad buy me a car? I want a Mini."

"Too expensive," I say. "But I'll buy you driving lessons—which otherwise you won't be able to afford—"

"Cool."

"—if, and only if, you start revising properly for your GCSEs. Tomorrow, first thing."

"Blackmailer."

I feel as if the ever-vigilant eyes of Marilyn Oxley are on me already. If they're not now, they soon might be, even if I stay up at this end of the street. She's probably got a long-range camera fitted to her roof and a bank of screens in her front room—like security guards in films, who always fall asleep at the exact moment that a balaclava-clad psychopath tiptoes through all the rooms they're supposed to be watching. Those movies need Marilyn Oxley; she wouldn't miss a thing.

I don't care if she sees me. I'm here to talk to other people, not her, and certainly not Kevin Cater and Fake Jeanette. I'm allowed to do that—or allowed to try, anyway. Today, my target is all the other houses. I need to find residents of Wyddial Lane that I haven't already spoken to.

"Can I come with you?" Zannah asks. "Or will that make us look like Jehovah's Witnesses? They always go in pairs."

"I don't think there's much chance of anyone thinking you're doing the Lord's work," I say, eying her gray T-shirt, which has "Gang Sh*t" printed on it in black. How did I not notice that before? "If you're coming with, you'll need to zip up your jacket," I tell her. "Did you have it zipped while we were talking to Lou Munday?"

"Irrelevant, since that's in the past." Zan snorts dismissively. "What, you think she'd have spilled everything she knows if I'd worn a Bambi T-shirt instead? Anyway, there's an asterisk, so it's not even a swear word. Which house shall we start with?"

"Let's just go door to door."

"Let's definitely *not* do that. We should pick the ones that look most chilled."

"Chilled? Oh, you mean—"

"Not refrigerated. Most of them look uptight and closed off—walls, fences, high gates. Kind of like luxurious prisons. There's no way people who live in houses like that are going to invite two strangers in and start chatting to them, answering a load of weird questions."

"So shall we start with the only one up at this end that doesn't look like that?" I point at it through the car window. On one of its gateless gateposts, there's a sign saying "No. 3." There's a wall, but it's low and crumbling. There's nothing to suggest that its owners want to hide themselves from prying eyes.

"Number 3 looks a good shout," Zan agrees. "Especially as it's got a wheelie bin at an angle outside its front door."

"Why? How's that relevant?"

"Think about it, Mother."

We sit in silence for a few seconds. Then I say, "Thought. Still don't know."

"It can't be bin day, or everyone's bins would be out on the pavement. Or a good few still would, at least—the ones belonging to people who aren't yet back from work. All these houses have massive gardens, loads of space on either side. But number 3's owners couldn't be bothered to wheel the bin a few feet farther and put it there, in that wooden bus-shelter type thing attached to the side of the house that's probably a bin store. They'd rather make the least possible effort, and leave it at the top of the driveway, where it makes the house look worse to anyone who passes by. I mean, who cares, right? I wouldn't either. There are bins in the world—deal with it."

"But that's your point," I say, getting it at last.

"Uh-huh. Number 3's owners can't be bothered with trivial shit. All their neighbors hate them for lowering the tone with their noticeable bin, and they don't care. Maybe they also won't care that it's not the done thing to tell strangers about what secret, twisted things your neighbors get up to."

"Okay. Number 3 it is."

I lock the car and we walk up the driveway. It's a wide house, as enormous as all the others on Wyddial

Lane, painted the color of buttermilk, with a redbrick chimney attached to its front. Next to the front door there's a sign that says "Low Brooms."

I ring the bell and we wait. "We might have to wait a while," I mutter. "Getting to the front door in a house this size . . ."

It opens surprisingly quickly. A woman who looks around my age, wearing cut-off bleached-denim shorts and a pink long-sleeved top, smiles at me and Zan and says, "Please say something nice!"

Not the response I was expecting.

Her frizzy brown hair has streaks of gray in it. Around her neck, on a leather cord, she's wearing a huge silver pendant that looks like a jellyfish, with a shiny dark green stone at its center. "I like your pendant," I tell her, hoping that's nice enough.

She beams at me. "That's the *best* thing you could have said. You can come again!" She laughs. "I couldn't adore it more, and I've worn it every day since I bought it and, do you know what? *No one* has said anything about it apart from you. No one's spontaneously said, 'What a beautiful piece of jewelry!' Look, it's two-sided. Nautilus with a malachite eye on one side, ammonite fossil on the other. Oh—that wasn't what I meant when I said, 'Say something nice!' I wasn't fishing for compliments!"

"Jellyfishing for compliments," I say, trying to present myself as the sort of person this woman would get on well with.

"Huh? Oh! No, a nautilus is very different from a jellyfish. Though in the grand scheme of things, they're both in the sea, so . . . hey!" She shrugs. "I'm sorry. You must think I'm high on drugs. I'm really not. I'm just kind of excited. I don't normally . . . wow, I mean, *shut up*, Tilly, stop blathering on at these poor people!"

"Hi, Tilly. I'm Beth Leeson. This is my daughter, Zannah." I hold out my hand. She shakes it. "Please don't stop blathering on our account. We came here to blather, as a matter of fact, so . . . if you blather first, I'll feel less guilty about my own blathering!"

I can feel disapproval radiating from Zannah. As soon as we're alone, she's going to list all the ways I handled this wrong.

Tilly from number 3 appreciates my act, anyway. She's laughing like a loon. "Okay, well, do you wanna come in?" she says. "Assuming you're not serial killers, or canvassers from an evil political party? They're all evil these days, let's face it. I'd vote Lib Dem but there are only about three of them left and one's a golden retriever." She throws back her head and cackles again.

"We're neither murderous nor political," I tell her.

"Fantastic. Come in, then." We can't. She's blocking the doorway. "I'll tell you what I meant. So. For months, I've not been answering the door when the bell rings. Justin and the kids are out all day during the week, and I've got those hours and *only those hours* to do all my work—I work at home—and clean, and cook, and the rest, you know how it is. So, my New Year's resolution was: no more rushing to the door when the bell rings. I stuck to it, too. Religiously. Unlike my other resolution, which was to cut out sugar and flour and alcohol, but hey! And at first it was *so liberating*. Understanding for the first time in my life that my doorbell—like my phone, like my email inbox— is there *to serve me*. Not the other way around! You know? And it's been amazing, I've been so productive since January, but . . . lately, I've started to think it's a shame. Who knows what those doorbell rings might be, you know? What if I'm too willingly closing myself off to new, fantastic experiences? So today, on an impulse, I thought to myself—I needed a break, to be honest—'Get off your bum and open that door.' And immediately panicked in case it was something dull like a survey about shopping habits. I never shop, anyway. Hate it. Waste of a day."

"If you want the opposite of dull, you're in luck," I

tell her. "I rang your bell in the hope that you'd answer a whole load of . . . unusual questions that no one else will answer honestly—about Wyddial Lane."

"What kind of unusual?"

"It's a long story. The short version is, I had some friends who used to live at number 16, and—"

"Number 16. That's the Caters, right? And before that . . ." She stops. Her eyes widen. "Lewis Braid? Is he your friend?"

"Not anymore, no. Not for twelve years."

"But you're here to ask unusual questions about him? Please say you are! That man is *crying out* to have unusual questions asked about him. Well, the opposite actually—he's not crying out for it, he'd hate it, but the world is, or at least, I am."

"I am too," I say.

She moves to one side and waves us in. "I'm so glad I opened the door," she says as we follow her across a wide entrance hall and into a messy kitchen with a red Aga and many blobby children's paintings stuck up on the walls. "This was meant to be—I truly believe that. Time to rethink that resolution!"

I try not to stare at the most eye-catching thing in the room: an enormous and scary-looking wall-chart calendar with boxes for all the days of the year, and black-and-white drawings of branches and leaves wrapped around them. There's tiny, spidery handwriting in many of the boxes in four different colors: red, green, purple and orange. It's weirdly beautiful, as long as you don't need to read the writing.

On a battered pine table at the center of the room, papers and forms are spread out. They look confusing and boring. Tilly's work, presumably. She sweeps them to one side, saying, "Fuck off, boring company tax returns!"

Does that mean she's an accountant?

"Okay, let's get this kettle on," she says. "Tea? Coffee? Rubis? And feel free to fire questions at me while I make drinks."

"What's Rubis?" I ask.

"You've not discovered Rubis? Oh, my good God! I'm about to become your favorite person. Oh." She frowns. "You're driving, probably. It's alcoholic."

"Tea for me, thanks," I say.

"Rubis is *heaven*. Imagine the most yummy chocolate that's *also* a delicious velvety red wine."

"I'll have some," Zannah says sweetly.

"You do right—as we Yorkshire folk like to say!" Tilly beams at her.

"Just a tiny bit," says Zannah's killjoy mother. Yorkshire? Tilly's accent couldn't be less northern if it tried.

She hands Zannah a bottle and glass, then puts the kettle on. I tell her a much-curtailed version of the story so far: that I saw Flora at number 16 and in Huntingdon, and that, despite this, the Caters and Lewis have all insisted that Flora's in America.

"Huh. Interesting," says Tilly. "As far as I know, they live in America now. Is it possible Flora was back, or is back, to visit the Caters?"

"Yes, but then why would everyone lie? On the phone, Lewis didn't say, 'Yeah, you might well have seen Flora, she's in England at the moment.' Flora herself rang me and said she was in Florida—no mention of any trip to Hemingford Abbots. And when I told her I was sure I'd seen her outside her old house, she said, no, no way, impossible. She ended the phone call after about ten seconds, having promised to ring me back, which she didn't. And then the next day, I bump into her in a car park in Huntingdon."

"That is deeply, deeply peculiar," Tilly says, handing me my tea. "Lewis is, though. Or was when I knew him. Maybe his wife is too. Maybe she was back, and didn't want to see you. Nothing against you, just a case of 'This particular trip is about *this* and I don't want to use any of it to do *that*.'"

"That'd explain her saying, 'How's things? Hope all's well! Gotta dash.' But lying about what country she's in when she knows I've seen her? And Lewis lying, and the Caters lying?"

"You're right," says Tilly. "No one would go to those lengths to avoid maybe having to have a coffee for half an hour with an old friend they'd rather not see."

Zannah says to Tilly, "You said before that maybe Lewis's wife is weird too, because Lewis is weird. Didn't you know Flora, when they lived here?"

"No. That was one of the weirdest things about Lewis: his wife, whom he worshipped—but no one ever saw her! It was the talk of the WLRC."

"What's that?" I ask.

"Sorry. Wyddial Lane Residents' Committee. We all decided Lewis's wife was a hermit who never left the house. Lewis was very sociable—came to every meeting and every drinks do, sometimes with his kids—but never invited anyone over to his place. *Ever.* Normally, that would make you unpopular—very keen on proper turn taking, is the WLRC; drives me crazy! Sometimes I can't face hosting a party for forty people! So shoot me!—but everyone loved Lewis because he'd make every party a success. He was a one-man show—and a brilliant one, too. And he'd always arrive laden down with booze and cakes and treats. But . . . yeah. We all wondered about the invisible wife. He talked about her nonstop but it was almost as if . . ."

"As if he wanted to make her feel like a presence in spite of her absence?" I suggest.

Tilly slaps me on the arm with the back of her hand. "That's it *precisely*. That very thing."

"Even if she didn't come to events, people must have seen her, though."

"Yeah. One or two did report having seen a dark-haired woman driving out through the gates but that was about the extent of it. And, actually, it's maybe unfair to label Lewis an oddball since *she* might well have been the weird recluse, and he was covering for her, trying to present a show of normal family life, but even if that was the case, what he did later . . ."

"What did he do?" Zannah asks. I notice that her glass is full. Last time I glanced at it, it was empty. I pick up the Rubis bottle and move it away from her.

"If I tell you, you must never tell anyone. Swear on all you hold dear. I've never told anyone on Wyddial Lane. Only Justin, my husband."

Zan and I promise not to tell anybody.

Tilly leans in conspiratorially. "He *stalked* me. Obsessed with me, he was. Lewis Braid, perfect husband and dad, turned into an honest-to-God creepy stalker."

**"What? *What?*"** says Dom, when I come to the bit about Lewis stalking Tilly. "I simply don't believe that. Sorry. No way!" His protests are so loud that I have to hold my phone away from my ear. Zannah and I are in the car in a service station car park on the A14. I'd been fobbing Dom off all day with quick, jolly "All fine! Talk later!" replies. I would have waited until we got home to tell him all this, except I've changed the plan again. Driving home isn't next on my agenda anymore.

"Why don't you believe it?" I ask him.

"I mean . . ." I hear something crunch in the background at his end, and picture him at the kitchen table, eating an apple. "I just don't."

"I want to hear why. It'll confirm what Zan and I think. Spit it out. Don't worry about being ungallant."

"You said she had frizzy hair, brown streaked with gray?"

"The essence of frizzy! So frizzy, you could barely see the individual strands of hair. If she's ever used conditioner, I'd be surprised."

"Did she have a pretty face?"

"She had a pleasant face, I'd say."

"Thin? Fat?"

"Neither. Maybe about like Mrs. Adlard."

"Who's that?"

"Dominic," I say flatly.

"What?"

"Mrs. Adlard is Ben's tutor."

"Oh, her. Right. So, not thin."

"But not fat either. Like, maybe a size 14."

"Lewis would think that was fat," Dom says without missing a beat. I give Zan a thumbs-up sign. One more subscriber to our opinion; we must be right. "If Lewis was going to stalk a woman, he'd pick a skinny, beautiful one. Someone who looked like Flora used to look before she had three kids."

"Zan and I agree. And he might pick that skinny, beautiful woman to stalk *because* Flora no longer looked exactly the way she did before she had three kids—he could easily be that shallow, with his constant search for perfection—but what he definitely would never do is become obsessed with a plain-but-pleasant-looking, not-thin, frizzy-haired, *gray*-haired person."

"Never."

"But I'm sure Tilly was telling the truth, that's the problem."

"She was," Zannah confirms. "Mum, put it on speaker. Aaand you have no idea what that means. Pass it here."

She fiddles with my phone, then balances it on the armrest between us. "Speak, Dad," she orders.

"Hello! Testing, testing."

"So lame. See, Mum, now we can both hear him.

Dad, she said they'd always been friendly, and Lewis helped her set up her own business, went above and beyond, came around at all hours of the day and night to provide support—but she didn't think anything of it because he was helpful to everyone, he was just that kind of guy."

"He was," says Dom. "That's true. He couldn't stand for anything to fail, and that included his friends' projects. Remember when I ran the marathon, Beth?"

"What happened?" asks Zan.

"Lewis nearly fell out with me because I wouldn't let him be my coach and personal trainer—even though he had a full-time job, wasn't a sports coach and had never run a marathon himself. Still, he wanted to take time off from work to make sure I succeeded and would barely take no for an answer. He couldn't imagine me being able to do it without his help. I did, though, and he was genuinely happy for me."

"At the same time as going on for months about how you'd have finished much faster if you'd let him coach you," I say.

"Sounds like how he was with Tilly's business," says Zan. "She thought, great, what a nice friend. Her business did well. The Braids moved. But he still kept turning up outside her house, *after* he'd moved to

Florida—spying on her from his car. The first couple of times it happened, he made crap excuses—like, really crap. One time she found him in her back garden and he said he'd been passing and heard something that sounded suspicious, so he'd gone to investigate. Another time she found him asleep on a bench in her back garden. On his chest was guess what? A pair of Tilly's silk pajama bottoms that she'd left to dry on the washing line."

"And . . . all this happened after the Braids moved to Florida? When the Caters owned the house?"

"Yeah, and when Lewis was working in America," I say. "Tilly, thinking it was all very odd, googled him and found that he definitely had a job in Florida at the time . . . but he also kept making time to come back and . . . fall asleep in her garden clutching items of her clothing."

"It all came to a head after the silk pajamas," Zannah tells Dom. "Tilly and her husband confronted him, told him they weren't going to pretend to believe any more excuses, and he broke down in tears and admitted it. He *cried*, Tilly said. Wept buckets."

"What did he admit?" asks Dom.

"That he'd fallen in love with her!" Zannah slurs. "He actually said that to her and her husband. Begged them never to tell anyone, especially not his wife, and swore blind that he'd never do it again. Which he didn't. The silk-pajama time was the last stalking episode."

"Zannah, you sound drunk. Beth, what's wrong with her?"

"Tilly gave her some booze."

"For Christ's sake, Beth!"

"Yeah, Mum." Zannah grins at me. "This happened on your watch. You tell her, Dad."

"Can you two come home now, please?"

"Not immediately. Dom . . . is it possible that there are two sides to Lewis? What if the perfection-seeking side of him makes him miserable, with the pressure it piles on? Tilly's dynamic, happy, relaxed. Doesn't give a damn about a few gray hairs."

"And Lewis had a secret urge to abandon his perfect life and run off with her? I mean . . . I'm not saying it's not possible, because anything's possible, but . . . Why aren't you coming home? What else are you doing?"

"Going to Wokingham. I need to try and find Flora's parents. They must know something about what's going on. Lewis Braid has been their son-in-law for twenty years."

"Her parents? Beth, you don't *need* to do that."

"I want to."

"Please don't. Beth, the time comes when you have to

draw a line. That time has come. Now. Today. Zannah needs to get back here and start revising. She's on exam study leave, not . . . crazy-dashing-around-the-country leave. Ben wants you to come home."

"Straight after Wokingham, I promise. Zannah was desperate to come with me, Dom. She's really interested in this."

"That's what worries me."

"No revision would have happened even if I hadn't brought her with me. You know as well as I do—she'd have done fuck all apart from paint her nails and watch reruns of *Love Island*."

"Hashtag when your parents believe in you," says Zan with a chuckle.

"She's got a brilliant mind and today, all day, that mind has been *working*." I was planning to say that anyway, but now it looks as if I only said it to ingratiate myself. Zannah makes a face at me.

"Do you want to hear what happened at Kimbolton Prep School?" I ask Dom.

Without waiting for his answer, I launch into a full account. He may be right: there might be a point at which one ought to draw a line, but I'm hoping there's also a point at which any intelligent person realizes that they have to find out what the hell's going on or it'll bother them forever. I reached that point some time ago.

I describe my conversation with Lou Munday.

"That all sounds . . . strange, horrible and worrying," Dom says when I've finished.

"Yep. I'd swear that secretary wanted to tell me *something*—more than she told me. Zannah agrees."

"I'm not sure I do," she says unhelpfully. "Maybe. Maybe Lewis Braid stalked her too."

"She didn't give me the brush-off in a normal, routine, off-you-go-you-nut kind of way. There was something she could have told me if she'd wanted to, if she'd not been scared of losing her job."

"Or scared of getting involved in something really unpleasant," says Dom. "Which you should be too, Beth. Whatever's going on in that house and with the Braids and the Caters, it's something our family needs to keep out of. Think about everything you've told me so far—Tilly, now the school stuff—it all adds up to a giant neon sign saying 'Stay the hell out of this mess.'"

"Typical graphic designer response there from Dad," says Zan. "Bringing signage and the visual into everything. Me and Mum aren't graphic designers so we can't see that sign."

Dom makes a disgusted noise. "Kevin and Jeanette Cater told us their children were called Toby and Emma."

"Uh-huh. And, don't forget, she turned up at the

car park wearing the same clothes Flora was wearing less than an hour before. Oh—and she isn't Jeanette Cater. Lou Munday told us Jeanette doesn't have a foreign accent. I forgot that bit."

"Who's that?"

"Memory of a goldfish," Zan mouths at me.

"Oh, the school secretary. Right. Well, whoever the woman at Newnham House was, she and Kevin Cater, assuming that's his real name—"

"Yeah, they fed us a load of bullshit," I say. *And you thanked them for it.*

"To our faces? While smiling and supposedly trying to help sort things out? I guess they must have, but . . . that's pretty twisted, isn't it?"

After more than forty years on this planet, Dominic has trouble believing that a civilized and solvent couple with an immaculate house could lie to him. He's still keen to believe in a version of the world in which everyone has each other's best interests at heart.

"They flat out lied." He still can't believe it.

"Yes. Dom, I have to go. I'll see you later tonight, okay? Bye." I press the end-call button before he can give me any more reasons for why I should come home right away.

# 11

There hours later, we're parked on Carisbrooke Road in Wokingham, outside a house that I hope still belongs to Flora's parents. I only came here once with Flora while we were students, but I'm sure it's the right place. I remember thinking it looked odd from the outside, and number 43 is the only one that fits that description. It's a lone detached house on an otherwise terraced street, and so narrow that its detachedness looks like a mistake—as if it's been cut off the row as an afterthought and shoved along a bit. It protrudes awkwardly from the low-walled private garden that's been built around it like a little green island.

"Would you mind waiting in the car?" I ask Zannah.

"Yes."

"I think they'll tell me more if I'm alone. They know

Flora and I were best friends for years. And confiding's easier to do with an audience of only one, I think."

"All right. If you insist. But remember everything they say. Even better, record it."

Recording a voice memo is one of the few things that my phone and I both know how to do. Dom showed me so that I could illicitly record Ben singing, with the most reluctance and embarrassment I've ever seen packed into one boy in a school hall, a song called "Piratical Style" from the musical *Pirates of the Curry Bean*.

"Wish me luck," I say to Zannah as I get out of the car. I'm not going to record Flora's parents if I'm lucky enough to find them—I'd feel guilty and it would show on my face—but Dom gave me some wise advice about a year ago, one day when I was crying because, yet again, Zannah and I were at loggerheads. He said: "Try this: say a direct 'No' as rarely as possible. If it's possible to not give in but not actually say, 'No, you can't' or 'No, I won't' then do it. It works like magic." I thought it sounded like the worst advice I'd ever heard, but I tried it and it worked.

I ring number 43's bell. The door is part glass, and through the leaded panes, I see a figure coming toward me along the hall. A tall man.

When he opens the door, I recognize him as Flora's

dad, Gerard Tillotson. Ged, his wife used to call him. His hair is white now and he's thinner.

"Mr. Tillotson?" I say with a tentative smile.

"Hello? You're not going to try and sell me anything, are you? Because I'm not buying—not today! Haha! I don't need any more dishcloths or clothes pegs."

I wonder if my two-tone hair has made him think I must be a gypsy. "It's nothing like that," I say. "My name's Beth Leeson. Perhaps you remember me?"

"At my advanced age, I remember very little, my dear. Here's my advice to you: don't get old. There's really not much to recommend it."

"I was at university with . . ." I stop and clear my throat. "For a long time, I was best friends with Flora. Your daughter," I add unnecessarily. His memory might not be what it once was, but he's likely to remember his only child.

"Is Flora all right?" he says quickly.

"Um . . . yes, I . . . I'm not here with bad news or anything like that." As I say this, I wonder if it's true. What if Gerard Tillotson thinks everything in Flora's life is fine? Should I tell him that I don't think it is? Would that be fair?

"Ah. Well, that's a relief." He looks down at his right shoulder, as if trying to decide what to do. "I'm afraid Flora's not here, if you came in the hope of find-ing her," he says eventually.

"Oh—no, I know that. It's not that. I was hoping to speak to you, actually. And Mrs. Tillotson if she's around." *Shit.* I shouldn't have said that. Flora's mum might be dead for all I know. "It's quite important."

If it were my child, I'd want to know. Whatever anyone feared or suspected, I'd rather be told so that I could try and sort it out, however old I was.

Gerard Tillotson says, "If you walk around the house, you will find—unsurprisingly—the back gar-den. At the far end of it is a little blue-painted struc-ture. It used to be a shed, but my wife spruced it up and now calls it the summer house. You'll find her in-side it, surrounded by her dress-making equipment." He closes the door without a good-bye. Through the glass, I watch him walk back down the hall and disap-pear into a room.

What am I supposed to do now? Shouldn't he be the one to go and get his wife? Would he have told me where I'd find her if he didn't want me to seek her out?

I walk around the side of the house. The blue former shed is there, as described, at the end of a long, taper-ing back garden. There are white net curtains at its windows, with small orange and green flowers standing out like birthmarks, raising the skin of the gauzy fabric in lumps. I knock on the door and it opens immediately.

Rosemary Tillotson's hair is as white as her husband's. Unlike her husband, she is now heavier than she used to be. I see a large cream-colored sewing machine behind her, a patchwork rug on the floor, and some peach-colored fabric spread out on a table.

"Oh!" She smiles, as if I'm a rabbit that's popped out of a hat. "This is a surprise. Can I help you?"

"My name's Beth Leeson. I'm . . . I used to be Flora's best friend. You've met me before, ages ago."

"Flora's . . ." Her mouth moves, but nothing comes out. Then she looks past me, into her garden, and says, "Is Flora here?"

"No, she's not, though I've seen her a couple of times recently. I was hoping to talk to you and your husband about her, if that's okay."

Rosemary Tillotson frowns. "I'm not sure if it is. You can't just come here. You can't just . . ." I'm preparing to defend myself when the angry words stop and Flora's mother bursts into tears.

**Twenty minutes** later, Zannah and I are sitting in the Tillotsons' long, narrow, bay-windowed living room. The four of us are drinking tea from blue and white pottery mugs. I was in the car, ready to give up and drive back home, when Flora's father tapped on the window and inclined his head to indicate that I should come back to the house. Since he had seen Zannah, I decided it would be strange if I didn't bring her in with me.

"I'd better tell you, and I hope you don't take it personally, that your visit comes as rather a shock to us," he says now. "Foolishly, selfishly, quite reprehensibly, I decided that my wife would be better able to cope with the shock and to deal with *you* than I would be myself."

Rosemary Tillotson hasn't said a word to me since she had her crying fit. She's sitting by her husband's side on the sofa, red-eyed and mute. He has apologized four times so far for her distress, and I've apologized for causing it.

Something is very wrong here, and I wish I knew what it was—whether it's the same something-wrong as at Newnham House. Are Gerard and Rosemary Tillotson, at this moment, gearing up to lie to me as thoroughly as Kevin Cater and Fake Jeanette did?

So far, I've seen this living room, the hall and bottom of the stairs, the bathroom under the stairs and the kitchen. That's the entire ground floor of the house. There are no photographs of Flora, Lewis or their children anywhere to be seen. Unusual for grandparents. My mum has photos of Zannah and Ben at every age plastered all over her house.

"Perhaps you could tell us why you're here?" Gerard Tillotson asks.

I'd intended to tell them the whole story. That was before I knew that a visit from their daughter's former best friend would prove so traumatic for them. With Rosemary's blotchy face in front of me, I can't bring myself to say that I saw two of her grandchildren last Saturday and they didn't seem to have aged in twelve years. Before I reveal too much, I need to know why my turning up has made the Tillotsons so distraught.

"I wouldn't have come if I'd known it'd upset you," I say. "It's just that . . . when Flora and Lewis moved to Florida, they sold their house in Hemingford Abbots to a family called the Caters. I happened to drive past the house the other day, on my way to take my son to his football match, and I saw . . . well, I thought I saw Flora there, outside the house. And then I saw her again in Huntingdon and . . . the way she behaved made me worry that something was really wrong. I spoke to her briefly on the phone, and to Lewis, and they both said she wasn't in England. According to them, she's in Florida—which makes sense, because that's where they live now, but I know what I saw and I can't think—"

"Do they?" says Gerard. There's a sharp edge to his voice. "Does Flora live in America?"

"Are you saying she doesn't? Have she and Lewis split up? Is he in Florida, but she's still in England?"

Zannah coughs and fires a harsh look in my direction. She thinks I need to shut up and give the Tillotsons a chance to answer.

Gerard takes a sip of his tea. He looks at Rosemary, who doesn't notice. She seems unaware of her surroundings and of the conversation.

"We've had no contact with Flora since May 2007," he says. "Nor with Lewis or the children. We know nothing about a move to Florida, I'm afraid, nor about the condition of our daughter's marriage."

My head and heart start to spin. How can that be true? Flora was closer to her parents than anyone I've ever known. At university, she would ring them every night to say good night and tell them she loved them. She kept this up even after she married Lewis. He used to tease her about it.

"We don't google, and we don't inquire," says her father. "No doubt Lewis is taking the world by storm in one way or another—he always was destined for great things—but we prefer not to know anything about it. It would be too painful for us to have to contend with regular snippets of information. All our friends and acquaintances know that, if they happen to hear anything, we don't wish to be informed."

"Did you say May 2007?" I ask.

"That's right," says Gerard. "Lewis and Flora sat where you and your daughter are sitting now, and Lewis explained that we wouldn't be seeing or hearing from them, or from our grandchildren, again. He meant it, too. Oh, we were in no doubt that he meant it."

My instincts are telling me that I need to get out of here and away, fast, so that I can think this through. I force myself to stay seated. Until last Saturday, the last time I saw Flora was in February 2007. Shortly before that, in December 2006, I felt betrayed by her for the first time in our long friendship. But what if . . . ?

I push the thought from my mind. If I get caught up in thinking it through now, I won't be able to concentrate on the Tillotsons.

"Why?" I ask. "Sorry, I don't mean . . . I understand why you don't want to hear any news and how upsetting that would be, but why aren't you in touch with Flora? The Flora I knew—"

"Might as well have died," says Rosemary Tillotson suddenly. "Afterward, she wasn't the same person. She wasn't our lovely, happy daughter. She was a stranger."

"Afterward?"

Rosemary nods.

"She means after Georgina died," says Gerard.

*Oh, God, please, no. No, no, no.* The room spins around me. For a few seconds, I can't breathe. All the air is stopped solid in my lungs.

"Mum, are you okay?" Zannah asks.

"Georgina died?" I say, once I'm able to speak. "How? When?"

"April the twenty-seventh, 2007. She was six months old. She just . . . stopped breathing."

"Cot death?" I say.

"Sudden Infant Death Syndrome, I believe they call it. Georgina wasn't the strongest baby to begin with. There were various complications. She was born six weeks premature, and there was something wrong with her right eye. She would have needed surgery to correct it at some point, or perhaps an eye patch would have done the trick. She wasn't as robust as both Thomas and Emily were as babies."

"Flora didn't . . ." *Of course she didn't tell you, idiot. She didn't tell you any of it. Don't you remember the sequence of events?*

"She stopped being Flora," says Rosemary. "The old Flora—the *real* Flora—would never have cut us off. Never. We'd done nothing wrong, nothing at all."

"Which of course is what parents who deserve to

be ostracized would say," her husband adds. "But we didn't deserve it. Not a bit."

*Then why? Why did it happen?*

I can't bring myself to ask them if, before she died, Georgina's nickname was Chimpy. It probably makes no sense that I still have the urge to ask this question. If Georgina is dead, how could Flora have been talking to her on the phone last Saturday?

"Would you like a hanky or a tissue?" Rosemary asks me.

"No, thank you." I sniff and wipe my eyes quickly with the back of my hand.

She says, "When Flora and Lewis told us that Georgina had died, I looked at Flora and I knew right away: she was gone. As gone as Georgina was. Somebody else was there instead. A different woman."

"We only saw them twice after Georgina's death," says Gerard. "Once when they told us the terrible news and the second time when Lewis said we would never see them again and that we mustn't try to contact them."

"But why would Flora want that?" I blurt out. "You say she'd changed—anyone would change after a tragedy like that, but to push away your own parents . . ."

"Please." Gerard raises a hand. He's telling me, as politely as he can, to shut up. "All the questions you're likely to ask are ones we asked ourselves, again and again. We didn't understand. Of course we didn't. After such a tragedy, to be bereaved again so unnecessarily— and if you think it's too dramatic to call being cut off by your daughter and remaining grandchildren a be- reavement, I can assure you, that's exactly how it felt and how it still feels."

"I can imagine," I say shakily.

*But it can't have been Flora's fault. None of it can. She'd never have cut you off if she'd had a choice.*

How the hell am I going to manage the long drive home after this?

Gerard says, "Since I'm no longer in touch with Flora, I obviously can't ask her why she made the deci- sion that she made. I have my suspicions, if you'd like to hear them?"

"Only if you don't mind telling us," says Zannah.

*Thank you, Zan. Thanks for speaking when I can't.* If Zannah or Ben ever cut off contact with me, I'd throw myself off a bridge there and then. I wouldn't try to be brave for anyone else's sake. I couldn't live in a world where my daughter didn't want to know me.

Gerard says, "I think . . . well, I *know*, from my own experience, that most people will go to extraordi- nary lengths to avoid unbearable pain. It's what we've done since losing Flora and the children. It's the reason your visit, and your mention of Flora's name, caused us such, uh, consternation, shall we say? Flora and Lewis knew that every time they saw us, every interaction they had with us in the future, they would have to confront *our* loss, the grief that *we* felt at losing Georgina. I don't think they could face that prospect. I must say, it doesn't surprise me to hear that they've moved to America. It fits with my suspicion: they want to surround themselves with people who have no memories of Georgina. It will make life easier for them. Perhaps it's the only way they can face living at all."

*People who have no memories of Georgina . . .* Not me, then. I remember Georgina very clearly, from her one visit to my house. Even if I'd never met her in person, there was no chance I would ever forget her.

Thoughts and memories crash-land in my mind, one after another: Flora on the phone, ending the call as soon as she could, promising to ring back and then not ringing back. Flora running away from me in a Huntingdon car park, Lewis on the phone from Delray Beach, Florida—happy to chat at length, confident he could sustain his lies for as long as I could keep him talking.

Flora wasn't confident or happy to talk, though she did her best to pretend to be. She could only stretch out her lies for a finite amount of time. And then she couldn't risk ringing back. When she saw me in the car park in Huntingdon, she didn't brazen it out, as Lewis would no doubt have done. She turned and ran.

She was scared. *Of me.* Shit, how can this not have struck me before? She was on her way back to her car, presumably strolling along in a reasonably normal frame of mind, and then she saw me and she freaked out. Ran away. I was the thing that caused that rush of fear—because she knew I'd ask after Georgina and she didn't want to have to talk about her death? But . . .

No. That can't be it. You might try and avoid an old friend in those circumstances, but the fear I saw in Flora's eyes, the way she turned and ran . . . that wasn't just reluctance to talk about a past tragedy. It was more and bigger than that. And then, to send that other woman back to the car park wearing her clothes . . .

"I'm worried Flora's in danger," I say before I can stop myself. "I'm not sure I can explain it very well, but . . . Flora and Lewis both lied to me. The people living in their old house lied. There are no pictures of Flora on Lewis's Instagram page—only of him, Thomas and Emily. I know none of this proves she's in danger, but I think something is really wrong."

"Beth, please try to understand," says Gerard. "We can't help you. We don't know the answers to any questions you might ask. You know more than we do, and

I'm afraid that conversations like this one won't do me or my wife any good at all. It's going to take us weeks, possibly months, to recover from your visit. Nothing you've said suggests danger to me so much as . . . well, hard though this might be for you to hear, I think it sounds as if Flora and Lewis don't want you in their life anymore—much the same way they felt about us."

"But they told you quite directly, didn't they? That's not what they're doing with me."

"Mum, we should go," Zannah says quietly.

"I'm sorry. Sorry to be so . . . relentless. Can I ask you one more question before I leave?"

"I'd rather you didn't," says Gerard, at the same time that Rosemary says, "Yes."

"Did you like Lewis? Were you happy to have him as a son-in-law? Did you ever worry that he might . . ." I can't bring myself to say it.

"Harm Flora?" says Rosemary. "No. Never. He adored Flora and the children. Treated them as if they were made of gold. I didn't like him, though."

Gerard makes a spluttering noise. He puts down his cup of tea and wipes his mouth. "Rosemary, of course you liked Lewis. We both did."

"I didn't."

"You did," he insists, looking perplexed.

"I pretended to. I've always pretended to, even after

they told us they didn't want us in their lives anymore. It was probably silly of me, Ged. You and I should have discussed it before now. I shouldn't have told you in front of people we hardly know."

"Never mind," he says. He looks as if he does, though.

"Why didn't you like him?" I ask Rosemary.

"It's hard to describe, especially at a distance of so many years. But whenever he came here, I felt as if I was a guest in *his* house and not the other way around. Not even a guest, actually. More of a servant. He always had an air of being in charge, even in places where he shouldn't have been. Even in my kitchen."

"He was always perfectly genial, as far as I recall," Gerard defends the man who told him he'd never see his daughter or grandchildren again. "Life and soul of every gathering."

"But we couldn't be ourselves around him, Ged. Not at all."

"I could."

"Well, I couldn't," says Rosemary in a shaky voice. "I always felt I needed to please and impress him, and that, if I didn't, my relationship with Flora would suffer. I worked out, very early on, what kind of mother-in-law he would most want, and then I pretended to be that person."

"When I spoke to Lewis on the phone, I asked after Georgina," I tell her. "I said, 'How old is she now?' Obviously, I had no idea she'd passed away. I said it in a 'Wow, she must be nearly a teenager' kind of way."

"Lewis won't have liked that *at all*," says Gerard Tillotson quietly. Something chimes at the back of my mind—some sort of alarm or warning—but it's gone before I can grasp it.

"What did he say?" asks Rosemary.

"He told me Georgina was twelve," I say. I know I've said enough, but I'm so furious with Lewis that I can't control it, and the rest spills out: "There was no hint of distress or unease in his voice. He sounded his usual, upbeat, extrovert self, even though, it turns out, he was telling me the most outrageous lie: that his daughter who died when she was six months old is alive and well and living in Delray Beach, Florida."

## 12

"Beth? It's pitch black in here," Dom complains. I'm in the bath, in the dark, with Kiehl's Lavender, Sea Salts and Aloe Vera bath foam and a few extra drops of essential lavender oil added for good measure, to make the scent stronger. My face is covered with a stiff, dried mask: Zannah's favorite—a blend of lavender and chamomile that comes as a powder. You have to add water and stir it into a paste.

Some people believe that tea is the answer to stress, and others resort to alcohol. For me, it's lavender.

"You want to talk yet?" says Dom.

I nod. I'm ready. It might be nearly midnight, but since getting back from Wokingham I've dealt with my work email inbox and had an hour or so to get my thoughts in order. The bath has helped hugely. I feel like I have a grip on things again. I've adjusted, digested all the new information.

"Good." Dom closes the door and locks it. Now we're in total darkness.

"Can I turn a light on?" he asks.

"No. Your eyes'll adjust in a minute."

He sits down on the floor, leaning his back against the wall. "We need to talk," he says. "Seriously."

"I agree."

"Great. I'm glad."

I know what's coming.

"You need to drop this now. Completely. No more driving to far-away places, no more hanging around schools. And don't turn this into 'My husband doesn't understand my point of view,' because that's not true. I do."

"I've literally never said those words, by the way."

"Zan told me what happened at Flora's parents' place. Something fucked up is going on with Lewis and Flora, big time, but it doesn't affect us. By which I mean: it doesn't need to, unless you keep your obsession stoked up. You've been lied to and fobbed off repeatedly—that means Flora and Lewis don't want you to know what's going on with them, they want you out of their lives. Let that happen—stop pursuing this—and we'll never see or hear from the Braids again. And that'll be *brilliant*, Beth. That'll be the best possible outcome."

"For who?"

"All of us. Me, you, Zan and Ben."

"And we're the only people who matter?"

"In this case, yes. No one's having their life threatened or endangered, are they? Flora's walking around, going about her normal business. She seems not to be in too terrible a state, apart from when she sees you stalking her."

"I'm not—"

"So you heard her talking on the phone outside her house and she sounded upset—so what? These people haven't been our friends for *twelve years*. Let them get on with their lives, whatever weirdness those lives might involve, and let's us get on with ours. The alternative is what? Letting down more clients? Isn't that going to harm your business? You've always been the one out of the two of us who cares about your job. Maybe you don't anymore, but it's not only about you."

*Here it comes.*

"Today, Zannah should have been at home revising. Instead, she was sticking her nose into other people's business and getting drunk. That can't happen again, Beth."

"I agree. It was a one-off."

"Yeah, well, it should have been a none-off." He sounds slightly mollified.

"I've made a decision. I need one more day, and then I'll stop. At that point I'll have done all I can. I've already rescheduled all the clients I canceled. They're all fine about it. Zannah's got some revision sessions coming up at school, which she'll go to. Our lives aren't falling apart, Dom. We're all fine."

"Right, and we're going to stay fine—by accepting that other people's lives are their business and their problem. I don't agree that you need one more day."

*I don't care.*

"What will this extra day involve?"

"I'm going to go to Huntingdon and try and talk to the police there."

"What?" Dom laughs. "Beth, no crime has been committed."

"I agree, there's no proof of any crime."

"But you think there is one?"

"I've no way of knowing, and no power to find out. I strongly suspect something is really horribly wrong. For all I know, it involves an element of crime. Generally, people don't go to such extreme lengths to hide whatever they're hiding unless it's criminal. One person alone might be desperate to hide a shameful personal secret, but four? Lewis, Flora, Kevin Cater and the woman who told us she was Jeanette?"

"Yeah, they're four liars who all know each other. It's hardly a huge underground network. And there's absolutely no reason to suspect a criminal conspiracy. But . . . you're not going to take my word for it, so let's go and see the police. Maybe if you hear them say, 'We don't think there's anything for us to investigate here,' it'll put your mind at rest."

"It won't stop me wondering what's going on. I don't think anything could, apart from finding out the answer. But I need to know that I've done everything I possibly could to help Flora and . . . whoever those two kids were that I saw outside her house. And the two in Florida. All of them."

"You said the two kids you saw outside the Wyddial Lane house last Saturday looked normal and healthy," says Dom.

"They did."

"And it's clear from Lewis's Instagram that Thomas and Emily are doing great. So there's no evidence that anyone's harming any kids, is there?"

"Dom, for God's sake."

"What? What did I say?"

I sit up and wash off the face mask. Once it's all

gone, I say, "How sure are you that those four children are fine—the two in England and the two in America? Really think about it, Dom. I heard Flora call the two little ones Thomas and Emily. They were outside Kevin Cater's house, and Lou Munday at Kimbolton Prep School told me that those are the Cater kids' names: Thomas and Emily. That means it's likely to be them that I saw."

"I know all this."

"The two kids I saw were absolutely beyond a shadow of a doubt Flora's children. Like teenage Thomas and Emily when they were little, they bore a strikingly strong resemblance to Flora. There's no way they aren't hers. So. Think about what that means."

Dom stands up. He walks over to the bathroom mirror and stares at himself. Eventually he says, "Flora had three children. One died. Then she had two more and called them the same names as the two children she already had."

"Except no one does that," I say.

"But *she* has." Dom turns to face me. He looks confused. "If everything you've just said is true, that the younger two must be Flora's, then that must be what happened."

"Must it? We've only seen pictures of teenage

Thomas and Emily on the Internet. The people in those pictures could be actors hired by Lewis."

Dom snorts. "Beth. Come on, get a grip."

"What? You think that's implausible? He pretended Flora was in Florida when she was in Cambridgeshire. He told me Georgina's twelve. She's not twelve—she's dead."

"Is she? If Lewis can lie so easily, maybe Georgina's alive. Maybe she's Chimpy, and you heard Flora talking to her on Saturday."

"Maybe I did." I've been thinking this myself. "All the options we've considered, all the ones we can possibly think of, are worrying, aren't they? Let's say all five kids are alive, but Lewis and Flora are telling Georgina's grandparents that she's dead. Or Georgina's two younger siblings have the same Christian names as her two older ones, and meanwhile their parents are telling weird lies and enlisting their friends to do the same. Does any of that sound to you like a family in which the kids definitely aren't at risk from the adults? Because it sure as fuck doesn't to me. I want to say all this to the police. I think there's something sinister going on that needs looking into."

"Unless . . ." I can tell from this halfhearted start that Dom knows the point he's about to make is a weak one. "My friend Anthony at university had the same first name as all his brothers: John. They were all known by their middle names, but—"

"Great. You can tell Huntingdon police that. I'll tell them Flora's two youngest kids are known by the names Thomas and Emily, which is what I heard her call them—the same names her first two were known by."

"Shouldn't you also be contacting the police in Delray Beach, Florida, if you think the original Thomas and Emily might also be at risk?"

"Huntingdon police can do that, assuming they agree with me."

"Christ, Beth." Dom covers his face with his hands. "Is that what you're hoping will happen? It won't. The police aren't going to lift a finger, however weird it all is. The most they'll do is send in social services."

"Fine. That's good enough for me."

*Liar.*

No matter what I tell Dom, nothing will be good enough for me unless and until I have the answers I need.

I say, "Flora's dad said that she and Lewis probably don't want anything to do with me now, just like they don't want Flora's parents in their lives anymore. If that were true, if that's all that's happening here, why wouldn't Lewis have said so on the phone? He was very direct when he cut off Flora's parents. Why not say to me, 'Sorry, Beth, we've moved on, you're pretty much a stranger now, we don't have to answer any of your questions, good-bye'? Why would it be any harder to say that to me than to Gerard and Rosemary?"

"It wouldn't. But a more diplomatic brush-off is always easier, and most friends would take the hint. Whereas parents need to be told more firmly. They don't let their kids go so easily."

"Maybe. But Flora's reaction in the car park was hardly diplomatic. There was no 'Oh, Beth, how lovely to see you after all these years—must dash now but let's catch up sometime.' Running away in terror is pretty undiplomatic."

"True," Dom concedes.

"And Lewis telling us we must come to Florida, and Kevin Cater inviting us around to his house, answering our questions . . . Showing us that picture of two kids I'd never seen before, lying about Thomas and Emily's names. He could have given us a polite version of, 'I'm sorry, I've no idea what your wife is on about. Now please leave me alone.' Do you want to know what I think?"

Dom sighs heavily. "Beth, I do, but . . . this has to *end*. For us, our being part of it."

"I know. I know it does. I just . . ." I close my eyes and inhale deeply. *Come on, lavender. Work your magic.* "This isn't a criticism, but I don't understand how you're not as curious as I am. Don't you want to understand it, whatever it is?"

"Not at the expense of our lives, no. Also, to an extent, I think I already do understand it. Not the finer details, maybe, but the more general explanation 'Lewis Braid is a massive weirdo' works for me. And I really don't believe anyone's in danger, Beth. I think Lewis is bizarre enough to have invented some mad reason to call his youngest kids after his oldest kids."

"Why did Flora run away from me?" I stand up, grab a towel and wrap it around me. I was planning to wash my hair, but the plan had a built-in loophole: that I knew I wouldn't bother in the end. I hate washing my hair. It's the annoying chore that looms in the shadows at the end of every nice long bath, potentially ruining it.

"I don't know why Flora ran away." Dom sighs.

"To avoid talking to me, clearly. But why? She must have been scared I'd ask something or scared to tell me something, scared I'd find out whatever the secret is. Maybe she thought I'd found out already, maybe Marilyn Oxley told her I'd been asking about the Caters and

Thomas and Emily. If the secret is something eccentric but harmless, her fear makes no sense."

"Maybe she was scared of you. Just you. Nothing to do with her secret."

My heart twists. *He can't know.*

"Why would she be?"

"I don't know. You tell me."

I turn away. I wish I could be indignant, but I can't. I've wondered the same thing myself. Though if Flora's scared of me because of what I did twelve years ago, that would be an absurd overreaction. She can't imagine that I'd . . .

"Beth, I'm sorry." Dom's voice cuts into my thoughts. "That was below the belt. There's nothing scary about you."

We all have things we'd rather people didn't find out about us. I don't want to, though. Not anymore. "I need to show you something," I say.

**Dominic and** I sit on opposite sides of our bed. Between us, lying on the duvet, is a cream envelope that I've dug out of an old handbag. The handwriting on the envelope is Flora's.

I couldn't bring myself to throw it away. Not at the time, and not at any point since. "Don't tell Zannah and Ben," I say. "I'm not proud of this and I'd rather they didn't know."

Dom nods.

I pick up the envelope and shake its contents out onto the bed: a Christmas card with a picture of Santa Claus and his reindeers flying over a snowy mountain. And a photograph of the Braids, with a slit that's been cut into it and a hole in the middle, where a small part's been excised . . . and then, lying a few inches apart from the other two items, the cutting from the picture, the person whose absence has made the hole: a tiny baby wrapped in a pink and white blanket, eyes closed. *Georgina Braid.*

I pick up the card and show Dom what's written inside it: "To Dom, Beth, Zannah and Ben, Merry Christmas and a Happy New Year! Lots of love from Lewis, Flora, Thomas, Emily and Georgina." Followed by three kisses, as per Braid family card-writing tradition. A perfectly ordinary message.

Georgina was two months old in the photograph. The last time the Braids came to visit us was February 2007, when Georgina was four months old, and two months before she died.

*If she died.*

Flora and I both knew that our friendship was over

in February 2007, but we were pretending otherwise, to ourselves and to each other. Dominic had no idea. I don't know what Lewis knew or didn't know. I made a special fuss of baby Georgina, aware that not long ago I'd deliberately taken a pair of scissors and cut her out of a happy family photograph.

"Not my proudest moment," I say to Dom.

"You? Oh. I thought you were going to say that this was how it arrived—with Georgina cut out."

"No. I did it."

"Why?"

I remember as if it happened earlier today, though it was twelve years ago: once removed from the photograph, Georgina landed on the kitchen floor. Seeing her lying there, so tiny and separated from her family, I felt immediately ashamed. What the hell was I doing? What if cutting a child out of a family photo was like sticking pins in a wax model of someone you hated? I would always be someone who had done that to a baby. I could never undo it, which made me feel weirdly doomed—as if, with one vicious, unjustifiable act, I had sealed my fate.

That was my immediate reaction. Overreaction. A few minutes later I realized that all I'd done was cut up a photo, and what did it matter, really? Impulse control had never been my strong point and I knew I'd behaved pathetically, but it was hardly likely to harm Georgina Braid in real life.

Still, I couldn't bring myself to throw the Braids in the bin, after what I'd done already. I put the card and the pieces of the photograph back in the envelope, which I stuffed into the side pocket of my handbag. I told myself everything was fine, that no one would ever find out I'd done something so petty and spiteful.

"Flora found out," I tell Dom. It's a relief to say it out loud. The horrible thing I'd done, and how bad it made me feel, was nothing compared with the shame I felt when Flora saw the evidence. Most people successfully hide the worst aspects of their characters from everyone they know, all their lives. I was unlucky.

"She found out you cut Georgina out of the photo she sent you? Jesus, Beth. I don't understand. At all."

"When the Braids came around for the last time . . . You probably won't remember, but you and Lewis went out to the Granta for a pint."

Dom shakes his head. Of course he doesn't remember.

"I knew Flora was thinking the same as me: we both wished you hadn't gone and left us alone—well, alone with the kids. We were chatting, trying to pretend everything was okay, but deep down we both knew it hadn't been normal for a while between us, and then suddenly Thomas started wailing. He'd pulled the skin off a blister on his heel and it was bleeding. Flora handed Georgina to me and started rummaging around in her changing bag, looking for a plaster. She didn't have one, but I knew I had one in my bag. I totally forgot, in that moment, that the cut-up picture was also in there. I sent Zan to look for the plaster. A few minutes later, back she came with all of that." I nod down at the photo pieces and the card. "She gave it to Flora and said, 'Look. This was in Mummy's bag. Someone's torn baby Georgina out of the photo.' She had no idea what she was doing, obviously. She just thought it was a weird thing she'd found, and that we'd want to know about it. I could feel myself turning bright red. One look at my face told Flora who the guilty party was."

Dom looks appalled, understandably. "Why the hell did you keep it? Why not chuck it in the rubbish once you've gone as far as cutting it up? What did Flora say? Anyone cut one of our kids out of a photograph, I'd punch their lights out."

"I didn't give her a chance to say anything. I started talking at a million miles an hour—saying how sorry I was, that I didn't know what had come over me. She was upset, but she said she understood. I explained how angry I'd been—that she'd not told me, and then sent the card and the photo, assuming I knew. She apologized for forgetting to tell me. She cried. It was a bit of an apology fest all around . . . and we both knew that was it, that we'd never see or speak to each other again."

"Jealousy," Dom says. "That was what came over you. Understandably, I suppose."

"What? No. You mean the miscarriage?" I try to fight the feeling of disappointment that's rising inside me. Dom's bound to think this. What else would he think? How can he know what I've never told him?

"Me losing a pregnancy had nothing to do with it," I say. "You might not believe that, but it's true."

"Then why the hell did you cut a baby out of a photo?"

"Because Flora never told me about her, and I was . . . more hurt than you can probably imagine. When she got pregnant with Thomas, she told me right away. When I knew I was pregnant with Zannah, I rang Flora within ten minutes of taking the test. I think I told her before I told you. You were in a meeting and I couldn't get hold of you . . ."

Dom waves impatiently to indicate that he doesn't care about not being told first.

"When we both got pregnant a second time, same thing: Flora phoned me immediately after she'd told

Lewis and her mum. I phoned her within an hour of knowing I was pregnant with Ben. With my third pregnancy, it was different. I told Flora because I always had before, not because I really wanted to. Lewis had inherited his fortune by then, and . . . I don't know if it was us or them, but somehow the idea of this huge wealth that they suddenly had came between us."

"Did it?"

"I didn't talk to you about it because I wanted to pretend it wasn't happening. You didn't notice or care, because Lewis never mattered to you the way Flora mattered to me. But we saw them a bit less, and it was awkward when we did see them. And I thought it had to be the money that had made things different, but . . . thinking about it now, the change happened at the same time that Flora must have found out she was pregnant with Georgina. Oh, God, Dom, I've been such a terrible friend."

"You mean cutting up the photo?"

"Not only that." I blink back tears. "I used to think that defacing a happy family photo like a psycho was the worst thing I'd done. Not anymore."

"Beth, what are you talking about?"

"I'm trying to tell you!"

"Sorry. Go on."

"When I had the miscarriage, I had to tell everyone who knew I'd been pregnant. Including Flora. She was really nice on the phone. Sympathetic. I thought, 'Maybe we'll be okay, maybe the awkwardness between us was just a blip and now things'll go back to normal.' We talked about meeting up and she said she'd ring me to arrange something, but she never did. We didn't see or hear from her or Lewis at all, for months. It was like they'd forgotten us completely. And then, just before Christmas, *those* arrived." I nod at the card and photo pieces.

"You mean . . . ?"

"Yep. Flora had been pregnant and had a baby *and not told me.* Not the day she found out, like she had with Thomas and Emily, and not ever. She went through an entire pregnancy and birth without telling me. I had no idea. And then suddenly, just before Christmas, a card arrives signed from all of them, including Georgina, and there's the photo of the five of them and . . . it's as if Flora's forgotten, or doesn't care enough to be aware of it, that she's had another baby and told me nothing about it. That's how I found out. From being sent *that.*" I point to the evidence: evidence of Flora's awful behavior as well as mine.

"I called her. Soon as I'd finished crying, cutting up the photo, hiding what I'd done—inadequately, as it turned out—I called Flora. She sounded normal. Well, normal for New Rich Flora. I thought, 'She has no idea why I'm calling.' I said, 'I got your Christmas card. Flora, I didn't know you'd had another baby. I didn't even know you were pregnant.'"

"What did she say?"

"She sounded puzzled at first. She said, 'Didn't you? You must have known!' Then there was this long, horrible silence, during which she must have realized I couldn't have known because she never told me. She's not stupid, and she knows I'm not either. We both knew that any charade of us still being best friends was finished."

"Maybe she didn't tell you because of the miscarriage," Dom says. "She didn't want to rub salt into the wound."

"No. There was no planning or strategy. If she'd thought about it, she'd have known that for me to find out in the way I did would be the most hurtful thing of all. She just wasn't thinking about me at all. At the time, I thought it was because she didn't give a shit about me anymore."

"But . . . if this phone call revealed that the two of you weren't close friends anymore, how did they end up coming around to ours with Georgina?"

"After that conversation, Flora briefly felt bad enough to make a bit of an effort. And I wanted to believe the friendship could still recover. But from the second they arrived, things were wrong and awkward and . . . bad. I assumed it was because Flora felt so guilty about not having told me, or maybe she didn't want to be there and was just doing a duty visit, for form's sake. I was wrong."

"How?"

"I'm scared you'll think I'm a terrible person if I tell you," I say tearfully. "I'm scared I *am* a terrible person."

"Don't be silly. Just tell me."

"All these years, I've been making it all about me. When Flora changed and seemed less interested in me, I put it down to Lewis's inheritance. When months passed and I didn't hear from her, it never once occurred to me that she might be in trouble. When she was pregnant and had a baby and didn't tell me, I used it to back up my theory: that she and Lewis were rich now so she didn't need to bother with the likes of me anymore. I didn't ever think, 'Flora wouldn't treat me like this unless something was really wrong.' And I should have thought that, Dom—because she wouldn't."

Finally, Dom sees what I'm driving at: "You think that whatever weird shit's going on now started then?"

"Yes, I do. And . . . after that last time they came

to ours, I drew the wrong conclusion again. Apart from their new address card, Flora never contacted me after the day she found out I'd cut up the photo. I assumed that was why . . . but it wasn't. Sure, she'd have been hurt by that, but it wasn't the reason. Flora never got in touch again because she couldn't risk having me in her life anymore. She couldn't risk being close to me—because if she was then I might find out the truth. The secret. Whatever that was. Is," I correct myself. "Dom, whatever it is, *it started before Georgina was born. Months before.*"

"I wish we'd talked about this at the time. I had no idea—about any of it."

"I didn't want to talk about it. I was . . . ashamed, I guess. People aren't supposed to feel jilted and have their hearts broken by their friends."

Sudden ringing makes me jump. "Is that your phone?" Dom asks.

I nod, reaching down to pull my handbag up onto the bed.

"Who'd call this late at night?"

My heart judders as I look at the screen. "It's Lewis," I say, recognizing the number I tried to call back so many times on Sunday evening.

"Answer it."

"Hello? Lewis? Hello?"

I hear muffled noise in the background. Movement.

"Is anyone there? Lewis?"

"Beth?"

"Who is this?"

"I meant to ring you back the other night, and then life took over and I never did. I'm sorry."

"Flora?"

"Hi, Beth! Say hi to Rom-com Dom from me!" Lewis Braid calls out in the background.

"Yes, it's me," Flora says. "Beth? Can you hear me okay?"

I can. It's definitely her. Definitely him, too; no one else calls my husband Rom-com Dom. It's Lewis and Flora Braid. In Florida, now. Together.

# 13

Whatever I was expecting when I imagined talking to the police, it wasn't PC Paul Pollard. I'd prepared myself for the brush-off, but when I met Pollard, I realized I'd expected the disappointing reaction to come from someone a little bit impressive, with an air of authority. Pollard seems not particularly bright and says, "Got it," every ten seconds. He looks about thirteen. The tea he's brought in for me and Dom, despite being in proper cups with saucers, has got tiny, reflective pools of what looks like grease spotted across the surface of the liquid. We thank him for it as he sits back down behind the table in the small, white-painted interview room.

"Right," he says. "So Mr. and Mrs. Braid phoned

you last night from America, you were saying—because she'd forgotten to call back on Sunday night?"

"She didn't forget." I've already told him this. "That was a lie."

"Got it. Yep. And how long did you speak to them?"

"About fifteen minutes. It wasn't us speaking to them, it was me speaking to Flora. Dom and Lewis didn't really say much apart from calling out hi and bye. It was the tensest phone conversation I've ever had—both of us on edge, trying to pretend we were chatting normally, catching up on news, when it was obvious we were both massively on edge. She flat out denied having been in Huntingdon. Said I must have seen someone else the two times I thought I saw her, because she hasn't been back to England recently."

"Got it." Pollard makes a note.

"After she ran away from me in the car park, they all must have decided urgent action was needed—an emergency trip to America for Flora. As if that would make anything more plausible!"

"Did you tell her you'd visited her parents, or that they'd told you her daughter Georgina had died as a baby?" Pollard asks.

"No. What's the point? She'd only have lied about that too if it suited her."

"Got it."

"I don't think Georgina Braid is dead," I tell him. "For some reason, Lewis and Flora wanted Flora's parents to believe that she was, so that's what they told them—and then broke off all contact so that their lie would never be discovered."

"There must have been a funeral, if Georgina died," says Dom. "I wonder if Gerard and Rosemary went to it."

"She didn't die," I tell him. "She's Chimpy—and she seems to be nowhere! From Lewis's Instagram, it seems as if she's not part of his life in Florida, and Lou Munday told me the Caters only had two kids, so she's not in Hemingford Abbots. Where is she?"

"Mrs. Leeson—"

"Call me Beth."

"Got it." Pollard rubs the index finger of his left hand across the skin between his nose and his mouth. It looks as if he's making an obscene gesture, or pretending to have a mobile mustache. "I can't see that there's anything criminal here to be investigated. I'm not saying it's not a strange story—it is—but you've not brought me any crimes I can investigate."

"I understand that. But when something's so strange that some element of criminal behavior behind it all seems likely, can't the police look into it?"

"If there's a solid lead, yes. But—"

"Four adults with presumably quite busy lives have gone to huge lengths—spent money on a transatlantic flight, even—to make me believe I can't have seen Flora in Cambridgeshire twice in the last week. Why? Who would bother doing that to cover up weirdness? Doesn't the sheer effort made to deceive me suggest that something criminal might be going on? I mean . . . Flora must have gone home after seeing me in Huntingdon, taken off her clothes and given them to that other woman to put on, so that she could come back to the car park wearing the same outfit and hopefully make me think I'd been hallucinating again. I don't believe anyone would go to those lengths unless it was to cover up something that could land them in prison for a very long time."

"By a solid lead, I mean evidence that points to a crime," says Pollard, whose expression reminds me that he has endured my little speech with great patience. "For example, if you'd seen someone at 16 Wyddial Lane causing bodily harm to another person. What you've told me is unusual but it's not enough. I can't do anything with it."

"Could you maybe find out for us if Georgina Braid is dead?" Dom asks.

"I could find out if I needed to, but I'm afraid I can't—"

"Of course. I understand. It's not your job to satisfy the curiosity of members of the public when no crime has been committed."

"Though safeguarding and child protection are your job, presumably?" I ask Pollard. "How will you feel in two weeks' time if you get an emergency call from Wyddial Lane and you arrive to find that something terrible has happened to Thomas and Emily Cater?"

"Mrs. Leeson—sorry, Beth—I understand that you're concerned, but you need to be careful. What you've just said could be construed as a threat to those children."

"*What?*"

"Beth wasn't making a threat, she was making a point," says Dom. "Her point was, it's better to be safe than sorry, and it's a good one. We might not have witnessed any physical harm to anybody, but I think there's enough in what we've told you to justify a quick check. You could talk to the head teacher at the prep school, ask her if she's aware of any issues in the family. Maybe he or she could tell you who the woman Beth and I met really is. She introduced herself to us as Jeanette Cater, but she had a non-English accent, and the school receptionist told Beth that Jeanette Cater didn't. She also told her the Cater kids are called Thomas and Emily, when Kevin Cater and that woman, whoever she was, said their names were Toby and Emma. Is that not sufficiently worrying? I mean . . . can you say with a hundred percent confidence that you believe the children in that house aren't at risk?"

Dom's words seem to be having an effect. *Please, please. See reason.* "PC Pollard, you didn't hear Flora on the phone last night. I did. She sounded the way someone would sound if someone had a gun to their head."

"Got it. Got it. Let me ask you something, Beth. Last Saturday, you were convinced you saw the Thomas and Emily you'd known twelve years ago getting out of that silver Range Rover. Correct?"

I nod.

"Yet all through our conversation, you've referred to the children living at 16 Wyddial Lane as Thomas and Emily Cater."

"As far as I know, their surname is Cater. That's what the school calls them." What's he getting at?

"But if they're Thomas and Emily Cater, five and three years old, then they can't also be the Thomas and Emily Braid you used to know. So which is it?"

"Are you asking me if I still believe that the two young children I saw on Saturday are actually the same people as the Thomas and Emily Braid I knew twelve years ago?"

"I am, yes."

I take a deep breath. "Then you think I'm either crazy or stupid. They can't be the same people, can they? It's impossible. People age. Children grow. Time doesn't go backward. Last Saturday, what I saw were two children who looked pretty much identical to my memory of the Thomas and Emily I knew. I heard them called by the same names. It was such a shock, I . . . for a while, a short while, I thought it was them and they hadn't grown. But obviously I soon realized that would be impossible."

"Got it." Pollard writes this down, smiling. He seems to have liked that answer. "All right, let me see what I can do to help here. How about if I arrange for someone who's more well versed in child protection is-sues than I am to have a word with a few people at the school? If any member of staff there has concerns about the Cater children's safety or welfare, that'll give us an angle to do more."

"That would be amazing," I say. "Thank you."

"Did you note down the registration plate of the sil-ver Range Rover?" Pollard asks me.

"No."

"Why not?"

"No particular reason."

"You seem to have been looking into the Caters and

the Braids fairly thoroughly, that's all. You've said you think the Cater children must be Flora Braid's because of the strong resemblance, and you think the photos of . . ." He looks down at his notes ". . . groups of birds on the wall at number 16 have to belong to Lewis Braid. The registration number's a way of knowing for sure who that car belongs to. I'm surprised you didn't write it down."

"I don't care who the car belongs to. Kevin Cater, Lewis—who cares? They're both involved in this, either way."

"Got it." PC Pollard stands up and gives his upper lip one final rub. "Leave it with me. If anyone at the school thinks the Cater children are at risk, then, as I say, we might be able to get somewhere."

**Ten minutes** later, Dom and I are sitting in his car outside the police station. "I think that went pretty well," he says. "Better than I expected. It's a relief to hand it over to the professionals."

Not for the first time in our twenty-three-year marriage, I wonder how two people can live happily side by side and sleep in the same bed every night—two people who would probably die for each other if necessary—and yet see the world in such profoundly different ways. I try to imagine how I might feel if I believed Paul Pollard was capable of resolving the problem. Why don't I believe it? Maybe I should try to.

Dom starts the car and we pull out of the car park and set off for home. "Beth, I need to tell you something," he says. "I don't think it means anything—beyond what we already know, that something messed up's going on—but I wouldn't feel fair keeping it from you. I was going to tell you last night, but then—"

"Just tell me."

"Yesterday, all the Braids' social media accounts disappeared. Every last one."

"What do you mean? Why would they disappear?"

"It'd only happen if they'd been deliberately deleted by their owners."

I swallow hard. "And . . . you didn't think this was worth mentioning to PC Pollard?"

"No," says Dom. "Because about three hours later, they all reappeared. I looked through them all—Lewis's Instagram and Twitter, Thomas and Emily's Twitter. Nothing looked different. All the stuff that had been there before was still there, so it's not like they did it because they wanted to delete stuff. You don't need to deactivate an account to delete individual posts anyway."

"How certain are you that nothing was different when the accounts reappeared?"

"Not infallibly certain, but I'm pretty sure."

"I didn't realize you were familiar enough with their social media accounts to know what was on them. I assumed you'd found them, had a quick look, then not looked again."

"Yeah, well." Dom smiles sheepishly. "You're not the only one who's curious."

Of course. Who wouldn't be curious? He's just given himself away. "You've been downplaying your level of interest in the hope of getting me to ease off," I say.

He doesn't deny it.

"If you're interested in how I feel about that? Not great. You could have saved me a few sleepless hours of wondering if I'm crazy because you, a normal person, just didn't seem to care that much."

"You're right. I'm—"

"What time did all this happen, the social media stuff?" I ask quickly, so that there's no time for him to apologize. Probably soon I'll forgive him for trying to manage me instead of communicating honestly, but not yet. Not for at least an hour.

"I noticed the accounts were gone early yesterday—nine-ish. By noon they were back up."

"And then later that same day, Flora rings up, supposedly for a friendly, news-swapping chat? What does that tell you?"

Dom shakes his head with a shrug.

"They're panicking. Whoever's running the show can't decide on a strategy. First it's 'Disappear, delete everything,' then it's 'Act as normal as possible, phone, pretend all's well.' There'd have been no point in telling Pollard about it because it's not a direct lead to a crime."

"That's what I thought."

"We'll never hear from him again," I say. "If we chase him for updates, he'll avoid us."

"I disagree," says Dom. "He's going to do something, and he'll let us know the upshot, once he has. But whether he does or not . . ."

"What?" From his tone, it sounds as if he's about to make another attempt at managing me.

"We're agreed that we're leaving this now, right? You and me. We take no further action. We don't even look at Lewis's Instagram. For us—apart from gratefully receiving any updates PC Pollard chooses to give us—this ends here. Yes?"

Bearing in mind his views about the benefits of avoiding a hard "no," I say, "I can't give you an unconditional guarantee that I'm not going to look at Lewis's Instagram and Twitter again. I'm sorry."

"And if I ask you to promise that's all you'll do? No more than that?"

"I could make that promise and then end up breaking it because of . . . something I can't foresee at this precise moment. Like: more and worse sinister shit happens, and PC Pollard turns out to be useless."

"You don't have to be the person who deals with every problem in the world, Beth."

"Really?" I snap. "Just remind me what global problems you're dealing with, currently?"

"I'm dealing with trying to keep our family in one piece."

"That's so unnecessarily dramatic! Our family's fine. Stop reciting lines you've heard in bad films that have nothing to do with our situation."

Dom takes a deep breath and goes on. "I'm trying to make sure that Zannah passes her exams, that you and I continue to do our jobs and earn money, that our life stays on track. I'm sorry if that doesn't feel like an ambitious enough project for you."

"I care about our family as much as you do, Dom. And I know we're okay and will remain okay. Caring about your own family doesn't have to mean turning a blind eye to something terrible that's happening in another family. I know it's not my job to make sure the Caters' kids are safe. It's Pollard's job. And if he does it . . . great."

Dom says nothing. He doesn't like any of my answers. Not one bit.

Gerard Tillotson's words come back to me: "Lewis won't have liked that *at all*."

By the time we turn onto the A14, I've worked out what it means—why it snagged in my mind as sounding strange at the time, though I couldn't work out what the significance was.

I say to Dom, "When Zannah and I were at the Tillotsons' house, he said something weird—Flora's dad."

Nothing. No response.

"I told him I'd asked Lewis on the phone how old Georgina was now, in a 'doesn't time fly' sort of way, and he said, 'Lewis won't have liked that *at all*.' As soon as he said it, I thought, 'No, that's wrong, there's something off about it,' but then the conversation moved on and I forgot about it until just now."

"Doesn't sound strange to me," says Dom. "If one of your kids is dead and you've decided to pretend they're still alive—though God knows why you would, but anyway—you're hardly going to welcome being asked about them and having to spout a load of bullshit to maintain the façade, are you?"

"You didn't hear how Flora's dad said it. It wasn't like 'Lewis will have found that deeply uncomfortable or upsetting,' it was more . . . wry and knowing. 'Lewis won't have liked that *at all*.' Almost as if he was thinking that, for Lewis, it would be more of a PR or image failure. Someone's seen through the image he was hoping to project and that's a disaster for his ego. Or maybe it was 'Lewis will have hated to learn that something he thought he'd gotten under control had escaped his control.' Either way, trust me, it wasn't Lewis's grief that Gerard was thinking about."

I'm not expecting a reply, but eventually Dom says, "You don't know Gerard Tillotson well enough to read his tone. His words make perfect sense in the context."

"The tone was unmistakeable. Whether he realizes it or not, Gerard knows that Lewis cares more about image management and controlling everything than he does about his dead daughter. Who isn't dead, I don't think."

"We don't know if she's dead," says Dom. "And I don't see how this gets us any farther forward. All right, Lewis is a control freak—everyone who knows him probably agrees, including Flora's dad—but so what? What's that bringing to the table? As people say in all the boring meetings I have to go to, where the only things brought to the table are boring ones. And the table's also boring."

I smile, knowing the joke is meant as a peace offering.

"Lewis is a control freak," I say. "He cares about image management and control. Exactly."

"Exactly what?"

"The Tillotsons also said Georgina was born prematurely. She wasn't robust, they said. She had various health complications. What if that wasn't good enough for Lewis, to have a not-perfect child?"

Dom frowns. "That baby that came around to ours was fine looking."

"But she had health complications from being premature." I think back, trying to remember the details. "I'm pretty sure Rosemary said she was going to need an operation of some sort. What if, for Lewis, that sort of imperfection was intolerable? He decided he'd rather pretend she was dead and just . . . get rid of her. He nicknamed her Chimpy because he didn't see her as fully human, and they put her in some kind of home, or care, or with a foster family."

"That's horrific." Dom grimaces. "No. That's not what happened."

"How do you know?"

"Because it's too horrible. It's not just Lewis, Beth. He might be capable of God only knows what, but what about Flora? Can you see her treating a child that way?"

"Not unless forced to by Lewis, no. That's why she

was crying when she was speaking to Chimpy on the phone."

"You're making me feel slightly sick," says Dom. "And . . . you're making all this up, Beth. Sorry, but it's morbid and depressing and there's no reason to think any of it's true."

"It would explain Peterborough too."

"What's that?"

"A city north of Cambridge."

He gives me a look.

"I heard Flora say 'Peterborough' on the phone. Maybe that's where Georgina is."

"Yes, because when you ring someone, you always randomly announce the name of the place where they are. If someone rang me now, they'd suddenly say 'the A14' in the middle of the conversation for no reason."

As if on cue, my phone starts to ring. I unzip my bag and pull it out. "Hello?"

"Is that Beth Leeson?"

"Speaking." I know the voice, but I can't place it.

"This is Louise. Lou Munday. We met when you came into the school."

"Of course, I remember you." I didn't give her my mobile number. I gave her the landline.

"Can we meet?" she says. "There's something I need to talk to you about."

# 14

Dom wasn't happy about handing over his car to me, once I'd dropped him at the Huntingdon station.

"Why am I the one who has to get trains and taxis home?" he asked.

"Please, Dom."

"I understand why you want to talk to this receptionist, but why do you need my car for that? Why can't I just drop you at the school? I assume this Lou woman has a car—can't she drop you at the station once the two of you have had your chat?"

"I don't know how it's going to go. If the conversation ends badly, I'll be in no position to ask favors by the end of it. I don't want to risk being stranded," I told him, wondering if he'd see through the excuse.

I'm meeting Lou after school finishes for the day. That's an hour from now. It means I can get to the car park well before that and be in position to catch another glimpse of Thomas Cater, and maybe Emily too, if she comes with whoever's picking her brother up today. Dom's car has tinted windows, making it unlikely that I'll be noticed inside it, though there's a chance that if Kevin Cater or "Jeanette" turns up, they'll recognize the car as the one that was parked on their driveway while they lied to us.

There's nothing I can do about that. I'm not sure it matters, in any case. I'll be there legitimately, to meet Lou, which I can say if anyone bangs on my window and gives me a hard time; I've been invited. Whether I'm watching or not, Thomas will have to walk out of the building and over to the car park area. No one will be able to stop me from seeing him. They're hardly going to put a blanket over his head so that I can't catch a glimpse of him.

*Who is "they"?*

Who will come to collect Thomas? I've got a strange kind of premonition in my mind, as I pull into the school car park, that I'm about to see Flora again. It doesn't strike me as impossible. Either Lewis could have worked out a way to make a phone call seem as if it's coming from America when it's not, or he drove

Flora straight to an airport after they made that call together. She could have flown at nine or nine thirty in the evening, Florida time, and landed before midday UK time. She'd probably be jet-lagged, but it would be just about possible for her to get to Thomas's school by three thirty.

I pick a parking space at the center of a grid of white-painted rectangular boxes on the ground. As and when other cars arrive, they'll have to park all around me, hemming me in. That will provide some cover.

I use my phone to send some basic, easy chore emails while I wait for school to finish: yes, Ben can go and see a production of *Len and Ezra*, whatever that is, and I'm willing to pay £30 for him to do so; yes, I can confirm that I'm expecting Pam Swain for a back, neck and head massage on Monday and that, no, I definitely won't need to cancel her again.

At three fifteen, other cars start to join me in the car park. I sit up straight in the driver's seat when I see the silver Range Rover, which is one of the last to arrive, at three twenty-eight. I haven't decided what I'll do if it's Flora. Will I get out of the car, walk over, try and talk to her? If I did, would she run away from me again?

It's not her. It's the woman who pretended to be Jeanette Cater. She steps out of the Range Rover, slams the door behind her, then walks briskly over to two other women, both younger than her, who are standing behind a larger group of waiting parents. Either Emily's not with her or she's waiting in the car. Today Not-Jeanette is wearing leopard-print leggings, a black V-neck sweater with a thick gold belt, and flat slip-on shoes that look as if they came from a child's fancy-dress box: glittery and gold, with bows on them and no visible soles.

I lower my window an inch or so and take a few photos of her with my phone. They're not great, but they'll do. I edit the best one to enlarge her face. Ideally, I'd like a photo of Flora too, to show Lou Munday. I do a Google image search for Flora Braid, Flora Tillotson and Jeanette Cater, but each one yields only photos of people I've never seen before.

I hear the muffled sound of a bell. A few minutes later, there's a burst of purple blazers rushing out of the building. Some of the children run to waiting adults, their faces lighting up with joy. Others slump and limp along, looking down at the gray concrete.

There he is: Thomas Cater. I recognize him immediately.

*No, you don't. You recognize five-year-old Thomas Braid. That's who this is. That's the face you know, the same face you saw last Saturday, and twelve years ago. Isn't it?*

I stare at his face, wishing he'd keep still so that I could see it better. Is it identical, or slightly different? Is this the boy who came to my flat in Cambridge in 2007, who pulled the skin off a blister on his foot and needed a Band-Aid?

Why am I allowing myself to think this way? I know it can't be the Thomas I knew, still five years old. Then I notice his shoes and feel as if I've caught my heartbeat in my throat.

I know those shoes. They're horribly scuffed after so many years. One of the soles has partly come loose and flops to the ground with each step Thomas takes. It's the same pair of shoes that Thomas Braid wore twelve years ago: black with a white star on the side and the lowest point of the star hanging down and curling under at the bottom, like a tail. I can picture them on my living room floor, amid the plastic toys, and Thomas next to them, barefoot, crying because he'd just pulled off his blister and now it hurt more and was bleeding.

Emily Cater, when I saw her outside the house on Wyddial Lane, was wearing hand-me-downs too: the "Petit Mouton" top I'd seen before on Emily Braid.

All parents know shoes are different. You don't pass them down from one child to another. If you care about your child's feet, you have them properly measured and buy shoes that are a perfect fit, unless you're too hard up and can't afford to. When you live in an enormous house on Wyddial Lane, you don't send your son to school in twelve-year-old shoes that are falling apart—not unless . . .

I can't bear to think about what the "unless" might be. An urge rises inside me: to leap out of the car, grab Thomas and take him home with me, where I can make sure no one harms or neglects him.

All the other children are coming out in groups, but Thomas is alone. He looks neutral—not happy or sad—and walks at a steady pace, neither quickly nor slowly. He seems unaware of his surroundings, and more focused on whatever's happening inside his head.

The two young women that Not-Jeanette is chatting to look more like au pairs than mothers. That might be why they're standing apart from the larger group of adults: the help in one cluster, the parents in another, no mixing.

Thomas eventually comes to a stop next to the glittery gold shoes. He doesn't do or say anything to attract attention. He stands and waits. Fake Jeanette, if she has noticed his arrival, shows no sign of it. Eventually one of the other two women nudges her and nods to indicate that Thomas is there.

Even now, there's no communication at all between the two of them. Pretend Jeanette hugs one of the women good-bye, then sets off walking toward the Range Rover, trailing her arm out behind her and waving her hand as if to say, "Come on, this way." Thomas follows her, but he hasn't looked at her, not once, and nor has she looked at him. They haven't spoken at all. It's as if there's no relationship between them, only indifference that goes both ways. The sole of Thomas's damaged shoe continues to flop beneath his foot.

I duck down in my seat and cover my face with my hand, so as not to be seen as they pass me.

Not-Jeanette opens the back door of the car and Thomas climbs in. She closes it. Still, there has been no interaction or eye contact between them.

*She's going to drive away with him . . .*

And now she has. And I did nothing.

*Because there's nothing you could have done.*

Telling myself Thomas will be fine, I get out of the car and start to walk toward the school's main entrance. Halfway there, I hear a voice calling my name.

I turn. At first I can't see where it might have come from. Then I spot Lou, in the driver's seat of a red Ford Fiesta. I didn't see her leave the building; she must have come out while I was watching Thomas. She gestures toward me, and I see that the passenger door is open.

"Get in," she mouths at me as I approach. She seems nervous, in a rush, as if we've just robbed a bank together and she's driving the getaway car.

I obey the order. Another incentive to make sure we part on friendly terms—I'm going to need her to drop me back here later so that I can drive home.

Is it naive of me to trust her? What if she's . . .

*No. That's paranoid. She's a school receptionist. What's she going to do—pull over and whip out a knife in broad daylight?*

If someone wants me out of the way, presumably there are plenty of thugs for hire.

If Dom knew that I was even thinking in this way . . . "Where are we going?" I ask.

"The Gallery," Lou says. "We can talk freely there."

**The Gallery** turns out to be a crowded, homely café in Huntingdon, with square tables and a comforting smell of baked potatoes. Lou and I take the last available table. I tell her it's my treat, whatever she wants to order, and thank her for being willing to talk to me, even though she's the one who's initiated the meeting.

"How did you get my number?" I ask her once we have our cups of tea in front of us. "My mobile phone, I mean. When you asked for my details, I gave you the landline."

"You'll think I'm a stalker." She looks embarrassed. "I tried the landline and no one answered, so I googled you. I found your massage business Web site."

With a photograph of me smiling, in my white work tunic, and both my phone numbers, mobile and landline, as well as my work email.

"Sorry," says Lou unnecessarily.

"Don't be. You're no more of a stalker than we all are these days. You could have saved yourself the bother, though, and spoken to me yesterday."

"I was too scared. I can't believe I'm doing it now." She shakes her head, as if at her own recklessness. "I could lose my job if I'm caught discussing families who are at the school. And I really need my job. My husband's business had to fight an expensive legal battle last year that nearly cleaned us out."

"That sounds rough. So . . . what changed your mind? About speaking to me. Was it the police?"

"Police?" Lou's eyes widen.

"Or social services? Has someone been to the school today, or rung up, asking about the Caters?" It's probably too soon. PC Paul Pollard might do something, but it will take him at least a day or two to get around to it. And the likelihood is, he'll do nothing.

"No. Why would you think that?" Lou asks.

"I'm trying to work out why you suddenly decided

you want to talk to me. Enough to look me up online and call me. That's a big change from yesterday. Did something happen?"

Her eyes are flitting around, not settling anywhere. "Look, I need to know before this goes any further," she says. "Are the police involved in whatever's going on? Please tell me. Don't lie."

I try not to be irritated by the suggestion that I would. Something I can't put my finger on makes me think that being completely straight with her is going to be the most effective strategy.

I take a long sip of my tea and start with my detour to Wyddial Lane last Saturday.

As simply and clearly as I can, I tell her everything. By the time I've finished, she's drunk all her tea. My cup's still full, and cold.

"And . . . you told all that to the police, everything you've just told me?"

I nod.

"Weren't you embarrassed?"

"Why would I be?"

"It's such a crazy-sounding story. It's . . . I mean it's *outrageous.*" She stresses the word. "I'm not saying I don't believe you, but I couldn't sit there and say all that to the police."

"It's not the first time I've been outrageous," I tell

her. "Sometimes you have to do the things no one else would do to get a result. My husband only got his first job because I applied for it on his behalf. Without telling him."

"As his wife?"

"No. Pretending to be him."

"Wow."

I can't tell if she's impressed or repelled. "I'd shown him the advert and he'd said, 'There's no way I'd get that. I'm too inexperienced.' And he was right, he wouldn't have got it, because he's not the sort of person who'd really sell himself in the bold way *I* could tell that particular company wanted. It was obvious from their ad. So I wrote an application letter basically saying 'I'm brilliant and you won't find better'—more subtly than that. It was a great letter, if I say so myself—witty, charming, but it made the point: 'I'm the best you'll get.' And he got the job!"

"You're very different from me," says Lou. "I feel terrible for being here."

"Then why are you?"

She stares into her empty teacup. I'm starting to feel the first prickle of impatience when she says, "If I talk to you about the Caters, will you swear never to tell anyone that the information came from me?"

"I can't promise to tell nobody," I say. "If the police

do end up looking into it and they come back to me with—"

"I don't mean the police. If there's an official investigation, that's different."

"I promise that whatever you tell me won't lead to you losing your job. You can trust me. I'm not going to land you in any trouble."

She nods. "Yesterday, you asked me about Jeanette Cater's accent, or your daughter did."

I wait.

"Jeanette Cater—the woman I know by that name—has an English accent. Like yours."

I show her the photo I took in the car park of the other woman. "Then who's this?"

"Yanina. She's the Caters' nanny. I don't know her last name. I think she's Ukrainian."

"And the woman you know as Jeanette—does she look a lot like Thomas, facially?"

"Yes. Oh! I might have a photo, from sports day." Lou rummages in her bag. "I'm terrified I'll lose my phone and then all my pictures'll be gone. I've got hundreds on there. Should back them up, really." When she pulls out her phone, a crumpled tissue and a hair clip fall out with it. She picks them up and stuffs them back in.

I sip my cold tea while she scrolls through her photos. "Here we are," she says eventually. "This is Jeanette." She passes the phone across the table to me.

It's Flora. Her face is flushed and she's wearing gray and blue running shoes, gray sweatpants and a red T-shirt. There are two women standing to her right, also wearing running gear. All three of them are smiling. Two of the smiles look natural and convincing. Flora's is the odd one out: stiff and uncomfortable, as if it's hurting her lips to make that shape.

"That was after the mums' race."

"This is Flora Braid," I say.

"Are you sure?"

"Positive."

"That's so odd," says Lou. "I wonder why she changed her name."

Another peculiar aspect of this whole bizarre business has just struck me: many of the strangest details involve names. The Ukrainian nanny, Yanina, pretended her name was Jeanette. Either Flora's doing the same in her dealings with her son's school and her next-door neighbor, or else she really has changed her name to Jeanette Cater. And, since Thomas and Emily Braid can't possibly have been frozen at the ages of five and three, then the Thomas and Emily I saw last Saturday in Hemingford Abbots must have been two different children—but their names are the same.

"It doesn't surprise me that Mr. Cater and Yanina presented themselves to you as a married couple," Lou says. "I've often thought they seem like more of a unit than Mr. and Mrs. Cater do. I'm not saying there's anything going on between them. They've never shown signs of being romantically involved, but they seem to be . . . together, somehow. Like, a pair."

"A pair but not a couple?"

"Yes. There have been a few times when all three of them have been in school together—Mr. and Mrs. Cater and Yanina—and it's as if Mr. Cater and Yanina are the grown-ups and Mrs. Cater's a child, trailing along behind them. More in the same category as Thomas and Emily—like their older sister or something. And those three sort of cling together in a way that's always struck me as a bit off."

"Which three? The Caters and Yanina?"

"No. Mrs. Cater and the two children."

"They cling together?"

"Yes, it's strange. Like she's determined to protect them. She wraps her arms around them as if she's terrified of the world on their behalf."

My mind is reeling. Flora, terrified of the world? Terrified for her children? She never used to be. She was always very relaxed about . . .

*About the other Thomas and Emily?*

I can remember her thinking it funny the way her mum used to say, "Aren't you worried about Thomas crawling upstairs?" and "Aren't you worried about Thomas sitting so near where you're cooking?" Flora was a far less neurotic new mother than I was.

"Have you ever heard any of them use the name Chimp, or Chimpy?" I ask. "Flora, Kevin or the nanny? It might be a person's nickname, or the name of a pet."

Lou looks blank. She shakes her head.

"What about Peterborough? Does that ring any bells?"

"Not in connection with the people we're talking about, no."

"Have you ever heard Flora . . . I'm going to call her Flora, since that's who she is to me. Have you ever heard her say she's very lucky?" I'm not sure why I'm asking this, except that I've heard her say it twice: once on the phone outside Newnham House and once in the background, the first time Lewis rang.

"No," says Lou. "She doesn't look as if she thinks she's lucky at all, though it's clear they've got pots of money."

"That's why you contacted me, isn't it? You have a sense that something's wrong in the Cater family?"

"Yes, but . . . I kept telling myself that *I* must be

wrong to think that. Since I've known Mrs. Cater, she's been clingy with her children, and reluctant to have conversations and interactions with anyone who *isn't* her child."

"She was reluctant to talk to you?"

"Always. She was painfully shy and wary. I used to think, 'What on earth does she think I'm going to do to her?' I'm the school's administrative manager, and we're an all-one-big-family kind of school. I have a lot of contact with families—selling tickets to school shows, fielding people who've missed deadlines for trips but decide three weeks later that their child simply has to go. I could say the most harmless, straightforward things and Mrs. Cater would mumble, 'Ask my husband' or 'Tell Yanina,' and then scurry off. As if she somehow . . . I don't know. Didn't want to be there. And I feel awful saying this about such a young child but Thomas's behavior ever since he joined the school has worried me. He's such a solitary soul—always on his own, talking to himself as if he's playing an endless imaginary game in his head, but he never seems lonely. He's quite content with his invisible wall around him, but if any of the other children or a teacher tries to engage him he clams up." Lou winces. "He does this strange thing where he sort of presses himself up against the nearest wall and touches it with his hands."

"Is the school worried about him? Officially?"

Lou's face hardens. "Nobody apart from me will admit there's a problem. We're nonselective, so we've got our fair share of special needs kids, and not enough SEN teachers, so everyone's determined to believe Thomas is just shy and eccentric. He's not unhappy most of the time, and he's manageable as long as you know to leave him to his own devices whenever possible. He's bright and polite, doing well with his literacy, brilliant with numbers—and everyone thinks that means he's doing fine. Shy is such an easy word, so they all trot it out, but it's the wrong word for Thomas." Lou sighs. "I don't know what the right word is, though, so I'm in no position to convince anyone. And I'd never have dared say it before you turned up and seemed worried about the Caters too, but I'll say it now: there's something wrong in the Cater household."

I want to hug her, but I restrain myself.

"The way Thomas presses himself against walls, and against his mother too. And Emily's the same. She's only been in with Mrs. Cater to collect Thomas a few times, but I've more than once seen the three of them move along the corridor like they're glued together. Thomas is quite different with Mr. Cater and Yanina. He never goes anywhere near them."

"That doesn't sound good," I say.

Lou's eyes fill with tears. "Yet I'd decided to put my worries to one side. I told myself I was being over the top. I feel guilty now. But what could I do, when the head teacher and all the other teachers kept telling me everything was okay?"

"Don't beat yourself up about it. You must see hundreds of strange families. More strange ones than normal ones, I bet, if my kids' school's anything to go by. There are fifteen-year-olds there who have never watched a TV show because their parents think television is the work of the devil."

Lou smiles.

"So is Thomas still in his first year at the school?"

"No. Second. He's very young for his year, so when he started with us he'd only just turned four. Too young to start school, if you ask me."

I can't remember Thomas Braid's exact birthday but I know it's in February. That wouldn't be considered young relative to other pupils in his year group, or old—just average.

"Did Flora ever chat to other mums? Was she friends with any of them?"

"Never that I saw. She kept herself to herself. Some people are good at projecting an air of self-containment, aren't they? Especially the dads."

"Tell me about it," I say. "All dads turn into

deaf-mute hermits at the school gates. My husband used to come back from collecting our kids in a mood of actual triumph if he'd managed to avoid being spoken to by any other parent."

"And those dads know where and how to stand so that no one will talk to them," says Lou. "Mrs. Cater did too."

"Did?"

"Does, I mean. Though, now that I think about it, she hasn't been to drop-off or pick-up in ages. Or if she has, I haven't spotted her."

"Has anyone else seen her? Recently, I mean?"

"I haven't asked them. We're all so trained to mind our own business, aren't we? It makes every aspect of life so much easier if we do."

"What's your impression of Kevin Cater and Yanina?" I ask.

"I don't warm to him at all," says Lou. "I think he's got too much free time on his hands. No idea what work he does, if any. Which is unusual. With most parents, we find out quite quickly. It comes up in conversation. Mr. Cater can talk and talk—unlike his wife. Sometimes you can't shut him up. That's usually when he's at his most pompous, finding fault with someone or something."

I roll the words "unlike his wife" around in my

brain. They feel so odd. Is Flora really Kevin's wife? If her relationship with Lewis is over, why was she in Florida with him last night? An equally unanswerable question is: why would Kevin and Flora pretend to be married if they aren't?

"If there's ever a mix-up or misunderstanding in communications, Mr. Cater's ready to pounce," says Lou. "Instead of drawing attention to it nicely, he'll write in indignantly, cc-ing everyone from the head teacher to the chair of the board of governors. It's like he's just waiting to dump his disapproval all over us, you know?"

"I didn't warm to him either," I tell her. "Before he lied to me, even. His manner was off-putting and un-pleasant."

"Yes, it is, generally."

"What about Yanina?"

"Hard to know what kind of person she is. Superfi-cial, would be my guess. She's friendly and smiley on the surface, but you can sort of tell it doesn't go very deep. It's more like she uses friendliness and charm as currency, to reach whatever her goal is at any given time. You know, the weirdest thing of all . . ." Lou breaks off with a shake of her head.

"What?"

"Everything you've told me: Mrs. Cater being the

same person as your friend Flora, Yanina pretending to be Jeanette, the Toby and Emma lie, the older Thomas and Emily who live in Florida with their dad . . . it's all so utterly creepy and beyond the bounds of normal behavior, but . . . no part of it shocks me. I don't disbelieve any of it. It was sort of a relief when you told me all those things."

"Why?"

"I don't know. I'm trying to work it out."

Next to us, a girl with blond curly hair in bunches starts to cry. Her mother leans across the table and says, "Jessica, you've already had one. You're not having another. It's bad for you."

Lou says, "I ought to find your story implausible from start to finish. I ought to be horrified, but . . . in a strange sort of way, everything you've told me feels *right*. All the suspicions I've had about the Caters and what might be going on . . . they've never been ordinary. I've never thought, 'Oh, maybe Mr. Cater's sleeping with the nanny and Mrs. Cater's furious about it.' I think I've always known, deep down, that something was really wrong, but not known that I knew it. Or not let myself know I knew it because it was too big and horrible. Does that make sense?"

I nod.

"But, like, at the same time, I don't see how it can be

true? I had no proof of anything. And if my intuition about it was so strong, how come none of my colleagues agreed with me that there was a problem?"

"Intuition isn't something most people have time for," I say.

"I suppose it's easy for me to say this now, but I do think I knew. Two things, really: that the behavior I saw, however unusual, wasn't half as odd as whatever was behind it. The cause."

I wonder how much she's allowing what I've told her to distort her memory of what she used to think. "What's the second thing?" I ask.

"That the explanation, whatever's really going on with the Caters, must be something so strange that I couldn't ever imagine it," Lou says. "No matter how hard I tried."

# 15

"It makes quite a difference," says Pam Swain, as I smooth away a hard knot beneath her left shoulder. Many people would say, "Ow!" or make distressed noises, but not Pam. She can handle my pressure. She's used to it. "It's funny, you wouldn't think I'd notice, with me lying facedown for the hour, but the purple's definitely more soothing and relaxing than the white was."

"It's not purple, Pam," I say mock-sternly. "It's aubergine. Remember?"

"Yes, sorry." She laughs. "Aubergine."

"I still love it—though I was worried I'd hate it as soon as I'd put down the paintbrush. But it works because it's deep in a soft way. Not bright."

"That's it exactly," says Pam.

She's fifty-nine, a nurse at the Rawndesley General Infirmary, and she's been coming to me for two years. Like so many of my clients, she's become a friend. Rarely do I give a massage in silence. All my regulars like to chat—probably because my massages aren't the kind that allow clients to zone out and nod off. The aim isn't inner peace or pampering. My work is about increasing flexibility and removing chronic pain. If you want someone to rub pretty-smelling oil into your back while a bland *Sounds of the Ocean* CD plays on repeat, I'm not the massage therapist for you. I don't apologize for any of this; I advertise it upfront, and my work diary is full of people still wanting more after years of coming to me.

"I wouldn't want more than one wall this color, but I'm glad I have one," I tell Pam. "I so nearly didn't do it."

"I remember. And you wouldn't have done it if Zannah and Ben hadn't already changed their walls from white to something else."

This is true. I've always been a strict white-walls-only person, but I persuaded myself that I was allowed to paint my treatment room aubergine by thinking, "No radical change is happening here. You are already somebody with two nonwhite rooms in your house."

Zannah's bedroom has mint-green-and-gold

diamond-patterned wallpaper that she insisted would look amazing and has hated from about a fortnight after it went up. She refuses to let me or Dom strip it or paint over it, though, because of something about the importance of remembering one's mistakes and learning from them—advice she got from a YouTube star's Pinterest quote board. Instead, across the whole of one wall, she has spray-painted the words "Big Mistake" in pale pink, graffiti-style. The other walls she's covered in collages of photographs so that the wallpaper is barely visible: pictures of her and Murad, friends, family.

When Ben heard Zannah lobbying to have her room redecorated, the principle of equality obliged him to join in, even though he didn't and doesn't care what his bedroom looks like. He chose pale gray for the walls, but couldn't be bothered to test the various shades, so Dom—who, despite being a graphic designer, also has zero interest in the difference between one color and another when it comes to doing up our house—picked one for him at random. It looks good. Zannah immediately said, "Ben, your room looks a hundred times better than mine, you little shit."

Ben chose a couple of posters of Kate Moss, the supermodel, wearing clothes with the word "Supreme" on them, and asked me to get them framed.

At the same time, he took down all the pictures that he thought were too childish, apart from the very first one I ever bought for him that was his before he was born—framed and waiting for him in his room. It's a black-and-white drawing of a five-bar gate in a field, with teddy bears sitting on the gate's bars and in a semicircle in front of it. The bears are all grinning happily. Most recently, they've been grinning at Kate Moss in her Supreme T-shirt across the no-man's-land of Ben's clothes-strewn floor.

"Change really is the most frightening thing," says Pam with a sigh.

I know my next line in this dialogue, and Pam just gave me my cue. "It's true," I say. "But change is good for us. If we never make any changes that scare us at first, we end up missing out." I vary the wording slightly each time Pam and I have this conversation.

"Yes," she says quickly. "I think one of the worst mistakes we make is investing so much significance in details of our lives that don't matter at all. We can just choose. It doesn't matter all that much, and maybe there's no wrong choice."

"Mm-hmm."

"It's like me, with moving house," says Pam, as if she's never said it before. "Or rather, not moving house. I know I could live somewhere nicer, quieter and for half the price. I don't like living on a busy street in the center of a town. But Ed loved the house, and I've lived in it since we got married. The thought of moving's frightening. I might not be able to be me in a different house—that's what I say to myself. But that's rubbish, of course."

"And you'll still be you if you stay where you are," I say cheerily. Here is where the discussion always stalls. Pam will change the subject now, and we'll spend the rest of our hour together talking about other things. I don't mind the repetitive element of my sessions with her. She seems to need it, and I keep hoping that one day she'll pluck up the courage to do what she so obviously wants, on some level, to do: sell her enormous town house that's much too big for her now that Ed's died and her children have all left home, and move to a cottage in a country village.

I swore to myself that I would never advise her directly, or tell her that's what I think she ought to do, even though sometimes I'm tempted to scream, "Just do it and stop fretting!" I'm not sure whether she would prefer a new house to her current one, but I'm convinced she'd feel happier and more confident if she demonstrated to herself that she's brave enough to take a risk once in a while and live with the consequences, whatever they might be.

"So, what's been keeping you so busy?" she asks. "It's not like you to cancel on me twice in one week."

"I know. I'm sorry."

"No need to apologize! I know you wouldn't do it if it wasn't necessary. You're so reliable. I was a bit worried about you, that's all. Is everything okay on the home front?"

"Fine. There was something I had to pursue. Something I can't really talk about, I'm afraid, but nothing for you to worry about."

"Well, you pursue away!" she says. "You're the sort of person who'd make a success of whatever you decided to do."

"Am I?"

"Oh, yes," Pam says confidently.

*Apart from persuading PC Pollard to check on the Cater children.* We still haven't heard anything from him. I wanted to ring him this morning, but Dom said we ought to give it more time. "If he doesn't get back to us by the end of Thursday, we can ring him then," he said.

It's Monday today. Pollard's already had long enough. I've spent the days since we saw him trying to prove to Dom that I can put the Braids and the Caters to one side and get on with normal life. He's been impressed and so have I. I've done better than I thought I would. Every time a new theory occurs to me and I'm about to say, "You know, another possibility . . ." I manage to stop myself in time.

If I ring Pollard on Thursday and find out he's done nothing . . .

"He will have done," Dom assured me this morning. "If he's doing it properly, through child protection channels, it might take a while. There'll be processes they have to go through. It's probably all underway. Be patient."

I think again of Thomas Cater's broken shoe, with its flapping sole. I don't want to be patient. I want to do something. I know what I want to do, but I've been pushing it down whenever it surfaces in my mind because it's too extreme.

"Beth? There's something worrying you, isn't there?" says Pam. "I'm not asking you to tell me what it is, but there's something."

"Sorry, Pam. I was miles away." I try to sound lighthearted. "Something I'm trying to figure out, that's all. How to take a particular project forward."

"You can't think how to get to where you want to be—is that it?"

"No, I know how to get there. It's whether I should

go at all—that's the problem. If and when I arrive, I might find it's the last place I want to be." It's hard to discuss it without any of the specifics.

"I've been listening to an excellent podcast," Pam says as I pour some more oil into my hands to rub into her back. "I tell you, since Ed died, podcasts have saved my life. Anyway, this one said that you can fear change and still allow change to happen if it's necessary."

"Sounds good, but fear's not my problem. It's more a straight choice. Deciding what to do between two options that are diametric opposites."

*1) Do whatever I have to do to find out what's going on with Flora and her family. 2) Leave it to PC Pollard.*

"Ah, well, this podcast had something to say about choices too," says Pam. "And indecision. Mind you, it hasn't managed to help me resolve to move house yet. Though if it does, it'll be thanks to one particularly useful piece of advice."

"What's that?"

"Imagine you could pursue both choices, in parallel universes."

"Like a *Sliding Doors* scenario?"

"What's that?" Pam asks.

"A film. Never mind."

"Imagine you make choice number one, and it goes as well as it possibly could."

"Okay." That's me taking action and finding out the truth. And then doing what? What if I can't prove it, or no one will listen? What if the truth is as bad as I'm imagining it must be, and I'm powerless to do anything about it?

"Now imagine you make choice number two," says Pam. "That also goes as well as it possibly could."

Which means PC Pollard finds out the truth, arrests whoever needs to be arrested, rescues Thomas and Emily Cater . . . who then go into the care system, because their parents are in jail.

Those parents, I realize with a jolt of shock, are Lewis and Flora. They must be. For the children I saw with Flora outside Newnham House to look so similar to older Thomas and Emily at the same ages, they must have both parents in common, not just one. In all four faces, there's an unmistakeable resemblance to Flora, but the eyes are different. They've all got the same eyes: dark and almond-shaped, not rounder and green like Flora's.

How the hell have I only just seen this? I've thought so much about the similarities between the two pairs of children, the ones living at Newnham House and the teenagers in Florida as they were twelve years ago—and then about how younger Thomas and Emily's faces reveal that they're Flora's, not Yanina's or any other woman's—that I've failed to think about the eyes and what they mean.

Flora used to say it all the time: that baby Thomas or baby Emily had looked at her with Lewis's eyes. "Not just his eyes, but his stubborn expression," she would say, laughing. "That 'Give me what I want or else' stare."

Last Thursday, as I watched Thomas Cater walk across the playground to Yanina after school, I told myself that he couldn't be the Thomas I knew in 2007; he had to be a different boy because it was in every way impossible that he was the same one, frozen in time, unaging—not because he didn't look identical to Thomas Braid. He did. Going only by the visuals, they could be the same person.

*Which means Thomas Cater has Lewis Braid's eyes. And is his son. And Emily is Lewis's daughter.*

Then why doesn't Lewis insist on having them in Florida with him? The Lewis I knew wouldn't allow any child of his to stay in a house where his wife was living with another man. He wouldn't let his youngest son go to school wearing broken shoes that barely covered his feet.

"Beth?" Pam's voice breaks into my thoughts. "Was it helpful? Or are you still trying to work out what both choices going as well as they could might look like? That's what the exercise is: you imagine that each choice goes amazingly well, and then you choose which of those ideal outcomes would be the most ideal. It's very clever."

I don't have time to answer. There's a loud rapping on the door of my treatment room.

"Beth, I need a word." It's Dom. No apology for interrupting when I'm working—something he's never done before.

"What is it?"

"It's urgent," he says. "It's Zannah."

I apologize to Pam, leave her in the treatment room on the table, and close the door behind me, my heart thudding like a maniac on the loose in my chest.

Dom's waiting for me in the hall. "What's wrong with Zan?" I snap at him. "Tell me quickly. Is she hurt?" She's supposed to be with Murad at a revision session at school. History.

"What? No, nothing like that," says Dom. "Physically she's fine."

*Thank God.* "Then what?"

"She just rang and said can I send you to school immediately. I told her you were with Pam. She said, 'This is more important than someone's stiff back.'"

"Important how?"

"She refused to say. I tried, Beth."

"Did she sound upset?" *Please, please, don't let Murad have dumped her, not just before her GCSEs.*

"No. More angry."

"Oh, God. Just angry, though, not scared?"

"It was hard to tell. Maybe a bit scared too, yeah."

I'm finding it hard to breathe. *Please let this not be too serious.* "Why didn't you make her tell you what's wrong?"

"You think I didn't try? She wouldn't tell me anything. She only said that it's important and you need to go to school immediately and text her when you get there. Don't go inside and ask for her—she stressed that quite a few times. Text Murad's phone from the car park and she'll come out and meet you. She wants you to hurry. Have you got his number?"

If she's asking me to text Murad's phone, they can't have broken up. Unless she had his phone for some reason, found something on it that shouldn't have been there, and is refusing to give it back. "Yeah, I've got his number. But, Dom, I've got Pam—"

"I know. Look, don't blame me. I offered to go instead, and got a firm no. Oh, and Zannah wants you there by eleven. Ideally before."

I look at the clock on the wall above Dom's head.

"I can easily do it. It's only ten past ten and it's a fifteen-minute drive. What about Pam, though?"

"She'll understand—it's a family emergency."

He's right. Back in the treatment room, I explain the situation to Pam, who's very reasonable about it. "Of course you must go," she says, buttoning up her flower-print blouse. "And try not to worry. Everything seems ever so serious when you're that age. It's probably just boyfriend trouble."

That's what I'm worried about. Zannah feels things deeply. Her love for Murad isn't a passing fad. If he's done something like cheat on her and she's just found out, I'll be lucky if I can stop her smashing his head in with the nearest heavy object. Maybe she has already. Dom said she was fine physically, but maybe Murad isn't. No, a teacher would have rung if there had been an injury, surely . . .

"Beth." Pam puts her hand on my arm. "Zannah is fine. If it was really serious, she'd have told Dominic what had happened, wouldn't she?"

I hadn't thought of this and it makes me feel slightly better. "Yes. If it was life or death, she'd have told Dom."

*But if it wasn't, she wouldn't interrupt you when she knows you've got clients all day that you let down last week and are trying to make it up to.*

"Unless she's pregnant," Pam announces cheerily. "She'd prefer to tell Mum than Dad that sort of news, I imagine."

Yes, she would. Oh, God. "Thanks for that," I try to smile. Zan and Murad have already thought of a name for their first baby: Truelove. Is this the news I'm about to receive—that Truelove Rasheed-Leeson is already on the way? Zannah knows how not to get pregnant; she and I have discussed it many times.

*But GCSEs are coming up. And she'd do anything to avoid them. And she hasn't revised.*

No. I shake the idea from my mind. She wouldn't— neither accidentally nor deliberately. Not my Zan, who's wise beyond her years.

"Stop imagining worst-case scenarios and go," says Pam. "You don't need to wait for me. It'll take me a while to put my jewelry back on. Dominic'll see me out, I'm sure."

"Thank you, Pam. I'll make this up to you—free massages for life, at this rate."

I grab my car keys and head for Bankside Park.

# 16

I follow Zannah's instructions: park in the visitor car park, text Murad's phone to say I've arrived. Immediately, three dots appear on the screen beneath my message. She's typing. Or he is.

Nearly a minute later, the typing is still going on, or so the jumping dots indicate. Maybe it's both of them together. What are they doing, writing an essay?

The message that finally lands has no name at the bottom, so I can't tell who wrote it. It contains directions for how to find the Art room on foot. The school has 2,000 pupils and is spread over four buildings if not more. Each one is a labyrinth of corridors. I'm to meet Zannah at a particular door, which she's waiting at.

What's she doing in the Art room, when she gave the subject up two years ago? She's supposed to be at a History revision day. And why can't she come and meet me in the car park?

I cross the wide rectangular yard and knock on the prescribed door when I find it, planning to ask all these questions. Zannah's voice calls out, "Mum?"

"Yeah. Open the door."

"I can't. There's an intercom, and I don't know the code." Her face appears at the window next to the door, which is open. She opens it wider. "Quick, climb in."

"What? Are you kidding? I'm nowhere near agile enough to—"

"Mum, it's a ground-floor window. It's easy. You might not be able to do it gracefully, but you can do it."

"All visitors are supposed to go through reception. If someone sees me . . ."

"They won't. Why d'you think I chose this room? In Bankside Park terms, this is the middle of nowhere. No one'll see you, unless you take four years to climb in."

"Can't you climb out?"

"No! Someone might see us together. Just do it, now."

I manage to get inside, but not quickly and not without injury. I land inelegantly on the large table that's pushed up against the wall beneath the window—perhaps by Zannah, to catch me—then roll onto the floor. The room I land in doesn't look like an

Art room. It looks disused, like a semiderelict space awaiting redecoration. There are no pictures up on the peeling walls.

"Please tell me this isn't really the Art room," I say.

"Was. This whole block's unsafe or something, so it's going to be done up. Oh, my God, have you ripped those trousers?"

"And grazed my knee." I bend down to inspect it. "Do you want to tell me why these indignities were necessary? It had better be good, Zan."

"Have you watched it yet?" she demands.

"Watched what?"

"You haven't!" She looks aghast. "I emailed it to you!"

"I was with a client, then rushing to meet you. I haven't had time to check my emails."

"Get your phone out," she orders, nodding at my bag. "You need to watch it now."

"All right, but . . . can you calm down?" Her rapid-fire manner makes me think someone's going to burst through the door at any moment and try to kill us both.

"Calm down, yes. Slow down, no," she says. "It's a time-sensitive situation. You'll need to log into school Wi-Fi, there's no 4G here. It's BanksideParkStaff, no spaces, capital B, P, and S and the password's—"

"Wait, there's no . . . Oh, I've got it. Password?"

"banksideparkers, no spaces, all lower case."

"Okay. Done. How do you know the staff Wi-Fi password?"

"Everyone knows it. Solid spy network."

I go to my email inbox, open the message from Zannah and click on the link that's the only thing in it.

It's a video clip of extremely poor quality, with muffled, shaky sound. I can just about make out Zannah's jeans and trainers, the ones she's wearing today, and another pair of legs that also end in Nike trainers—red ones that I recognize, with orange laces. "Is this you and Murad?" I ask. Zan nods. They're allowed to wear their own clothes when they come in for revision days.

In the film, Zan is laughing, telling Murad that he'd better put his panini away because "She's coming. I can hear her." A close-up of the panini fills the screen for a second. Then we're back to the trainers.

"It's fine," I hear Murad say. "S'a revision meeting, not a lesson. No one's ever said we can't eat in those."

Zan laughs. "Hosmer's going to say it in like, five seconds. No eating in classrooms."

"No, it's no eating in *class*," says Murad. "This isn't a class, per se."

"Oh, per-*say*?" Zan giggles. "Just put it away! Seriously, you want to provoke Hosmer? Why give her the chance to make your life a misery when you know there's nothing she likes more?"

"I'm hungry."

"Is it just you and Murad at this revision class?" I ask Zannah.

"Yeah, these sessions are voluntary. Everyone else was a no-show. And you think *I'm* unmotivated. Shh, listen."

"This is going to be brutal," says Recorded Zannah. "I'm going to film it: your blood dripping down the walls after she's cheffed you. Here we go. Too late to back out now!" There's another wobbly shot of the panini, then gray fuzz, then Murad's trainers again.

"What's that on the desk?" I hear an Australian voice ask.

Camilla Hosmer: head of History and a walking, impossible-to-solve, pros-versus-cons dilemma. She's conscientious, well organized and expert at transferring knowledge of her subject from her brain to her pupils' brains, which can't be said of most Bankside Park teachers, unfortunately. She's also a vigilant and passionate enforcer of every tiny rule on every single occasion, even if it makes no sense. The word "flexible" is not in her vocabulary. Murad knows this better than I do. I suspect his panini stunt is a deliberate attempt to entertain himself and Zannah by winding her up so that there will be less time for History revision.

"It's a panini, miss," says Murad in the video clip. The visuals have disappeared. I think I'm looking at the underside of a desk: just semidarkness with a few bumpy imperfections in it. "Bacon, avocado and Brie. It's delicious. Want some?"

Deliberate cheek. This isn't going to end well. I'm fairly sure that my being here is something to do with the forthcoming unhappy ending to this little scene. *Cheers, Murad. It's not like I need to earn money or anything.*

"This is a revision session, not a bistro," I hear Miss Hosmer say.

"But, miss, I'm starving."

"Get out! Now."

"All right, I'll put it away, miss."

"I told you to get out, Murad."

"But look, I'm putting it in my bag. There, it's gone."

"Take it out of your bag, put it in the bin and then. Get. Out."

"Miss, I'll go if you really want me to, but I'm not throwing my panini away. If I do that, I can't eat it later, can I?"

"How would you like it if I told your parents I'd

caught you eating a bacon sandwich?" Miss Hosmer snaps at him.

"What do you mean, miss?"

Murad says something else, but I can't tell what it is. Zan's voice obscures it; she whispers something.

"You know what I mean," says Hosmer. "You're letting yourself down, and you're letting your family down."

"Why? Because he's eating bacon?" Zan's voice. She sounds angry.

"Oh—do you think my family's Muslim, miss?" Murad laughs. "My dad kind of is. But my mum isn't. She's whiter than you, and a hippie. And we all eat bacon."

I look up at Zannah. "Fucking hell," I say.

"Watch," she orders.

Her recorded voice in the video says, "Why have you turned bright red, miss? Is it because you've realized you've messed up and you owe Murad an apology?"

"Throw the panini in the bin, and then leave this classroom, please," says Hosmer. She doesn't sound angry anymore, just cold and remote.

"No, I won't," says Murad. "I'll leave if you want me to, but I'm not throwing my lunch away."

"And I'll leave too, but only once you've apologized for your racism," says Zannah.

"I haven't got a racist bone in my body, Suzannah." Hosmer sounds tearful now.

"It might not be a bone," Zan quips. "Maybe it's a racist intestine."

"Or a kidney," Murad says.

I nearly drop my phone when there's a sudden burst of loud noise. Miss Hosmer has started to shout in a hysterical way that borders on shrieking. I can't make out her words but it's something about going to the head teacher right now. The clip ends abruptly, while she's still in the middle of yelling.

"Jesus," I say quietly. "So . . . ?"

Zannah's ready. She starts talking faster than I've ever heard her talk before. "So, what happened next is, I held up my phone and told her I'd recorded it all. She started screaming at me, how dare I record her without permission, how dare me and Murad accuse her of racism when she was the least racist person in the world, she was going to go and get Mr. Stevens right now and we had to wait there while she did, that was our only chance, or else if we dared to leave the room before she came back with Mr. Stevens, we'd be expelled, and she wouldn't care about the impact on our GCSEs to expel us right before them. All of that—how we wouldn't even get good references. It was scary, Mum! Not only her psycho screaming, but the threats—like, I reckon she could make Stevens expel us if she really wanted to? He hasn't got a clue what's going on half the time, and he relies on her to run the school, basically. Then she was about to leave the room to go and get him, and she turned back suddenly, marched over to me and yelled, 'Give me your phone!' Before I could agree or disagree, she *pulled it out of my fucking hand* and ran out of the room. I ran after her, because, like, she can't just do that? I couldn't see her. She wasn't in the corridor, and I should have been right behind her. You know where I think she was?"

I shake my head, stunned. Zannah cannot get expelled. That can't happen. This is a disaster. Dominic will think this is the end of the world.

"Hidden away in a classroom or a stationery cupboard, deleting the recording off my phone. She pulled it out of my hand before I'd had a chance to turn it off, so she had full access, no passcode needed. And guess what?" Zannah blinks away tears and sniffs. "When Stevens turns up and I tell him I've got footage of Hosmer being racist and then denying it, and he asks to see it, there's nothing there. No film. All gone. I tell him Hosmer's deleted it, she denies it—"

"Wait. Did she deny making the racist comment?"

"Yes!" A tear rolls down Zannah's cheek. "She flat out denied it. Said me and Murad had made up this lie, and it was serious and you can't just call people racist, you can't just lie about people, and I mean, like . . . exactly! You can't just *lie*!"

"But we can prove she's lying," I say. "I've got the film on my phone. How did you—"

"Soon as she started screaming at us, I thought, 'Shit, why did I tell her I had it recorded?' I was angry and I wanted to scare her, but then she lost the plot and starting yelling about me recording her without permission, and we're not even allowed to bring phones into school in the first place. They've decided to be really strict about it this term. I thought, 'She's going to confiscate my phone,' so I quickly put it on my knees under the desk and emailed the proof of her racism to you, while she ranted like a loony and stomped around the classroom."

"But, Zan, we've got the film. We'll go and see Mr. Stevens and—"

"Mum, I've accused a teacher of racism. Not just any teacher, either—one of the few who can actually teach. Don't you get it? They're *more* likely to expel me if I make them look bad than if I'm bad. They'll find a way—like the fact that I shouldn't have recorded Miss Hosmer without permission or even had my phone with me . . ."

"Zan, calm down. This is going to be fine."

"I've been told I have to go and see Mr. Stevens at eleven, on my own. We've told him our side already, and then they said they wanted to talk to each of us again, separately. They didn't like it when we were together because we backed each other up. Murad's in with Stevens now. He dropped his phone into my pocket before going with them, so I contacted you . . ."

"So that I'd bring my phone in with the video on it," I say when Zannah stops to breathe.

"No, so that I could ask you what the hell I should do, before I see Stevens. I don't know what to say. Part of me thinks if it was that serious he'd be ringing our parents, and he isn't, but, like, it felt *very* serious? And he and Hosmer *love* bringing parents in to make them as disappointed in us as the school is—so why's that not happening? I think he's going to offer us a deal: we apologize for disrespect, admit we lied about Hosmer being racist and then we'll get let off with some minor punishment. If we don't say we lied about the racism and the recording, we're going to get expelled." Zannah pushes her hair away from her face. "What should I do? I mean, I could just lie. It's not like I've never lied before."

Eleven o'clock. It's now ten to. Damn. I'm going to have to postpone another client, since its looks as if an important meeting has just added itself to my schedule.

"You're not going to lie and you're not going to tell the truth," I say, passing Zannah a tissue from my bag. "Wipe your eyes. You're going to sit quietly and let me do all the talking."

**Duncan Stevens** remains seated behind his desk as Zannah and I walk into his office. It's Camilla Hosmer who rises to greet us. She's surprised to see me and not in a good way; she can't hide it either. "Oh! Mrs. Leeson." She manages to produce a polite smile eventually, but it takes her some time. "We only . . . I mean, there was no need for you to . . ."

"You wanted Zannah on her own, I know. But I've got something to contribute, so here I am."

"That's probably a good idea, Mrs. Leeson," says Mr. Stevens. "This is quite serious. Miss Hosmer, since you're on your feet, can you pull over an extra chair for Mrs. Leeson, please?"

"There's no need," I tell him. "I'm not staying long."

"I think it might take longer than you think," says the head teacher. "I'm sure Suzannah has briefed you already, so . . . you'll know, I imagine, that a serious incident has occurred." Behind him, all over his office wall, are framed photos of Bankside Park pupils looking like happy high achievers: holding aloft trophies, cute rabbits, iced cakes, or with sports medals draped around their necks, or shaking hands with grateful-looking elderly women in wheelchairs.

I'd like to hit Miss Hosmer with a wheelchair. Even leaving today's disaster aside, I've had a petty grudge against her for more than a year, ever since she invited me in to give a talk about my massage therapy business. It was part of a series of lectures she was organizing at Bankside Park, designed to inspire the older girls to become the next generation of female entrepreneurs, rather than just the proud owners of cleavages rated "peng" and "flames" on Instagram by the upper school's male population.

Part of my talk was about why I'd been unable to stay in my original career. I'd told the girls that I'd felt my true talents were wasted in my old job, and that, although leaving felt like a huge risk at the time, I was so glad I'd taken that risk. Then I went on to say that fear stops so many people from fulfilling their dreams and ambitions, and that bravery is required to overcome the fear. All pretty standard stuff, I thought. The girls seemed to like it; they all applauded. Some stared at me vacantly throughout, but others looked inspired. Miss Hosmer thanked me afterward and I went home thinking it had gone well.

That afternoon, Ben came home from school red-faced with fury, having heard from one or two pupils in the older year groups that Miss Hosmer had used her afternoon registration period with her form group to undermine me. The girls, it seemed, had been a bit too inspired, and evidently this had annoyed her. "Please remember that Beth Leeson is extremely lucky that things have gone well for her, and she's probably the exception, not the norm," Miss Hosmer had apparently told them. "She left a well-paid, secure job and started a business that happened to be successful, but that doesn't mean it always works out that way. Job security is important too, and not everyone can be their own boss."

"But that makes no sense," Dom said when Ben told us. "Why would she bring you in for entrepreneurial inspiration and then say that?"

"It makes perfect sense," I told him. "She'd love to resign from Bankside Park but she's too scared to do it."

None of this is relevant to what's happened today, except that when I check the drawer of my benefit-of-the-doubt cabinet marked "Camilla Hosmer," I find it empty.

"I do know how serious it is, yes," I tell Mr. Stevens.

"Good, good. I'm surprised, because we've never had any trouble with Suzannah before, not in all the years she's been here, but Miss Hosmer has described her behavior this morning as disrespectful, disobedient and dishonest."

As he speaks, Hosmer brings a chair over—the rigid, plastic one that's clearly the least comfortable one in the room—and places it behind me, then gives it a little push so that the edge of the seat digs into the backs of my knees. Pointedly, I step away from it. "Disrespectful and disobedient, yes, but not dishonest," I say. "Zannah shouldn't have brought her phone in to school, so there's the disobedient bit. She spoke disrespectfully to Miss Hosmer, so a tick for that box too. And she did it because she doesn't respect her. Neither do I."

"I beg your pardon?" says Hosmer.

"You heard." I turn to face her. "You made a racist assumption about Murad and it turned out to be wrong. Just because he's got brown skin, that doesn't give you the right to tell him he shouldn't be eating bacon. If you saw a white kid eating chocolate during Lent, would you assume he came from a family of devout Christians and tell him he was letting his parents down, and Jesus?"

"Miss Hosmer is adamant that she said no such thing to Murad, Mrs. Leeson," says Stevens. "That's where the dishonesty comes in."

"True, if you mean Miss Hosmer's dishonesty," I

say. "Before she grabbed Zannah's phone out of her hand, Zannah had had the presence of mind to email me the film she'd recorded of the incident. Would you like me to play it for you now?" I brandish my phone.

Camilla Hosmer's mouth has dropped open. Stevens looks at her.

"Miss Hosmer? Shall I play the video for Mr. Stevens?"

Hosmer bursts into tears and runs out of the room, slamming the door behind her.

"She deleted it from Zannah's phone without permission, then lied about it to you," I tell Stevens.

He nods slowly, playing for time while he decides what to say. Whatever it is, it's not going to start with the words, "I'm so sorry," which means I'm not interested in hearing it.

"Mr. Stevens, one of my regular clients is the editor of a local newspaper that has a circulation of 8,000. She's become a good friend over the years. She's fond of Zannah, too. If I ask her to, she'll run a story about Bankside Park's racist head of History who lies and tries to punish pupils who call her out on her racism. The little film Zannah made would go up on the newspaper's Web site and get loads of hits. It could easily go viral. Do you think OFSTED will be impressed? I don't."

"Mrs. Leeson, there's no need to make unpleasant threats. Why don't we all calm down a bit, and then, once the dust has settled, I'll talk to Miss Hosmer and see if we can—"

"No, that sounds like bullshit," I say. "If you don't want me to contact my friend, you need to tell Miss Hosmer to apologize to Murad and Zannah. Right now. Go and find her in whatever toilet cubicle she's crying in and let's get on with it. I'm not leaving until I've heard those apologies."

"Nothing is going to happen right now," says Stevens, in the most patronizing tone of voice I've ever heard. "Why don't you and Zannah go home, and I'll contact you once I've had a chance to—"

"Give Zannah back her phone and we'll go, if that's the way you want to play it. But then I *will* be contacting my friend, and some of the national papers too, I think—the ones that have education supplements. Pieces will run, and the video will be shared far and wide."

"All right," Stevens snaps as he springs out of his chair. "All right. Wait here."

He leaves his office at speed. I turn to Zannah. Tears are streaming down her face. "Mum," she whispers. "What happened? Did we just . . . win?"

# 17

An hour later, we're at Mario's, the nearest half-decent café to Bankside Park. It's far enough away to guarantee that no one from school is likely to walk in, and the coffee and cakes are from heaven, even if the owner isn't. Silvia thinks she's a "character" and sings loud arias from operas whenever she feels like it, sometimes making it hard for customers to continue their conversations.

Zannah and I are eating her magnificent iced orange and cinnamon rolls, to celebrate our victory. "You're a ledge, Mum," Zan says. "I can't believe I got my phone back *and* an apology."

"Neither can I."

"Hosmer wasn't really sorry, you know."

"Who cares?"

"Ugh. She's such a . . . there's no word bad enough. I can't even insult her anymore. It'd be an insult to insults."

"Dad would have done the same as I did, you know."

Zannah wrinkles her nose. "No, he wouldn't. Would he have pretended to have a client who was a local news editor? I don't think so! He'd have said they were being unfair and asked for an apology, but he wouldn't have gotten creative and blackmailed them. And he'd have let them give me and Murad detentions for having our phones in school and being cheeky, when you were, like, 'That's not happening.'"

She's probably right.

"They gave me back my phone too late, though." Zannah giggles. "I wish I could have recorded you saying, 'Tell you what, Mr. Stevens—why don't you and your staff work on your own behavioral problems for a few weeks first and then maybe I'll allow Zannah to accept a detention from you.' Mum, you know what I'm gonna do?" Zannah brushes crumbs off her hoodie. "Revise the *fuck* out of my GCSEs from now till they're done."

"That's great, don't swear, and how come?"

"Nothing will piss Hosmer off more than me doing better than they all expect me to." Zannah peers at me. "What?" she asks. "What was that funny look?"

"You made me think of Tilly."

"Who?" Zannah says. "Oh, Rubis Tilly who got me drunk?"

"*You* got you drunk. Yes, that Tilly. And Lewis Braid. If the true explanation for someone's behavior is unusual enough, it's the easiest thing in the world to hide it behind a more obvious explanation."

"What's that got to do with me revising the *fuck* out of my—?"

"Imagine you get all 9s in your GCSEs, because you work really hard."

"Never gonna happen. But I could get all 6s and 7s, maybe."

"You would know that you'd only made the effort in the hope of ruining results day for Camilla Hosmer, but that would never occur to most people. If you said to a stranger, for example, that you did nothing, and did nothing, and did nothing, and then suddenly started revising like a maniac in the run-up to your exams, why would any stranger think you might do that?"

"Weird question. They'd probably think I suddenly panicked and was worried about failing."

"Right. So if you told them that was why, they'd believe you without a second thought. They wouldn't question it. Just like, if Lewis is hanging around out-side Tilly's house in his car when he should be in Florida, what's the obvious explanation there? If you keep turning up outside someone's house, and lie about why when they ask what you're doing there . . . well, it looks as if you might be an obsessive stalker, doesn't it?"

"So?"

She's impatient for the conclusion, but I'm not quite there yet. "Lewis Braid is the father of Thomas and Emily Cater. They have his eyes, just like older Thomas and Emily do. Flora was with him when she rang me last week. That means he's still around, still involved in whatever's going on at Newnham House." I raise my hand to stop Zannah asking questions before I've finished. "But he's not supposed to be. Think about the lies he and Flora have told me: Georgina's twelve and doing great; they have no young children, only the three they had when they moved to America, where they now live; they have no connection with Heming-ford Abbots anymore."

"I don't get it, Mum."

"Tilly kept finding Lewis loitering outside her house. Then she found him in her back garden clutching her silk pajamas, at which point he declared his obsessive love for her. She and her husband had a word with him, he promised faithfully to stop, and he did—he never bothered them again."

"Uh-huh."

"Stalkers don't just stop, Zan. Someone as deter-mined and driven as Lewis Braid wouldn't have given up so easily. Nor would he pick Tilly to obsess over. She isn't his type. So why would he pretend to stalk her and be in love with her?"

"I don't think he would," says Zannah. "You can't be sure—"

"I'm sure," I cut her off. "Think about what Tilly told us: the pajamas in the back garden and the crying and admitting it all—that came later. The first thing, she said, was that she noticed Lewis outside her house a few times. I assumed she meant he was lurking in her front garden near the house—number 3 doesn't have any gates, so that's possible—but she didn't say that. She said 'outside my house.' That could mean that *she* was in her front garden or on her driveway and she saw Lewis in his car, parked where we parked when we went to Wyddial Lane."

"If she just saw him in a car on the street, she wouldn't assume he was in love with her." Zan rolls her eyes.

"No, but if she spotted him more than once, she might think, 'Why does he keep turning up? I thought the Braids had moved to America.' And think about what kind of person Tilly is. She said the first few times she confronted Lewis, he made crap excuses for being there. That probably means she trotted enthusiastically up to his car, knocked on the window, said, 'Hi, Lewis! What are you doing back? I thought you'd moved to America.' And he was forced to lie.

"I've been to Wyddial Lane three times now. It's a silent, mind-your-own-business sort of place. Everyone's hiding behind their high walls and gates, not watching what's happening on the road. I'd bet everything I own that no one except Tilly on that street would rush up to a parked car and cheerfully demand to know the business of the person sitting inside it. Marilyn Oxley at number 14 is nosy and observant enough, but she's also keen on keeping her distance. You should have seen the effort I had to put in to persuade her to leave her house and come and talk to me through the gate. Anyone would have thought I was waving a bomb around or something."

"Okay, so Tilly saw Lewis parked outside her house, and she went and tried to chat to him," says Zannah. "She asked him what he was doing there, and he made crap excuses. I still don't get it."

Silvia picks this moment to wander over to our table. "You ladies want more rolls? More coffee?"

"No thanks," I say.

"They are very good, though?"

"Sublime, as always."

"Ah, you are very kind to me!" She wanders away. Mercifully, there's been no singing so far today.

I say to Zannah, "Lewis would have known his excuses for being there weren't remotely plausible. That will have bothered him. He'll have worried that he'd made Tilly suspicious. If the lie that he and Flora desperately want the world to believe is that they're living in Florida, done with Wyddial Lane, and a different family now owns their old house, a family that has nothing to do with them—"

"I get it!" Zannah flaps her hands. "So he starts acting like *more* of a stalker to Tilly and gets caught with her PJs in the garden deliberately."

"Yes. If he arranges it so that she 'finds out' "— I make air quotes with my fingers—"that he's been stalking her, and then breaks down and sobs and says he loves her wildly, then his crap excuses are no longer suspicious. Suddenly, there's an explanation that looks obvious."

"And it explains why he then stopped stalking her: because he never wanted to or really did in the first place. Wait: that only works if you're right about Tilly first spotting him in his car on the street, not in her garden."

"I'm going to contact her and find out," I say. "I

didn't take her number, but I know she runs a business from 3 Wyddial Lane. Shouldn't be hard to find."

"Another thing I just thought of," Zan says. "You know what Tilly said about none of the neighbors ever seeing Flora? What if that was deliberate? Lewis and Flora planned it so that no one saw her because they knew she'd be coming back as Jeanette Cater. They didn't want the neighbors to say, 'Wait, you're not Jeanette, you're Flora.'"

A shiver runs through my body. Pretending to be an obsessive stalker, hiding from the world so that you can come back with a different name . . . What can the Braids be so determined to hide that they'd go to such extremes? The more I know about the lengths they've gone to, the more convinced I am that the truth must be unbearable. For who, though? The Braids themselves, or for other people?

"Did Georgina Braid have Lewis's eyes like the other four?" Zannah asks.

"I don't know. Don't think I ever saw her with her eyes open. She was a tiny baby the only time they came around. Resemblances often don't become obvious till you're a bit older, anyway." Even in the photograph Flora sent with the Christmas card, Georgina had her eyes shut. The image of that tiny cutting lying on my kitchen floor flashes up in my mind. I push it away. "Why?" I ask Zannah.

"Dunno. I just wondered if she might have been Kevin and Yanina's baby, not Lewis and Flora's." Zannah laughs at my immediately alert expression. "Relax, Mum. That's not a brilliant new theory. I don't know why I said it."

"You wouldn't have said it for no reason." If Flora was never pregnant with Georgina, then what I was annoyed about never happened: she didn't fail to tell me that she was pregnant or that she'd had a baby—because she wasn't, and she didn't.

Zannah says, "Assuming you're right about the eyes thing . . . which, okay, I believe you. Then little Thomas and Emily are Lewis and Flora's, but everyone's pretending they're Kevin and Jeanette Cater's. But there is no Jeanette Cater, not really, and Yanina lives in that house too, and she and Kevin might be together . . ."

"And also might not be."

"It would be neat, though," Zan says. "A straight swap. Kevin and Yanina have Georgina and for some reason Flora and Lewis pretend she's theirs. Then a few years later, Lewis and Flora have Thomas and Emily number two, and Kevin pretends they're his."

None of this strikes me as impossible or even unlikely, given all that's happened and everything I know to be true. It would explain why Flora seemed distant and less interested in spending time with me in 2006, when she—or somebody—was pregnant with Georgina. If she knew she was about to have to tell the world the most outrageous lie and then sustain it, pretending that another woman's baby was hers, there wouldn't have been room in her mind or life for anything else. And . . . she wouldn't have wanted her parents around her, either. They knew her better than anyone; they'd have been able to tell for sure that she wasn't herself, that something was horribly wrong.

I was too wrapped up in what I thought was her rejection of me to worry about what might have been going on in her life. It's unbearable to think that Thomas and Emily Cater might be suffering now because of my failure to realize twelve years ago that not everything was about me.

Flora's suffering is more complicated. She has to be one of the main liars behind all this, whatever it is, but I've twice seen her behave like a victim.

"That could be what 'Chimpy' means, if Chimpy's Georgina," Zannah goes on. "Lewis and Flora and their kids are all perfect looking, aren't they? Kevin and Yanina's kid might not have been. From what you've said about Lewis, I can imagine him giving someone an insulting nickname, and expecting them to find it funny."

"Taunting," I mutter.

"What?" says Zan.

"You're right. Lewis liked to taunt people with nicknames, so you might be right about Chimpy. But what if he took it further?"

"How?"

"If you call your youngest two children names that your oldest two already have, and make them wear their old clothes and shoes . . . Couldn't there be an element of taunting there too?"

"That's creepy, Mum."

It is. And if it's not true, if it's miles away from the truth, then maybe I'm the sick one for dreaming it up. Flora would never willingly harm a child, especially not her own.

Lewis is a different matter. I have no idea what he's capable of, and I can't help asking myself the question: what if he chose to call his youngest children Thomas and Emily as a deliberate act of cruelty?

**Dom's hovering** in the hall when Zannah and I get home. "PC Pollard rang," he says, trying to sound matter-of-fact. In the short silence that follows, I hear the gloating he's trying so hard not to indulge in: *I told you he would.*

I drop my bag on the floor—something I frequently moan at the children for doing. "What did he say?"

"Tell me about school first."

"It's all fine. Sorted out."

"I was hoping for a bit more detail than that." Seeing my glare, Dom says, "Pollard went to 16 Wyddial Lane."

"Himself? I thought he was going to send child protection people?"

"I don't know. He said he went himself."

"Do you think that means he passed it on to child protection and they weren't convinced enough to do anything?"

"I've no way of knowing."

"Try letting Dad speak," Zannah suggests.

"He talked to Kevin Cater and Yanina, and also to the children: Thomas and Emily. Had a nice long chat with them all, he said. In his opinion, all's well and there's nothing to worry about."

"Nothing to worry about?" *Don't lose it, Beth. Don't scream. Think about how insane Miss Hosmer sounded on Zannah's video. You don't want to sound like that.* "What did you say, when he said that?" I ask.

"I thanked him for looking into it and for letting me know he had."

"That's all?"

"Yes. Should I have said something else? He'd done all he was going to do, and, let's face it, he needn't have done anything."

"But, Dad, you know there's something to worry about: all the things that still don't make sense."

"Pollard knows about those things too," I say quietly.

Dom looks past me into the middle distance, as if listening intently to someone behind me that I can't see or hear. I've got a strong feeling that person is begging him not to lose his temper.

"You're right, Beth. Pollard knows everything that's happened, he's been to the house, and the net result of all that is what I've just told you: he's satisfied nothing more needs to be done."

"And so we should be too? Did he go to Thomas's school? Did he talk to Lou Munday?"

"I don't know. He didn't say anything about the school."

"Course he didn't go to the school," says Zannah.

"Did he find out if Georgina Braid is dead or still alive?"

Dom looks puzzled—as if this is the last question

he'd have expected me to ask. "He didn't mention Georgina at all."

"And you didn't either?"

"No, I didn't."

"Did he speak to any of the Caters' neighbors? Did you tell him about the shoes?"

"The . . ." He looks puzzled. Then he remembers. "No, I didn't tell him about Thomas Cater's fucking shoes!" Dom snaps. "I'm sick of this, Beth. Do you want to know why I didn't ask all the questions you wish I'd asked? I don't care anymore! Whatever the Braids are up to, I don't give a shit, as long as I can get my life back—the life that didn't involve talking about the Braids and the Caters every waking second of every day."

"That's understandable," I say. Now that he's lost his temper, I feel calmer. "I've been expecting you to share my level of obsession. It wasn't fair of me. I'm sorry, okay?"

Dom eyes me suspiciously.

"I promise I'll stop talking to you about this soon," I say, knowing he won't notice the "to you," or think about what it might mean. "I have one more question: did Pollard say anything else, apart from what you've told me? Anything at all."

"Yes." Dom looks trapped. I know how he feels. I

also know I'm not prepared to feel it for much longer. "He told me Kevin Cater admitted lying to us about his children's names. Cater told him he'd been reluctant to reveal the real names because he was worried you had a strange obsession with his children."

"Did he or Yanina admit that they both pretended she was Jeanette when we went around?"

"I don't know. That wasn't mentioned. And that was a second question. You said only one. I mean it, Beth. You can let this take over your life if you want, but I'm not letting it take over mine. If you want Pollard to do something else . . ."

"I don't want him to do anything."

"He spooned it." Zannah's voice rings with contempt.

"I'm the one who needs to find out what's going on," I say, thinking about Pam Swain's podcast exercise: *you imagine that each choice goes amazingly well, and then you choose which of those ideal outcomes would be the most ideal.* It doesn't work at all. My choice number two was leaving it up to Pollard to do what needs to be done. That's the one I chose, in my head, and look how it's turned out.

Or maybe Pam's exercise works brilliantly . . .

*Yes. It does. You can't choose between two alterna-*

*tives without thinking realistically about the people involved.*

With Pollard being who he is, with his level of interest and care, and doing things in the way that he does them as a result, choice number two has already gone as well as it could have. For it to go any better, you'd need to replace Pollard with someone more determined, more obsessed, more willing to do whatever it takes—ideally, someone who once loved Flora Braid and her children.

I'd need to replace him with me. Which means choice number one is the right answer. "I have to do it myself," I tell Dom. "I'm the only person who can or ever would."

"What does that mean?" he asks. "Please don't say what I think you're about to say."

"It means going to Florida."

# 18

From: beth.leeson@triggerpointtherapy.co.uk
To: DominicL@Logonomika.com

Hi Dom,

I'm at Heathrow. My plane's delayed by two hours—great!

I don't think it's ever happened before that I've left the house with you refusing to speak to me or say good-bye. For what it's worth, I don't think it's fair. We've never disagreed about anything serious before, not once in our whole marriage. About this one thing we disagree, and that ought to be fine. Married couples don't always have to agree about everything.

You think a trip to Florida is an unnecessary expense. I don't. I need to do this. I think Flora and

her kids might be in real trouble, and I can't just ignore that fear. No, she's not my friend anymore, but
if I hadn't been so blinkered and pig-headed twelve
years ago, maybe she still would be. I have to do what
I can, and either I'll be able to help or I won't. Or I'll
find my help isn't needed and I've been wrong about
everything. Either way, I'll be glad I tried. And if I'm
creating drama where there's no need, if I find out
that I've been totally wrong to make a fuss, then I'll
be relieved—and it will have been worth the money
to find that out, because you're not the only one who
wants their life back. I do too.

I wouldn't force you to go to Florida and spend
more time on this, knowing you didn't want to. That
wouldn't be fair. Can't you see that you trying to stop
me when I feel I need to go is unfair too? I don't think
it's irresponsible of me to go. I think it's the opposite.

All right, I'm going to stop now because I sound
like a two-year-old: "It's not fair!" I'll be back as soon as
I can, and the kids will be fine. Work will be fine. I sent
a nice email to all my regulars and they all got back to
me saying they understand completely, even though
I hardly told them anything. I don't think I'm going to
lose a single client. Zannah says she'll help around the
house while I'm gone, and Ben won't worry as long as
you don't panic him by making him think I've done

something crazy. Instead, you could tell him that you support my decision to go to America, or at least that you understand it.

I'll ring you when I get to my hotel if it isn't too late.

B xxx

From: DominicL@Logonomika.com
To: beth.leeson@triggerpointtherapy.co.uk

I'm glad you emailed. Sorry I was off with you when you left. I'm just worried. But, yeah, I could have expressed it better. At the risk of sounding like a selfish twat, your safety is all I care about, not Flora's, and I don't like the idea of you walking up to Lewis Braid and calling him a liar to his face. The guy's not right in the head. He never was. We just didn't care because we were young and undiscriminating, and he threw great parties and was fun to hang around with (except when he wasn't). But I've been thinking—imagine being Flora all these years, having to live with him and deal with his bad side as well as his good side. He was always dead set on getting his way, and that tendency'll only have gotten worse as he's aged. For me, that explains why Flora's stressed and miserable, and why she ran away from you. If she feels trapped, if their relationship has turned ugly and she's too scared to leave him, she might not want you to see that. Neither of them would want you to see it.

Maybe I'm being over the top. I heard something on the radio this morning about coercive control in relationships. Some of the behaviors that were discussed sounded a bit like Lewis even as he was before, even without the getting-worse-with-age factor. That might have influenced me. Just don't meet him alone in any secluded places, okay? He might make a pass for all you know, and not take no for an answer.

This memory has just come back to me, a second ago: Lewis and I were having a drink at The Baron of Beef once and I said, "I wouldn't put anything past you, Braid" (I can't remember what made me say it) and he said, "You'd be right not to, Rom-com Dom." I still don't think he'd harm any children, though. That'd be a step too far even for him. But you're right: we can disagree about that. I just want to know that you're fine. Stay safe and come home soon.

D x

# 19

It's a little after eight in the evening, Florida time, when I arrive at the Delray Beach Marriott Hotel. According to my stiff body and aching brain, it's past one in the morning. The check-in desk, less than a minute's walk from the entrance doors, looks unfeasibly far away. Instead of feeling as if I've arrived, I'm looking at the reception staff and thinking, "Right, last leg of the journey, one final push." The prospect of having to fish out my passport and credit card, sign forms and make small talk makes me want to lie down on the floor and close my eyes.

The high-ceilinged lobby smells of several things all at once: mainly the sea, grilled meat, leather and suntan lotion. There's a heap of suitcases on the floor that looks as if it might once have been a pile. Children hop around them, try to sit on them, end up pushing them over. Grown-ups scoop their offspring up off the tiled floor and try to shush them. One little boy breaks free of his mother, runs over to a potted tree by the side of the entrance door and sticks his hands into the soil it's planted in.

Eventually, the suitcases and families are all processed and I'm at the front of the line for the reception desk. I hand over what I'm asked for and sign where I'm told to. Eventually, I get to my room, which contains two double beds. I lie down on one of them, stretch out and think about what I need to do before I can go to sleep: ring Dom, eat something . . .

Then I'm opening my eyes, feeling groggy. My throat is dry and my bladder is uncomfortably full. What time is it? How long have I been asleep?

It takes me longer than it should to find my bag where I dropped it, on the far side of the other double bed, and pull out my phone.

It's 4 a.m., local time. My phone changed time zones in the taxi from the airport to the hotel, when I checked Lewis, Thomas and Emily Braid's social media accounts. None of them had posted anything new since I last looked.

Four a.m. That means I've been asleep for seven hours straight: conked out in my clothes, without brushing my teeth. And now I can't get into bed properly and sleep because I've done my night already and done it wrong.

I go to the bathroom and turn on the light. Good: there's a bathtub as well as a shower. And a little bottle of bubble bath lined up alongside the shampoo and conditioner. A long, hot, scented bath should be all I need to make me feel better. And food. Breakfast probably doesn't start till 6 a.m., but I can't wait till then. I'm starving.

What time will Lewis Braid get to his office? Seven thirty?

*Or not at all, maybe. He might be on his way to the airport to fly to Japan on business, and you'll have wasted your time and money.*

My stomach lurches at the thought. Then I realize it's not necessarily true. I might be able to find out more with Lewis gone than with him here in Florida. He won't have warned his colleagues not to tell me anything because it wouldn't occur to him that I'd turn up. If he's away on a business trip, I might be able to get his home address from someone if I play it right. I could go to the house, and if Flora's still here, which she might well be if Lewis wants to keep her well away from me . . .

*Don't get carried away. Flora might not have been in*

*America when she rang you. Lewis could have rigged it so that it looked as if that was where they were calling from.*

They might both be in England.

*Then where are seventeen-year-old Thomas and fifteen-year-old Emily? Home alone?*

I need to think of a way to make Lewis's colleagues give me his home address. I searched online in the hope of finding a home address but nothing came up, so my obvious first port of call is Lewis's workplace, which was easy to find.

I chose this hotel because the offices of VersaNova are only a seven-minute drive away. *So close.* I try not to let myself believe this means I'm close to getting the answers I want. The more I hope this is nearly over, the more disappointed I'll be if my trip achieves nothing.

I dial the number for room service and skim-read the menu while I wait for someone to answer. Breakfast doesn't start till five thirty, so I order a pepperoni pizza from the all-night menu, telling myself that Italians must do it all the time. Then I brush my teeth, run my hands through my hair and wash my face, so that the waiter I'm about to meet won't mistake me for a scarecrow. The food, when it arrives, is delicious. I sit at the long black desk beneath the large TV screen on the wall, enjoying my early, inappropriate breakfast, and knowing I'd enjoy it more if I didn't think I might soon be face-to-face with Lewis Braid.

I've witnessed Lewis's anger a few times. Once in a restaurant, he yelled at a group of women at the next table who were making too much noise, and made such a forceful impression on them that they paid up and left before their main courses had been served—but I've never seen him angry with me. Not yet. How will he react when I turn up at his office, uninvited? Will he morph into a monster the way Camilla Hosmer did in Zannah's low-budget film?

Or maybe he's a monster already. It's so easy to believe that the label only fits infamous historical figures and mug-shot faces we see on the news. When it's someone in our personal life—someone we've sat laughing with in a pub, someone who's punted us down the River Cam singing "Sit Down, You're Rockin' the Boat" in a cheesy American accent—it's hard to believe that their true nature might be monstrous.

I think again about the incident in the restaurant. It happened while we were all still students. Flora and Lewis had only been an item for a few months. Two of the women from the noisy group were crying as they left the restaurant. I can't remember precisely what Lewis yelled at them, but it wasn't only about the racket they were making; it was more personal than that. He insulted their appearances and their intelligence—wittily and with his usual articulate brio, since every occasion and opportunity had to be The Lewis Braid Show. He wanted to solve the noise problem, but not as much as he wanted to make everyone else in the restaurant laugh.

None of us did. We looked down at the floor and wished it would swallow us up. I remember feeling ashamed to be out for dinner with someone who could behave in that way. Flora turned bright red and mumbled, "Lew-*is*," as she always did. He never normally had trouble raising a laugh, but he misjudged his audience on this occasion and took it too far.

Assuming I find him today, I'm going to need to talk to him alone in order to get anywhere.

I wonder if he'll deem it worth staging The Lewis Braid Show for me alone. Probably. One person is still an audience, though a small one. I expect his first move will be an attempt to lavish hospitality on me. *"Beth! What a fantastic surprise! It's so great to see you. Let me take you on a boat trip/to the best beach for miles around/to a baseball game!"*

When he realizes that I'm as determined to know the truth as he is to keep it from me, will the friendly façade slip? And the question that really interests me: if it does, what will I see?

**By 8** a.m., I'm already so tired that I could sleep for another seven hours if I let my eyes close. No chance of that. Not with Lewis Braid maybe about to arrive at any moment.

I'm sitting in the back of a taxi in the vast outdoor car park that belongs to his company, VersaNova. My driver called it a "parking lot." It's so well landscaped and generously proportioned, it almost seems to be the main point of this whole exercise—as if someone designed an enormous, attractive car park first, for its own sake, and then said, "You know what? It's a shame to waste this—let's put the head office of a multi-million-dollar tech company next to it."

Despite the early hour, I'm not the only person here. There are plenty of other cars around. None, yet, looks expensive enough to belong to Lewis Braid.

Now that I'm here at his workplace, in the full light of a day that promises to be warm and sunny, the thoughts I was thinking in my hotel room a few hours ago seem almost deranged. I came pretty close to wondering if Lewis was evil. He and Flora might be mixed up in something strange and unsavory—I'm certain they are, in fact—but there's a lot of distance between unsavory and monstrous. Lewis Braid is hardly a murderous villain.

*You can handle him. You can handle the encounter you're about to have.*

Assuming he comes into the office today.

I stare at the tanned, tire-shaped bulges of skin at the base of my taxi driver's skull and wish I could feel as calm as he seems. He's been luxuriating in silence all the way from the Marriott to VersaNova, as if wanting me to notice that it's a deliberate lifestyle choice. When I asked if he'd be happy to wait for as long as I need him to this morning, he did some slow, relaxed nodding. He has the manner of someone who would only emit words if you pierced a thick plastic seal inside him, turned him upside down and squeezed him hard.

I sit up straight as a car that looks like a contender pulls into the lot. It's low, flat, waxed to a powerful shine. No roof.

*It's him. Lewis.*

I open the taxi's passenger door. "I'll be as quick as I can," I say to my driver as if he's urged me to hurry. His eyes are half closed. I'm not sure he's fully awake.

Lewis is quicker at getting out of cars than I am. By the time I'm out, he's several feet ahead, swinging a large black leather bag around and humming a tune—a gratingly fast-paced, bouncy one, if you're jet-lagged. Whatever he's hiding, he doesn't seem unduly worried about it.

He hasn't seen me. He's marching along briskly. Soon he'll reach the building, go inside, and then I'll have to deal with doormen, receptionists and probably security checks in order to get to him. He'll have a choice about whether to see me or not, whereas if I can get his attention now . . .

I open my mouth to yell his name, then notice that he's stopped suddenly, on the steps up to the revolving entrance door. He pulls a phone out of his pocket. Slowly, I move closer. He's facing the building, and has no idea that I'm approaching.

If he turns around and sees me, I'll say, "Hi, Lewis," as if I wanted him to notice me. Which I did, until this phone call happened. Now I'm hoping I can get close enough to listen, unobserved. The change in his body language tells me it isn't a run-of-the-mill conversation that he's having. He looks braced, somehow—as if the outcome of the call matters to him a lot. Maybe this is what all high-powered business calls look like.

I creep as close to him as I dare, then duck in between two cars and kneel down so that I won't be visible if he decides he'd like a change of view while making his call. I hear him say, "Are you ready for Daily Responses? What?" he snaps. It sounds as if he's been told something he wasn't expecting to hear and doesn't like it much. "Ten minutes late, yes. Where are you?" he barks at whoever he's speaking to. "And where should you be?" he asks in the exact same tone after a short pause.

From cheery, haven't-a-care-in-the-world tune hummer to ice-cold Condemnatron boss in a few seconds. This is familiar; Lewis's demeanor used to change with dazzling speed when I knew him. In a minute he might be humming merrily again.

I hope so. That'll make it easier for me to pop up as soon as this phone call is over with my carefully rehearsed, "Hey, Lewis. You said I should come and visit you in Florida, so here I am!"

"And *what* are you?" he asks whoever he's speaking to.

Is he hoping for a response along the lines of "I'm a complete and utter fool whose entire life is a comprehensive failure"? It sounds like it. I wouldn't be surprised if someone's out of a job before the day is over.

"Good," says Lewis, sounding placated. Evidently his interlocutor has said the right thing. "I'll see you later."

Maybe the correct answer to "*What* are you?" and the one supplied, was "On my way in right now to apologize profusely and beg your forgiveness."

I wonder what Daily Responses is. Is Lewis on his

way there now? It sounds like a strange kind of religious service—like the masses I used to attend at my Catholic school. They involved prayers and responses. VersaNova must have a daily ritual that's the secular equivalent. This being America, it probably involves yoga, green tea and affirmations.

If Lewis's colleague is ten minutes late, doesn't that mean he is too? Maybe the colleague is supposed to be there already, before him.

He puts his phone back in his pocket, turning slightly. I duck down lower. Having him see me is one thing; being caught eavesdropping is another.

*That could happen. He could, at this moment, be striding toward my hiding place.*

All I can do is wait, crouch and pray. Time passes. No one appears. Once I think it's safe, I stand up and rub the small of my back.

The steps are empty. There's no sign of Lewis anywhere in the car park. He must have gone inside.

*Damn.*

Though it's not necessarily a bad thing. Talking inside beats talking in a car park, assuming he agrees to see me. And if he refuses, I'll know for certain that I'm on the right track. A Lewis Braid with no guilty conscience would come bounding out of his office to greet an old friend.

VersaNova's lobby is covered, bottom to top, in glossy veined stone of an indeterminate noncolor. At its center is a reception desk made of the same stone that looks as if it has grown up out of the floor. Three receptionists are lined up behind the desk, looking like hopeful contestants in a game show with a ludicrously high budget. Above their heads, there's a large silver plaque embedded in the wall, bearing VersaNova Techologies' logo.

Two of the receptionists are smiling too hard at me. I walk over to the third. She looks the least suspiciously radiant. "I'd like to speak to Lewis Braid," I tell her. "I just saw him arrive." On her name badge it says "Wayna Skinner" and, beneath that, "I make sure to want from a feeling of abundance."

As I suspected: yoga, green tea and affirmations.

I can't see the badge of the receptionist on the far left—it's too far away—but the one in the middle, Lisa Pearce, has some words of wisdom on her badge too: "Failure only lasts forever if I'm too scared to try again." I might suggest they introduce similar badges at Bankside Park: "Camilla Hosmer. Lies, false accusations and sporadic racism keep me looking young."

I think about what Lewis said on the phone about having a favorite life coach. Was it his idea to pin inspiring messages to the company's receptionists? It wouldn't surprise me, though the Lewis I knew had no time at all for new-age nonsense. America might have changed him, I suppose, or he might be cynically playing the corporate game. I wonder if he'll be willing to miss Daily Responses in order to talk to me.

"Do you have an appointment with Dr. Braid?" Wayna Skinner asks me.

"No."

"Then you'll need to make one. He doesn't see anyone without an appointment."

"Can you tell him Beth Leeson is here? I think he'll see me. Tell him I've come all the way from England, in response to his invitation the other night. I'm an old friend."

"Oh, I see. Awesome. Let me see what I can do for you." She picks up the phone. "Martha? It's Wayna. There's a lady here to see Dr. Braid. A Beth Leeson. She's an old friend he invited over. Thank you."

I wish I could witness the moment of Martha telling Lewis I'm here: downstairs, in his building. What will he think? How will he react?

"I sure will. Thank you, Martha." Wayna hangs up the phone. "He'll see you. Please stand in front of the camera and I'll take a photo for your pass."

"Camera?"

"Up there. Can I see your ID? Passport?"

Luckily I still have it in my bag, from the airport. I trust my own ability to look after my handbag more than I trust any hotel safe.

With her friendly smile fixed in place, Wayna stares at my passport photograph and me for longer than anyone in an airport ever has. "My hair was different then," I tell her.

Finally she places a laminated pass in my hands with excessive care, as if she's granting me access to the country's nuclear codes. The photograph VersaNova's camera has taken of me from on high makes my head look huge and my body tiny and tapering.

"Take the elevator up to five and Martha will meet you there," she says. "Have a great visit!"

The elevator is good company. It lets rip with an exuberant, prerecorded "Level! Five!" as we come to a stop. The doors open and I step out into a beige-carpeted reception area. There are two sets of white double doors and four orange leather chairs lined up against one wall, but no Martha. I'm wondering if I ought to do anything apart from wait when one of the doors swings open.

"Lewis."

"Beth! It's really you! Is Dom with you?"

"No. Just me."

"You should have brought the whole family. What a

treat it is to see you!" He strides over and wraps me in a hug. I think about resisting, even as I hug him back. In his best moments, this was what was great about spending time with Lewis. He could make you feel as if you were his favorite treat in a way that no one else could.

"Maybe some other time," I say. "I came alone because . . . I'm not on holiday. This isn't a fun trip for me."

"Isn't it?" Lewis laughs. "So you're here to work? Great! Our latest prototype needs to be ready for market in five months. Want to help with that?"

"I want some answers. Ones that are true." I try to say this hopefully, as if I believe he's going to help me.

"Well, you've come to the right place. I'm always happy to give true answers to true questions. But let's hold this Q and A in my office, where we can have some privacy—in case this turns out to be like the drinking games we used to play. Remember those? Share a sordid secret or down one more shot."

Something about his manner makes me wonder if he's prepared for this. Did he expect that one day I'd come here and appeal directly to him? Did he take steps to make sure I soon ran out of other options, relishing the prospect of using his charm to turn Beth-the-problem into Beth-who's-no-threat-at-all?

I laugh and try to look impressed and amused, knowing that's what he wants. I need to choose my words carefully—to make this The Beth Leeson Show, directed by me and not Lewis, unlike every other interaction I've ever had with him.

"I haven't brought any alcohol with me, but we could maybe play a variant of that game," I say as I follow him along a gleaming white corridor.

"Without the best bit? How would that work? Would there be any refreshments at all? I've got the wherewithal to make us some beautiful mint tea in my office."

"Great. So the new game can be sordid-secret swapping," I say smoothly. "We can drink mint tea and swap secrets." It's not as hard to talk like this as it would be to anyone who wasn't Lewis. I'd forgotten this about him: in order for a conversation with him to work, you often had to imitate his manner, and you hoped no one heard you doing it.

"I refuse to believe you have any sordid secrets, Beth." We've stopped. He opens a door and gestures for me to go in.

"Maybe not sordid, but I do have secrets," I say, staying where I am, in the corridor. "Doesn't everybody?"

"I don't think so. Imagine that." Lewis looks serious

suddenly. "Imagine having none at all. Wouldn't that be horrible?"

"I'm not sure."

"Nothing that you'd mind everyone knowing about you, nothing that you keep just for you and maybe a few trusted friends? I'd hate it."

*Don't ask him to tell you his secret. Not yet. It's too soon.*

"Am I your trusted friend?" I say instead.

A grin spreads across his face. "I could slip easily into people-pleasing mode and say yes, but you said you wanted true answers, so. I don't know, Beth. You and Dom disappeared from my life in kind of a weird way. What was that all about? Flora would never tell me. She wanted me to believe we'd all drifted apart but I don't think that's what happened, is it?"

"No."

"No. I told Flora I didn't believe that story, so she made up a better one, hoping I'd like it more: some nonsense about you cutting up a photo of our children."

"That's true. I did. But I don't think that's why our friendship ended."

"It's *true*?" Lewis laughs. He looks delighted—as if it's the best news he's heard in a long time. He reaches out and squeezes my shoulder. The doors at the far end of the corridor open and two women appear.

Lewis waves in their direction without really looking at them, then gestures again through his open office door. "Come on in," he says. "I haven't got long, but I want you all to myself for the time we do have. Something tells me you and I are going to have *fun* today."

# 20

There's a framed photograph on Lewis's desk: of him, Thomas and Emily sitting outside a beach-front restaurant, under a green-and-white-striped awning. All three of them have lobsters in front of them and they're all laughing.

"No Flora?" I say, pointing to it. "No Georgina?"

"In that particular photo?" says Lewis. He moves over to inspect it more closely. "I've never seen either of them, and I work next to that photo most days of my life. But let me know if you spot something I've missed. Mint tea? Once I've made it, I'll take the photo out of its frame and you can cut it up if you like. It's okay, I've got plenty more." He grins to make it clear he's joking.

"You didn't want a reminder of all four of them on your desk?"

"I'm fascinated by these questions." Lewis arranges white square mugs in square saucers at the drinks station beneath his huge, metal-framed window. "I change the picture all the time," he says. He sounds gleeful. If he wishes I hadn't turned up in his new American life, he's doing an excellent job of concealing it. "This week it's Thomas and Emily's turn in the frame. Everyone gets a turn. Just like, at home, I change my colleague picture regularly. On the mantelpiece in the living room, I currently have a framed photo of Aaron and David from Marketing."

I laugh. I think it's convincing.

"So, when does the secret-swapping start?" Lewis asks, handing me my tea.

"Soon as you like. I'll go first. I cut up a family photo Flora sent me—one that came with a Christmas card. Actually, I didn't cut it up completely. I just cut Georgina out of it."

I watch Lewis's face to see if anything changes when I mention her name. It doesn't. All I see is intense curiosity and relish, no discomfort or guilt. No sadness either.

"Go on," says Lewis. "I'm intrigued."

"I'd have thought you'd be disgusted, or furious," I say. "Georgina was only a tiny baby. I cut her out of a photograph of your family. She fell on the floor."

"So what?" Lewis chuckles. "This was more than ten years ago. Whatever you did, you did it to a piece of paper, not to my daughter. I'd love to know why, though." He walks over to his desk, sits behind it, then uses it as a footstool, putting his feet up on a pile of glossy brochures.

I try to focus on his face, not the soles of his shoes. "When I saw the picture, I realized Flora had been pregnant and had a baby, and not told me. I took that as evidence of how little I mattered to her. The photo she sent was the first I knew of Georgina's existence. I was upset, and I overreacted. Then I felt terrible about it. Flora found out I'd done it, which didn't help our friendship, but that wasn't the cause of the rift between us. That was something else."

"Was it a rift? Is that what it was?" asks Lewis. "A rift sounds dramatic and exciting. You're telling me a rift happened and I missed it? I'll be honest: I always thought the root cause was envy."

"Because you suddenly had money? No. For a long time I thought it was the money that had changed things between us, but I was wrong."

"Then what was it?"

"That's what I'm waiting for you to tell me."

"Well . . . let's see." He smiles conspiratorially, as if

we're both enjoying the game. "I've never cut up any photographs of your children."

"You know what I want you to tell me, Lewis."

His face changes. The smile is gone. Now he's staring at me earnestly, with sympathy in his eyes. "I think I do," he says. "I think you want a story that explains why you've seen Flora in England recently. The thing is, Beth, you can't have. Flora hasn't been in England. She's been here, with her family. I don't know who you saw, but it wasn't her."

"Maybe I saw the woman who lives there now," I say.

"Quite possibly."

"Jeanette Cater?"

"I can't remember her name, if it's even the same family that we sold to."

"Don't you remember Kevin and Jeanette Cater?"

"Kevin Cater . . . Yes, I think that is who we sold to."

"You used to work with him."

"No, I didn't."

"He worked at CEMA while you and Flora were there."

"Did he?" Lewis looks mildly interested in this coincidence. "You could be right, but I didn't know him.

Flora might have. Beth, are you all right? You're starting to worry me."

"I'm fine. Do you have a current photo of Georgina? I'd like to see one."

"Not with me, no."

"None on your phone?"

"No."

"How come?"

"Do you know about Georgina?" Lewis asks. "I suppose you might have found out if you've been scouring the UK in search of Flora."

"What's there to know?"

"That she died," Lewis says simply. "Which . . . you knew. Okay. Did Flora's parents tell you?"

"Why did you lie to me? I asked you how old she was now and you said twelve."

"I didn't want to discuss the death of my daughter with someone who's not part of my life anymore. My aim was to get on to a new subject as swiftly as possible. I miscalculated, clearly, because now we're having the conversation I didn't want to have, only face-to-face."

*No.* He sounds so plausible, but it can't be true. Or rather, what he's told me so far might be true but he's saying it to obscure the bigger truth, whatever that is. If he really had nothing to hide, why would he allow someone he hasn't spoken to for twelve years to intrude into his morning with a barrage of strange questions? He wouldn't. He'd ask me to leave.

"I'm sorry Georgina died," I say.

"Thank you. Me too." Lewis smiles sadly. "This game turned out to be less fun than I hoped it would be."

"Tell me the truth, Lewis. Please."

"I just have."

"The whole truth." I'm not scared to push him further. What's he going to do, leap out of his chair and punch me? I'm assuming he cares what the people in this building think of him and so wouldn't risk it. "If you and Flora are still married, why are there no photos of her on your Instagram? Why is she living with Kevin Cater in your old house, and calling herself Jeanette? Whose are the two children that live in that house? They're yours and Flora's, aren't they? So why are they living with Kevin Cater? I've *seen* them, Lewis. I know you're their father."

"Are you lonely, Beth?"

"No. I'm not lonely at all."

"Are you fulfilled?"

"What do you mean?"

"You've flown all the way from England to sit in my office and fire strange accusations at me. They do sound like accusations, whether that's your intention or not—as if you're a TV detective trying to crack a case.

Which casts me in the role of 'villain you've exposed, about to be locked up at Her Majesty's pleasure.' In fact, I'm someone who's done nothing wrong and who used to be your friend. Whose third child died tragically many years ago, and who didn't and doesn't want to talk about that with someone he's no longer close to. There's nothing in my life that justifies a manic interrogation, so . . . this has to be about whatever's going on with you. I'm wondering if you're okay."

I decide to try a new tactic. "Tell me the truth, Lewis. I don't much care what it is. All I want is to know. People are trying to tell me I didn't see something I know I saw, and I've had enough. At least confirm that it was Flora I saw, even if you won't tell me anything else."

A flicker of impatience passes across his face. "Beth, I can take you to Flora right now if you like."

"She might be in Florida now, but she wasn't the two times I saw her."

"Yes, she was." Lewis raises one hand, finger pointed upward. "I've thought of a solution.

"Can you tell me the exact dates and times of your alleged Flora sightings? There's rarely a day that she doesn't see someone—her friends, charity committee ladies, tennis club people. I can probably track down whoever she was with when you claim to have seen her in the UK."

"To provide an alibi, you mean?" An extremely well-paid one, no doubt. "I'm sure you could, but why would you? If you're telling the truth and nothing suspicious is going on, why would you indulge my irrational obsession?"

"The very question I'm asking myself at the moment." Lewis smiles again. "Because you were once a good friend, I guess. As for something suspicious . . . even if Flora was in the UK, which she wasn't, how is that suspicious? She has a passport. She's allowed to travel."

"The two children living at 16 Wyddial Lane are called Thomas and Emily."

Lewis laughs. "Yeah, right. Of course they are."

"I heard Flora call them by those names. They look identical to . . ." I point at the photo on his desk. "To the way *they* looked at the same age. That's how I know they're yours."

"Wait, wait . . ." For the first time since I arrived, he looks as if he doesn't know exactly what to say next. "Beth, I don't want to hurt your feelings, but . . . do you realize how unwell you sound?"

"I might sound that way to someone else, who knew

nothing, but it's not how I sound to you. To you, I sound like someone who knows a bit too much. Whereas to me, I sound like someone who knows too little."

"This is verging on pathological now," he says.

"We could easily sort it out once and for all."

"How?"

"Take me to see Thomas and Emily. If they tell me Flora lives with you all and hasn't been in England recently, I might believe them."

"You know what?" He sounds angry. Finally. "I'm not going to do that. I'm not going to introduce my kids to someone displaying pathologically obsessive behavior. Even if she is an old friend."

"All right. Never mind. They'd probably lie for you anyway if you paid them enough. If mine are anything to go by, teenagers are generally bribe-able."

"Are you listening to yourself? Can you hear how you sound?"

"Who's Chimpy?"

"Chimpy?" I see a flash of what looks like genuine confusion. "I have no idea who Chimpy is. Who is it?"

"I don't know. I think you do, though." As I say it, I'm aware that it doesn't feel true.

He doesn't know. Everything else I've said, even if he wasn't expecting it, he knew it might come up. But not this. Not Chimpy.

"What's happened to you, Beth? Hearing you say these things . . . it makes me ashamed for you. How have you become this? I can withstand any attack you want to launch at me, but it makes me sad for you."

"Nothing you say is going to work on me," I tell him. "Not until you tell me the truth."

"All right, well . . ." He shrugs. "I guess we're done here."

"Are we? You're not curious about anything I've said? If you don't believe the two children living in your old house are called Thomas and Emily, you could easily check. Ring Huntingdon police and ask for PC Paul Pollard. He'll tell you."

"The police? You went to the police about this?"

I nod. "I'm worried about the children. And Flora. She would never have cut off her parents and stopped them from seeing their grandchildren. Not of her own free will."

"Ah, I see. You think I'm controlling Flora? Stopping her making her own decisions?"

"She was always scared of you. I didn't see it at the time, but now I see it as clearly as I see you standing here in front of me. All those times she mumbled, 'Lew-*is*,' when you were off on one of your rants. I always assumed she was embarrassed, but she wasn't. She was scared. That was her way of begging you to stop—and even that she could only bring herself to do in the mildest way. That's why I didn't recognize it for the fear it was. And I think it must have gotten worse and worse. The last time you all came around was the worst I've ever seen it. Do you remember ordering Flora out of our living room so that we wouldn't catch a glimpse of her breasts while she fed Georgina? She obeyed without question. She always obeyed you, but on that day she looked properly scared. I was too wrapped up in my own guilt about that stupid photo to notice at the time, but I remember it vividly. That was fear I saw on her face. Fear of you."

"I feel this is where I should say, 'Much as I'd like to spend the morning talking about my wife's breasts . . .'" Neither of us laughs. Lewis says, "You're scraping the barrel, Beth. Her *breasts*? I don't know what you're talking about. I don't remember . . . No, I'll go even further. I don't think anything like that happened the last time we all got together. In fact, I'm sure it didn't. Flora sunbathes topless on beaches all over the world. You know she does: you've been on holiday with us enough times to know. People in every continent have seen her tits and I don't give a shit. Wow." He exhales slowly. "That's something I didn't expect to be saying this morning."

"You're not going to make me doubt myself, Lewis. I've spoken to Tilly from number 3 Wyddial Lane. The woman you stalked, remember?"

"You want to talk about stalking?" He's not quite shouting, but he's almost there.

I'm in the middle of the room. He's behind his desk. I could make a dash for the door and I'd get to it before he could stop me.

If I need to. I still don't think he'll turn violent. His losses of temper were always verbal only. I never saw him hit anything or anyone. He wouldn't risk me running out of the room yelling that Lewis Braid had assaulted me.

"What is it that you're doing if not stalking, Beth? Coming all the way to America to tell me about some children that are nothing to do with me . . . My life, Flora's life, it's none of your fucking business. I owe you nothing. No explanations, nothing! You have the nerve to say Flora's scared of me? You're the one she's scared of. Not me. *You*. She never runs away from *me*."

My breath catches in my throat. Does he realize what he's done? Lewis closes his eyes. He slumps a little in his chair.

*Yes. He realizes.*

"So you admit Flora was in Huntingdon—that I saw her there, and that she ran away from me in the car park? There's no point in denying it now. We both heard what you just said."

I count the seconds, waiting for an answer. Finally, he gives a small nod.

*Thank you. I wasn't wrong and I'm not crazy.*

"Why would Flora be scared of me?"

"Because she needed you to leave her alone, and you wouldn't. Instead, you turned into a stalker."

"Needed me to leave her alone, or wanted me to?"

"I can't answer that," Lewis says wearily. "I'm not her."

"What do you mean?"

"You'll find out soon enough. Come on." He pushes back his chair and stands up. "I'm not having this conversation without Flora."

"Where are we going?"

"Do you want answers? I thought that's why you came here—for answers?"

"It is."

"Then you need to trust me, or you won't get any. Which might be better for everybody, but it's too late for that. You won't leave it alone, so you're going to get your answers—whatever the cost, right?"

"What do you mean?"

He looks as if he's weighing whether to say what's on his mind. "Since Georgina died, Flora hasn't been . . . She's not the same person you remember, as you've so observantly noticed. Seeing and speaking to you will make her much worse. *That's* why we've been trying to keep you at bay. It's not going to help Flora to share intimate details of our life to satisfy your curiosity. It's not going to help me either, as the person who has to look after Flora—which is why I'd very much appreciate it if you'd turn around, go home and forget all about us. But you're not going to do that, are you?"

How has he done it? How has he gone from lying brazenly to my face to making me feel guilty?

*He's a liar. The guilt you're feeling is a lie. Don't let him see it.*

"If you want to protect Flora from having to talk to me, you could easily do that," I tell him. "Give me an explanation that makes sense."

"It wouldn't be fair to do that without involving Flora. It's her story to tell as much as mine. Where are you staying? A hotel?"

"The Marriott, Delray Beach."

"Go there now. Flora and I will meet you there in an hour, hour and a half. Soon as we can."

*Will you? Or will you take Flora and the kids and run?*

I can't think of any way to stop him from leaving his office and going wherever he wants. I can hardly block his way to the door, or lock him in.

*Locked up at Her Majesty's pleasure . . .* Lewis said it before and it stuck in my mind.

*Wait. What if . . .*

An idea is starting to form in my mind. Of all the expressions Lewis might have used, he chose that one. *He* chose it: Lewis Braid.

I'll need to check to see if I could be right. A simple Internet search will sort that out.

"I'll see you at the Marriott," I say as evenly as I can manage.

"Are you all right?" Lewis asks. "You look a bit . . ."

"I'm fine."

"What room are you in at the hotel?"

"We won't be going to my room," I tell him. "I'll meet you in the lobby."

We leave the building together. Lewis smiles and waves at the three receptionists on his way out. I hand my laminated pass back to Wayna.

Once we're outside, Lewis heads for his car without looking at me or saying good-bye. I walk over to my taxi, more grateful to be reunited with my silent driver than I would have believed possible.

As we pull out of VersaNova's car park, I fumble in my bag for my phone. It won't take long to search for the name that I might have invented . . .

A few seconds later, I have the confirmation I need. And no idea at all what it might mean.

# 21

I'm sitting in the lobby of the Marriott, facing the main doors, when Lewis and Flora walk in. *At last.* It's nearly two hours since Lewis and I left VersaNova together. He looks preoccupied and determined, as if he's in the middle of completing an important task and nobody had better interrupt him until it's done. He's still holding his black leather bag, the same one he had with him at the office. Flora looks at me, then quickly looks away, as if she might still avoid an encounter with me if she plays this right.

It occurs to me only now, when I see them together: he looks a lot younger than she does. That never used to be true. Whatever they've been through, she's come out of it worse.

I stand up and walk toward them. Flora stops. For

a moment, I wonder if she might turn and run again. Lewis drapes his arm over her shoulder. Anyone else in the hotel lobby who observed the gesture would think it was affectionate: a man putting his arm around his wife. To me it looks as if Lewis also fears Flora might try and escape.

None of us says hello. Lewis says, "Let's go to your room, Beth."

"I told you, I'm not doing that. We can sit there and talk." I point to an octagonal space nearby, marked out by eight white floor-to-ceiling pillars. Between the pillars, on a raised platform, there are tables and chairs. "No one's sitting there. We'd have it to ourselves."

"I'm not doing this in a public place," says Lewis. "Either we go to your room or Flora and I leave. What do you think we're going to do to you, Beth?"

My room has a balcony that overlooks the swimming-pool terrace, where there are bound to be a good number of people sunbathing or reading on loungers. If I leave the door to the balcony wide open, so that I can shout for help if I need to . . .

"Can I see what's inside your bags before you bring them into my room?" I say.

"From TV detective to airport security." Lewis shakes his head.

I don't care how disappointed he is in me. I don't

trust him and I'm not taking any risks. I've never trusted anyone less, in fact. He needn't be here, with a story he's reluctant but prepared to tell me. There's only one reason why he'd bring Flora here and give up his working day to explain things to me that—as he correctly pointed out—are none of my business: he's still hoping to control me. He wants to satisfy my curiosity because he fears what will happen if he doesn't.

"You can look in Flora's bag." He pulls it off her shoulder and hands it to me. "Mine's full of confidential documents. I can leave it in the car, if it bothers you?"

"Yes, please."

"Fine. Give me five minutes." Flora tries to follow him when he moves to leave the lobby. "What are you doing?" he asks her.

"Coming with you."

"Why? Wait here."

He leaves. Flora stares down at the ground.

"Are you angry with me?" I ask her.

"No. Of course not."

"I wish you and I could talk alone."

"We can't," she says quickly.

"Now? Or ever?"

"We won't see each other again after today."

"Why? Because Lewis won't let you see me again?"

"We only agreed to meet you so that you'd leave us alone. You need to stop . . . what you're doing. Stop following me around." She looks up at me. There are tears in her eyes. "I don't want to see you."

"I'm not here because I want us to be friends again," I say. "If you don't want that then I don't either. All I want is to know that you and your children are all right—your two youngest children, who have the same names as your two oldest. Don't they?"

She says nothing. Her eyes flit back and forth.

"Why, Flora? Why would you do that? I've seen Yanina picking Thomas up. They didn't look at each other or speak to each other. I'm worried for him and Emily. I saw him walking along with the sole of his shoe hanging off. Even if you don't care about yourself, you should care about those children."

"I care," she says.

"Well, then, you must know they're not okay. And you're not okay either. Let me help. Tell me what's going on before Lewis comes back. We don't have to wait here for him. We could go somewhere else where—"

"I don't need your help. I don't need you to worry about me."

"If you don't want to talk to me, why are you here?"

"Lewis says we have to, otherwise you won't ever

leave us alone, and that's all I want: for you to leave me alone." Instead, Lewis has left her alone with me. Why? He could have easily let her go with him to the car.

It would have looked odd, though—her trotting after him like a slave. And he knows he's trained her well enough that she won't say anything. Unless . . . No. Unless nothing. Every time I find myself starting to wonder if maybe Flora's the one in control, I think back to the way she and Lewis were when I knew them before.

He's the boss. Always was, always will be.

"Who's Chimpy?" I ask.

Flora looks puzzled, as I expected her to. "Chimpy? I don't know."

"I'm sorry about Georgina," I tell her. "When I saw you outside your house in Hemingford Abbots, you were talking on the phone. I heard you say that you were very lucky. To lose a child isn't lucky."

"You think I don't know that?"

"Why did you describe yourself as lucky? It might sound like a strange question, but I heard you say it twice. Once was outside the house and the other time was when Lewis first rang me, after I sent him a message on Instagram. I heard you in the background saying those exact same words: 'I'm very lucky.' "

"I *am* lucky." She looks away. "Only people with

nothing to live for are unlucky. Do you think that because Georgina died, I have nothing to live for? I have other children, and I love them."

"How many?"

"What?"

"How many other children do you have? What are their names?"

"How can you do this to me?" she whispers. "I've told you I don't want it. The children are fine."

"Flora, they're not. They're . . ." *Too late.* Lewis is back. My time alone with Flora has run out. I try not to feel frustrated. It's not as if the conversation was going well.

"I'm good to go," Lewis says. "No bag, no concealed weapons." He twirls around. "Do you want to pat me down?"

"Wait here," I say. "I need to use the bathroom. Then we can go up."

"There's probably one in your room." He smiles. "I'll help you find it."

"I'm not leaving the two of you alone in my hotel room."

"Worried we'll snoop around in all your private stuff? I think that's what they call projection."

"Wait here. I won't be long."

Locked inside a cubicle, I repeat to myself the

words, "You are not at risk of physical harm" until I believe them. Then I pull my phone out of my bag, go to Voice Memos and press the "Record" button. I don't know what story I'm about to be told or if any of it will be true, but I want it on record, whatever it turns out to be.

**Up in** my room, I decide I'm not going to open the door to the balcony. Now that we're all here, the feeling that I might be in danger has evaporated, and the only thing worrying me is that I'm about to waste more time listening to lies. How would I know?

Lewis and Flora sit in the two chairs opposite the desk and TV. I sit on the edge of the bed nearest them. "Well?" I say, putting my bag down on the floor in front of my feet. Hopefully it will be close enough for the recording to work.

"What do you want to know?" Lewis asks. "We'll answer your questions on two conditions. One: that you leave us alone afterward and don't reappear in our lives at any point in the future, for any reason. Can you give us that guarantee?"

"If you tell me the truth, and if the children aren't at risk of harm."

"The children are fine. Though I'm not sure which children you mean. Presumably the younger two?"

Lewis raises a hand to silence me. "Between us, Flora and I have four children. All of them are safe, loved and well looked after."

"What's your other condition?" I ask him.

"Confidentiality. You can tell Dominic. I know him well enough to know he won't say anything. I assume he's still a fan of the path of least resistance?"

"He won't tell anybody."

"Good. Impress on him that he mustn't. And you tell no one apart from him. Understood?"

I nod. Lewis must be delusional if he thinks it's a real promise. I'll tell whoever the hell I feel like telling—whoever I think needs to know.

"Thank you," he says. "It's all yours, Beth. Ask away."

"Why did you lie? Why pretend you and Flora are still together? You're not still together, are you?"

"No."

"And Flora's married to Kevin Cater?"

"Yes. Though she's not called Flora anymore. Her legal name is Jeanette Cater."

I turn to Flora. "Why did you change it? And if you're married to Kevin Cater, why do you live in the same house you lived in with Lewis? Why call your children Thomas and Emily when you've already got two children with those names?"

"Flora?" Lewis prompts. "I'm not doing this on my own."

"And why are they *your* children, if she's with Kevin now?" I ask him. "They're not Kevin's. I've seen them. They're yours. They have your eyes, like the other Thomas and Emily. I thought they were the same people. I thought the Thomas and Emily I knew hadn't grown in twelve years—that's how similar they look."

"They're Kevin's children," says Flora. "Mine and Kevin's. You're right, they look like . . . their older half-brother and sister, and their eyes aren't Lewis's. There are brown-eyed people in my family. My mum has brown eyes like that. Maybe they're her eyes. I know I always said they were the spitting image of Lewis's but I never really believed it."

"She only said it to keep me happy," says Lewis. "They both had her face, and she thought I'd mind. I probably would have, in those days. I was still an emotional child when we had our kids."

"Why did you give the children you had with Kevin the same names?" I ask Flora.

"Georgina's death . . ." she starts to say.

"What? What about it?"

She seems to have frozen. We wait for nearly ten seconds. Then she turns to Lewis. "I can't," she says. "You."

She sounds like a small child. *You do it, Daddy.*

Lewis rubs his temples with the flats of his hands. "Me," he says in a low voice. "All right. You want my version? Flora's never heard my version before, not in my words. Why would she? She already knows the story, so I've never needed to tell her, but she seems to want to hear it now. She won't like it much, but okay. You sure you don't want to take over?" he asks her.

She shakes her head.

Lewis looks at me. "You won't like it either. Georgina didn't die of natural causes. Gerard and Rosemary no doubt told you it was Sudden Infant Death Syndrome. It wasn't. It was neither natural nor unavoidable. Georgina died because Flora made two bad decisions. One: to have Georgina sleep in our bed. Thomas never did, Emily didn't . . . but Georgina was premature and Flora was neurotic about her. For no reason that I could fathom, she wanted Georgina in bed next to her every night. Insisted it would be better for her. Fine—she was the mother, and I assumed she knew what she was talking about. I moved into the spare room. Couldn't sleep properly with a snuffling baby that close.

"One night, I came home to find Flora halfway down a bottle of white wine. I was surprised. She didn't normally drink, but she'd had a tough day with all three kids being difficult in some way. Still, I told her to take it easy. She said she was fine, she'd only had a couple of glasses. I told her that was more than enough and she swore at me—said it was none of my fucking business. It was the first time she'd ever spoken to me like that.

"We had a big row. I went up to my office—my office at home—slammed the door and worked for the rest of the evening. Flora gave the children their baths. That was supposed to be my job, but that night I didn't care. I was too angry. I heard Flora putting Thomas and Emily to bed, heard them asking why Daddy wasn't joining in. Then she must have taken Georgina and gone to bed because I didn't hear anything else. At about ten thirty, I realized I hadn't eaten and was starving. Flora hadn't brought me up any supper, which I took to mean that she was still angry with me. I looked in the fridge and the oven—nothing. So I went out. Drove into Huntingdon, got myself a curry. Came home, went to bed in the spare room. I was still pretty angry, and wondering what I'd do if Flora didn't apologize first thing in the morning. There was no way I was putting up with treatment like that. I went to sleep."

He seems to be steeling himself to continue. Finally he says, "A few hours later, I was woken by screaming from Flora. I ran to our bedroom and found Georgina lying there, dead. In our bed. She was blue. Not breathing. It was the worst moment of my life."

"I killed her," Flora says, her voice no more than a whisper. "I didn't murder her deliberately. What I did was worse, because I didn't want her to die but I still caused it to happen: the opposite of what I wanted. Even though I'd drunk that wine, I still put Georgina down by my side, as I always did. Normally it was fine."

"And this one night it wasn't," says Lewis. "Flora rolled on top of her and suffocated her."

"So now you know." Flora looks at me. "I'm a woman who got drunk and killed her baby."

"That's why you cut your parents out of your life," I say, starting to understand.

"Not just them," says Flora. "Everybody. Lewis, Thomas, Emily. You."

"What do you mean?"

"Lewis didn't want our marriage to end. Even after what I'd done. It was me. Lewis tried to help me. He was heroic. I didn't want help, though. I wanted to pretend it had never happened—and that meant getting far, far away from anyone who had known or cared about Georgina. The other two children, and Lewis . . ." Flora shakes her head. "They were my victims as much as she was. I'd deprived them of a sister, a daughter. I'd deprived my parents of a grandchild. I had to get away from all of them."

"And me?"

"No!" She says it as if having me in her life would have been the worst torment of all. "We'd been so close, Beth. You'd have sensed I was hiding something and dragged the truth out of me. And even if you hadn't, don't you understand? I couldn't tolerate any continuity with my old life. The only way I could live at all was in a world that had never known Georgina. If I could have erased everyone's memory . . . Obviously I couldn't, but I made Lewis vow never to tell the others what had happened."

"By the others, do you mean Thomas and Emily?" I ask.

Flora nods.

Lewis says, "It was bad enough that they'd lost their baby sister. Neither Flora nor I could stand the thought of them knowing the full truth: that their own mother's negligence had killed her. And no one else could know the truth either, least of all the authorities. Flora might have gone to prison for all we knew. Then Thomas and Emily would have a mother behind bars, I'd have a wife who was a convict. No. Intolerable. Believe me, Beth, I was as keen to conceal the truth as Flora was."

A tear rolls down Lewis's cheek and he wipes it away. I've never seen him cry before. I don't like it; it feels wrong.

"It was much easier to say that we'd found Georgina

dead and had no idea why she'd stopped breathing," he goes on. "Thomas and Emily were too young to connect that with the row they'd overheard the night before, me telling Flora to stop drinking."

"I couldn't go to prison," says Flora. "That would have been the thing . . ." She trails off.

"What?" I ask her.

"I was too scared to take my own life, after Georgina died. I wanted to, more than anything—to never feel anything ever again. Couldn't make myself go through with it. But if there was even a chance I'd go to prison I'd have done it."

"So you called it cot death and everyone believed you?"

"The parents don't get to call an infant death anything," says Lewis. "Doctors decide. We told everyone that we'd found Georgina in her cot, blue and not breathing. People couldn't have been more sympathetic. There was no hint of any suspicions in our direction. But Georgina had been born premature, and was maybe going to need surgery on her eye when she was a little bit older, so perhaps they found it easy to think of her as a flawed specimen."

Flora flinches.

Lewis lets out a ragged sigh. "It was a tragedy, and we were in shock and grieving, but we could have survived it. We could have rebuilt our lives—but Flora wouldn't allow that to happen. She couldn't give us that chance."

"I couldn't live with them and pretend," she says. "How could I stay there, knowing what I'd done? I didn't deserve beautiful children and a husband who loved me. And I couldn't live a lie, no matter how much Lewis wanted me to. What I really wanted, *all* I wanted, was to die. I prayed it would happen, without me having to do anything."

"There were moments when I could have killed her," says Lewis. "Not because of Georgina—because she was proposing to leave me, when all I'd done was protect her and our family."

"So you left?" I ask Flora. "You abandoned them all?"

"That's exactly what she did," says Lewis. "And cut off all contact. With everyone. I had to go with her to tell her parents. She begged me to do the talking, and I did it. I fucking did it, Beth. Then I had to tell Thomas and Emily that she couldn't be part of their lives anymore. Flora and I came up with the least upsetting story we could think of in the circumstances: Georgina dying had caused her to have a breakdown, and now she wasn't herself anymore and couldn't be around anyone, including them. It was devastating for them to hear that, but what could I do? I could hardly say, 'Mummy'll be back any minute now, she's just nipped to the shops.' She wasn't ever coming back to us. She'd made that clear, and I could see it. Even sitting in a room with me, having the conversations we needed to have, she couldn't stand it. It was like she'd developed an allergy to all of us—me and the children."

"To myself," Flora corrects him. "You reminded me, that's all—of the difference between what I used to be and what I'd become. It was better for Thomas and Emily not to be around me, given the state I was in. Lewis was a good dad, Beth. *Is* a good dad. Any damage I did by abandoning the family, he repaired."

"I'm not going to deny that. Fuck it." Lewis shifts in his chair. "I'm not. We had a rough few years, but slowly, steadily, Thomas and Emily—whose names Flora refuses to say, have you noticed, Beth?—grew into the happy, secure teenagers they are now. Thanks to me. And it has to stay that way. Over my dead body are they going to find out now, after all these years, that Georgina's death wasn't a tragic accident."

"I won't say anything," I tell him. What good would it do, at this late stage? "I'm so sorry. I can't imagine how awful it must have been."

"Well, what can I say?" Lewis laughs bitterly. "Thank you, Beth, for making this little trip down

Memory Lane possible. Can I go now? I need to get back to the office."

"Without me?" Flora asks expressionlessly.

"Yes, without you," he snaps. "I'm going to take a little break from trying to help you, if that's okay."

"But how will I get back to the house?"

"You'll figure out a way." Lewis stands up.

"I've got more questions," I say.

"Oh, I bet you have. Flora can answer them." In an angry, singsong voice he says, "Flora has decided today is a talking day. Good-bye, Beth."

Without another word, he leaves the room.

# 22

I stand up and walk over to the window, to give Flora a chance to compose herself. She started to cry when Lewis left and hasn't stopped since. Sunlight is streaming into the room, streaking the carpet and furniture with stripes of gold. They create a bar-like effect and make me think of prison—something that was in my mind even before Lewis and Flora came up to my hotel room, thanks to Chimpy.

There's a darkness in here that's almost suffocating; the light from outside can't touch it. The shimmering turquoise swimming pool, palm trees and orange sun umbrellas on the other side of the glass look as implausible as a stage set that's way too good to be true.

I flick the catch, slide the balcony door open and step outside. The hot air hugs my face. It's a welcome relief. When the heat gets too much, I slide the door closed again.

"You should tell the truth, Flora. To your parents, the police, everybody. Instead of walking around like a shadow, hiding a horrible secret. You shouldn't have to live like this for the rest of your life."

"It's better than having everyone know. Don't tell me it isn't. You can't imagine how it feels to have done what I've done. It would destroy my parents if they knew."

"And Thomas and Emily?" I say, wondering if Lewis is right about her unwillingness to say their names.

"Them too. I don't want to hurt Lewis's children any more than I already have. He's been good to me. No one deserves any more pain."

"Including you?"

"I deserve nothing," she says quietly. "Nothing good, anyway."

"They're your children too, Flora. Not only Lewis's."

"Not anymore."

"How much of what you've just told me do Kevin and Yanina know?"

"Nothing." An impatient look passes across her face. "Why do you think I married Kevin? If he'd known, I wouldn't have gone anywhere near him. After Georgina died, when I left everything behind, I thought I'd be alone forever. That was what I deserved and what I wanted. Then I met Kevin, and he . . . he pursued me. I realized that I could maybe have a family again. As long as no one in my new life knew the truth. I'd changed my name by then, to Jeanette Dawson. Dawson was my mum's maiden name. You won't be able to understand this, but . . . I convinced myself I was a different person."

"You didn't tell Kevin you'd been married before?"

"He knew about Lewis, but not that I'd had any children with him. I lied about that. When I was pregnant with . . ." She stops. Starts again. "I made sure he never came to doctor or hospital appointments. It wasn't hard. He had no interest in them. He's not interested in much, Kevin. I don't love him or particularly like him."

"Then why . . . ?"

"Can't you guess?" Flora smiles through her tears. "I wanted more children. Knowing you don't deserve something doesn't make you stop wanting it. I was weak. I shouldn't have let myself accept Kevin's proposal, but once I did, the rest just—" She breaks off and frowns. "No, it didn't just happen. That's not true. I let it happen. I was Jeanette now, so it was okay. That's what I told myself—that it would be okay."

"So you had two more children? With Kevin, not with Lewis?"

"They're Kevin's, Beth."

"You had two children, and you called them Thomas and Emily."

"You know I did. That's why you're here."

"Why did you choose those names?"

She stares at me. Is she hoping I'll withdraw the question?

"Why, Flora?"

"I don't know. I can't explain it. I wanted what I'd lost, I suppose. Kevin would have let me call them anything. Up to me, he said."

"How did he feel when you told him you were going to Florida suddenly? If he knows nothing about what happened in the past, how did you explain this trip? Isn't Kevin wondering what the hell's going on?"

"I blamed it on you," says Flora.

"Me?"

"When Lewis rang me to say you'd been in touch, my heart nearly stopped right then and there. I hadn't seen or heard from him in twelve years. I was a nervous wreck. There was no way you'd contact Lewis after so many years unless you suspected something—I knew that. And Marilyn Oxley, my neighbor . . . she'd told Kevin that you'd asked her if our children were called

Thomas and Emily. I had to get away from you, Beth. To make sure *this* didn't happen. I didn't want you to know, and I knew I could so easily break down and tell you if we met. You were my best friend for so long. We knew everything about each other, didn't we?"

I nod.

"I couldn't risk that. Lewis knew it was a risk, too. He said, 'Cast iron rule: you don't see her, you don't speak to her, you don't let her come anywhere near you.' So I did everything he said, like I always have, apart from that one night—the night Georgina died, when I wanted a drink and then another drink so badly that I ended up killing my own daughter."

"What happened to Georgina was an accident, Flora. If you want to say it was an accident that only happened because you made a bad decision, then tell yourself that . . . but even so, you should stop torturing yourself. Everyone makes bad decisions. And it was twelve years ago. Isn't it time you forgave yourself?"

"What an excellent idea." She eyes me coldly. "I'll just do that, then, shall I?"

"Has Lewis told you you should forgive yourself? If you always do what he says—"

"He said it when it first happened, before I told him I was leaving. Hasn't said it since." She smiles as if at a fond memory. "Lewis has always been extraordinarily selfish. Breathtakingly so, really. If I was going to remain as his wife and the mother of his children, then he didn't want me to torture myself. It would have a terrible effect on them—his family. But if I'm leaving? Well, then he's certainly not going to tell me to forgive myself, is he?"

"You said a minute ago that he'd been good to you."

"He has, purely for his and his children's sake. He doesn't care about me anymore. Couldn't you tell? I don't mind. I still appreciate his help. I'm as obedient an ex-wife as I was a wife." Flora laughs as if we're having an ordinary conversation. "When he rang to say you'd contacted him on Instagram, I followed his instructions to the letter: pretended we were still together and living in Florida, a happy family of five. Going along with his plans was my only option. He could think straight and I couldn't."

"And you told Kevin what? 'Someone I want to avoid is poking around in my business, so I'm going to have to go and stay with my ex-husband in Florida'?"

She recoils. "I'm not staying with Lewis and his children. I'd never do that. He wouldn't allow it, either. Lewis arranged another house for me to stay in. I'm not part of their life anymore, and we both want to keep it that way. I'm a coward, Beth. I'm not confident and brave like you."

"I asked about Kevin," I remind her.

"Kevin understood, yes. He doesn't pry into my business. That's one of his best qualities."

*Got it. Prying is bad. Message delivered, loud and clear.*

"So together, you and Lewis made a plan to mislead me because you thought the questions I was asking might lead to the truth coming out." As I say it, I try to imagine the conversations they must have had if this is true. I picture Kevin Cater, not privy to these discussions, saying to Yanina, "Flora and her ex-husband must have some unfinished business to deal with, relating to this old friend. I'm not going to pry."

"We knew you knew about the names," says Flora. "How could I explain to you why I'd used the same ones? I knew it was the first question you'd ask me if you got the chance. There's no explanation that makes any sense apart from the truth! And if I told you I was estranged from . . . from . . ." She covers her face with her hands.

"From your oldest two children," I say. "From Thomas and Emily Braid."

"If I told you that, you'd have asked why. You'd have demanded an answer. You remind me of Lewis sometimes, with your determination to get the result you want. I'm not a strong person, Beth. You'd have broken me down eventually. Lewis and I both knew that. We agreed that the best thing to do was get me out of the way, where you couldn't find me."

"Except I did."

"You did." Is that hatred in her eyes, or something else? "Here you are."

"And here *you* are, telling me the story. What if I go to the police now?"

"You promised Lewis you wouldn't tell anyone but Dom."

"Flora, Lewis might be your lord and master, but he's not mine. What if I break the promise I made?"

"You won't. You wouldn't do that to me, or to any of the other people who would suffer if you did. Georgina's been gone twelve years. What would it achieve to stir things up now? Have some compassion for Lewis, if you've got none for me."

"Flora, how can you say that? That's so far from—"

"He isn't my lord and master, but he is my savior," she talks over me. "He says he's not doing any of it for me, but I still get the benefits. He made this escape plan for me. He's helped in all kinds of ways—like letting me and Kevin have the Hemingford Abbots house, which he didn't have to do. It was still his, he hadn't sold it. And once he'd moved to America—"

"Flora, I know you're lying." The words spill out of

me as a sudden realization hits hard. How did it take me so long to see it? "You're so intent on cutting all ties with your old life that you disown your kids, change your name, cut off your parents—something you'd never do, by the way—*and then you choose to live with your new husband and bring up your new children in the house where Georgina died?* You expect me to believe that?"

Flora stands up. "I don't have to talk to you," she says. "Not anymore. You already know the only thing I wanted to keep from you. Do what you want with it, I don't care."

"Really? That's not plausible either—that you suddenly don't care about the effect it would have on your parents, for example, if I were to go to them next week and tell them the truth."

Flora moves toward the door. I try to block her path, but she shoves me hard. I land on the bed on top of my bag.

"Flora, wait!" I call out. The door slams.

Rubbing my sore side, I get up and run after her, but there's no sign of her in the corridor in either direction.

**I don't** want to go back inside and shut the door to the outside world. Not yet. Instead, I stay in the corridor, leaning against the wall, watching my hotel room through its wide-open door and half expecting somebody to burst out of it. That doesn't happen, and won't, since there's no one in there. All I see is an ordinary, unremarkable room: suitcase spread open with clothes spilling out, rumpled duvet cover, cushions scattered on the floor. No hotel guest who passed now and glanced in would see any sign of unusual activity.

Maybe it's not unusual. Thinking about it, it can't be. It must be absolutely standard: people lie to each other in hotel rooms all the time.

If I'd run down to the lobby as fast as I could, determined to find Flora at all costs, would it have done me any good? If I'd tracked her down, would she have told me the truth, and would I have believed her if she did? I've lost count of the number of times she's lied to me.

*It has to be another lie: all of it.*

I slide down the wall into a seated position and start to make a mental list of all the reasons why I'm certain the detailed story Flora and Lewis just told me is not true.

I don't believe that Kevin doesn't know what's going on between Flora and Lewis. Any spouse would demand to know the details before saying, "Fine, you go off to America with your ex. I'll stay here and mind my own business." When Dominic and I met Kevin Cater, he had the manner of someone who was in on the plan.

There was an in-charge air about him. Everything I can recall of his behavior that day makes me think he knows all the details there are to know. He also knows why it matters that Dom and I should be kept in the dark. Yanina knows too.

Lewis feigned resentment when he told me the story; so did Flora. They hadn't wanted to tell me, they didn't want to be in my hotel room unburdening themselves, but I'd been so persistent, I'd left them no choice. *A lie.* I knew Lewis Braid well for years, and people don't change—not that much. There's no way he'd ever dance to anyone else's tune. The more reluctant to talk he seemed, the more I was likely to believe the story—that was his thinking.

Then there's the eyes. Thomas's, Emily's. Flora can lie all she likes, but I've seen their faces. Yes, Rosemary Tillotson has brown eyes, but she doesn't have *those* brown eyes. All four children are Lewis's. That links to another part of the lie: Flora told me that, when Lewis rang her to say I'd contacted him, she hadn't seen or heard from him in twelve years. That can't be true, if the two of them had two more children together.

The truth is that Lewis came back to Hemingford Abbots and, while there, got Flora pregnant. Twice. Tilly, his former neighbor at number 3, saw him, and, to explain away his presence, he pretended he was obsessively in love with her, when really he was there to see Flora.

The Lewis Braid I knew would never leave me to decide his fate. He has no idea if I'll keep the promise I made to tell no one but Dom, and he wouldn't take that risk.

Another lie, possibly the most insulting one of all, is Flora's claim that she distanced herself from me because she feared I'd drag the truth out of her. Doesn't she think I have a functioning memory? Her altered behavior toward me started long before Georgina's death. In fact, it started many months before she was born, when Flora must have been just a few weeks pregnant. Whatever made her push me away, it had nothing to do with the guilt she felt after killing her daughter.

*Maybe she didn't kill her. If the rest was a lie, why not that too?*

The main proof of Flora's dishonesty, as I told her, is the house on Wyddial Lane. No one determined to cut all ties with their former life would willingly live in the house where the tragedy occurred that had brought their whole world crashing down. No one.

Then there are the things that seem more like contradictions or details that don't add up than outright lies. Lewis was right: I knew from our various holidays with them that Flora often sunbathed topless and he never minded, so why did he scream at her when she breast-fed Georgina in front of me and Dom, as if there was something objectionably immodest about it?

If Flora did cause Georgina's death, and her and Lewis's aim was to stop me finding out, they could have succeeded. Easily. Flora could have brazened it out in the car park in Huntingdon. "Lewis and I have split up," she could have said. "Our kids are with him in Florida, apart from Georgina who died tragically—cot death—and I'm not part of their lives anymore. He won't let me see Thomas and Emily." When I asked her, as I certainly would have, why her children with Kevin Cater were also called Thomas and Emily, she could have said, "I wanted to annoy Lewis. It was a bit petty, but I didn't care."

What could I have done if she'd told me that, even if I didn't believe her? She and Lewis could have told me that exact story today, instead of telling me the very thing they've supposedly gone to all this trouble to stop me from finding out.

I go back into my room, unzip my bag and pull out my phone. I press the red button to stop it recording. Whenever I want to, I can listen to all those lies again—lucky me.

I lock the door to my room, slip the key card into my

bag and head down to the lobby, telling myself there's zero chance of me finding Flora still in the building. She'll be long gone by now.

What should I do next? I can only think of one thing: go back to VersaNova and tell Lewis I've seen through his and Flora's little performance.

*And he'll say you're deranged and throw you out. He'll say, "Look what happens when I try to talk to you, Beth. You don't listen. You don't believe me. Why should I bother wasting any more of my time?"*

What will happen if I go back to PC Paul Pollard with Flora's taped confession that she killed her daughter? Would she be brought in for questioning? What about Lewis, who admitted to misleading the authorities to protect his family? Does my recording count as admissible evidence? I have no idea how these things work.

There are lots of people in the hotel lobby, but Flora isn't one of them. I approach the concierge, who stands smiling behind his lectern by the entrance doors, unoccupied. I describe Flora to him and he listens attentively. "Did you see her leave?" I ask. "It was about ten minutes ago. Did she ask you to get her a taxi, maybe? She didn't have a car with her. Or maybe her husband came to pick her up?" I describe Lewis.

The concierge shakes his head. "No husband, but I think I know the lady you mean. She asked the quickest way to the beach from here."

"The beach?" I suppose there must be one, though I haven't seen any sign of it. "Delray Beach?"

"Yes, ma'am."

"Can you give me whatever directions you gave her?" I ask him.

Outside the hotel, I cross the busy road. On the pavement opposite, there's a sign in the shape of an arrow that says, "To the beach." I have a strange feeling: that if I find Flora like this, I'll have found her too easily.

Except finding her isn't the challenge. Getting the truth out of her is the hard part.

I follow a roped-off path until I arrive on a long, wide, sandy beach. Stretching out in both directions are two long rows of blue sun umbrellas and wooden recliners with cushions, mainly occupied. The blue-green sea is calm, barely moving apart from where it's being disturbed by people determined to have fun in it. I take off my shoes and hold them in my hand as I walk between the rows of sun loungers.

It doesn't take me long to find her. "Flora," I say, half expecting her to get up and run away.

She's sitting on the sand, in a large patch of shade

from the umbrella in front. There's some shade left over, so I sit down next to her. "I'm sorry," I say, and mean it. Provoking her so that she ran away was a bad strategy. "I shouldn't have accused you of lying."

"I don't mind." She says it as if there was never a break in our conversation. She looks peaceful; almost content. "You don't see why I'd want to stay in the same house. I understand that."

"But you did want to?"

"Yes."

"Why?"

She gives a small laugh. "It's funny that I still want to hide things from you even after I've told you the worst. Don't you think that's funny?"

I wait.

"Lewis only offered me the house once I was pregnant with Thomas—my Thomas. Not newly pregnant but quite far gone. I'd already had the twenty-week scan and knew I was having a boy. Kevin and I were living in a tiny flat with only one bedroom. He was doing one short-term contract after another for tech companies, and couldn't seem to find a full-time job. No one would have given us a mortgage at the level we needed. I knew Lewis hadn't sold the Hemingford Abbotts house—"

"How did you know that? You told me you and he

hadn't been in touch for twelve years until he rang you to talk about me."

"That wasn't true. The truth would have sounded too weird."

"Try me."

"We've always kept in touch. Kevin knew nothing about it. It was Lewis's initiative, not mine. He liked to check on me, so he rang me every few months. To check that my situation was stable."

"Didn't you mind, if you wanted to cut all ties with your old life?" Is this a new lie I'm hearing or, finally, some of the truth? I wish I knew.

Flora shakes her head. "Turned out I had the same need he did: to check he'd said nothing, told no one our secret. Neither of us could let the other one drift too far out of reach."

"So, what, every few months you'd talk?"

"Not for very long. They weren't warm, friendly chats between friends. Far from it. Just . . . updates about our life situations. I told him when I changed my name, when I met Kevin, then later when I married him. Lewis needed reassurance that I wouldn't confide in him about . . . the past."

"Presumably you told Lewis about being pregnant with Thomas the second, then?"

"Don't call him that," says Flora.

"Shall I call him Thomas Cater?"

"Yes, I told Lewis. He knew Kevin and I were hard up and couldn't easily afford a house that was big enough for the new family we wanted to start, so he very kindly offered for us to live at Newnham House—which he still owned. He'd rented it out intermittently, but it had been empty for a while at that point."

"And you said yes," I state the obvious. "I still don't understand why."

"I knew by then that I was having a boy and that I'd be calling him Thomas," says Flora. She stares at me with a plea in her eyes, as if urging me to work it out.

"And . . . you thought that with a child called Thomas, in the same house you'd lived in before, you could almost pretend that nothing bad had ever happened?" I say.

From Flora's expression, I can see that I've guessed correctly.

"Georgina had been dead for quite a few years by then," she says. "At first, yes, I wanted to get as far away from any reminders as I could, but I felt differently after I got pregnant again, and especially once I knew we were having a boy and what I was going to call him. Then, I wanted to try and . . . I don't know, re-create what I'd had, I guess."

"And the house helped with that?"

She nods eagerly.

*Is it possible?* I don't know why I'm bothering to ask myself. I can't bring all the relevant facts to mind and listen to Flora at the same time.

"Beth, never mind the house," she says suddenly. "Do you understand about my need for Lewis and his for me, even after everything?"

"I think so."

"I never really loved Kevin."

"Yeah, you said." Is this going where I think it's going?

A large yellow and blue beach ball rolls past us. Gleefully screaming children run after it, kicking sand in my eyes. I blink to get the grit out.

"You were right," says Flora. "Thomas and Emily, they're . . ." Again she looks hopefully at me, inviting me to fill in the blanks.

"Thomas and Emily Cater are Lewis's children," I say.

"Yes. Kevin has no idea. Please, please don't tell him. Lewis'd kill me if he knew I'd told you."

The idea of me telling Kevin Cater anything nearly makes me laugh. "What would you have called Emily if she'd been a boy?"

I'm expecting an "I don't know," but Flora says, "I wouldn't have let that happen. I knew I needed to have a girl next. I paid for an early blood test. Luckily, it was her. It was Emily. I know what you're going to ask me next."

"Please make it so that I don't have to," I say, shivering despite the heat.

"I'd do it if I could," Flora says so quietly it's almost a whisper. "Another Georgina. Lewis won't, though. After Emily, he . . . he said it wasn't good for me; it was twisted. He said he wouldn't let it happen again, and he hasn't."

*Another Georgina.*

She's staring out toward the sea with the trace of a smile on her lips.

"Flora, you have to listen to me." I reach over and squeeze her hand. "You need help. Professional help, to deal with all this trauma properly. *I'll* help you. If you don't like Kevin or love him, you can leave him."

"He loves me, though. And the children. They're his in every way that matters. He's the one they call Daddy."

"Does he treat them well?" I'm not sure I intended to say this out loud, but I have and it's too late. Might as well press on. "Is he kind to them? Is Yanina?"

Flora's expression is guarded. It wasn't before I asked the question. "Stop it, Beth. You can't keep doing this. I've told you everything. You need to leave me alone."

"Flora, please. Look at me. Kevin doesn't treat Thomas and Emily very well, does he? Are you sure he doesn't know they're Lewis's children and not his?"

She stands up, dusting the sand off her clothes. "I'm going. Don't follow me. That wouldn't be fair. I've tried to be as fair to you as I can, and now you need to stop. Go back home. You've got a family of your own, haven't you?"

"Flora!" I call after her as she walks away. I could chase her, but what good would it do?

I stay where I am, watching as she gets smaller and smaller. A man in a baseball cap leans down into my view and asks me if I want to rent a sunbed instead of sitting on the sand. I tell him I don't. By the time he's moved aside, I can't see Flora anymore.

# 23

I run all the way back to my hotel room, flop down on one of the beds with my phone and ring the landline at home. I count the seconds. Someone picks up at the exact moment I'm starting to worry about why no one's answering. It's Dom. "Is everything okay?" he asks. "What's happening?"

*You've got a family of your own, haven't you?* Flora's words have been ringing in my head since she said them, wrapped in the fear that I'm somehow risking the people I love most by taking too much of an interest in another family. I know that's not true, but it didn't stop me wanting to check.

"Everything's fine," I tell Dom. "I just wanted to hear your voices."

"I'm afraid I've only got one."

"What?"

"Voice."

I smile.

"I'll do my impression of Chandler from *Friends* if you ask me nicely."

"Please don't. It's terrible."

"Fair enough. What's happening there, Beth?"

"I've spoken to Lewis and Flora," I tell him. "They've told me a story, and for all I know it's true, but . . . it's not *the* story."

"How do you mean?"

"I think Kevin Cater and Yanina are harming the children at Newnham House. That's what Lewis and Flora are scared I'll find out. I don't know why they want to protect two mistreaters of children—*their* children—but I think they do." This was the conclusion I came to, running back from the beach. "There's a whole other long story about Georgina, but . . ." I don't have the energy to explain it all now, and I know Dom won't mind if I don't. "Can I speak to the kids?"

"They're both out."

"Where?"

"Zannah's at Murad's, and Ben's with Lauren at the cinema. Reluctantly. He'd have preferred to stay at home and play Fortnite, he said."

"Then he needs to convey that message to her, not you."

"That's what I told him. Oh—that woman rang for you."

"Who?"

"Lou Munday, from the school. She rang about ten minutes ago."

"The landline?"

"Obviously. She doesn't have my mobile number, does she? I told her she might get you on yours."

"I'd better go, then. She might be trying to call me now."

"Hang on. I want to hear about—"

"I'll call you back later. Love you. Look after the kids. I'll take care and be safe, I promise."

Once I've pressed the red button to end the call, I inspect my phone. There's no evidence of Lou having tried to ring me while I was talking to Dom. Luckily, I have her number stored. I take a bottle of Diet Coke from the minibar in my room, open it and go and sit out on the balcony.

Lou answers on the second ring. "That's so weird," she says. "I was just—"

"I know. My husband told me. Has something happened?"

"Kind of. I took a call today at school, from a woman calling herself Jeanette Cater."

"You mean Flora? I mean . . . the woman you know as Jeanette, with the English accent?"

"No. That's what was so odd. It sounded like someone putting on an English accent."

"Yanina, then?"

"I think so. I'm almost positive."

"Go on."

"She was phoning to give notice for Thomas. He wasn't in today, and apparently he won't be coming back to school at all. And Emily, who was due to start with us in September, now won't be coming."

My heart is pounding. I lay my palm flat on my rib cage, as if that will make any difference. Why would this happen today of all days? What have they done to Thomas? Have they only taken him out of school, or have they done something worse?

"Did you tell her that you knew she was lying? That you knew she wasn't Jeanette Cater?"

"No. I wasn't sure letting her know that I knew was a good idea."

If Yanina's planning to harm those two kids . . .

This is all happening because of me, because I couldn't leave things alone.

"Beth, are you there?"

"Yes."

"Are you okay?"

I'm not. I'm terrified that, by trying to protect Thomas and Emily Cater, I've placed them in greater danger. I take deep breaths and try to calm down.

"What else did she tell you?" I ask Lou.

"That they're leaving the country. Moving to America."

"When?"

"In the summer. She didn't say where they were going more specifically. Just said America."

"If they're leaving in the summer, why take Thomas out of school now? Why not let him finish the term?"

"Exactly. That's what I thought," says Lou.

If Thomas remains at school, other people can observe his behavior, and the behavior of anyone who goes there to drop him off or collect him. *And that's the last thing they want.*

"There's more," Lou says. "I told her—Yanina, assuming it was her—that she needed to talk to the head teacher about something as important as that. I can't just cancel school places and take children off lists without it going via the head teacher. There's all kinds of things to do with notice and fees that need to be dealt with. She said, okay, she'd ring the head. Then the phone rang again, straight away, and I answered it, and it was him: Mr. Cater. 'I believe you just spoke to my wife?' he said."

"Go on."

"He then tried to tell me the same thing. It was as if he thought it might work better if it came from him. I thought he was going to quibble about money and the notice period, try and save himself a term's fees, but he didn't."

"Why did you think he would?"

"He's complained about the fees before, many times—which got me thinking. Most parents pay as soon as they receive the bill, but some don't. A hand-ful always wait until we send our final demand. I'm talking every term. I don't know what they think will happen. Maybe they hope that one day we'll forget to chase them about it."

"Are the Caters part of this late-paying group?" I ask, trying not to spill Coke as I press the cold bottle against my forehead. It's too bright. I can't stay out here for much longer.

"Yup," says Lou. "Anyway, I told Mr. Cater the same as I'd told Yanina—that he'd need to speak to the head. Then I emailed the head and the bursar and told them what had happened, the nanny pretending to be Mrs. Cater, and the bursar sent a reply saying exactly what I'd thought: that there would probably be some wrangling over the notice period in a last-ditch attempt to save some cash, and then she said something else—one line that leaped out at me."

"What line?" I ask.

"Let me get it up on my screen," Lou says. "Here it is: 'I don't know why the Caters complain about cost—it's not like the money's coming out of their accounts.'"

"They don't pay Thomas's school fees? Then who does?"

"That's what I wondered. I emailed right back and asked."

"What did she say?"

"She had no idea. As long as the fees arrive, no one questions whose account they come from. Sometimes it's a grandparent paying the fees. In this case . . . well, it doesn't sound like that's what's going on here, given what you've told me."

"What do you mean?"

"Thomas Cater's school fees so far, and Emily's deposit to reserve her a place, have all been paid from a bank account based in Florida."

"What's the name of the account?" I ask, thinking the answer to my own question at the same time.

As if she's reading my mind, Lou says, "Lewis Braid."

**An hour** later I'm sitting on the floor in the middle of my hotel room, waiting for my swirling thoughts to arrange themselves into some kind of recognizable order. The sun's edging away from me inch by inch, as if it doesn't want to get involved in whatever mess I've got myself embroiled in. There's a hollow feeling in my stomach. I should probably order something to eat, but every time I try to think about where I might have put the room service menu, my brain slides back to what it prefers to think about.

Lewis Braid. Lewis is paying the school fees of Thomas and Emily Cater.

That could make sense. They're his children, and he has plenty of money. There's only one problem with this explanation, and it's a significant one: according to Flora, Kevin Cater doesn't know Thomas and Emily are Lewis's. He believes they're his. Doesn't he wonder why his wife's ex-husband is willing to pay the school fees of her children from her second marriage?

Is it possible he doesn't know that Lewis pays the fees? Perhaps Flora has told him they're coming out of a separate bank account she's got that her parents have put money into, or something like that. Or maybe Kevin knows that Lewis plans to pay for Thomas and

Emily's schooling, doesn't care why, and is simply happy to be spared the expense.

None of these theories satisfies me. I think about my encounters with Kevin and Yanina—not what I've been told about them by anyone else, only what I've witnessed and experienced myself. The confident way they produced the photograph of two completely different children . . . *Toby and Emma*. And then they told PC Pollard they'd given those names because they were afraid I was a dangerous obsessive.

I shake my head, though there's no one here to see me do it. Kevin and Yanina weren't afraid of me. They knew I was no danger to the children at Newnham House. They were attempting to manipulate me, and confident they'd succeed. I know this is true, because I was there.

I trust my senses, my instincts and my judgment. I always have, but since that first Saturday on Wyddial Lane, I trust myself even more.

*What does your judgment say about Kevin and Yanina?*

I've been so busy puzzling over Flora, Lewis and the children that, until now, I haven't spent much time thinking specifically about Kevin and the nanny. She might not be a nanny—that's the first thing that occurs to me. A Ukrainian nanny with a foreign accent is so easy to believe in. It's a familiar stereotype, and people rarely question those. More likely, Yanina is a woman who happens to have an accent that isn't English, and who's in the house for some other reason, not to look after Thomas and Emily.

What kind of nanny collects a child from school and doesn't even make eye contact with him? And why would anyone—Lewis, Kevin, any person in charge of children—invest in full-time live-in child care when they won't spend a much smaller amount on new school shoes to replace ones that are literally falling apart?

The more I focus on them, the more convinced I am that Kevin and Yanina are central to whatever's happening at Newnham House. They aren't just two minor players in a drama created by Flora and Lewis, a drama they don't fully understand because many of the details have been kept from them. Flora lied about that, like she lied about Kevin being happy not to pry into the details of her past life. Of course he'd want to know what had made his wife feel she had to rush off to Florida with almost no notice to be with her ex-husband. Any husband would. Most, I think, would raise significant objections.

Kevin Cater didn't mind at all. He was in his element when I met him, all ready to pretend the nanny was his wife for the benefit of anyone who happened to drop by. He played the part of the innocent, inconvenienced family man brilliantly. They could have told Dom and me then that Yanina was the nanny, but they decided, probably after discussing it with Lewis, that it would be more effective to have her play the part of Jeanette Cater. The hope, the assumption, was that I'd then think she must have been the dark-haired woman I'd seen outside the house with the two children. She thought she and her partners in deception were going to deal with me easily, neutralize the threat, persuade me to doubt my own perceptions and believe the lies instead, believe that my mind was playing tricks on me. Lewis will have said to them all, "Don't worry about Beth Leeson. We can handle her, as long as we all stick to the script."

In the car park that day in Huntingdon, Yanina didn't flinch. She played her part so convincingly, fully believing in her assured victory. She was the outraged, innocent car owner, shocked to find a stranger in her car. Except she wasn't shocked at all. The four of them will have agreed that she should return to the car park dressed in Flora's clothes, to make me think I was losing my mind. Yanina might not have known she'd find me *inside* the Range Rover, but she knew I'd be there.

They must all have been prepared for me to say, "Why are you wearing Flora's clothes? I've just seen her wearing those same clothes. Don't tell me I haven't." Yanina was trusted, evidently, to be convincingly aghast and uncomprehending if I reacted in that way.

Lewis had no worries about Kevin and Yanina. That's why they were allowed to invite me and Dominic to Newnham House. Flora, Lewis decided, was the only possible weak link, the one who couldn't necessarily be trusted not to let something slip. Better to move her to a different country, to be on the safe side. Meanwhile, he knew he could trust Kevin and Yanina to take charge of all the lying that needed to be done in England, while he and Flora lied with a matching confidence and determination in America—determination to win, to make sure that what they've all hidden so successfully remains hidden.

The terrible secret. What could it be? If I'm right about everything I think I've worked out so far, then someone might be in prison . . . but who? And for what?

The crime involved, because it has to be a crime, must be worse than what Lewis and Flora told me—worse than Flora accidentally killing Georgina and disowning her family, worse than her and Lewis misleading the authorities about the cause of Georgina's death. No one trying to hide their guilt would invent something more likely to land them in jail than the truth. Lewis Braid is hardly an ordinary person, but I can't see any reason why even he would do that.

Which means the truth must represent a greater threat than the story he and Flora told me. And Kevin Cater and Yanina know exactly what it is. There's no detail they don't know. They're not being deceived, like me, or even partially deceived. They're fully informed and trusted participants in the deception. Whatever's going on, they and Flora and Lewis are equal partners.

*Great. Good luck convincing PC Pollard of all this, or anyone else who can do anything about it.*

My stomach rumbles. I tell myself I can find the menu and order food any time. I don't need to do it right now. There's still so much I need to think through . . .

Flora in the background when Lewis first phoned me, saying that she was lucky. She wasn't in Florida then. It was the day before I saw her in the car park in Huntingdon. Which means Lewis had a recording of her voice saying, "I'm lucky," because there's no way she was there with him in Delray Beach at the time.

Why would he have that on tape? It seems too much of a coincidence that he'd record her saying the very same words I heard her say outside Newnham House. Though a bigger question, maybe, is why she would arrive home on a Saturday morning and have that particular conversation while getting out of the car. If Flora needed to talk to someone and say not what I thought I heard her say at first but what I now believe I heard her say that day, then why wouldn't she wait until she was . . .

My heart starts to thud as another answer slots into place.

*Nobody's in prison. No one at all.*

Adrenaline combined with an empty stomach makes me feel light-headed. It's so obvious, once you think of it. It's only taken me this long to see it because of an assumption I made, a stupid one. Then, immediately after leaping to the wrong conclusion, I found plenty of evidence that seemed to prove me right. It wasn't evidence of anything, though. I just chose to believe it was.

Now I know what was really going on. But what does it mean? How does it alter or add to the overall picture? I still don't know that.

I need to talk to Flora again. Whether she wants to talk to me or not, she's going to have to. And she will because . . .

*Because people can make Flora do things she doesn't want to do. Lewis can, Kevin and Yanina can, and you can too.*

If the answer that's just come to me is right, and it has to be, then Flora can't be playing her part in all this by choice. Can she?

*No. You know she isn't. You saw her face. You know her. She's your best friend.*

I pick up my phone and ring Lou back. "Can you access school records from home?" I ask her.

"I'm not at home—" she starts to say.

"Can you access the records from wherever you are?"

"Only my emails and the main school Web site, which is public. Why?"

"Could you get into the building if you went now?"

"Yes, I've got the code for the—"

"I need you to go. I need the mobile number you've got on record for Jeanette Cater. That'll be on a database somewhere, won't it?"

"It should be. We encourage all parents to give us all their contact numbers. We require it, actually. Doesn't mean all of them do it, though."

"I need that number," I tell her.

"Is it so important that it can't wait till tomorrow?" she asks. "You can say if it is."

I don't know how to answer. Will anything terrible happen tonight if I don't make Lou interrupt her evening?

"It is, then," she says, when I fail to answer. "It's fine. I'll go in now. Sit tight. I'll let you know, soon as I can."

I pace up and down the room, turn on the TV and mute it immediately like Zannah and Ben do at home. I press the Channel Plus button on the remote control until I find something I can bear to look at: a kitchen. Two men are sitting at a table while a large older woman, a redhead with her hair pulled back into a ponytail, walks around behind them. I stare for a few seconds, then switch the TV off again.

I have no idea how to pass the time between now and when Lou rings me back. The desire to eat has left me completely. I don't think I can stay in the room either.

I grab my phone and key card and head downstairs and outside. I walk around the building, through the lush greenery of the gardens toward the pool terrace, where I soon realize I can't stay. Everyone here looks far too relaxed, sprawled out on sunbeds with their eyes closed, cocktails in fruit-decorated glasses on tables next to them.

I walk around to the front of the hotel and cross the road, planning to go back to the beach, but halfway along the narrow, roped-off path I change my mind and turn back.

Finally I admit it to myself: I have no idea what I'm

doing or where I'm going. This isn't good. I need to get my head together if I'm going to speak to Flora again. Instead of running around frenetically, I need to keep still and focus.

I force myself to walk slowly back to my room, breathing even more slowly. By the time I get back, I feel a little more composed. As if to reward me for sensibly taking myself in hand, my phone starts to buzz in my pocket as I push open the door to my room.

"Lou!" I hope it's her. I didn't stop to look.

"You're in luck," she says. "I've got Jeanette's mobile number for you."

## 24

Back in my hotel room, I sit down in the hard chair at the desk and stare at the number Lou has sent me. It doesn't look familiar. It can't be the same one Flora had twelve years ago. I think I'd probably recognize that number if it was in front of me, though I can't call it to mind.

I key in the digits, press the dial button and wait for her to answer. Each of these stages feels as if it lasts an age. How many more stages will there be?

It doesn't matter. However many there are, I'll be here for them.

"Hello?"

"Flora, it's me."

"I told you to leave me alone."

"I know. And I let you think I might. I should have

been clearer. I can't leave you alone until I'm sure that you and the children are safe. Flora, listen, this is important. I *know* you're not okay. I knew it the second I saw you get out of that car outside your house in Hemingford Abbots. I knew when I saw the look of pure fear in your eyes in the car park in Huntingdon. I know you've lied to me and I understand why, but you've miscalculated here. You think if you lie convincingly enough, I'll disappear, and you're scared of what they'll do to you if you don't help to make me go away—I get that—but you need to believe me now. I'm not *ever* going to drop this. And when they see that I haven't dropped it, they'll blame you."

I stop in case she wants to try and deny any of it. I hear her breathing.

She says nothing.

"They're not going to blame themselves, are they?" I go on. "People like them never do. Lewis isn't a good person. I think you know that better than anyone. I should have realized it long before I did. Kevin and Yanina aren't good people either. But you are, Flora. You were my best friend for years. I *know* you want to help make sure Thomas and Emily aren't harmed any more than they already have been."

She doesn't respond. All I can hear is her breathing.

"I've spoken to people at Thomas's school. The staff

are worried about him." Only one member of staff, but Flora doesn't need to know that. "They know there's something wrong at home. Shall I tell you what I've been told? That you cling to Thomas and Emily as if you're terrified something bad will happen to them."

I hear a sob. *It's working. Keep going.*

"What do you think Lewis is going to do if you follow his instructions to the letter? Treat you well? When did he last treat you well, Flora? Not for a while, I don't think. I'm right, aren't I?"

Silence.

"What will Kevin and Yanina do if you obey their orders? What will your reward be, for helping to get rid of nosy, pushy Beth? Will they suddenly treat you and the children kindly? Have they ever done that? You've obeyed orders for a long time, haven't you, and where's it got you? Nowhere."

Where's this approach getting me? I have no way of knowing, and no plan. I'm acting on instinct—saying anything I think of that feels true, praying I'm right. I can't show any doubt if I want her to believe I can help her.

"We're going to do it differently from now on, Flora. You're going to listen to me, not them. I want to help you and the children. I know I can help, but you have to talk to me and tell me the truth. And you need to understand that if you don't do that, you won't get to avoid your fear. The opposite. You'll make the fear last longer. You'll create more of it if you carry on lying and avoiding me. You know why? Because I'm not going to leave this alone. Whatever you're all so terrified of, it's going to happen. I'm going to find out. It's only a question of when. It might take me a year, maybe two. Do you want to live in fear for that long? You can't keep the secret forever. None of you can."

She's letting me say all this—not shutting me down, not interrupting. That has to mean something.

"When did someone last try to help you, Flora?" I try to think of anything I can say that might flip that switch in her mind. "You know how persistent I've had to be. And I was your best friend for years. What if no one ever really tries to help you and the children again? What if I'm your only chance?" *Shit.* That sounded too threatening. In a softer voice, I say, "There's a better, more sensible choice you can make: you can tell me the truth right now and have an ally."

"Why does it matter to you?" She's crying. "Why can't you forget about me, forget about all of us?"

"Because there's something badly wrong," I tell her. "The children—Thomas and Emily Cater—are being harmed somehow. I'm not sure how but I know it's happening. Lewis is the driving force behind it. Lewis was and is *always* a driving force—that's all he knows how to be. And you're being harmed by it, whatever it is. Maybe that's your choice—to stay in that house with those people and let them hurt you in whatever way they're hurting you. Maybe you don't want to be rescued, but how can you deny your children the help you know they need?"

"You don't know anything! You don't understand!"

I wait a moment, then carry on as evenly as if her outburst hasn't happened. "There's a lot that I don't understand. That's true. I've worked out part of it, but not all. There are some things that still make no sense to me. Maybe you can explain them. If I'm going to help, I need to know what I'm dealing with. Why did Lewis make such a fuss about you feeding Georgina, the last time you all came to see us?"

"What? What are you talking about?" She sounds genuinely thrown off course by the question, as if I've asked her about a complicated algebra problem.

"You must remember the last time we all got together. You found out that I'd cut up the photo you sent me of you, Lewis and the kids. We both knew we'd never see each other again, though we didn't say it explicitly."

"I'd forgotten that you did that," Flora says quietly.

"You forgot that I cut Georgina out of a photograph?" I pause to consider this. It takes me a moment to realize what it means. "I suppose that's possible, if you had a lot on your mind, and you did, didn't you? You'd been distancing yourself from me for a while before that day. Months. Something else was going on in your life. It started around the time you got pregnant with Georgina. Maybe that was it, the thing that changed everything: the pregnancy. Whatever it was, there was something you couldn't talk to me about and didn't want me to find out. Bit by bit, you started to vanish from my life. You didn't really want to come around that last time, did you?"

"I remember it now," she says. "Lewis and Dom went to the pub."

"Yeah, for a bit. Then they came back, and they were in the kitchen, and we were in the living room with all the children. Georgina was a tiny baby. She'd been asleep all afternoon. Then she started to stir and you picked her up to feed her. You seemed on edge—more than you'd ever been with Thomas or Emily. I assumed it was because of the tension between you and me. You'd just found out about the photo, and I thought that explained the atmosphere that you could cut with a knife. That wasn't the explanation, though, was it? You and Lewis had brought the tension with you. He came into the room while you were feeding Georgina and yelled at you. I'd never heard him shout at you like that before. Other people, yes, but never you.

"I wish I could remember exactly what he said. It might have been as simple as 'What are you doing?' as if feeding your child in front of your best friend was a cardinal sin and you ought to know better. He looked and sounded appalled, and it made no sense."

"Yes, I remember," says Flora.

"I didn't get it. I still don't. You'd fed Thomas and Emily in front of me and Dom a million times—older Thomas and Emily—and Lewis had never batted an eyelid. He said so himself when I asked him about it earlier today: he reminded me that you used to sunbathe topless on the beach on holiday. He never minded that. So why the sudden move toward prudishness?"

Blindly following my instincts, I press on. "It wasn't about modesty, was it? Lewis had never insisted that no one should see your body except him. It was about Georgina. Somehow, this is all about her. That was when everything changed: when you got pregnant with her. You didn't tell me when you found out you were pregnant, or when she was born. And then she died. None of the other children died. Only her."

"Do you really want to help me, Beth?"

"You know I do."

"Then don't ask me. Help me by . . ." I hear a ragged

gasp. Then she says, "I don't want anything to happen to you. You say you don't want me to come to harm? I want the same for you. The used-to-be-best-friends thing goes both ways."

I close my eyes. There it is, finally—an admission. A cold, heavy feeling lands in the pit of my stomach. Fear. She's telling me there's something to be afraid of, something for *me* to be afraid of, if I don't drop this.

I'm scared of what will happen if I do. If I abandon Flora, Thomas and Emily to whatever mess they're in, I'll hate myself.

And I was right. I've been right all along. Does that mean I'll be right if I listen to the part of me that's saying I have to stay and see this through?

*Right all along? Like when you thought Thomas and Emily Braid might not have grown a day older in twelve years?*

I haven't got time to doubt myself. "Who was Georgina's father?" I ask. "Was it Lewis? Or was it Kevin Cater?"

"Lewis," Flora says quietly. "Why would you think it was Kevin?"

"I wondered if maybe Lewis didn't want you to feed another man's baby. I can't think of any other explanation that makes sense."

"No. I was never unfaithful to Lewis. I never would have been."

"When he yelled at you, you ran out of the room like a frightened mouse, clutching Georgina—as if you thought you'd really screwed up."

"I don't remember much about that day."

I get up, walk over to the balcony door and slide it open. This room, beautiful and comfortable though it is, is starting to feel like a cage. How long before I can go home?

*You can go any time you like. Back to your family, back to safety . . .*

"Want to hear something stupid?" I ask Flora.

She doesn't reply.

"Remember in the lobby before, I asked you who Chimpy was?"

"I don't know that name. It means nothing."

"I know. I made a mistake. The first time I saw you in Hemingford Abbots, you were talking on the phone and crying as you got out of the car. I knew then that something was wrong. It's not like I'd never seen you upset before. I had, loads of times, but those were all normal upset. What I saw in Hemingford Abbots looked different. It sounded different. More serious."

"Stop," Flora whispers.

"I thought I heard you say 'Hey, Chimpy,' and then, a few seconds later 'Peterborough.'"

"Please, Beth."

"But I didn't. What you said was 'HMP Peterborough,' the name of the nearest prison to Hemingford Abbots. Hey Chimpy, HMP. They sound so similar. If it weren't for Lewis, I'd never have worked that out. He said something in passing this morning about 'Her Majesty's pleasure'—a phrase I'd not heard for years. It's such a weird expression. I thought, 'Is that why prisons are called HMP?,' and then suddenly it came rushing at me: 'Hey, Chimpy.' It sounds almost exactly the same as 'HMP.' That's why I had a strange echo in my mind."

"I don't know anyone who's in any prison," says Flora.

"No one's in prison. Least of all you. Right?"

After a short silence, she says, "Plenty of people are in prison. I don't know anything about any of them."

"I know what that phone call was, Flora. I know what it means. You were almost too upset to speak. I don't blame you."

"You can't possibly know who I was speaking to and what it was about," she says.

"I see why you'd think that, but I can and I do. Now I understand why it was such an effort to force out each word. That's why there was a break between the two parts of the prison's name, HMP and Peterborough, a break just long enough to make me hear them as separate. I thought I knew exactly what you'd said, and got fixated on the wrong questions: what was the relevance of Peterborough and who was Chimpy? I thought Chimpy might be Georgina."

"Then you're not as clever as you think you are."

"What do you mean?" I ask her.

"Lewis never allowed nicknames or shortenings. Don't you remember? I was never allowed to say 'Tom' or 'Emmy.'"

This feels different, suddenly. As if we're having a real conversation. "I knew you never called them anything but Thomas and Emily. I didn't realize Lewis had forbidden it."

"He never explicitly said, 'I forbid it.' He didn't have to."

I'm wondering how to respond to this when she says, "He used to be horrible about Zannah's name."

"What?" Rage rears up inside me. It always does when someone criticizes Zan or Ben, even if the criticism is perfectly valid.

"Not about *her*," says Flora quickly. "Only the name. Lewis always liked her. He used to say in an admiring way, 'That child has a steely edge.'"

I don't want to hear anything Lewis has said about my children, but I'm afraid to say so in case it discourages her from talking about other things.

"He thought we should call her Suzannah at all times, I suppose?"

"Yes."

"Where did he stand on Ben?"

"Benjamin."

I turn and lean against the balcony rail so that I'm facing the room. The view that should lift my heart is starting to irritate me: the open sun umbrellas like spiky blue and white wheels, the rectangular, six-pillared building at the far end of the pool that makes me think of an Indian shrine.

"Rom-com Dom was fine, though," I say, trying to work out how to move the conversation back to HMP Peterborough in a way that doesn't feel forced.

"That was a joke," says Flora. "Chimpy wouldn't be very funny as a nickname. More of an insult. I would never compare my own child to a chimpanzee. Why did you think I would? Because of the strabismus?"

"The what?" I picture a polished violin made of dark wood.

"Lewis said you spoke to my parents. Did they tell you?"

"I don't know what you're talking about. What's a strabismus?" Is it a car?

"Weakness of the eye muscles," says Flora. "Georgina would have needed an operation. Well, she might have. There were other options. A patch might have cured it."

Yes. Flora's parents did tell me. One of them said something about Georgina maybe needing an operation. I can't remember if they mentioned her eye, but Lewis did. He told me this morning that Georgina would have needed eye surgery, if she'd lived.

"So . . . it's like a lazy eye?" I ask Flora. A girl at my primary school had one. She wore a patch for months. She still looked a little cross-eyed afterward, but nowhere near as much.

"That's amblyopia," Flora says. "They're connected, but they're not exactly the same thing. Why are we talking about this, Beth? Georgina's dead."

"I know. I'm sorry. I . . . Why would you think there might be a link between the name Chimpy and Georgina's eye condition?"

"There's no connection in my mind. I thought you might think it. To think that Chimpy might be a nickname for a beautiful girl . . ." Her voice shakes. "A girl who looks like a chimp would be ugly, and Georgina was beautiful. She was *beautiful.* Her eye made no dif-ference. It didn't make her ugly."

"Flora, I never said it did. I would never say or think that. I now know that Chimpy is nobody's nickname, so it's irrelevant, but I don't think it implies ugliness at all. Dom and I used to call Zan and Ben little chimps and it was nothing but affectionate. We certainly didn't think they were—"

The words fall away as my brain races ahead. No, we didn't. We didn't think our children were ugly, and Flora didn't think Georgina was ugly because of her eye problem.

Someone did, though. "Lewis thought Georgina was ugly," I say. "Because of her eye."

The other four all have his eyes. Georgina might have had too, except her eyes were flawed. And Lewis can't handle flaws. He never could.

"Flora, did . . . did Lewis . . ." I can't bring myself to ask. If the answer is yes, how does it fit with what's happening at Newnham House now, with Kevin and Yanina and little Thomas and Emily having the same names as their older brother and sister?

"Can you come over now?" Flora says, making my heart jolt. This is how she used to sound, at univer-sity and when we all lived in Cambridge. It's what we'd both say when we rang each other, if there was something new and entertaining to gossip about. "Lewis isn't here. I'm in the house he put me in, on my own. He won't be coming back today. It'll be safe."

"Yes, of course. Tell me where and I'll get there as soon as I can."

There's silence.

"Flora?"

"We'll have to be quick," she says. "I don't think he'll come back today, but there's a chance he might in the evening."

"That gives us plenty of time." Plenty of time to get her out of there.

There's a taut silence. I can't even hear her breathing. If this chance slips away, I'm not sure I'll be able to bear it. "Flora, please. You can trust me."

"I know."

"Then tell me. Where are you?"

She gives me an address.

# 25

Delray Beach's North Fayette Boulevard is grander than I thought it would be. It's the kind of street where I'd expect to find millionaire film stars behind every door. The houses are all enormous and all in different architectural styles, a bit like Wyddial Lane except this road must be thirty times as long. The house number Flora gave me was 4451. I've never been to a four-figure address in England. I'm not sure there are any.

I get out of the taxi, pay the driver and walk up the long drive that's lined with square-trimmed shrubs in square silver planters. 4451 is the only modern-looking house on this stretch of the road. The others mostly look like oversized doll's houses, with wrap-around verandahs, pillars, protruding porches and porte cochères, and rows of cute-looking wooden sash dormer windows with shutters and roofs of their own poking out from red-tiled roofs that tweak up at the edges like slightly lifted skirts. This house, by contrast, looks futuristic: a huge geometric puzzle that someone has expertly solved by slotting together an angular white object and a dark gray one.

I ring the bell and Flora opens the door. Behind her, I see more smooth expanses of white and dark gray, as if the same materials have been used inside as out. There's a sunken bar area with a glittering array of bottles and beautiful wood and leather high stools arranged in a crescent shape around it. Next to the bar is a shiny cylindrical column that goes up through the ceiling. I think it might be a lift. *An elevator.* Yes, it must be; there's a door in it, discreet but visible.

There are white and gray rugs, white and gray sofas, white and gray cushions. It looks immaculate, like a movie set before the cameras and cast arrive. The only details in the scene that jar are me and Flora. If someone had told me three weeks ago that today I'd be here, in this place and this situation, I'd have said it was impossible. I was never going to see Flora again. That was something I was sure of until recently, until knowing anything for certain started to feel impossible.

Flora's eyes are red, her skin pale, her hair pulled

back into a short ponytail. She's wearing a blue bath-robe over black leggings and a white T-shirt. "Come in," she says.

"Whose house is this?" I ask. "Does Lewis own it?"

"His company does. Usually it's for work contacts who need somewhere to stay."

"Figures. That's why it looks perfect inside and out."

"How did you guess?" says Flora.

"What?"

"That Lewis thought Georgina was ugly because of her eye. You said it on the phone before as if you knew, but you can't have known. My parents couldn't have told you. I didn't say a word to them. Neither did Lewis."

"You told me, Flora. When you said Georgina was beautiful. You said it so vehemently, as if you were ar-guing with someone who thought the opposite. That someone wasn't me. It wasn't hard to figure it out from there."

"So you understand why Lewis overreacted in the way that he did," she says, walking away from me. Reaching the other side of the room, she turns on a tap and fills a glass with water. "Want some?"

"No thanks." I don't think she does either. She didn't like standing too close to me.

The kitchen part of the open-plan ground floor has a wall made of glass that reveals a neatly landscaped terrace at the back of the house with a rectangular swimming pool embedded in it. As I move nearer Flora, the artworks on the walls of the living room area become visible. My breath catches in my throat.

Murmurations. Framed black-and-white photographs of large groups of birds making graceful shapes against a variety of skies. Exactly like the pictures in the living room at Newnham House.

Flora looks at me as if to say, "Don't come any closer." I'm worried she's going to run away from me again. The glass looks as if it might slide open if the right button were pressed.

"How did Lewis overreact?" I ask.

"The last time we came to see you."

"You mean when you fed Georgina? No, I still don't understand that. Tell me."

"She was so little, and premature. She slept nearly all the time, and her wakeful periods were in the night, always. That was the only reason Lewis said yes, when you invited us that last time. When she was asleep, there was no problem at all. She looked as perfect as Thomas and Emily had, even to Lewis. It was only when she opened her eyes that you could see the flaw."

Flora sips her water. I wish I'd asked for some.

"She slept nearly all that afternoon, do you remember? Even when Thomas started wailing about his blister, she didn't wake. I'd promised Lewis that she wouldn't. He said, 'Good. I don't want anyone knowing I've got a cross-eyed daughter.'"

"That's—"

Flora puts out a hand to silence me. "Please don't say it's awful or terrible or anything like that. You're going to want to say that so many times if I tell you the truth, and I already know it's terrible. You saying it doesn't help."

I nod.

"That afternoon, the last time we saw you all as friends, I'd promised Lewis that if Georgina showed signs of waking, I'd take her off somewhere so that no one saw. I knew he had no need to worry. She only ever woke when she was hungry, and the second she started to feed, her eyes always closed again. I promised him I'd make sure no one saw her with her eyes open, and I kept my promise. No one saw a thing. Lewis was paranoid about it, though. As far as he was concerned, feeding meant she was awake, which meant there was a risk she'd open her eyes. He thought I was being reckless—that I might expose the shameful family secret: a nonperfect child. That's why he screamed at me."

I don't know how I'm supposed to listen to this story and not react. My face must be expressing all the things I'm not saying in words.

"I had other strict instructions that day too," Flora says.

"Like what?"

"Not to say anything about Georgina being premature. Lewis insisted: you and Dominic couldn't know that my body had failed and ejected her too early. That's how Lewis saw it. Zannah and Ben had both turned up on time, healthy and perfect, and Lewis needs to feel superior in order to find life bearable. For the first time, he didn't. He blamed Georgina and me. Mainly me. Even Lewis understands that you can't blame a baby for anything. He used to say it all the time: 'It's not her fault I don't want her.' Sometimes it was, 'It's not her fault I wish she'd never been born.'"

"Flora . . ."

"It wasn't only the strabismus," she goes on. "He never wanted a third child. He had his perfect boy and girl and he wanted to stop at two. He always said two was the perfect number, and that was how many children we were going to have. I should have listened. If only I'd listened . . ." She covers her face with her hands. Her body heaves and she says something I can't make out. I think it was "None of it would have happened."

"So you and Lewis didn't agree to have a third child?" I say.

Flora shakes her head. "He'd never have agreed. Never. I tried to persuade myself that I didn't want another baby, but . . . When you want something so much, you don't think straight, do you? I kept telling myself, 'You're so lucky already, you've got Thomas and Emily,' but the urge didn't go away, and I thought Lewis would . . ." Her face contorts in pain. "I miscalculated. I hadn't seen the worst of him then—never directed at me, anyway. I'd seen him lay waste to other people, but . . . you remember how it was, Beth. He was so hard to resist when he was on your side and you had his approval. It made you feel invincible. I felt like the luckiest woman in the world when Lewis saw me as an asset. Then I went against what he wanted and got pregnant again, and everything changed."

"But if he knew you were trying to get pregnant and he didn't want to . . ."

"I didn't tell him." Flora looks at me with pity. "You think I'd have had the nerve to defy him openly? No. I said it was an accident. 'Good,' he said. 'Then you won't mind getting rid of it.' And he saw the look in my eyes and knew everything: that I'd disobeyed him, which would have been bad enough all on its own, and that I'd lied about it."

"What happened? How did he react?"

She stares into the distance. Finally she says, "You can't imagine, Beth. He looked at me and I knew: everything was finished. He would never love me again. I was condemned. Lewis doesn't give second chances."

"He used to boast about that." It was a feature that he had and we all lacked. There was a quote he liked, about it being your fault if someone hurts you more than once. He presented it as hard-earned wisdom, not intransigence, and we never questioned it. His belief in himself was so strong, we all fell in with it.

"I begged him to forgive me, said I'd end the pregnancy. It was the last thing I wanted to do, but I'd have done it. I was so scared, even then. Not scared of what he might do at that point, just scared of what my life would be like if I wasn't the beloved wife of the great Lewis Braid anymore."

All of this happened when Flora found out she was pregnant with Georgina. That's why telling her best friend was the last thing on her mind. "But you kept the pregnancy. How come, if you knew Lewis was against it?"

"He told me to. Said, 'No, you won't be having a termination.' As if he was in charge of me. I told him I didn't want one, I thought it was what he wanted, and he said, 'No, it's not. Not now that I've had a chance to think about it. You chose to get pregnant, and now you're going to see it through. We're both going to live with the consequences of your unilateral decision.' Do you want to hear the most ridiculous thing of all? I was relieved! I thought maybe he was coming around to the idea of a third child. He was still sounding so cold and . . . different from the Lewis who'd loved me, but if he was telling me to keep it, I thought . . ."

"You allowed yourself to hope."

Flora nods. "I was sure that when the baby arrived, he'd love it. But that was never going to happen. He ruled that out, the second he saw through my 'accidental conception' lie. He might not have made his whole plan on day one, but he drew a line that was going to stay drawn forever. I should have known. If I hadn't been so desperate for another baby, I *would* have known. It was deluded wishful thinking. Lewis doesn't change his mind, and to think that he would after I'd gone against him like that . . ." She shuts her eyes.

"What if Georgina hadn't been born prematurely?" I ask. "If she'd appeared bang on time, if she hadn't had the problem with her eye?"

"It could so easily have been fixed." A tear rolls down Flora's face. "One operation—that's all it would have taken. I told Lewis that. He said, 'Do you know what the trouble with you is, Flora? You don't know how to think properly.' I asked him what he meant. He said I had to work it out; he wasn't going to tell me—part of his effort to improve my thinking capacity. I did in the end. Work it out, I mean. Even if Georgina's eyes were fixed, even if she was the most flawless-looking, healthy child in the world, it still wouldn't be okay that she was there. She was never supposed to exist. We were supposed to be a family of four."

I wish she hadn't hidden all this from me. I nearly say it, then realize there's no point. It's not going to make her feel any better to think that if she'd told me every-thing then, all those years ago, Georgina might . . .

*Might still be alive? Why?*

I'd have told her to take the kids and get as far away from Lewis as possible. Would that have worked, though? Or would he have made a different plan to punish her? "His whole plan," she said.

"Flora?" I can't put off asking any longer.

"What?"

"Did Lewis murder Georgina?"

She looks away.

"Flora?"

"It was my fault."

"Georgina's death was your fault?"

She nods.

"The story you and Lewis told me about the wine and the argument you had, how it led to Georgina's death—that was true?"

"No."

"Tell me what happened. How did Georgina die?"

I wait.

"Flora? I think Lewis killed her. I think he's the one who belongs in HMP Peterborough. Not you."

She shudders. "What do you mean?"

"You know what I mean. Daily Responses."

"How do you . . ." Her mouth gapes open.

"Lewis took a phone call this morning on the way into work. He didn't know I was behind him. I was about to call his name, but then his phone rang, so I didn't. I eavesdropped instead. He spoke very briskly, as if to a business associate, and said 'Are you ready for Daily Responses?' It sounded kind of religious, like a ritual. Then I went inside and all the VersaNova receptionists were wearing badges with cheesy new-age mottos on them. Stupidly, I assumed Daily Responses was some kind of corporate mindfulness bullshit, but it isn't. Lewis wasn't talking to a colleague on the phone. He was talking to *you*."

She stares at me blankly.

I go on, telling her what she already knows. "It *is* a ritual—I was right about that part. A daily ritual, I assume, if it's called Daily Responses." Lewis giving it a name makes it even sicker. "I only realized later that the questions I heard him ask fit perfectly with the things I heard you say just over a week earlier, when you got out of your car in Hemingford Abbots in the middle of a phone call. No wonder you were crying. It's a form of torture. Has it been going on ever since Georgina died?"

Flora nods. "Some days I can get through it fine. Others, I go to pieces. You must have seen a bad day."

"Daily Responses: three questions and three answers, the same each time. I heard Lewis ask you the questions this morning: 'Where are you? Where should you be? And what are you?' And that day on Wyddial Lane, the first time I'd laid eyes on you in twelve years, I heard you recite the replies."

*Question 1: Where are you?*

*Answer: Home.*

*Question 2: Where should you be?*

*Answer: HMP Peterborough.*

*Question 3: And what are you?*

*Answer: Lucky. I'm very lucky.*

"He must have recorded you saying it at some point,"

I tell her. "When he phoned me the first time, I heard your voice in the background saying answer number three."

Flora turns on the tap and pours herself more water. She doesn't offer me any.

"Maybe he records it every time." I wouldn't put it past Lewis to collect Flora's Daily Responses and file them away. "He didn't this morning, though. The thing is . . . I don't think you do belong in prison, Flora. I don't think you killed Georgina. Lewis did, didn't he?"

"I think so," she says.

"What does that mean?"

She opens her mouth and lets out a sigh, long and loud. "It's a relief to say it after so many years. I've never said it before. Yes, I think Lewis murdered Georgina. The story he told you about me and the wine was a lie. Not the wine part—that was true. I did have a couple of glasses. By then, I needed at least a glass a night just to keep me from screaming and falling apart. I kept thinking 'There must be something I can do' but I had no idea what it might be. My husband hated me and one of our children, and had no intention of relenting. I couldn't leave him. That would have meant leaving Thomas and Emily too—he'd never have let me take them away from him, I knew that. What I didn't know was that he'd made a foolproof plan to take them away from me. Forever. And then make me suffer, forever. Killing Georgina was only stage one. There was plenty more to come."

We stare at each other in silence. Now I see what she meant. To say, "That's horrific," or "That's evil," could never be enough.

"Tell me about the night Georgina died," I say, though I'm not sure I can bear to hear it.

"I started to feel unusually sleepy. I felt so bad, I had to mention it to Lewis, who accused me of drinking too much. Now it seems so obvious that he drugged me, but it didn't occur to me then. However grim things were between us, I wouldn't have suspected he'd do that. I thought I must be coming down with something. Lewis told me to go to bed and said he'd look after the kids. I didn't want to leave Georgina with him, but I could hardly keep my eyes open."

"Did you fear he'd hurt her?"

"Not in the way he did. I thought I knew exactly what he'd do. It was what he'd been doing since she was born: being Wonder-Dad to the other two and ignoring Georgina completely. Since I'd told him I was pregnant with her, he'd shut out both of us as much as he could. The only time he turned on the charm was if he thought Thomas or Emily might notice something was wrong. He still wanted to preserve the illusion of the perfect family for them, so he'd make a point of being nice to me when we were all together, and sometimes he'd cuddle Georgina too, though he never looked at her. The second Thomas and Emily left the room, the act would end and the coldness would resume."

I want to kill him. I've never had this feeling before, about anyone.

"I remember just before I fell asleep, worrying that he might leave Georgina unchanged and unfed," says Flora. "She would always cry if she was hungry or uncomfortable, though, and there was nothing wrong with her lungs. She could scream loud enough to make your hair stand on end. But she never did, or if she did, it didn't wake me, thanks to whatever Lewis put in my food. I know he drugged me. I know exactly how much I drank that night—two glasses of wine, same as most nights. There's no way that would have knocked me out. If wine was all I'd had, I'd have woken up when Lewis came into my room and . . . stopped Georgina breathing."

"I'm so sorry, Flora."

"He probably used a pillow." Her voice shakes. "I woke up in the middle of the night to find him shaking me and telling me the same lie you've already heard, the one he made me tell too: I drank too much wine, took

Georgina up to bed, rolled over and smothered her to death by accident while in a drunken stupor. All a lie. When I dragged myself up to bed, she was still downstairs with Lewis. But he said my memory couldn't be trusted, because I'd drunk so much. He sneered at me. Said how could I deny I'd taken her up with me when he'd seen me do it. Even if I had, I'd never have put her in bed with me, not when I felt as bad as I did. I'm not an idiot. I was a good mother."

"I know you were. You don't need to convince me. I'm on your side."

"*Now* you are," Flora mutters.

"What do you mean?"

"Nothing." Her face twists, and I see how much she wishes she hadn't said it. She takes her glass of water over to one of the gray sofas and sits down. "You didn't know, and you couldn't have rescued me and the kids even if you had. I couldn't rescue us. It was crazy of me to think you might be able to, but I couldn't stop hoping. I thought, 'Surely she'll suspect something's wrong, and—'" She breaks off with a shrug. "I don't know what I thought you could do, but I had to cling to something."

"And I did nothing," I say, my words falling like stones. "I decided you'd lost interest in me because suddenly you were rich, and I gave as good as I got—that's how I thought of it. I saw you withdrawing from our friendship, took it personally and did the same. I'm so sorry, Flora."

"You're here now." She almost smiles.

"I felt so guilty, too, for cutting Georgina out of the photo."

"When I saw that, my first thought was that maybe you and Lewis . . . but then I told myself you'd never collude with him to hurt me. Then I remembered you'd had a miscarriage, and realized how hard it must have been for you to have me turn up with a baby I'd told you nothing about, and I forgave you immediately. I hope I said so."

"You have now. We can't change the past, Flora. We need to—"

"I so nearly didn't send you our new address post-card when we moved to Wyddial Lane," she talks over me, staring out through the window at the pool terrace. "Lewis told me not to. Thank God I did. I'm glad you found me eventually, even if there's nothing we can do. You tried. That means something."

Her mournful tone worries me. She sounds as if she's given up.

"I'm still trying, Flora—present tense—but you need to tell me everything. You woke up, Georgina was dead, Lewis was saying you'd rolled over, drunk, and smothered her. What happened after that?"

"Threats. Lots and lots of threats. I wasn't allowed to have you in my life anymore, or my parents. You and they were the people Lewis feared most. He knew that if I broke down and told anyone what a monster he was, it'd be them or you that I'd tell. You were easy to shake off. You disappeared as smoothly as if you'd helped draft Lewis's master plan. My parents." She flinches. "It was the second worst moment of my life, telling them our relationship was over. Lewis did the talking. He wasn't fazed by it at all. It was just something that had to happen. The first of many things."

"Tell me," I say.

"There's no point. It's over."

"What do you mean?" The words spill out of me in a panic.

I hear Lewis's voice behind me. "You'll see what she means if you turn around."

# 26

He's holding a gun. He points it first at Flora, then at me.

*No. Please, no. This can't be real.*

"Hey, Beth," he says casually, smiling the same way he did when he came out to greet me at VersaNova this morning. The suit and tie have gone. He's wearing black tracksuit bottoms, brown boots, a black hoodie. Apart from the boots, he's dressed like one of Ben's friends.

*Or like someone about to commit a crime, using the weapon in his hand.*

"You didn't think I'd have someone at the Marriott, ready to follow you wherever you went?" Lewis asks me. "I like to cover all bases. I'd have thought you might anticipate that."

My mind feels as if it's falling down and down and

down. I don't want it to land, don't want to look at where it's heading.

The gun can't be real. Fake ones must be as easy to come by here as real ones.

*Don't think like that, idiot. Believe it's real. Act like it's real.*

Flora hasn't reacted to his arrival at all. She must have seen him come into the house behind me. Yet she didn't show any shock, or even surprise. Suddenly, I understand why.

"You knew," I say to her. "That's why you started sounding like you'd given up. How did you know he was here?"

"She saw me from the window," says Lewis, pointing to the glass part of the kitchen wall. "My wife is excellent at giving up, Beth. Yeah, you heard that right. *My* wife. She never married Kevin. She and I never divorced. And she might be known as Jeanette Cater when she's hanging around Nowheresville, England, but legally her name's still Flora Braid." He balls his free hand into a fist, raises it and spreads his fingers wide. "Blows your mind, huh?"

My mind has been blown since I first saw Flora on Wyddial Lane with two children who seemed not to have aged in twelve years. I can't say any of this. All I can do is think about the gun.

"You, Beth, are terrible at giving up," says Lewis. "I'm never going to tell anyone the story of how and why I killed you today, and not only for all the obvious reasons. Imagine if I told my employees a story about two best friends . . ."—he moves the gun to indicate me and Flora—". . . one of whom always gives up and the other who never does, and it turns out that it's the determined, brave optimist who gets shot in the head, while the defeatist coward walks away without a scratch. That's not a message that packs a great motivational punch, is it?"

"You're not going to kill me," I tell him. My mouth is numb. The words sound as if they're coming from a hundred miles away. He can't do it. He must know that. I have children who need me to be alive.

Lewis sounds reluctant to correct me when he says, "I am going to kill you, but I'll say this before I do: I admire you. More than that—since I know my good opinion of you won't count for much—I'd say it's an objective fact that you're an admirable person. Whereas there's nothing admirable about Flora. If I'd married you instead of her, maybe I wouldn't have had to . . ." He stops and shakes his head. "But I never would have. You're not physically attractive enough."

"Don't, Lewis," Flora says quietly.

"Don't insult her looks or don't kill her? Which?

Aww." He feigns sympathy. "What, tongue-tied now, are you? You were doing so well: I made threats, you were saying, after Georgina died. Lots of threats. Go on." Keeping the gun pointed at me, Lewis walks over to a white sofa, sits down and puts his feet up on the low table in front of it. "Finish the story if you want to."

"What's the point?" she mutters.

"Beth, tell her what the point is."

My throat closes. I can't breathe.

"I'll tell her, then," says Lewis. "You want to know everything. Everything Flora and I know, you want to know it too. That's what this has been about, your whole little crusade. Right?"

"I want to help Flora and all of her children who can still be helped," I manage to say.

"That's sweet. And not true. Yeah, you wouldn't mind helping, but that's not what this is about for you. It's about your need to know. To make sense of what you saw, and everything that's happened. There's nothing wrong with that. Intellectual curiosity's a good thing. A *great* thing, actually. Flora . . ." Lewis gestures with his head. "Finish telling your story. It'll be cathartic for you to unburden yourself—all the therapy you've not had, all these years? Now's your chance. And then you'll be able to go back to your life in England with a different attitude. A better one."

He turns back to me. "I'm always telling her, Beth: when you can't change a circumstance—and Flora can't change her life circumstances, only I can do that—then all you can do is change your thoughts *about* the circumstance. That's the only way you get to feel better. Flora—tell the story. No, wait. Beth, you give the order."

"What order?"

"Ask her to tell you. Tell her how much you still want to get those missing pieces of information into your brain, even knowing you'll only enjoy the benefit of satisfied curiosity for maybe five minutes before you die. Or maybe you don't care anymore. Maybe now all you can think about is your fear of death, and that you'll never see your family again."

That's the one thing I can't afford to think about. "Tell me," I say to Flora. Lewis has had the gun on me for more than a few minutes now. I'm still alive. No one in this room knows for certain that I'm going to die.

"I can't," Flora whispers.

"Do it," Lewis snaps.

*Please, Flora. Talk. Start talking and don't stop.*

"Don't be a selfish bitch, darling. If you clam up, it's all over for Beth. She has no extended story time in which to work out how not to die. Right, Beth?"

If I look at him, I might fall apart. I fix my eyes on Flora instead.

Silence fills the room like poisonous gas.

Finally Lewis sighs and says, "You were telling Beth that first I killed Georgina and then I made threats. All true."

Flora's face twitches.

"Is that all I get by way of a reaction?" Lewis asks her. "She's never heard me admit to our daughter's murder before, Beth. This is a big moment. It's okay, I'm not worried. She'll never tell. I'll shoot you in front of her and still she won't breathe a word. I'd like to say it's loyalty but it's not. It's cowardice. What did I threaten you with, Flora?"

"You said I had to—"

"Don't tell me, you stupid bitch. Tell *her*—the one who doesn't know." He waves the gun at me.

"He told me I had to go away," says Flora. "That my drinking and my negligence had caused Georgina's death, and I had to pay the price. The price was that I'd lose Thomas and Emily too. I wasn't fit to be a mother, he said."

"I was actually pretty reasonable," says Lewis. "I could have told everyone that I'd found Georgina life-less and smothered in the bed with Flora, who'd passed out from too much drink. I didn't say that. I protected my wife. I knew she wouldn't have survived a week in prison—and yes, I believe some mothers who recklessly endanger their newborns do end up behind bars, even if they cry and say it was an accident. So I told everybody that Flora wasn't to blame, that I came in and found Georgina in her cot. Blue, not breathing. I said nothing about the wine Flora had drunk."

"Flora *wasn't* to blame," I say. "You were."

Lewis frowns. "I know. Don't let terror turn you stupid, Beth. I didn't pin the blame on myself, obviously. My point is, I could have told the world that Flora killed Georgina, and I didn't. I spared her that ordeal and that shame—possibly a criminal record too. I did all that willingly, because I didn't want to be unnecessarily vindictive."

Flora makes a strangled noise.

"But for an offense so severe, there had to be a price," Lewis goes on. "Oh, wait—you think I'm talking about the killing of Georgina? No. Not that offense. Tell her, Flora."

"The offense was that I got pregnant when Lewis didn't want another baby," she says mechanically.

"Deliberately, Beth. That's not on. You won't admit it now, but you know it's something no decent person would do. Then she gave birth too early, to a cross-eyed creature that was certainly no part of the amazing family I wanted—the one I *had* until she ruined everything. Did Flora cause Georgina's death? Yes, in a way. Without her scheming, there'd have been no Georgina. No one would have needed to die. That would have been better for all of us—you too, Beth. Flora's lucky still to be a free woman."

*Where should you be? HMP Peterborough.*

"Anyway, we very much were where we were, at that point." Lewis shrugs. He stands up with a heavy sigh. "As I say, I offered Flora a solution to our predicament that I hoped would work for all of us. She was to detach herself, immediately, and disappear. I'd cover all expenses. Thomas, Emily and I would then be free of her taint, and Georgina's, and able to get on with the rest of our lives. We agreed that after she'd gone, I'd tell the children that she'd had a breakdown and couldn't face being part of our family anymore after what had happened to their sister. And that was that. Separate lives. That's how it would have gone, if I hadn't been too soft-hearted."

"You aren't soft-hearted." Flora steps forward. Her words spill out in a messy rush, barely distinct from one another. "You're the opposite. You say you didn't want to be vindictive, but you did. You still do. You want me to suffer as much as possible."

Lewis nods. His eyes flash, as if her disagreement has given him new energy. "Interesting interpretation, Mrs. Braid. I've not heard any of this before, Beth. Flora never talks back. I wouldn't allow it. Today's different, though. It's True-Feel Reveal Day here in Delray Beach, Florida!" He chuckles. "Go on, Flora, have your say. I'm sure you're not afraid of anything, are you?"

"What should I be scared of?" she says. "You're never going to kill me—you've got your playhouse on Wyddial Lane with all your toys in it and I'm the main one, aren't I? Without me to torture, you'd have no interest in playing your game, and you *love* your game. You're incapable of loving any human being properly, but you love the game, and the power it brings you."

"She calls it a game, Beth," says Lewis in a voice designed to sound sad. "I call it giving her another chance. I think we need someone more objective than either of us to be the judge—you, for instance. Sure, you're on Flora's side against me, but you've got a good brain. Did I do her a favor or am I the sadist she thinks I am? Tell her the story, Flora. Actually, wait."

Using his free hand, he pulls his phone out of his pocket and sets it down on the table. "I'm going to record this. It's good to have it all stored, for the official record. In case one day I write my story." He grins. "Who lives, who dies, who tells *your* story, Beth?"

His eyes flit up and down as he sets the phone to record. They're never off me or the gun in his hand for long enough to give me a chance.

"Recording," he says, looking at Flora. "On your marks, get set, go. Let's let Judge Beth decide."

"He said I had to go," Flora says in a dull voice. "Far away from all of them. Lose my family. He would pay for my new life, but it had to be somewhere where there was no danger I'd bump into any of them by chance. First he sent me to Scotland. Until the job opportunity here came up, and he made a different plan: to put me back in the house where he . . ." She chokes on the words. Starts again. "Where it happened. And keep me there. He'd keep an eye on me, he said, to check I was coping. He didn't care what happened to me, but he pretended to. That's what he does: pretends or uses the truth as it suits him, so that I never know what to expect. Him keeping tabs on me was a control thing. That was how the phone calls started. The Daily Responses."

"Beth won't know what those are," says Lewis wearily, as if Flora's a toddler who's testing his patience to the limit.

"She knows."

"And if you didn't go to Scotland, and then back to Wyddial Lane, if you didn't do his sick phone ritual every day, what did he say he'd do to you?" Hearing myself ask the question, I realize I'm not as scared as I was at first. I don't know why not. Lewis still has a gun pointed at me. Maybe burning hatred flowing through you for long enough makes you braver. "Did he threaten to tell Thomas and Emily that Georgina's death was your fault? That you'd been a bad mother and killed her?"

Flora nods. "My parents too. It would have destroyed them. They'd have believed me over him if I'd told them everything, but I couldn't risk it because he'd threatened something far worse than exposing me as a killer, even if he hadn't stated the threat in words."

"If I didn't say it in words, Flora, how could I have made the threat?" asks Lewis.

"Innuendos, suggestions," says Flora. "You know how you did it, and I knew exactly what you meant: if I didn't keep my mouth shut and obey you, always, in every detail of what little life you'd left me, then you'd kill someone else I loved. Thomas and Emily, probably. Or my parents. Maybe all of them. There's nothing too evil for you, and you don't care about anyone apart from yourself."

"That's not true." Lewis looks angry. Insulted.

I watch his face carefully, not quite believing what I'm seeing.

"I cared about my family. You corrupted it beyond repair," he tells Flora.

"Even if you cared once, that changed," she says. "Your obsession with making me suffer took over. You got addicted to it at some point. I'm not sure when. Maybe when the Florida job prospect came up and you realized you could force me to live—" Flora stops with a strangled sob. "Live in *that* house again—the last place I'd ever want to go back to. The house where you killed Georgina, the house you make me live in."

"Who are Kevin Cater and Yanina?" I ask.

"Is that a trick question?" Lewis sneers. "They're Kevin Cater and Yanina. Yanina Milyukov. Kevin Cater used to work with me years ago, when we all still lived in Cambridge. Yanina's his girlfriend. I'm glad you brought them up." There's an edge of grim determination to his voice. "They're the people I pay to keep things running smoothly. Flora's not reliable these days, as you can see for yourself. She has two young children, whom she'd be incapable of looking after properly on her own. When I say 'pay'—" He breaks off and laughs. "'Through the nose' is the only way to describe it. I pay Cater and Yanina a fortune, in fact. Not that I mind—they're worth it. Most people would ask awkward questions, or want a say in what happened in the house. Not them. They do as they're told."

"And they don't know the rest. They have no idea how much they're *not* told," says Flora. "I've always been too frightened to say anything. They don't know you're a murderer. They don't know that every time you pop back from Florida you . . . you . . . *I hate you!*" She screams at him, bending double as if someone's snapped her in half. "I wish you were dead, I wish *I* was dead," she sobs.

As if nothing has happened, Lewis says to me, "I pay Thomas and Emily Cater's school fees too. They're not cheap. I do all of this so that Flora can have a second chance. A new family."

"Pretending to be Kevin Cater's wife?" I say. "That's her second chance? While his girlfriend pretends to be the nanny?"

"Flora's a mess," Lewis says dismissively. "No one would have believed in her as the nanny. Plus, I wanted her to be able to play Mummy again. Yanina's got a Russian accent, as nannies often do. It worked better that way."

I look at Flora. "How could they go along with it?" I ask her. "Are they monsters too?"

She shakes her head slowly, woodenly. There's a

puzzled look in her eyes, as if she's searching for the right word to describe Kevin and Yanina.

"You've never had a really large amount of money, have you, Beth?" Lewis says. "Life-changingly large, I mean. Cater and Yanina have. I've never explicitly told them that Flora's drunken binge caused Georgina's death, but I know it's what they both think happened." He looks pleased with himself. "Remember, Flora has also 'gone along with it,' as you put it. All these years. She could have walked away from that house any time she chose to. She could have gone to the police if she thought what I was inflicting on her was so terrible. But she never did, and she never will. That ought to tell you something."

"Because I know you'd kill my children," Flora tells him. Like an everyday wife reminding her husband of the bad thing that will happen if they don't both take care to avoid it. I know what I'm hearing, yet part of me is still thinking, "Is there anything else that this could all mean? It can't mean what I think it does."

"You're making that up." Lewis sneers at Flora. "I've never said it."

"Why are they called Thomas and Emily?" The gun in his hand is no longer pointed at me. I didn't notice him lowering his arm, which is now by his side. If he fired, the bullet would hit the floor.

"Who?" Lewis asks me. His face breaks into a grin. "*Think* about it," he says.

"Thomas and Emily Cater. I know they're both yours," I tell him.

"Of course they're mine." He looks impatient. "Who else's would they be?"

I wait.

"What more do you want to know?" Lewis asks. "I told you, I felt sorry for Flora. She'd deceived me and trashed my family, and I knew exactly what she deserved, but . . . I don't know. I hate to admit it, but maybe on some level I still loved her. I had Thomas and Emily, and she had no one. She was still my wife, still *mine*. I had to do something with her, I couldn't just leave her to rot. Then I realized there was absolutely no reason why she shouldn't have a second family." His face hardens. He stares at me, eyes wide, as he says slowly, "One. Baby. At. A time."

I stare back at him, full of a cold numbness. Is this what it feels like to look at the worst thing you've ever seen? I'm not really feeling anything, not anymore.

He says, "While Flora was pregnant—this time *with* my permission and without hers—it came to me. Of course the baby had to be called Thomas, if it was a boy. And a girl would be Emily. Same house, same names. Are you starting to understand, Beth? I saw a way of giving Flora some of it back, some of her old life. Me, from time to time. Every day, on the phone. A Thomas. An Emily." He walks toward Flora. "And one day soon, I hope, a Georgina," he says quietly. "We'll just have to keep trying, won't we?"

Any second now, if he keeps walking, he'll be facing away from me.

*And you're going to do what? Run at him, try to overpower him? Risk getting killed sooner?*

"I'm not lucky. I'm not lucky," Flora repeats as he walks toward her, her voice rising. "I'm unlucky."

"You're not as lucky as you could have been if you'd been more resourceful," Lewis says. "You could have made friends if you'd wanted to: mums at school, neighbors. You chose not to. It was your decision to become a virtual recluse, to sit around all day stewing in your misery."

"I'm not going to get pregnant again. I'm in my forties." Flora backs away from him as he approaches.

I stand completely still. How many chances to escape have I missed already? Do I have one now? This might be my one chance and I'm missing it because I'm thinking this instead of . . . I can't bring an alternative to mind. I'm frozen. Action feels impossible.

"Forties is nothing," says Lewis. "You're fit and healthy."

"Every time, I order my body not to get pregnant," Flora says. "Every single time."

Lewis laughs. "Well, it's ignored your orders twice already."

"You're a rapist," I tell him. "A rapist and a murderer."

"Everything you've done, you've done it to torture me," says Flora as he moves closer to her. "Making me live in that house, making me have more children, calling them the same names." She's breathing hard and fast, as if she's been running. In my head, I'm running away from Lewis. I wonder if she is too.

"The lies you made me learn by heart to repeat to Beth, while my children that I haven't seen for *twelve years* are just around the corner, and I can't see them, not even once, for a second. What's next? Let's say you get your way and I have another baby—what's next on your torture list after that?"

"Why are you saying all this now?" Lewis asks her.

There's a pause. Flora looks at me. Then she says, "I don't know."

"Your friend's here, and you've got some moral support for the first time in years. Clearly it's gone to your head. But Beth's not going to be here for much longer. Maybe you aren't either. Did you stop to think of that?"

He's going to kill us both. And if he does that, if he's

killed once and will happily kill twice more . . . "Why has Thomas been taken out of school?" I ask him as he raises his arm to point the gun at Flora's head.

Her eyes fill with fear. "What?" she says.

"Ignore her," says Lewis. "She's talking shit."

"I'm not. Thomas isn't at the school anymore. And Emily's place has been canceled. Kevin and Yanina . . ." The missing words stick in my throat.

What did Kevin and Yanina do? And why, if Lewis knows nothing about it? They're supposed to do what they're told in exchange for life-changing money.

"What the *fuck*?" Lewis swings around and points the gun at me. It makes a clicking noise. Everything inside me starts to shake. His face is twisted: a mixture of rage and confusion.

Flora lunges at him from behind. The gun falls from his hand and lands on the floor. He trips and tumbles, taking her with him. She lands half on top of him, with a noise that's halfway between a scream and a howl. Lewis lunges for the gun, not quickly enough. It's in my hand.

*It's in my hand.* I stare down at it.

Lewis lunges toward me.

"Beth!" Flora screams.

"Lewis, don't!" I say, aiming the words at his phone on the table. "Don't kill me. Please."

He was about to lunge again, but he stops. Confusion spreads across his face. He can't think why I'd say those words when I'm the one holding the gun. "Don't do it!" I cry out. There's nothing fake about the panic in my voice.

"What . . . ?" Lewis tries to scramble to his feet.

I fire the gun.

# 27

"Why did you turn it off?"

"You're not saying anything. No point me recording silence."

"I've already repeated it twice."

"I know. And I'm sorry to have to ask you to go through it again. You've been so incredibly helpful."

"Wasn't the recording on his phone clear enough for you?"

"Loud and clear, ma'am. You have no idea how grateful I am to have it. But I need to hear the story from you, in your own words. I know you've already told Detective Gessinger, but—"

"And then can I call my family?"

"Absolutely for sure. Don't worry, they know you're safe. I reached out to your husband myself."

"Can't we do this after I've phoned home? And slept? I've missed a whole night's sleep."

"I have an idea: how about if you only tell me about the last part, for now? Then tomorrow we can talk properly, once you're rested."

"Where's Flora?"

"Detective Gessinger's with her now. She's hanging in there. Her parents are on a plane, on their way over."

"And her children? She's got four children!"

"Mrs. Leeson, please let us take care of everything. There's nothing you need to concern yourself with. Trust me. We've got this."

"Okay."

"Now, I need you to tell me what happened. From the beginning."

"All right. I—"

"Wait a second. Resuming the interview at 1100 hours. Detective Sophia Steel interviewing Mrs. Elizabeth Leeson. All right, Mrs. Leeson, I need to hear your account of how Mr. Braid lost his life."

"He had a gun. He'd come to the house to kill me—he made that clear over and over again. Kept saying it. I don't know about Flora. I didn't think he was going to kill her—I think he might even have said he wasn't—but then later he implied that maybe he would. It's all in the recording, just listen to it."

"Go on. You're doing great."

"He would have done it. He'd have killed both of us. I had no idea that my question would throw him in the way it did. I assumed—"

"Wait, back up. You asked him a question while he was pointing the gun at you?"

"I think . . . I'm trying to remember. I think he was facing away from me, pointing the gun at Flora, when I asked him why Thomas had been taken out of school. I assumed he knew that had happened, but he didn't. He was shocked. We both saw it, me and Flora. Any second, he was going to kill us. We both knew it. When he turned around to say something to me, she ran at him and either grabbed him or shoved him, I don't know which."

"And then?"

"The gun fell out of his hand. Landed on the floor. Oh—he'd clicked it just before that happened, like people do when they're about to shoot."

"What happened after the gun fell?"

"I picked it up and started to back away toward the front door. I was thinking I could open it, run outside and scream for help. Lewis and Flora were both on the floor at that point. She'd landed on top of him. He was struggling to climb out from under her. Then he did, and he grabbed a knife from the block on the kitchen island. He started walking toward me, holding the knife like this—his hand was level with his head, in position to stab down."

"Go on. This is what we need. You're doing well."

"I was close to the door, and he was coming toward me slowly. I thought I'd have time to get out before he got to me, but the door was locked. He must have locked it when he first came in. I couldn't unlock it, not at the same time as keeping the gun on him, and if I didn't do that . . ."

"I understand."

"He was coming closer. I couldn't get away. There was nowhere for me to go. I knew he was going to kill me if I didn't do something, so I aimed the gun at his right arm—or I thought I did. I never meant to hit his head."

"You've never fired a gun before?"

"No. Never."

"Then the odds were against you hitting him at all. How much distance would you say there was between you when you fired that shot?"

"I don't know. The closer he got, the more scared I was. I fired when I knew . . ."

"It's okay. Take your time."

"When I knew that if he came any nearer I'd freeze and it'd be too late. I remember thinking, 'Soon he'll be too close and there'll be no point.' I shouted at him not to do it, not to kill me—"

"Excuse the interruption. You were the one holding the gun, and Mr. Braid was not yet close enough to reach you, and *you* shouted 'Don't kill me'?"

"I told you: he was walking toward me with a knife. Holding it like this."

"But you had a gun. Wasn't he worried you'd kill him? I mean, that's what happened, yes? You killed him."

"No, he wasn't worried. He still totally believed he was going to walk away without a scratch after killing me and Flora. He didn't think I'd ever fire the gun. He thought I was too weak. So did I, until I did it."

"All right. Thank you, Mrs. Leeson. We'll let you have a little rest, maybe call your family in England. And then—I'm sorry, but it's necessary—you're going to need to go back a little further and talk me through all this from the very beginning. How it all started."

# Epilogue

**Four months later**

The narrow road winds around and around, perilous zigzag corners all the way up the hill. Every so often we pass a large pile of rubbish, bagged in multicolored plastic sacks, that's been dumped by the side of the road and left to rot in the sun. There's a strike going on according to Dom. I don't know how he knows anything about the work disputes of Corfiot refuse collectors; I never got to find out. When he started to tell us, Ben and Zannah both groaned and put their earphones in, and he gave up with a sigh.

"How can there be any more turns?" he asks. "I mean . . . this is it. We're at the top. But I think I'm supposed to turn right again here. Didn't Flora's email say turn right at the Lavandula bar?"

"Yeah. We must be nearly . . . Look, there. There's a sign saying 'Villa Agathi,' with an arrow."

"Okay," Dom says in a low voice. He sounds as if he's readying himself for an ordeal.

"It'll be fine," I tell him.

"Will it?"

"Yes. The kids aren't worried." I adjust our rental car's rearview mirror and inspect each of them in turn. They're half asleep, undisturbed by the loud music that's pouring into their ears.

"What are you expecting to happen?" I ask Dom.

He shakes his head, keeping his eyes on the bumpy track ahead.

"We're not going to walk into an awful scene of pain and anguish. Is that what you're worried about?"

"I wouldn't say I'm worried, exactly."

"It'll be fine. They're on holiday."

"We're not, though. Are we?"

"Not in the same way, no."

"Not in any way. This doesn't feel like a holiday to me."

"It's a short visit. Who cares what we call it?"

"I just want to be prepared," Dom says. "I don't know. Maybe that's impossible."

I put my hand on his arm. "Relax. Flora could have invited us any time in the past few months, to her parents' house, but she invited us *here*. To a villa on the top of a hill in Corfu. I think that means she wanted us all to meet in good circumstances this time. Happy circumstances. I know that's what it means."

"It's not all of us, though, is it? Will that be mentioned?"

"I don't know." It's a good question. "Flora and I will probably talk about it at some point. You can avoid it if you want to. You'll be able to go off somewhere with Ben, maybe."

"I can handle a conversation about unpleasant things, Beth. It's not that I'm worried about."

"Then what?"

"I don't know. Awkwardness, I guess. Not knowing what's going to happen."

"Here's what'll happen. Flora's going to say hello and ask how we are, like a normal person. Thomas and Emily will probably be jumping around on a trampoline, or splashing in the pool. Flora's mum or dad will offer us a cup of tea."

"I want a beer," Dom says. "I'll need one."

"And it won't be awkward. Not for more than about two seconds, anyway. Flora's doing okay, Dom. She says the kids are too. They're getting better, all of them."

"And the other Thomas and Emily, the older ones? Do we mention them at all, or just carry on as if they don't exist? It's not that I want to bring them up, but . . ."

"No. Definitely don't."

"It's so horrible for Flora."

I agree, but I say nothing. Even saying, "Yes, it's awful," would make a terrible situation feel worse somehow, by officially confirming its existence. Not that it can be denied or changed. Thomas and Emily Braid are living with Lewis's mother, who has relocated to Delray Beach, in the same home they lived in with Lewis. They won't see Flora. She's written to them several times and so have I. So has Detective Sophia Steel. They've been told the true story of Georgina's death and everything that happened between their parents before and after that, and they don't believe it. Lewis's mother doesn't either. Their version of events, the one they're determined to stick to though there's no evidence for it, is that Flora and I conspired to murder Lewis, who never did a single thing wrong in his life. The one and only time I spoke to Emily Braid on the phone, a month ago, she said, "Why should I believe the mother who abandoned me and Thomas and who killed my little sister? I know that's what happened—Dad told us when he thought we were old enough to know. And she never once tried to make contact in twelve years. And then you and she plotted to murder him and get away with it. You make me sick!" I was cut off before I could say anything in Flora's or my defense.

*It's not true, Emily. The truth is that only I planned to murder your dad, during those few seconds that I had the gun in my hand, when I realized that I could. I planned it alone, with no help from Flora. I made up the lie about the knife and him coming at me with it in his hand, I said what I wanted Lewis's phone to record for the police to listen to later; I thought of all of it, the whole story and how it would play out, in those few seconds, while I clung to the gun with my trembling hands. All Flora did was corroborate.*

*Then I lied to Detective Steel. I didn't aim for Lewis's shoulder. I aimed for his head, and, even with my hand shaking violently, I must have aimed well. And maybe in a looser sense it was self-defense, but I'm never going to be able to think of it that way, knowing how much I wanted him dead, how deliberately I pointed the gun at the spot right between his eyes, willing the bullet through the air and into his warped brain.*

*And then I lied to Dom. And to Zannah and Ben. And I'll never know their opinion of what I really did, whether they would praise me and say, "I'd have done the same" or disapprove because I killed a man, deliberately, wanting him to die. Praying for it with every cell in my body, and feeling proud once it was done. That's the truth, Emily.*

"Maybe they'll change their minds one day," Dom says as we pull up outside turquoise-painted gates with a white sign on them: "Villa Agathi." Flowers have been painted around the name. "If Kevin Cater and Yanina can overhear *one* conversation between Thomas and Emily and change their minds about everything after taking Lewis's money for years . . ."

"But how will Thomas and Emily Braid ever hear their younger siblings' account of the things the horrible man from America used to say to Mummy when he appeared? Even if they did, they might not change their minds. They're believing what they want and need to believe because they loved Lewis. They adored him."

I don't believe Kevin and Yanina truly changed their minds, but I don't want to say so. Not now. I can't prove it's a lie, and I couldn't bear to hear Dom stick up for them. I'll never believe that they suddenly realized, after being unaware for years, that they were involved in something appalling, and took immediate steps to get the children to safety. They must have known, and tolerated it. Then I turned up, and they saw that they'd failed to convince me there was no cause for concern. Lewis's instructions were becoming ever more alarming and bizarre—Yanina dressing in Flora's clothes, Flora having to be flown out to Florida without the children—and then a policeman turned up asking questions, and Kevin and Yanina's convenient, lucrative gig started to feel more risky.

Then, maybe, they overheard Thomas and Emily talking and discovered that Lewis's treatment of Flora was a little bit worse than even they'd imagined. But I can't believe they cared, at that point. If their worry for the children's safety was genuine, surely they'd have bundled Emily into the car, gone to fetch Thomas from school and gone straight to the police or social services.

There's something that doesn't convince me about them phoning the school and handing in formal notice, canceling Emily's place. There was no need for them to do it, and it feels staged to me. Performative. So that they could claim, later, that they feared reprisals from Lewis to such an extent that they made a decision to take the children and flee to a different part of the country—which was what they did. Even if you did plan to escape, why think about giving notice to a school? Why not just go? Flora thinks they probably wanted to be upfront and end the relationship there and then, so that there would be no phone calls or inquiries the next day when Thomas didn't turn up for registration in the morning. Perhaps that's true. Flora will never ask Kevin or Yanina about it, or speak to them ever again, so there's no way of knowing.

"Are we here?" Ben asks as Dom switches off the car's engine. He stretches. "I'm tired." Tired or not, he's out of the car in seconds; Dom too. It's an old family joke: when we all drive home from somewhere, Dom and Ben are usually inside the house and halfway through watching a football match by the time Zan and I drag ourselves out of the car.

I turn and prod her leg. Her eyes snap open. She blinks.

"We're here," I tell her. "Sorry to wake you."

"You didn't," she says, stuffing her phone and earphones into the bag on her lap. "I was thinking . . ."

"Come on, you two," Dom calls out.

"What?" I ask Zannah.

She looks hesitant, then decides to go for it.

"Maybe I could try talking to Thomas and Emily

Braid. I think I could maybe . . . I don't know. I don't know what I could do, but I'd like to give it a go. I'm the same age as them."

"No," I say. "I don't want you involved."

"And yet look where I am." Zan nods toward the villa.

Damn. Why is she so good at winning arguments?

"They'd tell you horrible things about me, Zan. They'd call me a murderer. I don't want you to have to deal with that."

"I can deal with whatever they say, Mum. Seriously." Looking out of the window, she adds casually, "I could also deal with you being a murderer as long as you only ever have one victim and that victim is Lewis Braid."

Does she know? Is that possible, even though I haven't told her?

"Shall I try and contact them, then?" She smiles innocently at me.

*She knows.*

I've no idea how I feel about that. My daughter knows I lied. My daughter knows what I did in Florida.

"Thomas and Emily Braid?" I say, playing for time.

Zannah nods. "I won't mention it to Flora now, in case it doesn't work. I just . . . I reckon I could convince *anyone* that having a mother is a great thing, not to be missed," she says solemnly.

"Okay. You can try, if you want to." My eyes prickle with tears. I blink them away.

"Er . . . hello?" Dom leans into the car. "Did we come here so that Ben and I could stare at a wall, or . . ."

As he's speaking, the villa's blue gates open and Flora appears, with Rosemary behind her. She waves at us. She's smiling.

# Acknowledgments

I am immensely grateful to the wonderful team at Hodder, especially Carolyn Mays—my dream editor and also, luckily for me, my real-life editor. Thanks to Peter Straus, the best agent in the world, and Matthew Turner, and all at Rogers, Coleridge & White. Thank you to my wonderful American publishers, William Morrow, and to my amazing film and TV agent, Will Peterson.

A huge thank you to Kate Jones and Faith Tilleray for all their practical help and support. Thank you to my family—Dan, Phoebe, Guy and Brewster, who get a thank you and a dedication this time. Thanks to Adele Geras and Chris Gribble for reading and commenting on an early version, and to Emily Winslow, whose editorial advice improved this novel immensely.

Special thanks to Chris Ferguson, from Twitter, who gave me some very useful information about youth divisions of football teams. Thank you to my Dream Author program members who are just the best in every way! And last but not least, thanks to all my readers who write and send lovely messages all the time. Knowing that you're eagerly awaiting the next book makes me want to write it even more.

# HARPER LARGE PRINT

We hope you enjoyed reading
our new, comfortable print size and found it
an experience you would like to repeat.

**Well – you're in luck!**

Harper Large Print offers the finest in
fiction and nonfiction books in this same larger
print size and paperback format. Light and easy to read,
Harper Large Print paperbacks are for the book lovers
who want to see what they are reading without strain.

For a full listing of titles and
new releases to come, please visit our website:
**www.hc.com**

## HARPER LARGE PRINT